Christmas Gifts

Five festive stories from Carole Mortimer,
Diana Palmer, Leanne Banks,
Rebecca Winters and Lucy Gordon to
warm the heart this Christmas

Christmas Gifts

Carole
MORTIMER

Diana
PALMER

Leanne
BANKS

Rebecca
WINTERS

Lucy
GORDON

MILLS & BOON

Mills & Boon, an imprint of Harlequin (UK) Limited, Eton House, 18-24 Paradise Road, Richmond, Surrey TW9 1SR

CHRISTMAS GIFTS © Harlequin Enterprises II B.V./S.à.r.l 2013

His Christmas Eve Proposal © Carole Mortimer 2007
Silent Night Man © Diana Palmer 2008
A Man in her Stocking © Leanne Banks 2002
The Tycoon's Christmas Engagement © Rebecca Winters 2006
A Kiss for Mr Scrooge © Lucy Gordon 1993

ISBN: 978 0 263 91033 9

024-1013

Harlequin (UK) policy is to use papers that are natural, renewable and recyclable products and made from wood grown in sustainable forests. The logging and manufacturing processes conform to the legal environmental regulations of the country of origin.

Printed and bound in Spain
by Blackprint CPI, Barcelona

CONTENTS

*His Christmas
Eve Proposal*

CAROLE
MORTIMER

Carole Mortimer was born in England, the youngest of three children. She began writing in 1978 and has now written over one hundred and eighty books for Mills & Boon. Carole has six sons, Matthew, Joshua, Timothy, Michael, David and Peter. She says, 'I'm happily married to Peter senior; we're best friends as well as lovers, which is probably the best recipe for a successful relationship. We live in a lovely part of England.'

CHAPTER ONE

'JUST LEAVE THE coffee on the side, Donald, thanks.' Hawk called out from his bathroom to his English factotum, after he'd heard the other man knock on his bedroom door before entering. 'I'll be out in a couple of minutes,' he added, as he continued to towel-dry his hair after taking his morning shower, not expecting an answer; Donald Harrison was efficiency personified, and Hawk congratulated himself once again for having found the man ten years ago.

He continued humming to himself as, draping the towel about his shoulders, he took a couple of seconds to contemplate the view from his bathroom window, relishing the blanket of snow that swept across the whole of the foothills towards the Canadian Rockies, which he could see towering majestically in the distance.

Home. It was a stark contrast to the warmth he had left behind in Los Angeles yesterday; he'd been able to feel the biting cold as soon as he stepped out at Calgary airport last night. But Hawk had dressed with the

Canadian weather in mind, his sheepskin jacket, faded denims and the boots that had seemed so out of place in Los Angeles ideal for the refreshing coldness that he'd known he would find here.

He instantly felt part of the impending festive season now that he had the weather to go with it. It was unthinkable for him to even contemplate spending Christmas anywhere else but here. No matter where he was in the world, he always flew back to what had once been the family home for the holidays.

His parents now lived in Florida, as the warmth there was much kinder to the arthritis his father suffered after years of working on the land. They would arrive in three days' time at the five acres and house that were all that remained of the family farm. Hawk's younger sister and her husband—the city slicker— would fly in from Vancouver at the weekend, with their two young children.

No doubt the scores of female fans who avidly followed the movie career of Joshua Hawkley would find his family Christmas a pretty tame affair, probably imagining him instead to be on some Caribbean island, soaking up the sun on a golden beach and drinking piña coladas with a half-naked female at his side!

The half-naked female didn't sound half bad, but the rest of it could take a hike.

He turned to study his reflection in the slightly steamed-up mirror over the sink, rubbing the dark stubble on his chin as he debated whether or not to shave. He decided not; he had three more days before the parents arrived to just wind down and relax after all the razzmatazz that had gone along with attending his latest movie premiere last weekend, and not shaving was part of that process.

No doubt his mother would have some comment to make about his longer hair, though, he acknowledged ruefully as he looked at the dishevelled damp locks that rested on the broad width of his shoulders. He was due to start filming the long-awaited sequel to *The Pirate King* next month, and had grown his dark hair in preparation for the part.

If they could find a replacement leading lady, that was. A five months pregnant female pirate captain wouldn't exactly look right, and Hawk's schedule was such that filming couldn't be delayed until after the baby's birth.

Oh, well—that was the director Nik Prince's problem, not his. Hawk shrugged dismissively to himself as he strolled through to his bedroom.

'Donald, I think I might—who the *hell* are you?' Hawk rasped. He came to an abrupt halt in the bathroom doorway to stare across the room at the young woman standing in front of the window and drawing back his bedroom curtains.

There was no mistaking that she was a woman. Her long red waist-length hair gave that away, flowing down the slenderness of her spine the colour of rippling fire against a body-hugging black sweater.

But even without the hair it was impossible not to recognise that the tall, leggy figure belonged to a female. Her skin-tight black denims were doing everything they could to prove the point, Hawk saw with a frown.

At the same time he knew there shouldn't be a female—tall and leggy or otherwise—within several miles of here!

Rosie had turned at the first sound of the unmistakable, sexily husky voice of the actor Joshua Hawkley, taking in a sharp breath as she found herself gazing upon his nakedness.

Joshua Hawkley, thirty-five years old, the most sought-after film star in the world for over a decade, was standing in front of her—gorgeously, gloriously and magnificently naked!

Her throat felt dry, her lips and tongue numb, as she continued to stare at him with wide green eyes.

She had never been the sort of teenager—had never been *allowed* to be the sort of teenager!—who'd hung posters of pop and film stars on her bedroom wall. But if she had, this man would definitely have had pride of position!

Joshua Hawkley—or simply Hawk to his friends—at a height well over six feet, had a body Adonis would have been envious of: his shoulders were wide and muscular, and dark hair grew on the broadness of his chest and down over the flatness of his stomach to—

Wow.

Gasp.

Whoa!

A sudden rush of saliva moistened her throat and

mouth as she found it impossible to remove her gaze from his perfect manhood.

As if becoming aware of the avidness of her gaze, Hawk moved one hand to casually pull the towel from his shoulders before draping and fastening it about his waist.

Rosie blinked, as if waking from a spell, before dragging her eyes back up to his face. Colour warmed her cheeks at the knowing smile curving those sculptured lips in a face that could have—*should* have—been carved by Michelangelo. A face dominated by cobalt-blue eyes above a long aquiline nose, that lazily smiling mouth and the strongly squared jaw. Long dark hair, damp and dishevelled after his shower, did absolutely nothing to dispel his air of masculine perfection, only adding to his ruggedness.

'I have absolutely no idea how you got in here,' Hawk bit out impatiently as the girl continued to stare at him unblinkingly. 'But I seriously advise you to get yourself out again!' he added, with none of the tolerance he usually felt towards his more enthusiastic female fans.

This was his bolt-hole, damn it, and it shouldn't even be public knowledge, let alone accessible to some desperate woman who had got in here because she either wanted to share his bed or use a relationship with him to acquire a movie role!

How on earth had she got past Donald?

The girl—for she was no more than that, Hawk was sure, despite her height and the fullness of her breasts and those curvaceous hips—moistened the sensual softness of her pouting lips.

Her eyes, between lush dark lashes, were a deep, mesmerising green, her nose was small and pert, and covered with a smattering of freckles and her chin was stubbornly pointed in a heart-shaped face. And all of her elfin beauty was surrounded by that long flame of pre-Raphaelite-style hair.

At any other time, Hawk knew, he would have found her untamed beauty fascinating. But not when she had invaded the privacy of his home. Not just his home, but his bedroom, for heaven's sake!

'If you aren't out of here in two minutes I'll have no choice but to forcibly remove you,' he warned her harshly, and he ran an impatient hand through his tousled hair, his previous good humour having completely evaporated, to be replaced by impatient anger at this girl's intrusion.

She moistened her lips a second time before speaking, those green eyes huge and haunting. 'If you would just let me explain, Mr Hawkley—' Her voice was throatily soft, her accent distinctly English.

'Keep your explanation and just get out of here!' he cut in irritably, his gaze narrowing suddenly as he saw the tray bearing a cafetière and coffee cups on the bedside table. She must have brought it in with her. 'Where's Donald?' he rasped suspiciously.

'That's what I was trying to explain,' Rosie answered, with some relief.

'You were?' His stance was challenging now, muscles rippling as he folded his arms across his chest.

He really was as gorgeous as he looked on screen, Rosie acknowledged slightly breathlessly, and his semi-nakedness made him more immediately so in the intimacy and privacy of his bedroom.

But it was also pretty obvious from Joshua Hawkley's comments that he was in complete ignorance of who she was or what she was doing here. That Donald hadn't told his employer that she was even staying here.

Joshua Hawkley's aggression was understandable now that she realised he had thought she was an intruder—an over-enthusiastic female fan?—in his home.

She shrugged. 'My—er—I don't know if you noticed, but Donald wasn't at all well yesterday when he picked you up from the airport…' She grimaced as Hawk gave a puzzled shake of his head. 'No? Well, this morning he woke up shivering and with a high temperature. I think he probably has the flu,' she finished.

Three things became obvious to Hawk from that statement.

First, this girl knew exactly who Donald was, and so wasn't an intruder at all.

Second, she had come to an abrupt halt after beginning her statement with 'My—'

And third, perhaps she didn't need to complete it. She had obviously been around to see what Donald had looked like when he woke up that morning…!

CHAPTER TWO

IN THE LIGHT of those realisations, Hawk re-evaluated the young woman standing beside his sleep-tousled bed.

She looked vaguely familiar to him—as if he should know her... Where had he seen her before? He knew he had never met her.

And obviously she was here to see Donald...

She had to be in her early twenties—but then Donald was only in his early forties. A twenty-year-odd age difference wasn't an insurmountable barrier.

Hawk had never found the need to discuss Donald's private life with him, but he supposed that his assistant must have one. He knew that the older man liked to listen to classical music, and that when their schedule allowed Donald took off to go to live concerts in one part of the world or another.

But, despite his cultured tastes, there was still no doubting that Donald—even with his prematurely white hair—was still an attractive guy, and in possession of all normal male needs.

Even so, Donald could have warned Hawk that he

had invited a female guest to stay when Hawk had returned home last night. Donald had arrived two days earlier, so that he could prepare and warm the farm-house for his employer's arrival.

Hawk scowled, feeling at something of a disadvantage now, after his first assumptions about this lady. 'Does Donald need to see a doctor?'

'I don't think so.' Rosie shook her head, somewhat relieved that Hawk wasn't probing for intimate details of her relationship with his long-term employee. 'I've given him some medication to bring his temperature down, so he probably just needs to go back to sleep for a while. Something he's loath to do without speaking to you first,' she added. The reason for Donald's urgent need was becoming obvious now that she knew of this man's ignorance regarding her identity.

Joshua Hawkley gave a terse nod. 'I'll get dressed and come straight through.'

'I—yes. I'll make fresh coffee, shall I?' she asked with a grimace, as she picked up the untouched tray she had brought in earlier.

Hawk felt a brandy might be more beneficial after the jolt of unexpectedly finding this woman in his bed-room, but as it was only ten o'clock in the morning coffee would have to do. 'That would be great,' he accepted briskly, turning away, eager to put some clothes on so that he could go and speak to Donald.

He pondered the fact that if Donald had relation-ships, then he had never brought any of his women home with him before. But at the same time Hawk recognised it was the holiday season—a time when everyone wanted to be close to somebody.

Which meant he would probably have to accept Donald's red-haired and wildly beautiful friend staying for a while.

A thought he found strangely disturbing...

The fresh coffee had barely finished percolating when Joshua Hawkley entered the cosy warmth of the open-plan kitchen, with its green and white tiles and oak cabinets.

'The medication seems to have served its purpose,' he drawled, as Rosie turned to give him a guarded look. 'Donald is already asleep,' he elaborated. 'Which means that any explanations will have to come from you,' he finished dryly, and he moved to sit on one of the stools at the breakfast bar, looking across at her enquiringly.

He was a little less overwhelming now that he was wearing a navy blue sweater, faded denims and scuffed cowboy boots, Rosie acknowledged. But only a little; the dark good looks that so captivated cinema audiences, that held millions of women in his thrall, were no less disturbing in reality, and the long length of his hair was giving him a piratical appearance.

Which was probably the idea, Rosie allowed, knowing he was due to start filming the sequel to his previous million-dollar box office hit *The Pirate King* some time in the New Year.

She deliberately turned away from his piercing blue

gaze to pour his coffee into a waiting mug, playing for time, not really sure how much Donald would want her to tell his employer. The fact that Donald hadn't told Hawk anything about her at all only increased her reluctance!

'Pour yourself a cup and join me,' Hawk invited huskily, once she had placed the steaming mug of black coffee on the breakfast bar in front of him, along with milk and sugar.

After all, just because she was Donald's friend it didn't mean she had to wait on him.

Hawk watched her through narrowed lids as she reluctantly complied with his suggestion, the movements of her graceful hands economic, her slender body willowy—apart from the pert fullness of her breasts as they thrust against her sweater.

For all that he had been surprised to find her here, Hawk certainly couldn't fault Donald's taste in women!

He waited until she had seated herself on the stool opposite, her gaze not quite meeting his, before speaking again. 'Perhaps we should start with your name?' he invited mildly.

It shouldn't have been a difficult question, but nevertheless Hawk sensed her hesitation, the slightly searching look she gave him before answering.

'Rosie,' she finally told him, those graceful hands wrapped around her coffee mug as if drawing strength from its warmth.

Hawk kept his expression deliberately mild. 'Rosie what?'

'Look, Mr Hawkley.' She looked up at him, obviously seriously uncomfortable with his questioning. 'I really think you should talk to my—Donald about this.'

Again Hawk heard that hesitation after 'my'...

'My' what? Friend? Lover? What?

Hawk found himself with an overwhelming curiosity to know the answer to that question.

So he waited, knowing from experience that an expectant silence on his part would eventually bring a response. He didn't have to wait long.

'If my being here is an inconvenience, then you only have to say so and I'll leave,' she began flusteredly.

But the mere suggestion of her doing any such thing seemed to make her cheeks pale and those deep green eyes look haunted...

Why? Hawk wondered. What was this woman hiding, or running away from? More to the point, why had she chosen Donald to run to?

He regarded her with hooded eyes. 'I'm not saying so,' he drawled. 'I'm merely wondering. Have you and Donald known each other long?'

Had she and Donald known each other long? Rosie pondered. Surely that depended on what was meant by *knowing* each other?

'A while, yes,' she finally answered huskily.

Hawk nodded. 'And you're here to spend the holidays with him?'

'Possibly.' Again her answer was noncommittal.

Only having arrived in Canada herself yesterday, Hawk's imminent arrival and Donald's early flu symptoms had proved a distraction to any deep conversation she might have had with Donald, so Rosie had no idea what her short or even long-term plans were. No idea whether Donald would even want her to stay and spend the holidays with him.

The only thing that had consumed her yesterday, as she'd thrown things into a suitcase in readiness for her flight, was the thought of the white satin and lace wedding dress that hung on her wardrobe door—a constant reminder of just why she had to get away. She'd needed to go somewhere where no one would think of looking for her, hopefully where no one would recognise her either. Joshua Hawkley obviously hadn't…

Rosie had been puzzled, a few days before, when, taking her passport from the box where her mother kept all the family's papers, she'd seen a piece of paper there too, on which Donald's telephone number was scrawled. Her puzzlement had turned to shock when curiosity had made her call the number and Donald had answered. She had discovered it was his current mobile number!

She didn't know which of them had been the more surprised to hear the other's voice, although Donald had readily agreed when she'd asked him if she might fly out to Canada to see him.

Hawk was still watching her from between narrowed lids. 'You aren't being very—forthcoming about your relationship with Donald,' he finally murmured impatiently.

Her relationship with Donald? Did she have one?

She wasn't sure any more. But perhaps that was part of why she had come here—to find out…?

She straightened. 'I really think you should talk to him about this.'

Hawk shrugged broad shoulders. 'He isn't up to talking about anything at the moment.'

And Donald hadn't been yesterday, actually, Rosie accepted. Donald's flu symptoms were obviously worse today, which was making this situation more difficult for her than it needed to be.

It had all seemed so simple when she'd arrived yesterday and discovered that Donald had his own suite of rooms over the garage adjoining the farmhouse. It was an arrangement that meant Joshua Hawkley didn't even have to be made aware of her presence if Donald decided otherwise.

But waking up this morning to find Donald incapacitated in his bed had changed all that—even more so when he had asked her to take Joshua Hawkley's morning tray of coffee up to his employer. A request Rosie had very reluctantly agreed to when it seemed it was the only way to stop Donald's growing agitation.

She roused herself to reply to Hawk's comment. 'Then I suggest you wait until he's feeling better.'

Hawk found himself bristling at her dismissive tone. He was being reasonable about this, wasn't he? Considering he had found a strange woman wandering around his bedroom only a short time ago, he really thought so!

What—?

'Hawk!' A distraught, tousle-haired and robe-covered Donald staggered into the kitchen, the ravages of the flu evident in the paleness of his lined face. 'I meant to tell you—' He looked at the two of them seated at the breakfast-bar. 'I just felt so ill last night that all I wanted to do was fall into bed—' He gave a frustrated shake of his head as he swayed slightly. 'I hope Rosie has explained?' he added weakly as she stood up.

Hawk's mouth twisted ruefully as he also stood up. 'Not so far, no,' he drawled ruefully. 'But I'm living in hope,' he added, with a mocking glance at her flushed face.

Donald looked across at her dazedly. 'You haven't told him...?'

Told him exactly what? And how much? Rosie frowned.

The situation had felt so difficult last night—the gulf between Donald and herself so wide that the two of them hadn't had a proper chance to talk yet, let alone involve a third party. And that third party was Joshua Hawkley! A man who lived in the limelight himself, who once he knew her full name might add two and two together and come up with the correct answer of four!

The fewer people who knew who she was, the less likelihood there was of—

'Rosie is my daughter, Hawk,' Donald turned to tell the other man before she had a chance to stop him.

Hawk's cobalt-blue eyes widened on her incredulously, telling Rosie that this was the last explanation he'd been expecting!

CHAPTER THREE

DONALD'S daughter…

Whoever Hawk had thought this young woman might be, it certainly wasn't the other man's daughter!

He hadn't even known Donald had been married, let alone that he had a daughter of—what?—twenty-two, twenty-three?

But maybe Donald hadn't been married. Maybe this girl was the result of a brief relationship all those years ago. Whatever—it didn't make her any less than *Donald's daughter*.

Hawk had never once heard Donald mention her in the ten years he'd worked for him, let alone seen her!

But had *Donald* seen her during that time? Hawk supposed that he must have done. After all, his employee had holidays, free time, and he certainly didn't owe Hawk any explanations about his personal life.

Where had Rosie suddenly appeared from? Because he was pretty sure that Donald hadn't known she was going to join them here when he'd come ahead from Los Angeles a couple of days ago.

More to the point, *why* had she come...?

Hawk felt a little dazed. 'Perhaps we should get you back to bed,' he murmured, as Donald coughed painfully. 'Rosie can tell me anything else I need to know,' he concluded, with a narrow-eyed glance in her direction.

But Rosie had no intention of telling him anything more than she absolutely had to!

Hawk's surprise at discovering she was actually Donald's daughter, rather than the lover he had clearly assumed her to be, had been pretty obvious. But, if anything, he looked more disapproving of the true explanation of their relationship than he had of his previous assumption!

She shrugged off the movie star's disapproval impatiently. Her father might work for Hawk, and as such owe him some sort of explanation as to why she was here, but that didn't mean Rosie was answerable to him too.

Not even if she was to be a temporary guest in his home?

No, not even then, she decided stubbornly.

'Let's go and finish our coffee,' Hawk suggested, softly but firmly, as they settled Donald back in his bed. The effort of coming downstairs seemed to have tired out the factotum, and he lay back exhausted against the pillows.

'Would you like me to stay and make you some tea?' Rosie offered gently, at the same time pointedly ignoring Hawk. 'Or bring you a glass of cool juice?'

Donald gave a weak smile. 'No, I—I'll be fine. You go and talk to Hawk,' he encouraged huskily.

Not what she wanted to do at all, Rosie reflected, as she turned and preceded Hawk from the flat and back down the stairs to the kitchen in the main house, all the time thinking of what she actually needed, *had* to tell, this disturbingly attractive man.

Not that much, really, she decided. The bare bones of the truth should do it. She hadn't had a chance to tell her father everything yesterday, about her reasons for being here, and there was no need to tell Hawk either.

'Have you finished deciding how much I need to know?' Hawk probed wryly once they were seated back at the breakfast bar, knowing by the way her cheeks became flushed that he had scored a direct hit with his question.

She raised her pointed chin defensively. 'My father has already told you all there is to know, Mr Hawkley—'

'Hawk,' he put in firmly, elbows resting on the breakfast bar as he studied her across its width. 'Somehow I don't think that's true, Rosie,' he persisted. 'For instance, the glaringly obvious thing Donald hasn't told me is why I didn't know of your existence until today!'

Auburn brows rose over her cool green eyes. 'Perhaps he didn't consider it any of your business,' she dismissed.

Hawk was starting to feel seriously irritated by this woman's deliberate rudeness. She certainly hadn't looked so cool earlier, when he had strolled out of the bathroom stark naked!

If he were honest, he hadn't felt that cool himself when he'd first became aware of her in his bedroom— the tell-tale stirring of his body had been proof of that! He studied her closely now, noting the golden ring circling the green of her eyes, making them appear almost luminous, and the freckles that covered her nose, making him wonder if she had freckles anywhere else. And what it would feel like to kiss every one of them…

He straightened, impatient with his own wandering thoughts. He wasn't involved in a relationship with anyone at the moment, but he had only left Los Angeles yesterday—the land of plenty when it came to beautiful available women. Finding himself attracted to Rosie Harrison, who took the phrase 'woman of mystery' to a whole new level, was a complication he certainly didn't need. Now or at any other time.

'Are you here to spend Christmas with Donald?' he enquired tersely, the thought of Rosie sharing the flat over the garage with Donald during the holidays robbing him of some of his contentment at the contemplation of a quiet family Christmas.

'That hasn't been decided yet,' she answered noncommittally.

She brought a whole new dimension to that saying about getting blood out of a stone too, Hawk acknowledged impatiently, deciding he had had enough of this verbal fencing for one morning.

'Although the fact that he's obviously ill does rather change things, doesn't it?' Rosie suddenly opined.

Hawk eyed her warily. 'It does?'

'Well, of course it does,' she came back waspishly. 'Apart from the fact that he's ill and will need looking after, he's obviously also unable to work. As I understand it, you're expecting the rest of your family to descend on you in the next few days...?'

'Yes...' Hawk confirmed, wariness in his own tone now.

'And Don—my father,' she corrected awkwardly, 'was supposed to shop for food, put up the decorations and things?'

'Yes.' Hawk nodded, very aware of the fact that she seemed to be having difficulty actually calling Donald her father.

Damn it, why did Donald have to get the flu now? Because Hawk was pretty sure he was going to have to wait until his assistant was better before he got any helpful answers to his questions!

No matter how much she was determined not to answer Hawk's questions, Rosie was also aware that if he chose to tell Donald she couldn't stay on here her father would have no choice but to ask her to leave. And the truth was, at this moment in time, she didn't have anywhere else to go to...

In the circumstances, it wasn't in her best interests to be completely uncooperative...

'Well, I could do those things for you instead—if you would like me to,' she offered lightly. 'If you'll just point me in the direction of the nearest supermarket and tell me where you keep the Christmas decorations…?' she prompted, at Hawk's lack of a response to her offer.

He raised dark brows over mocking blue eyes, a slightly derisive smile curving the sculptured mouth that was set so arrogantly in his ruggedly handsome face. Rosie's pulse fluttered slightly as she was once again forcibly reminded of exactly who this man was.

Only a woman who was deaf, blind or totally insensitive to blatant sexiness could fail not to tremble slightly with awareness in his presence.

But she was a woman running away from her wedding day, from a man she neither loved nor wanted to marry, which should have made her totally immune to the attractions of any other member of the opposite sex.

But it didn't…

She tried to break her gaze away from the compelling blue of Hawk's eyes. And failed. Instead she felt as if she were drowning in their dark depths, as if she were trying to swim against the tide, and the effort to resist rendered her slightly breathless and trembling.

This wouldn't do, she told herself firmly. Joshua Hawkley might be one of the most dangerously attractive men she had ever met, but he was also her father's employer—her father's over-curious employer! She would be wise to keep that in mind.

It took some effort, but she finally managed to drag her gaze away from his, staring at a point somewhere over Hawk's left shoulder. 'Unless you would prefer to do those things yourself—?'

'Hell, no! You feel free to carry on, if that's what you want to do,' he bit out as he stood up.

Rosie sighed. 'I merely offered because I'm sure my father would expect it,' she explained.

'I've already said it's fine, Rosie,' Hawk drawled. 'I still have to shop for gifts, anyway. One more to add to the list now,' he added pointedly.

Rosie gave him a startled glance. Surely he didn't mean her…?

'Please don't bother on my account,' she told him hastily.

She'd brought some cash with her, which she had changed into Canadian dollars at the airport, but those funds were limited, and certainly wouldn't last very long if she had to go out and buy Christmas presents for Joshua Hawkley and his family. She'd had no choice but to use her credit card when she booked her air ticket, but was loath to use it now. Canada was a big country, but paying with her credit card would certainly give away her location to anyone unprincipled enough—determined enough—to use that method to track her down.

Her caution would probably seem a little dramatic to anyone else, but she had come to know only too well the ruthlessness of her pursuer…

In the last few minutes Hawk had watched all the different emotions as they'd flickered across the beauty of Rosie's face. Emotions too fleeting for him to be able to fully comprehend. But he had registered her slight panic at his mention of buying Christmas presents.

What was this woman hiding? Hawk wondered frowningly, as he continued to watch her anxious features.

Because he was pretty sure from the way she avoided answering his direct questions that she was hiding something…

CHAPTER FOUR

'I'LL drive you to the mall, if you like,' Hawk told her briskly. 'You can shop for food while I go off in search of gifts for my family.' Even as he made the suggestion he could see that it didn't sit too well with Rosie Harrison. Her slender hands trembled slightly as she collected up their empty coffee mugs and put them in the dishwasher.

At least he thought it was his suggestion that was making her tremble...

It was difficult to tell what she was thinking or feeling when she continued to avoid his gaze!

She shook her head. 'I don't think my father would approve of my putting you to any trouble on my behalf—'

'It isn't on your behalf if you're going to be shopping for food for my family,' Hawk reasoned. 'Besides, I'm going into Calgary anyway,' he added firmly, feeling a sudden determination, now that he could see her reluctance, to take her with him.

How contrary was that?

Very, Hawk acknowledged ruefully. But after years of being a public figure, of being pursued by some of the most beautiful women in the world, it was something of a novelty to find a woman who was so obviously reluctant to spend any more time in his company than she had to.

That wasn't conceit on his part either, only fact; his place on the Hollywood A-list made him an easy—and possibly useful—target for any woman who was trying to make it in the movie business.

Besides, he might be able to get Rosie Harrison to open up a little more about herself if he spent some more time with her...

She gave another small shake of her head, her glorious red hair shimmering like a living flame as she did so. 'I don't think it's a good idea to just leave my father on his own when he isn't well.'

Considering Donald hadn't been well several times during the last ten years—whether with other bouts of flu or stomach upsets—and had managed pretty well without the attendance of his daughter, Hawk didn't think her being here this time was going to be of any relevance to the other man's wellbeing or recovery!

'Like all men, I know for a fact that Donald prefers to be on his own when he isn't feeling well,' Hawk assured her. 'But I'll go up and check on him while you get ready—explain what's happening if he's awake, if that makes you feel happier about going,' he assured her.

Rosie wasn't fooled by Hawk's lazily relaxed tone

for a moment. She knew by the look of determination on his face that he wasn't about to accept any of her arguments against going to Calgary with him. Much better to just give in gracefully.

'I'll only be five minutes,' she told him reluctantly. 'What?' she prompted, when she saw his sceptical expression.

'If you do only take five minutes to get ready to go out, then you'll be the first woman of my acquaintance to do so!' he explained wryly.

Rosie gave him a narrow-eyed glare. 'I can only assume that must be due to the type of woman you're acquainted with!'

'You're probably right!' Appreciative laughter glinted in his deep blue eyes as he gave a grin, his teeth white and even against his tanned skin. 'I'll go up and see Donald in a couple of minutes,' he confirmed, his gaze slightly mocking.

She hadn't taken the complication of this dangerously attractive man's presence here into account when she'd arranged to come to Canada so suddenly, Rosie acknowledged to herself as she hurried from the kitchen up to her father's flat. If she had thought about it at all, she'd have believed the actor would be too busy with his own family to even notice her. And if her father hadn't become suddenly ill, then he probably wouldn't have done.

All of which made absolutely no difference to the fact that he *had* noticed her, and that she was about to accompany him into Calgary in order to do his grocery shopping for him!

What would she have been doing if she were in England now?

Considering the time difference, she would most probably have been in bed. Although she doubted very much that she would have been asleep. Sleep seemed to be something that had eluded her more and more as her wedding day had approached and she'd realised what a mistake she was making.

But it was a mistake she had now done something about, she reminded herself firmly. Before it had been too late.

In fact, now that she thought about it, she didn't even want to contemplate what would be happening now if she were still in the UK!

She was going to take one day at a time, deal with one problem at a time—and what she had to concentrate on right now was getting ready in the five minutes she had assured Hawk that she would take!

'I'm impressed,' Hawk announced, as Rosie hurried down the stairs to join him at the front door—still with ten seconds of the allotted five minutes to spare!

He was a little disappointed that the wild flame of her hair was hidden under the black woollen hat she had pulled on over her ears. She was wearing a black coat too, which reached from her neck to her booted feet. Only the lively beauty of her face, dominated by those challenging green eyes, gave colour to her appearance.

He looked down at her assessingly. 'You shouldn't

wear black,' he said disapprovingly. 'It drains all the colour from your face.'

Colour—angry colour—heightened the paleness of her cheeks. 'When I want your opinion, I'll ask for it!' she snapped, before preceding him out of the door he was holding open for her, more annoyed with the fact that she knew he was right than with his actual comment.

But almost every item of clothing she owned was black, so he was going to be disappointed if he expected his criticism to elicit any change in her wardrobe!

She drew in a sharp breath at the extreme cold she encountered as she stepped outside. Snow had started to fall some time in the last ten minutes or so, landing stingingly on her face as she turned to look up at Hawk. 'Perhaps we should wait until this storm blows over…?' she voiced uncertainly.

He grinned down at her, seeming completely unconcerned by the flakes landing in the dark thickness of his hair. 'If you stayed home every time it snowed in Canada you would never go anywhere,' he assured her as he used a remote to open the garage doors.

Rosie knew that a blizzard like this in England would bring everything—public transport and private cars alike—to a grinding halt. But if Hawk said it was okay, then she would have to take his word for it. She certainly wasn't about to let him think she was worried by a little thing like a snowstorm!

She had to admit that everywhere looked very beautiful as they travelled into Calgary. And there were lots of other drivers on the road who obviously felt the same reluctance as Hawk to have their movements dictated by the weather.

As they entered the shopping mall together, Rosie heard the Christmas carols that were playing over the public tannoy, saw the real pine tree that was at least twenty feet high, decorated from head to base in glittering red and green and lit by gold lights, and was suddenly struck by the realisation that it was going to be Christmas in a few days' time...

How ridiculous that she hadn't really thought of it before!

But she knew it was the thought of her wedding on Christmas Eve that had driven awareness of anything else from her panicked mind.

How long had it been since she had been free to actually enjoy Christmas? To listen to Christmas carols? To go to a mall like this and see all the excited expectation on the other shoppers' faces?

Too long, she acknowledged heavily.

But she was free to enjoy it now, she assured herself determinedly, at once brightening at the thought. It might even be fun to spend Christmas here in Canada with her father—

'Feel like sharing the secret?' Hawk asked huskily at her side.

She turned to give him a startled look. 'What secret?' she snapped warily.

He shrugged his broad shoulders. 'You were looking

serious, and then you suddenly began to smile; I merely wondered what had brought about the transformation.'

Well, he could go on wondering!

Too many of her freedoms had been curbed these last ten years, but her thoughts were most definitely her own!

'Hey, Hawk,' a man called out in greeting as he walked past them. 'Looking forward to seeing your next movie!'

'Thanks,' Hawk returned with a smile.

It was the first of many such greetings as they continued to stroll down the mall.

It was interesting to Rosie that although people obviously recognised Hawk as the actor Joshua Hawkley, and smiled or spoke to him as they passed, he met their attention with a languid charm that, while it was not unfriendly, didn't invite further conversation either. A manner they all accepted with good humour.

She turned to give him a curious glance, feeling Hawk's hand beneath her elbow as they strolled towards the grocery store. 'Doesn't it bother you?' she questioned. 'All this attention,' she explained as he raised dark brows enquiringly. 'People talking to you? Watching you? Talking about you?'

He gave the question some thought. 'If it was going to bother me, then I shouldn't have become an actor and put myself in the limelight,' he finally replied.

Rosie couldn't help admiring his pragmatic attitude. Even if she didn't share it...

But then, becoming a public figure in the UK had never been her choice, had it?

'Are you going to be okay doing the grocery shopping on your own?' Hawk enquired as they reached the store entrance. 'If not, I could always—'

'No, I'm sure I'll be fine,' she assured him quickly. 'I just—do you have any cash?' she asked awkwardly. 'My credit card is maxed out from booking my flight, I'm afraid.' Having mulled her difficulty over during the drive into the city, she had decided this was the best excuse she could come up with.

Hawk looked at her for several long seconds before answering her. 'Just wander about for half an hour or so, picking up what you think we're going to need, and then I'll meet you at the checkout and pay for it all,' he finally decided.

Rosie turned away on the pretext of collecting a trolley so that he wouldn't see the embarrassed colour that had stained her cheeks under his probing gaze. Not feeling it was safe to use her own credit card was going to be more difficult than she had imagined if Hawk was going to look at her in that totally sceptical way too often…

'How many people am I shopping for?' she asked briskly as she rejoined him.

'Seven adults and two kids. Donald normally joins us for Christmas dinner,' he explained.

Maybe that was what Donald normally did during the holidays, but he had his own daughter here with him this year—and Rosie certainly didn't want to be included in the Hawkley family Christmas.

But standing outside a supermarket, with Hawk still attracting curious glances, wasn't the ideal time to argue that particular point!

'Traditional fare?' she enquired efficiently instead.

'Very traditional,' Hawk answered dryly. 'My mother is British. Anything less than turkey and all the trimmings is sacrilege in her traditionalist's eyes!'

Rosie felt a little unsettled at the knowledge that Hawk's mother shared her own nationality. It made him a little less of the unknown quantity that she would have preferred him to be.

Hawk felt himself smiling with hard satisfaction as he saw that knowing his mother was British had unnerved Rosie slightly. She was far too cool and self-contained for his liking, and anything that gave him an edge had to be a positive thing.

'She will have made a Christmas pudding and will bring it with her, so don't worry about that,' he instructed.

'I wasn't worrying,' she assured him tartly.

'Do you cook, Rosie?' He quirked his dark brows.

'Why?' she countered suspiciously.

Hawk shrugged. 'It's always useful to know.'

Her mouth tightened. 'No, Mr Hawkley, I don't cook.'

'Pity.' He grimaced. 'In that case, it looks as if we'll have to put up with my cooking for the next few days!'

Rosie stared up at him wordlessly for several long

seconds, looking as if she would like to argue his use of the word 'we', and then thought better of it as she snapped, 'If you'll excuse me? I'll go and do your food shopping for you now...' She moved off with her shopping trolley.

Hawk stood and watched her go, knowing a quiet satisfaction that he had managed to rattle her cool control slightly.

Rosie had been in the bathroom getting ready when Hawk had paid his visit to check on Donald. The older man had been dozing—not peacefully so, but caught somewhere between sleep and slight delirium as he muttered to someone who clearly wasn't there...

'Don't worry, Gloria... Going to America...won't be coming back,' Donald had mumbled. 'Won't forget the money, Gloria.' Then, with startling clarity, the feverish man had bitten out, 'Don't bring our daughter up to be a money-grasping bitch like *you*!' before lapsing back into his troubled slumber.

'Our daughter...'

Rosie...?

The young woman who had felt no qualms just now at asking Hawk for cash to buy the groceries even though she must have known he was good for it—that he would have reimbursed any money she had paid out on his behalf?

Had the absent Gloria brought her daughter up to be a money-grabber, after all?

He didn't know—couldn't fathom what sort of

woman Rosie was from the little she was prepared to tell him about herself.

It was a situation that would need watching.

And for all that he didn't quite trust her, or her motives, Hawk knew he would be more than happy to watch Rosie…

CHAPTER FIVE

'HERE—let me do that.'

Rosie barely had time to register that Hawk had rejoined her in the supermarket before she felt him move to take over pushing the trolley.

Except she hadn't let go of it yet...

Hawk's hands covered hers. Big hands. Warm, protective and strong hands.

So very strong, Rosie thought, and she felt the equivalent of an electric shock run along the length of her fingers and up her arm.

She snatched her own hands quickly away. What was that? What had just happened?

'Did I hurt you?' Hawk had turned to her with concern, reaching out as if to take her hands in his so that he could inspect them.

Rosie thrust her trembling hands behind her back as she stared up at him. Hurt her? No, he certainly hadn't hurt her. She wasn't sure what had happened...

For years she had imagined that some strong, dauntless man would come along and sweep her off her feet.

A man who would rescue her and take her away from a life that had become more of an ordeal than the enjoyment it had once been.

But Joshua Hawkley, although certainly strong and dauntless, certainly didn't want to rescue her! More the opposite—she had the definite feeling that since he had realised she was Donald's long-absent daughter he thought her father was the one who needed rescuing from her!

She moistened her lips before speaking. 'Just an electric shock from the trolley handle,' she dismissed, apparently unconcerned.

Those blue eyes darkened speculatively. 'Are you sure—?'

'You're back early,' Rosie interrupted brightly. 'Couldn't you find anything?' She looked at his empty hands.

The same hands that had just evoked such a strange trembling inside her…!

He grimaced. 'I made the mistake of going into a toy store first, and realised that I have absolutely no idea what to buy for a six-year-old boy—let alone a seven-year-old girl! I don't suppose you have any idea what I could get them?'

'Me?' Rosie echoed incredulously, that moment of complete awareness starting to fade. From her trembling body if not her memory!

'I guess not,' Hawk said, thinking that it had probably been a silly question; as an only child Rosie probably had no more idea of what children were into these days than he did. At least, he *assumed* she was an only child…

'You guess right,' Rosie confirmed dryly.

'I'll give Jen—my sister—a call later, and check it out with her,' he returned as he gave Rosie a considering look. 'Aren't you hot in all that gear…?' She was still wearing the thick woollen hat, as well as the heavy coat that covered her all the way from her throat to ankles, and her face was no longer pale but flushed from her stroll around the heated grocery store.

'It's easier than carrying them,' she replied tautly, before turning her attention to the rows of pasta on offer.

Deliberately? Yes, he believed so, Hawk decided frustratedly. What was it with this woman? Why was it such hard work even just trying to talk to her?

And what had happened just now when he touched her?

Because something had…

'Do you need any help putting that away, or can I go up and check on my father?' Rosie asked politely, once she had helped Hawk carry the bags of groceries from the garage into the house.

Enough groceries to feed an army rather than a family over Christmas—Hawk having added lots more things to the shopping trolley after joining her.

That was okay with her; it was his money, after all. Besides, once she had actually got inside the supermarket she had realised that, apart from buying the turkey and some accompanying vegetables, she knew absolutely nothing about feeding nine people over the Christmas period.

When she stopped to think about it, she couldn't remember the last time she had actually been at home for Christmas. She seemed to have spent the last five or six of them in some hotel suite somewhere in the world. And even when she and her mother had been at home, they certainly hadn't celebrated Christmas in the lavish way that Joshua Hawkley and his family were obviously going to.

What must it be like to be part of a big family like that? Rosie couldn't even begin to imagine—

Stop prevaricating, Rosie, she told herself firmly.

Stop pretending that nothing had happened!

Because it had. It most certainly had!

This wasn't about Christmas. This was about what had happened when Hawk had touched her in the supermarket. And no amount of prevarication on her part was going to make that go away!

That lowering of her guard—or the opening of her eyes to the joy of the people around her—seemed to have opened her up to all sorts of other emotions too.

Since then—since Hawk had touched her—no matter how she tried to deny it she had been totally aware of him, had trembled with awareness every time she looked at him.

She wanted to call a halt to the wild thoughts rushing through her brain, to make these new sensations go away. But, as hard as she tried, she hadn't been able to do it.

Maybe because, after this morning, she knew exactly what Hawk looked like beneath the thick sweater and denims he was wearing. How his muscles rippled across the width of this chest and arms when he moved. How silky the dark hair was on his tanned chest…

How much she longed to run her hands over the width of his shoulders and down the length of that muscular chest!

That was all she'd thought about since the moment Hawk's hands had touched hers in the supermarket!

In a supermarket, of all places!

She knew what it was, of course. She wasn't that naïve.

Sexual attraction.

Something she had never known before. Never felt before. But she knew she was feeling it now. Her whole body was trembling with her awareness of him, her senses singing with that same emotion, her breasts tight beneath her jumper, their nipples sensitised, aching.

Which was why she had to get away from Hawk for a while. Had to go somewhere she didn't have to look at him any more. Had to try to make some sense, gain some control, over these totally unexpected yearnings.

'Sure—you go and check on Donald,' Hawk agreed distractedly, as he began to open kitchen cabinets and put the food away, his muscles rippling as Rosie had known they would. 'It must be some time since the two of you last met up?'

He voiced the question casually, and yet Rosie knew it wasn't casual at all...

'A while,' she answered evasively.

Hawk turned to look at her, the intensity of his gaze easily holding hers. 'How long is a while?' he persisted.

Rosie's mouth tightened. 'Several years.'

'Years!' Hawk echoed incredulously, trying to put that knowledge together with Donald's fevered mumblings earlier. Although, when he thought about it, he knew Donald and Rosie hadn't spent Christmas together in the last ten years, because Donald had spent those Christmases with Hawk and his family! But still... 'You haven't seen your own father for *years*?'

Her gaze was challenging as she met his. 'No.'

'How many years?' he tried again.

'A few,' she bit out unhelpfully. 'Now, if you wouldn't mind, I really would like to go and see how he is...'

Hawk did mind. Very much. He was growing tired of this woman's guardedness, was becoming more and more convinced that her reasons for being here weren't innocent. 'I'll get the two of us some lunch when you come back—'

'I'm really not hungry,' Rosie cut in, not liking the turn this conversation had taken—deliberately so on Hawk's part, she was sure.

She was desperately hoping it was only tiredness after their morning out that was filling her with the fanciful longing to see Hawk naked once again...

'I—think jet-lag is catching up with me, or something.' She looked down at the floor to hide her discomfort.

Hawk's gaze narrowed as he continued to look across the kitchen at her. She had finally taken off the black woollen hat and her long coat, but was still looking a little pale, and her eyes seemed to glitter almost feverishly as she scanned the tiled floor. 'You aren't coming down with the flu too, are you?' he asked gently, and he moved across the kitchen towards her.

'No!' she protested, looking up suddenly and stepping back. 'No, I'm sure I'm not,' she repeated bristly, the smile she attempted not quite happening. 'A couple of hours' sleep and I'm sure I'll be fine,' she added, with forced, bright dismissal, her gaze not quite meeting his now.

Hawk stood only inches away from her and continued to look down at her searchingly. There was a slight flush to her cheeks now, and her eyes were definitely feverish, but somehow he didn't think that was caused by the onset of flu...

Her breathing was shallow, her breasts barely rising up and down with the movement, and yet he could see the clear outline of her nipples against the wool of her sweater. Aroused nipples. Engorged and thrusting...!

His eyes returned to her pinkened face—a face she raised to his now in defiant challenge, her jaw set, mouth firm, her green eyes defying him to voice what they were both aware of.

Rosie Harrison was completely physically aware of him!

A dangerous realisation when he was completely physically aware of her too! In fact, he couldn't remember the last time he had been so attracted to any woman, and that feeling had stayed with him since their hands had touched in the supermarket—

It was madness on his part to want Rosie! Not only was she the daughter of his employee, but Hawk also didn't yet trust her, or her motives for this sudden reappearance in Donald's life. And he would need to know a hell of a lot more about her before he did!

Damn it, for all he knew her reason for suddenly popping up in Donald's life could be as simple as the fact she was just another woman on the make, using her father in order to get close to *him*. Other women had tried much more daring exploits to gain his attention—including the one who had climbed from her tenth floor balcony over to his adjoining hotel suite in an effort just to say she had met him.

Unfortunately, it went along with the territory of being such a public figure.

It was also the reason that he had never even considered marriage.

He wanted the sort of marriage his parents had. One of complete giving and taking by both parties. Wanted to know that the woman he loved wanted him for himself, and not because he was Joshua Hawkley, movie star.

A tall order, he knew, when that was exactly who he was. But he wasn't willing to settle for anything less.

And Rosie Harrison, with her mysterious past as well as her present, certainly wasn't that woman.

The sooner Donald rallied and was able to answer some of Hawk's questions about his daughter, the better Hawk would like it!

'I'm sure you will be too,' he rasped, before stepping back. 'If Donald needs anything, let me know, hmm?' he added abruptly.

'I'll do that,' she replied sharply, turning and walking determinedly away from this man who tormented as well as attracted her.

What was wrong with her? Rosie berated herself as she climbed the stairs to her father's flat and closed the door firmly behind her. A little Christmas cheer, and the previously unknown luxury that for the first time in her adult life she was free to do whatever she wished, plus the first single, sexy man she had been in contact with for longer than she could remember—if ever!—and she responded like some gauche schoolgirl.

Worse, Hawk had *known* she responded!

She had seen that knowledge in his eyes just now, as he'd looked down at her so searchingly.

She gave a self-disgusted shake of her head before going through to the bedroom to check on her father. He was asleep, his temperature down when she touched his forehead, so she quietly left him to rest.

Without thinking about it, it seemed, she took her violin from its case, cradling it to her like a precious child. Which to her it was. It went with her wherever she travelled.

She wondered how long it had been since she had last played the precious instrument and known that same singing pleasure as her body had known when Hawk's hand had so briefly touched hers? Since she'd had the freedom to express in her playing the same excitement just looking at Hawk, imagining touching him, having him touch her, had given her...

Too long, she suspected.

How long before she would play like that again?

If she ever did...

CHAPTER SIX

'COME on, sleepyhead, let's get you moved to somewhere a little more comfortable!'

Rosie felt herself being lifted up in strong arms. A part of her wanted to protest, but her eyelids were too heavy, and she couldn't seem to find the words either, so instead her arms moved up over strong shoulders and she snuggled more comfortably against the hardness of a male chest beneath her cheek.

Her father had always carried her up to bed like this when she was a child and had fallen asleep in front of the television—carrying her up the stairs before tucking her warmly beneath her duvet—

Her lids flew open, wild with panic as she remembered she wasn't a child any longer. That she wasn't at home, but in Canada! That she had been too tired earlier to do any more than change into a soft cotton nightshirt and plait her hair before pulling the duvet over her and falling asleep on the sofa.

And her father was in bed himself, in the adjoining

bedroom, suffering with the flu, so he couldn't possibly be carrying her anywhere.

But Hawk was!

He gave a wolfish grin as he looked down into her wide, startled eyes. 'Don't look so worried, Rosie. I'm only taking you to one of the bedrooms in the main house.'

Which bedroom? His own? Had her arousal earlier been so obvious to him that—

'It suddenly occurred to me that there's only one bedroom in Donald's apartment,' Hawk rasped as he easily read—and didn't appreciate—the panicked thoughts going through Rosie's tousled head.

Hell, what sort of man did she imagine he was, to even think that he might be about to take advantage of her half-naked sleep-befuddled body?

His mouth tightened. 'There's no way you can sleep on the sofa for the whole of your stay, Rosie,' he said firmly.

'I'm sure that my—Donald and I will be able to sort something out once he's feeling a little better...' She trailed off, a frown creasing her creamy brow as she looked up at Hawk. 'You can put me down now!' she exclaimed. 'There's absolutely nothing wrong with my legs!'

There was nothing wrong with any part of her that Hawk could see. And he could see quite a lot. The nightshirt she wore was only knee-length, and showed a long expanse of shapely bare legs. Long, silky legs that would wrap around a man as he—

He gritted his teeth, his arms tightening about her as he felt the stirring of his body. Great. He had just taken umbrage because she obviously thought he had less than innocent intentions towards her—and now his body had hardened with desire for her!

'We're here now,' he said tersely, and he kicked open a door and carried her inside.

Where was here? Rosie wondered anxiously, as she looked around the room.

It was a bedroom, certainly, and the lack of any personal items on display meant it was probably one of the guest rooms in the main house.

'I can't stay here,' she protested, even as Hawk laid her down on the duvet-covered bed.

'Why can't you?' he rasped, as he straightened to look down at her. 'The farmhouse has four guest bedrooms, so there's plenty for everyone.'

She looked extremely defenceless, lying amongst the gold-coloured cushions scattered on top of the duvet, her white nightshirt patterned with pink roses, her hair no longer flowing loosely about her shoulders but secured back in a single plait that ran the length of her spine.

She gave a shake of her head. 'Your family—'

'Would be disappointed in me if I let you continue to sleep on Donald's sofa,' Hawk assured her huskily, and he sat down on the side of the bed.

He hadn't meant to. He'd told himself to get out of there. Now. But his body had ignored the instruction!

She really was the most delicately beautiful woman he had ever seen, he acknowledged, even as his gaze roamed appreciatively over her face and body. Her features were so perfect, the green of her eyes so mesmerising, the gentle curves of her body softly alluring, her breasts pert, her waist tiny and her thighs shapely above those long, long legs.

Hawk's gaze returned to her face, and he frowned slightly as again he processed the feeling that *he had seen her somewhere before.*

'Hawk…?'

His dark gaze moved to meet hers, seeing the question in her eyes as she looked up at him uncertainly. He placed his hands either side of her head and he began to lower his head towards hers.

Damn it, what had happened to his not taking advantage of her half-naked, sleep-befuddled body? Hawk remonstrated with himself, and he paused with his mouth only centimetres away from hers.

To hell with that! He *wanted* to kiss her, to touch her. And Rosie didn't seem to be fighting him off either, if the way her arms had moved up about his shoulders was anything to go by!

Just one kiss, he promised himself. Just to know the feel of her lips against his. To know the taste of her…

Rosie's whole body turned to molten fire as Hawk's mouth finally claimed hers, her lips parting instinctively as they explored him the way he was exploring her.

The awareness she had felt earlier today was nothing to the heated pleasure she found now in his arms as their kiss deepened and Hawk's arms moved about her to pull her up hard against him.

Rosie melted into him, seeming to become a part of him as her legs entangled with his.

She groaned low in her throat as one of his hands moved the length of her, skimming the curve of her hip and waist before moving to cup the thrust of her breast, the pad of his thumb moving across its hardened tip.

Her body arched instinctively against his caressing hand, her lips opening wider to the assault of his tongue as it thrust in moist rhythm to the wild beat of her heart. The hardness of Hawk's body lay half across hers, telling her of his own arousal.

So this was what it was like—what it felt like to make love, Rosie realised wonderingly, in the small, joyful part of her brain that could still function.

It was more beautiful, more wonderful, than anything she could ever have imagined, and she knew no sense of denial as Hawk's hands began to restlessly roam the length of her spine, before cupping her bottom as he pulled her more tightly against him.

Rosie pushed her own hands beneath his sweater, touching him as she had so longed to do, her hands moving caressingly across the broad width of his back.

He felt good. So very good.

But she wanted more. Needed more. Wanted to feel—

She fell back against the pillows as Hawk wrenched his mouth from hers and held her away from him, to look down at her with eyes turned navy blue and a face pale beneath his tan.

Hawk breathed shallowly, moving determinedly away from Rosie even as he saw the hurt confusion in those dark green eyes at his sudden rejection.

He stood up to move across the room and stare out of the window. The same snowy scene that he had found so soothing earlier this morning did absolutely nothing to calm his chaotic thoughts now.

What was he doing?

He didn't even know her. Not that that was a prerequisite to making love to a woman. Normally. But Rosie wasn't just *any* woman. She was Donald's daughter. The daughter of the man who had been his friend as well as his employee for the last ten years.

Donald's daughter—whom Hawk distrusted as deeply as he desired her!

He leant his forehead against the coldness of the windowpane as he fought for the control that had so readily deserted him minutes ago.

Well, he knew what Rosie tasted like now: of heat and sensuality. Of a sweetness that had made him want to kiss her and carry on kissing her until his body was joined with hers and he found release inside her.

It was a need he was determined not to satisfy!

He dragged deep, controlling breaths into his lungs, tensing his shoulders before turning back to face her.

She no longer lay back amongst those pillows but sat on the side of the bed, her face very pale against the vivid fire of her hair, which was no longer confined in that plait but had come loose to swing protectively forward and cover the swell of her breasts.

Breasts that seconds ago had fitted so perfectly into his hands and had responded to his lightest touch…

His mouth tightened as he firmly closed a door on those memories. 'Who are you, Rosie?' he snapped harshly.

She blinked her confusion. 'You know who I am—'

'Donald's daughter.' He nodded impatiently. 'But that's not who you really are, is it?' he accused.

Rosie frowned across at him warily, even as she fought an inner battle to put her defences back in place. Defences Hawk had so easily knocked down only minutes ago as he kissed and caressed her…

But she mustn't think about that now—had to concentrate on what he was really asking her.

Hawk hadn't seemed to know anything about her at all this morning—not even that she was Donald's daughter. But had that changed in the last few minutes? Despite his earlier ignorance about her identity, had Hawk now recognised her as the world-famous virtuoso violinist Rosemary Harris? As 'La Bella Rosa', as the enthusiastic Italians had long ago dubbed her?

CHAPTER SEVEN

HAWK'S gaze narrowed speculatively as he easily saw the pallor deepen in Rosie's face, those deep green eyes once again taking on a haunted look.

So he was right after all, he acknowledged heavily. Rosie *was* hiding something. And with Donald too ill as yet to enlighten him—if indeed he even knew what secret his daughter was hiding—it would have to be Rosie herself who satisfied his curiosity.

From the guarded look on her face it was something he didn't think she was going to be too willing to do!

He thrust his hands into his denims pockets. 'You're—what? Twenty-two? Twenty-three?' he prompted harshly.

'Twenty-two,' she confirmed shakily.

He nodded. 'Then who have you been for the last twenty-two years, Rosie—because you sure as hell haven't been Donald's daughter!'

'Don't be ridiculous!' she came back with a derisive laugh. 'If I'm Donald's daughter now, then I must have been his daughter for the last twenty-two years too!'

The laugh had been a mistake, Rosie realised as she

saw Hawk's gaze darken dangerously. But what else could she do? She didn't want Hawk to know who she was—that in the world of classical music—a world he obviously wasn't in touch with—she was as well-known and successful as he was. She didn't want anyone in Canada to realise she was Rosemary Harris. She wanted—needed—to maintain her anonymity for a little longer.

Perhaps it would be better if she left here now?

She hadn't seen her father since he'd walked out on her and her mother when Rosie was twelve years old—had only come to him now because she had known it was the very last place her mother and Edmund—the man Rosie didn't want to marry on Christmas Eve or at any other time!—would think to look for her.

But Hawk was proving to be a complication she hadn't bargained for. And not just because of his persistence in trying to find out more about her...

He disturbed her. Excited her. Aroused her. Gave her an insight into emotions she hadn't even guessed at.

Which might be a positive thing with regard to her interpretation of the music she played, but was of absolutely no help at all to the peace of mind she was so desperately seeking.

The peace of mind she needed if she was to discover if she ever wanted to play again...

Which meant she had to concentrate on finding that peace for herself. And she couldn't find it around Hawk!

She shook her head. 'It's obvious you would rather I didn't stay on here, Hawk, so—'

'It's "obvious", is it?' he repeated scathingly. 'After the way we just were together?'

Well...no. But he certainly wasn't too pleased about his own response to her a few minutes ago, was he?

She shrugged narrow shoulders. 'I think that's something better not repeated, don't you?' she said carefully.

Hawk gave a humourless laugh. This woman really was something else. But what? That was the real question...

'Am I to take it from that comment that you're not sure, if you *do* stay on here, that you'll be able to keep your hands off my body?' he derided mockingly.

Her cheeks coloured at the taunt, her eyes sparkling angrily as she raised her chin challengingly. 'You really aren't that irresistible, Mr Hawkley,' she bit out coldly.

This time his laugh was genuine. 'Touché, Rosie,' he murmured appreciatively. 'But as for your leaving...' He sobered, shaking his head. 'I somehow don't think Donald would appreciate my driving his daughter away before the two of you have even had a chance to spend any time together.'

'This is your home, not my father's,' she replied evenly.

Yes, it was—and his stay here wasn't turning out to be the relaxing time he had expected it to be. But all the same he knew that Rosie's leaving wouldn't stop his curiosity to know more about her. Or the way he still wanted her!

'Then I'll ask you to stay on, Rosie,' he said tersely. 'I also suggest that we call a truce until Donald is feeling better.'

She raised auburn brows. 'I didn't realise we were at war...'

Not at war, Hawk conceded, but they were certainly a challenge to each other.

'Okay, Hawk. I'll stay on at least until I've had a chance to talk to my father,' Rosie decided. 'Talking of which...' She stood up, no longer looking at Hawk as she felt slightly self-conscious dressed only in her nightshirt. 'I really should go and check on him.'

'Do that,' Hawk agreed. 'Then perhaps you would like to come down and join me for a late lunch?'

Rosie gave an uncertain frown. 'I can easily get myself something in my father's kitchen...'

'Why bother when I'm cooking? Besides, I owe you something for waking you up so suddenly.'

Rosie searched his ruggedly handsome face for signs of mockery of the way in which he had woken her. But she could read nothing from his bland expression. Considering what a talented actor he was, maybe that wasn't so surprising!

Was having lunch with this man a good idea? Was *not* having lunch with him a good idea? Hawk seemed to have developed a relentless curiosity about her sudden appearance in her father's life, and he obviously felt protective towards the older man. As if he suspected that for some reason she had come here to hurt Donald.

Years ago she might have thought she would like to

hurt her father, in the way he had hurt her when he had deserted her and her mother so completely ten years ago. But maturity had brought with it the knowledge of just how impossible her mother was—how ruthless she could be when she set her mind on a course of action. Who could blame her father for wanting to escape from *that*?

Hadn't she just done exactly the same thing…?

No, she hadn't come here to hurt Donald. If anything she just wanted to talk to him—to find out why, when he'd left her mother, he'd had to abandon her so completely too. But that was all she wanted. It was too late—far too late—for anything else between them.

'Come on, Rosie.' Hawk cut cajolingly into her thoughts. 'Surely it doesn't take this long to decide whether or not you want to have lunch with me?'

Or maybe it did after what had just happened between them…

Not the most sensible thing he had ever done, he thought self-derisively. But being sensible had been the last thing on his mind once he had held Rosie in his arms and touched her!

'Okay.' Rosie accepted the invitation slowly, suddenly aware that she was hungry.

Something she hadn't felt for some time—weeks, possibly months—as the wedding had loomed ever closer. Always slender, she knew she had lost several pounds in weight in the last month or so. Even the idea of eating had made her feel nauseous.

But she felt really hungry now. Her mouth was

watering, and her stomach was cramping slightly as she remembered she hadn't eaten anything at all since consuming a sandwich last night after she'd arrived.

Perhaps the arousing of her sensual appetite had awakened her appetite for food too...

What a disturbing thought!

'If you could wait fifteen minutes or so?' she said briskly. 'After I've checked on my father, I would like to take a shower,' she explained, at Hawk's questioning look.

'Fine.' He nodded. 'Perhaps you would like to move your things in here while you're at it?'

Rosie looked around the room, appreciating that it would be much more comfortable than sleeping on the sofa in her father's flat. But she was also aware that if she moved in here it would bring her out of her father's domain and into Hawk's—almost as if she really were an invited guest. Not a good idea, in the circumstances.

Once her father was feeling better, and the two of them had talked, she had every intention of leaving. To go where, she still had no idea. But Hawk was far too curious about her for her to stay.

'I think I'll continue to stay in my father's flat, thank you,' she told him firmly. 'I would like to remain close while he's feeling ill,' she added challengingly, sure from Hawk's expression that he wasn't convinced by her concern for Donald.

And he was wrong to feel that way; she might not have seen her father for ten years, but as soon as she had met him again at the airport yesterday she had known an upsurge of the adoration she had felt for him as a child. It was an emotion she had quickly controlled, but nonetheless she had felt it. She certainly didn't intend hurting her father in any way. She had a feeling, from what she had come to know of her mother, that he had been hurt enough in the past.

Hawk's mouth twisted derisively. 'Your concern is touching,' he drawled. 'If a little late in coming!'

Rosie's cheeks flamed with the anger she obviously felt at his rebuke. 'Considering you know absolutely nothing of my relationship with my father, perhaps you aren't in a position to judge!' she snapped coldly.

From what he had already learnt, Hawk very much doubted there had been any relationship between Donald and his daughter for years!

But she was right. He wasn't in a position to judge. Yet. He gave an abrupt inclination of his head. 'I apologise.'

His apology obviously surprised her. Her eyes widened slightly as she eyed him suspiciously.

But Hawk was aware that he might just be wrong in his suspicions about this woman. Might be. Maybe…

'We can decorate the two trees Donald has placed in the sitting room and family room later this afternoon, if you would like?' he offered lightly.

Rosie still eyed him warily. 'Fine,' she agreed, her gaze guarded as she walked to the door.

What was it about this woman that made his pulse race and his body tighten with desire? Hawk wondered, even as he felt the renewed stirring of his body. At this rate *he* would need to take a shower before lunch himself. A cold one!

Rosie was a beautiful woman, yes. But no more so than many of the women he had known intimately over the years. Her body was willowy. But again, not startlingly so. In fact, she could do with putting on a few pounds.

So why, in spite of his uncertainty about her motives for being here at all, did he feel so attracted to her?

'Oh, and, Hawk…' She paused at the door to turn and look at him from beneath lowered lashes.

His gaze narrowed warily. 'Yes?'

A slight smile curved those sensuously full lips. 'I'm afraid I lied to you earlier,' she murmured throatily.

Hawk's wariness increased, his shoulders tensing. 'Oh, yes?' he prompted hardly.

'Yes.' She nodded, that smile widening as her eyes openly mocked him now. 'I *can* cook!' she taunted, before turning lightly on her heel and leaving him alone in the bedroom.

The little—!

That was why he was attracted to her, Hawk realised frustratedly. Unlike most other women he knew, Rosie, while obviously aware of his suspicions, had absolutely no interest in what he did or didn't think about her. In fact, she behaved as if his opinion of her was of no importance to her whatsoever.

Which, although she might not be aware of it, only succeeded in deepening his interest.

Perhaps, with Donald as ill as he was, it was up to

Hawk to find out more about this previously unknown daughter of his?

Donald's mutterings about Rosie's mother earlier certainly didn't inspire any confidence in Rosie's innocence.

Yes, perhaps he should employ some other way of seeing if he couldn't find out more about her…

CHAPTER EIGHT

ROSIE CONTINUED to smile as she walked down the hallway to the door that led to her father's flat. It had been fun teasing Hawk just now, taking his suspicions about her motives for being here and turning them back on him.

Perhaps she was finally getting her sense of humour back?

About time too!

Returning Hawk's kisses, his caresses, hadn't been such a good idea, though...

Her smile faded as she thought of her response to him, of just how much she had enjoyed being kissed and touched by him. Something that had never happened to her before.

He was Joshua Hawkley, top Hollywood movie star. Of *course* she had melted when he kissed her. What woman wouldn't?

Keep telling yourself that, Rosie, she told herself, as she went into her father's flat. Maybe with time she might even come to believe that was the only reason she had responded to him so absolutely.

Maybe…

'Oh, good, you're awake.' She smiled at her father as she entered the bedroom. He was sitting up slightly, so that he could drink some of the juice and take the medication she had left for him earlier on the bedside table. 'Are you feeling any better?'

'A little.' Donald gave a wan smile as he dropped back onto the pillows, the effort of sitting up at all obviously having weakened him. 'I still can't believe you're actually here, Rosie,' he croaked.

He reached out to grasp hold of her hand as she stood beside the bed, letting her know that his skin was hot and clammy. If Rosie had needed anything else to tell her how ill he still was, she could see how his hair was sticking damply to his brow, his face was flushed and his hazel-coloured eyes feverish.

'Promise me you won't just disappear again until after I'm better and we've had a chance to talk!' he pressed hoarsely.

Her own cheeks flushed guiltily as she acknowledged that, minutes ago, disappearing was exactly what she had been thinking of doing. If she could have thought of somewhere else she might go, that was!

'I won't just disappear,' she assured him huskily, squeezing his hand slightly before awkwardly letting go. Even this brief physical contact with the father she hadn't seen for years was opening up old wounds, filling her with questions she knew Donald wasn't well enough to answer yet. 'Hawk and I are going to decorate the Christmas trees,' she told him lightly.

He smiled at this mention of his employer. 'What do you think of him?'

She was trying *not* to think of Hawk!

She avoided her father's gaze. 'He seems—pleasant enough,' she replied awkwardly.

'Pleasant?' Donald echoed incredulously. 'That's the first time I've heard a woman call him *that*!'

Rosie felt the blush deepen on her cheeks. 'He's Joshua Hawkley, Father; what else is there to say!'

Donald frowned, a pained look on his face. 'How long have you thought of me as "Father" instead of "Dad"?' he queried gruffly.

Too long. But it had become easier, less painful, to think of him in that way than to remember the man who had spoilt and loved her for the first twelve years of her life. The man she in return had adored.

At least he had stopped talking about Hawk...

'We're strangers now—'

'No!' Donald protested. 'Never that. Not you and I, Rosie. We have a lot of catching up to do—things we need to talk about—but I've never stopped loving you. Never stopped loving my little girl. You have to believe that!' He looked up at her pleadingly.

She had never stopped loving him either. But it had been *ten* years!

'All of this can wait until you're feeling better,' she soothed, as she saw how pale he had become from the strain of talking at all.

'Yes,' he breathed raggedly. 'We have time now, don't we...?' he murmured, before drifting off into sleep once again as the medication obviously kicked in.

Rosie stared down at him for several more minutes. Apart from his prematurely white hair, he still looked the same to her as he had ten years ago. Was he still the man in whom she'd had total faith then? Whom she'd believed would never let any harm come to her?

Why had he abandoned her? Why hadn't he taken her with him when he'd left her mother? Why hadn't he tried to at least *see* her in the intervening years?

No matter how much she might know she had to get away from Hawk, Rosie knew she couldn't leave here until after she had the answers to those questions...

'We aren't going to get the trees decorated by standing around looking at them,' Hawk commented dryly, as Rosie stood staring up at the huge pine tree that dominated the sitting room.

He had taken the opportunity of her delay to come down and light the fire in the open hearth that served both the sitting room and the family room, and its warmth and flames added to the Christmas atmosphere.

Even the snow was falling again outside, to add to the festive spirit!

But Rosie seemed mesmerised by the tree.

It was a beauty, Hawk had to admit—smelling strongly of pine, at least twelve feet high, its branches lush and green.

'Rosie...?' he prompted softly.

She blinked, turning to stare at him as if she had forgotten he was even there. Once again he noticed she was wearing black—yet another black sweater, with black denims.

What was it with this woman and black?

Admittedly it brought out the vivid red of her hair, which was at the moment tied back in a ponytail. But it also made her face way too pale.

'Sorry.' She gave a rousing shake of her head. 'Where do we start? Do we put the lights on first, or the decorations?'

'The lights, of course,' Hawk answered, slightly puzzled. 'Haven't you ever dressed a Christmas tree before?'

Not that she could remember, no...

Probably she had helped her parents to decorate a tree when they were all still together, but Rosie certainly couldn't remember having done so since then.

Her mother considered real Christmas trees messy, smelly things, and preferred to buy an artificial one, already decorated, that could be stored in the attic after Christmas and brought down again each year.

With the fire burning so merrily, and the snow falling softly outside the windows, this setting was just too enchanting for Rosie not to be affected by it.

'Not one like this.' She avoided a direct answer. 'Lights first, then,' she added briskly, to avoid any further discussion on the subject.

'Lights first,' Hawk confirmed slowly, his gaze still narrowed on her speculatively. 'Why do I get the idea that you somehow haven't been living in the real world these last few years, Rosie...?'

Probably because she hadn't!

Her life had seemed so bleak and empty after her fun-loving father had left. She had retreated into herself, withdrawing from her friends to become something of a loner.

But all that had changed the day her music teacher, trying to encourage her to take an interest in music, had persuaded Rosie to pick up a violin.

From the moment Rosie had touched the instrument it had felt right, as if it were a part of her; just touching the polished wood, holding the bow, filled the empty void inside her.

More amazing was the fact that although she had started fairly late in life, after a couple of false starts she had actually known how to play it!

Instinctively.

Intuitively.

She hadn't even been able to read music at the time, and yet as she'd held that violin in her hands she had *known* how to play it.

So she had played it and played it. And that had released her from the prison of loneliness in which she had locked herself away.

And maybe if her music teacher, overwhelmed by the discovery of her amazing ability, hadn't called her mother in and told her of Rosie's natural talent—if her mother hadn't realised just how lucrative having a musical protégée for a daughter could be—Rosie's bewilderment and pain after her father had left might have been healed, allowing her to be a teenager.

Instead normal life had ended for ever the day her mother had discovered her gift for playing the violin...

'Don't be ridiculous, Hawk,' she snapped back at him. 'My mother employs staff to deal with the household tasks, that's all,' she elaborated, inwardly wincing at how snobbish she knew she must sound.

The knowledge was reflected in the flash of anger in Hawk's eyes before he masked the emotion.

He had met this woman—what...seven, eight hours ago?—and during that time she had aroused surprise, curiosity, amusement, anger and desire in him. More emotions than he had felt for any woman he had known ten times that long!

Right now he felt angry. He wanted to bring her out from behind that shield of coldness she was hiding herself with.

That it was a shield, Hawk didn't doubt. He had seen the real warmth of this woman when he'd held her in his arms such a short time ago.

She had wanted him then. As he had wanted her.

As he *still* wanted her, damn it!

'Is that how you think of your father?' he prompted softly. 'As a mere member of staff whose function is to carry out household tasks for me?'

'Of course not!' Rosie gasped, her cheeks blazing with heated colour. 'When I made that reference to staff I wasn't talking about my father—'

'Weren't you?' Hawk scorned. 'I think that you were—'

'I don't give a damn what you think, Hawk—'

'No, I know you don't!' he rasped.

'And that bothers you?' Rosie looked at him, her whole body tense with challenge now. 'Does it irk you that I don't bow and scrape before the mighty film star Joshua Hawkley?'

Add absolute fury to that list of emotions, Hawk thought, even as he clenched his hands into fists to stop himself from expressing his anger as he had so longed to do minutes earlier.

Mainly because he wasn't sure, if he touched her, that he would be able to stop there; the desire they had shared earlier was lurking only just below the surface of this conversation.

As it had been since they'd first met this morning…!

'I don't expect *anyone* to bow and scrape before me,' he grated out between clenched teeth.

'No?' Her chin was raised and she looked at him with challenging green eyes. 'But it seems to me that's exactly what everyone does!'

She was deliberately trying to annoy him, Hawk suddenly realised with calming clarity.

Why? Because he was getting too close? Because he was daring to ask her questions she would prefer not to answer?

He had called a friend of his in England earlier and asked him to see what he could find out about one Rosie Harrison. But he didn't expect to receive a call back for some time, so perhaps it would be better if he just backed off for a while.

He forced himself to relax, his smile derisive. 'You're entitled to your opinion,' he dismissed with a shrug, before turning to take the lights from the box. 'Do you want to hold the bottom of the step-ladder while I take these to the top of the tree?'

She wanted to knock him off the damned thing altogether, Rosie realised bad-temperedly, even as she moved to steady the ladder while he climbed up it.

He was rude.

He was persistently inquisitive.

He was also wildly, ruggedly, good-looking. So powerfully sensual, so exquisitely male, that he made her legs go weak at the knees!

She didn't want to feel this way. Didn't want to want this man.

But she did. Even now she wanted to reach out and touch him, to feel the warm strength of him beneath her hand, longed to feel his hands on her again.

Why *this* man? Why—?

'Damn!' Hawk swore as his mobile began to ring. Resting the lights on one of the branches, he reached to take it out of his back pocket. 'Yes?' he barked irritably into the mouthpiece.

Rosie watched his face as he took the call, his initial irritation quickly followed by frustration. 'No, I don't have any comment to make,' he snapped. 'Jeff, just find out which newspaper has it and see if you can stop it.

Then get back to me. Yes, now,' he bit out tersely, before abruptly ending the call.

Rosie eyed him warily as he looked down at her with piercing eyes. 'What?' she voiced uncertainly. 'What's wrong?' Because she knew from his face that something was.

Hawk sat down on top of the ladder, running a hand through the long dark thickness of his hair before replying. 'How do you feel about having your photograph in the newspaper?' He sighed.

'What…?' she gasped weakly, hands gripping the step-ladder so tightly now that her knuckles showed white.

'That was my agent on the telephone,' Hawk bit out grimly. 'He's been contacted by a reporter to see if I have any comment to make about the woman I'm spending Christmas with!'

She gave a dazed shake of her head. 'But how—? You said something about a photograph—?'

'Apparently some resourceful soul took a photograph of us with their cell-phone when we were out shopping this morning,' he explained hardly. 'A reporter now has it, and is intending to have it published in one of tomorrow's newspapers.'

No, Rosie inwardly protested.

This could not be happening!

CHAPTER NINE

'HEY, IT MAY not be that bad!' Hawk encouraged, as Rosie staggered back to drop down into one of the armchairs, her face pale. 'Jeff will get back to me and let me know how damaging the photograph is,' he added, as he climbed back down the ladder.

Damaging!

That there was a photograph of her in Canada at all, with or without Joshua Hawkley at her side, was more damaging to Rosie than he could ever imagine!

'Rosie…?' Hawk came down on his haunches at her side. 'It isn't the end of the world—'

'Maybe to you it isn't!' she came back heatedly, her eyes stormy in the pallor of her face.

She shook her head. Hawk didn't understand— couldn't understand—that any photograph of her that appeared in the newspapers now was sure to bring repercussions. She was supposed to be in England, taking time off to prepare for her wedding. Not in Canada, with the charismatically sexy actor Joshua Hawkley!

Hawk looked at her searchingly, obviously confused.

'Aren't you overreacting a little?' he attempted to ca-
jole. 'The speculation about the two of us will be a
nine-day-wonder, and then—'

'Nine days?' she repeated, stricken.

In four days' time, as far as the general public was
still concerned, Rosemary Harris was due to marry
world-famous conductor Edmund Price!

Edmund knew she wasn't going to marry him, of
course. She had told him so three days ago, when she'd
given him back his ring. The point was, her mother
would know it too now. But there had been no announcement of the wedding's cancellation made in the
newspapers yet, and any photograph of her with another
man—let alone the wildly handsome Joshua Hawkley!—was sure to be more than a nine-day-wonder!

She shook her head. 'You don't understand…!' She
buried her face in her hands like a child, as if not being
able to see Hawk would make all of this go away.

Once she'd realised her father's employer was the
famous actor Joshua Hawkley she should never have
stayed here. She should have just gone to some dis-
creet hotel on the other side of the world and made
herself 'disappear', until the supposed wedding day
was over and the speculation that was sure to follow
had died down.

Instead of which she had now been photographed
shopping for food in a Canadian mall with Joshua
Hawkley!

'Look, Rosie,' Hawk reasoned softly. 'I would be

very surprised if your own mother would recognise you, covered up in the way you were!'

How unintentionally ironic—when it was her mother she didn't *want* to recognise her!

Gloria would be over here on the next plane if she knew which province Rosie was in. Of course her mother couldn't work out exactly where she was staying in Calgary. But Rosie, of all people, knew how tenacious Gloria could be when she got an idea in her head...

For example, the idea of Rosie's marriage to maestro conductor Edmund Price...

Rosie should never have allowed things to get as out of control as they had, of course. But her mother was like an express train when she decided on a course of action—she had absolutely no hesitation in knocking down anything that got in her way, including Rosie's own reluctance about the marriage!

As far as Hawk was concerned, he felt Rosie was overreacting to this. Okay, so it wasn't very pleasant, having an innocent excursion like this morning's shopping expedition taken out of context and blown up into something it wasn't. But it really wasn't the end of the world.

At least, it shouldn't have been.

Except to someone he suspected was hiding something...

'Rosie, why don't you tell me what's wrong?' he encouraged huskily. 'A problem shared is a problem halved, and all that...'

She gave a humourless laugh. 'You have no idea!'

'Then tell me, damn it.' His voice hardened in his frustration with the situation.

She looked at him for several searching seconds before shaking her head. 'There's nothing to tell,' she bit out tightly.

Hawk's frustration deepened as he realised that Rosie had obviously looked at him and decided he couldn't help her. 'We both know that isn't true,' he returned scathingly. 'It's been obvious from the first that you're running away, or hiding from something. If you tell me what that something is, maybe I can help…?'

Rosie swallowed hard as once again she looked at him searchingly.

Could she tell Hawk the truth? Could she tell him— explain how her life had been during the last ten years? How her mother's single-minded pursuit of fame and fortune for her daughter, and ultimately for herself, had made Rosie's life so restricted and lonely? Could she tell him of the wedding she had fled from so urgently because she had known she simply could not, *would* not, marry a man she neither loved nor wanted to be with, but who her mother saw as yet another step up on the ladder of Rosie's already meteoric musical career?

Could she tell Hawk any of that and have him understand…?

How could he, when she knew from her conversation with him earlier at the mall that he accepted the public adulation his career attracted, the invasion of privacy that accompanied being in the public eye. He would never be able to understand why she didn't.

As for her broken engagement to Edmund Price, a man years older than her, goodness knew what Hawk would make of *that* after the way she had responded to him earlier!

She gave another shake of her head. 'There's nothing to tell,' she repeated firmly.

'Damn it, Rosie—' Hawk broke off his angry outburst as his cellphone rang for a second time. Frowning his irritation, he stood up to take the call. 'Yes?' he barked, turning away from her.

Rosie didn't doubt that the call was from his agent. With more news on the photograph, no doubt.

How had that happened?

Why had it happened?

Wasn't it enough that Hawk was over-curious about her presence here, without someone actually taking a photograph of the two of them together?

She still couldn't believe that someone had done that and then sold it to a reporter, who in turn had no doubt sold it to the newspaper who would pay the most.

She stood up and moved over to stand in front of one of the windows, staring out at the snow-covered landscape. It was so beautiful here. So quiet. Like stepping out of time—stepping off the world for a while.

Except that reality—first in the form of Hawk, and now with the existence of this photograph—kept intruding!

'Rosie…?'

She turned back to Hawk, her expression deliberately bland as she looked at him enquiringly.

'It's already too late to stop the photograph being published in tomorrow's newspaper,' Hawk explained with a grimace. He easily guessed that her calmness now was only a pose, that the dismay she had exhibited earlier wasn't far beneath her surface coolness. 'Jeff is e-mailing a copy of it over for us to look at, so that at least we'll know what's coming,' he finished heavily.

She didn't look reassured, he acknowledged ruefully; her face was starkly white against her black clothing and the fiery colour of her hair.

'Let's hope that at least they haven't caught me pushing the shopping trolley,' Hawk joked, in an attempt to lighten the situation. 'That would do nothing for my swashbuckling image!'

Rosie's mouth tightened. 'I'm glad you find all of this so funny!' she cried.

He didn't. Not the fact that the photograph existed, nor Rosie's reaction to it.

But it wouldn't be the first time he had been photographed when he would rather he hadn't been. And he doubted it would be the last either.

He sighed, pushing his hands into the back pockets of his denims. 'Maybe if you explained—'

'I don't owe you any explanations, Hawk,' she countered emotionally. 'A few kisses—totally unwise on my part—do not entitle you to my life story!'

Hawk's hands again tightened into fists in his pockets, even as he breathed deeply in an effort to control his temper. Because he was sure she was doing this deliberately—that she wanted to antagonise him by deliberately belittling their time together earlier. And he wasn't about to give her that satisfaction.

Rosie wasn't going to succeed in pushing him away that way!

And she *was* deliberately pushing him away.

Why? Because he had got too close?

Well, she had got too close to *him*—had somehow succeeded in getting in under the radar that had always alerted him before to the dangers of getting involved.

And he *wanted* her life story!

He wanted to know what she had been like as a little girl. Whether she had found her teenage years as awkward as he had. Wanted to know what her hobbies were. What food she liked. What she liked to do. What work she did. Whether there was anyone special in her life…

Most of all he wanted to know the latter!

Rosie Harrison had seriously got under his skin, Hawk acknowledged, slightly dazed. He had known her only a matter of hours, but already he wanted to know everything there was to know about her.

Contrarily, Rosie didn't want to share any part of herself with him.

'The e-mail, Hawk?' Rosie reminded him tightly, having no idea what he was thinking right now, but pretty sure her efforts to annoy him and so put him at a distance had succeeded.

'Yeah.' He sighed resignedly. 'My lap-top is in the

study.' He gave a half-smile before turning and striding from the room.

Rosie resisted the impulse to follow him, knowing she had already betrayed her anxiety enough without that.

If the photograph was as damning as she thought it would be then she knew she would have to leave here before its publication tomorrow—with or without that conversation with her father.

She would have to leave Hawk too.

Something, she realised with sudden consternation, that she was already loath to do...

CHAPTER TEN

'IT'S A GOOD photograph of you, isn't it?' Rosie spoke brightly as she tried to hold back her relieved laughter now that Hawk had downloaded a copy of the photo.

Her own face was shown only in profile, totally unrecognisable beneath the black woollen hat pulled low over her ears—as it had been meant to be!—whereas Hawk's worst fear had been realised: he was indeed depicted pushing the shopping trolley!

He looked at the photograph on the computer screen disgustedly. 'The PR team for Prince Movies are going to love this!'

Rosie wasn't so out of touch that she didn't know of the famous movie company owned and run by the three Prince brothers. The same movie company that was due to start filming the sequel to *The Pirate King*, starring Joshua Hawkley, in the New Year…

'As you said—not exactly the swashbuckling image required, is it?' She smiled.

Hawk closed down the computer file, then turned to look at her. 'You're enjoying this, aren't you!'

Considering that only minutes ago she had been worrying about the repercussions that might follow the publication of this photograph—an anxiety she now knew had been totally unnecessary—yes, she *was* enjoying Hawk's obvious discomfort!

Her eyes glowed with laughter. 'The only thing that could have been less macho would have been if the shopping trolley had been a baby buggy!' She grinned, soon dissolving into full laughter as Hawk gave her a reproving look beneath raised brows.

She was lovely when she laughed, Hawk acknowledged. Twin dimples appeared in her creamy cheeks, her teeth were very white and even between sensuous lips, and her eyes gleamed like emeralds.

'So you think it's funny, do you?' he murmured throatily as he slowly began to advance on her.

Rosie continued to smile even as she took a step backwards. 'That all of those female fans are going to have their fantasies about you dashed when they see you doing something as mundane as food-shopping? Yes, of *course* I think it's funny!' she confirmed with another chuckle.

In truth, Hawk wasn't in the least bothered by the photo. He was more interested in the amusement it was affording Rosie, and how that amusement had banished her earlier strain and replaced it with happy laughter.

He still had no answers as to why the photograph should have bothered her so much in the first place, but at that moment he didn't particularly care either.

His gaze was intent upon the pouting sensuality of that smiling mouth.

Rosie saw the danger just a little too late. Her eyes widened, her hands moving up in protest as Hawk's arms moved about her and he pulled her in tightly against his body, his lips descending to claim hers.

Too late to protest, she realised, even as her lips parted beneath his, her hands moved up his chest and over his shoulders, and her fingers become entangled in the dark thickness of his hair as she pulled him close to her.

Hawk needed no further encouragement. His lips were plundering now, taking her response and giving one back, his tongue slowly circling her lips before claiming the moistness within.

Rosie's pleasure rose swiftly, wildly. The hours since they had last been together like this seemed never to have passed—their kisses were fierce, demanding, and they couldn't seem to get enough of each other.

Her arms clung about his shoulders as she felt herself lifted up and then placed on the long sofa. Hawk briefly raised his head to hold her gaze with his as he moved to lie down beside her, then his mouth claimed hers once more.

He felt so good, tasted so good, she discovered as she ran her tongue fleetingly against his lips. She was almost afraid of her own response, but not wanting him to stop. Never wanting him to stop!

His hands caressed her restlessly from breast to thigh, igniting, setting fire wherever they touched, so that the whole of her body, it seemed, burned and quivered at his slightest touch.

Her neck arched as his lips moved from hers to the creamy column of her throat, to taste and gently bite, sending shivers of pleasure down her spine, creating a throbbing warmth between her thighs.

'And what are *your* fantasies, Rosie...?' he encouraged.

'Touch me, Hawk!' she groaned huskily. 'I want you to touch me!' Her plea turned to an aching sigh of pleasure as his hands pushed her jumper aside and he bared her breasts to his questing hands and lips.

Rosie stopped breathing altogether as she felt the moisture of his tongue encircling the throb of her nipple, slowly licking that hardened nub before drawing it into the moist heat of his mouth, suckling first gently, and then more deeply, as she arched instinctively against him.

The warmth between her thighs turned to heat, hot and molten, and she moved against him in rhythm, spiralling out of control, taking her with it, until she thought she would totally disintegrate with the force of the pleasure Hawk was giving to her.

She pushed his own jumper aside, skin against skin now, and the friction of the dark hair on his chest was arousing against her bared breasts. Hawk groaned low in his throat as her hands travelled down the length of his spine to cup him to her, to feel the hard throb of his own need against her.

He raised his head to once more capture her mouth

with his, his kiss hard and demanding even as he moved a hand between them and dispensed with the fastenings and zips on both pairs of denims. He pushed the material impatiently aside, his hardness against her as his hand once again captured her breast, to caress its fiery tip with the soft pad of his thumb.

Rosie's hand moved to touch him. Steel encased in velvet, throbbing, pulsing. So good to touch. So powerful, and yet so velvety smooth.

She wanted him inside her. To fill her. Wanted him to assuage the need inside her as she wanted to assuage the need she could feel pulsing inside him. They—

Hawk suddenly wrenched his mouth from hers. 'We have to stop, Rosie!' he groaned regretfully, moving to rest his forehead against hers as he breathed raggedly in an effort to regain control. 'We can't make love here,' he went on softly, his expression regretful, his eyes dark as he pulled her jumper down to cover the temptation of her breasts, still full and roused from the caress of his hands and mouth.

He hadn't wanted to stop. Never wanted to stop kissing and touching this woman. He wanted nothing more than to bury himself in her softness, to move against and inside her, taking them both over the edge of that pleasure as they found release.

But a part of him had remained aware, even if Rosie wasn't, that they weren't completely alone in the house—that Donald, as unwell as he was, could quite easily walk in on them at any time. And he doubted Rosie wanted that to happen any more than he did.

'Rosie—'

'Don't!' she choked, no longer looking at him, her face once again pale. 'Please let me up,' she pleaded tautly as she pushed ineffectually against his chest.

Hawk reached out to grasp the tops of her arms. 'Rosie, you have to listen to me—'

'Why do I?' she demanded, all her earlier laughter having gone now as she glared up at him. 'Isn't it enough that you've obviously made yet another conquest without having a post-mortem about it?'

Hawk was shocked. 'Is that what you imagine this is?'

'Well, isn't it?' she challenged. Not waiting for him to move, she scrambled to the bottom of the sofa and stood up to turn away from him as she refastened her denims and straightened her jumper. 'Obviously that photograph dented your ego a little more than I had appreciated!' she turned to add scathingly.

Hawk stared up at her incredulously. One minute so hot and aroused in his arms, and now she had all the softness of a spitting tigress!

He shook her head. 'It wasn't like that—'

'Wasn't it?' Rosie scorned, absolutely devastated by her uninhibited response to him seconds ago—a response that still made her body ache! 'Let's face it, Hawk, I'm the only available female around for miles for you to seduce!' she exclaimed, sure she was hurting herself more with her scorn than she was hurting him.

Hawk sat up, his gaze dark on hers. 'And are you?'

he said softly. 'Available?' he added pointedly at her surprised look.

She blushed slightly. 'Of course I'm available! What sort of woman do you think I am?' she cried.

'I wish I knew...'

'What's that supposed to mean?' Rosie demanded.

Hawk looked at her levelly. 'You've told me so little about yourself. How can I be expected to know what sort of woman you are...?'

She had walked right into that one, Rosie realised belatedly. Well, if he thought he was going to get anything out of her that way, he was mistaken!

'The point is, Hawk,' she emphasised, biting her lips, 'you don't *need* to know what sort of woman I am! I'm here to visit Donald, not you. In fact,' she continued hardly, 'I think it might be better if I keep to my father's flat for the rest of my stay here!'

Which was going to be extremely confining. But, as she intended leaving as soon as she and Donald had had their talk, it hopefully wouldn't be for too long.

'You mean because we don't seem to be able to be in the same room together without taking each other's clothes off?' Hawk taunted, and he stood up to pointedly fasten his own jeans.

Rosie gave him a frustrated glare before turning abruptly on her heel and marching determinedly from the room.

And she didn't stop walking until she had reached the sanctuary of her father's flat, closing the door behind her as she desperately tried not to think about Hawk, or the things he had said.

But Hawk was right. She knew he was right. They *didn't* seem to be able to be together without wanting to take each other's clothes off!

In fact, she accepted shakily, Hawk, and the undeniable attraction she felt towards him, had become much more of a danger to the peace of mind she was seeking than anything or anyone else had ever been...!

CHAPTER ELEVEN

'YES?' ROSIE STOOD squarely in the bedroom doorway of her father's flat the following morning after opening the door to Hawk's knock—looking bright and alert, Hawk noted impatiently, after probably sleeping for almost sixteen hours.

The same number of hours *he* had spent trying to make some sense of his feelings towards her—and coming to absolutely no conclusion. The hot desire he felt for her was at complete odds with his usual caution towards romantic involvement.

He willed himself not to react to her challenge now, knowing that was exactly what he had done last night. As he had been *meant* to do, he had realised, once she had walked away from him.

But Hawk wasn't feeling in a good humour himself this morning. For good reason! 'I came to check on how Donald is this morning,' he replied tersely.

Rosie seemed to relax the tension in her shoulders slightly. 'A little better, thank you,' she answered with cool politeness. 'In fact, he's taking a shower right now.'

Hawk had so many questions he wanted to ask this woman. Questions that had only increased after he'd read the newspaper this morning…!

'I guess he's out of the shower now,' Hawk observed, as he heard the sound of music playing in the bedroom—one of the classical CDs Donald often liked to play in the car when he drove Hawk. Although *that* was no longer the reason Hawk recognised it!

'I guess he is,' Rosie acknowledged, appearing distracted. 'Look, I'll tell him you enquired after him—'

'Oh, no, you don't!' Hawk managed to put his foot inside the door just as Rosie was about to shut it in his face. 'I would rather come in and speak to Donald myself, if you don't mind,' he asserted, as he pushed the door back open.

'And if I *do* mind?' Rosie faced him challengingly, eyes sparkling, deeply green.

He shrugged. 'As you pointed out yesterday—it's my house.' His gaze narrowed on her warningly.

When he was filming his work schedule was such that he often went short of sleep—so it wasn't last night's insomnia that was making him so irritable this morning but his rapidly increasing anger towards this woman. A woman who, if the way he couldn't stop thinking about her was anything to go by, had got to him more deeply than any other. A woman who had totally deceived him…!

Rosie's mouth thinned. 'So it is,' she acknowledged mockingly, and she stepped back to allow him to come into the flat.

The music her father had on the CD-player in the bedroom could be heard more clearly. It was a piece that Rosie recognised all too easily. She should do— *she* was the violin soloist, and she was playing the concerto that she had written herself…!

'Here—I went out and got this earlier.' Hawk held out the newspaper that Rosie hadn't noticed he had been carrying under his arm. 'Page three,' he added hardly, as Rosie slowly took the newspaper from him.

She gave him another brief glance before opening the paper and turning the pages, her curiosity such— despite the melancholy strains of music that now filled the flat—that she couldn't *not* have opened it.

It was the same photograph that Hawk's agent had e-mailed to him yesterday. Perhaps not quite as blurred as the downloaded copy had been, but there was still too little of her face visible for her to be recognisable.

Nevertheless, her hands shook slightly as she shut the newspaper abruptly and put it down on the coffee table. 'I—It seems harmless enough,' she dismissed stiffly, still slightly thrown by the fact that it was *her* CD her father was playing in his bedroom.

Her latest album—a compilation of her music that had only been released the previous month…

'Don't you have something to tell me, Rosie?' Hawk queried, his impatience growing by the second.

She looked surprised. 'Something to tell you…?' she repeated slowly. 'I don't think so.'

Hawk was pretty sure he was going to put this woman over his knee and spank her delicious little bottom in a minute! A shapely bottom, encased in blue denim this morning, and a green sweater the same vivid emerald as her eyes…

Better. Much better, Hawk decided, glad that she hadn't chosen black today.

Although that didn't alter the fact that he had received just about all the evasion he intended taking from this woman. He wanted answers—answers that only Rosie could give him. Something she didn't seem inclined to do…

He reached out to grasp her arm as she would have turned away. 'Maybe you should read a little more of the paper this morning, Rosie,' he warned. 'The second photograph of you—of Rosemary Harris!—is much more flattering!' he added grimly.

Her face became haunted as she glanced at the paper she had thrown down so dismissively only seconds ago, her wariness increasing. 'What—?'

'Hawk!' Her father greeted him warmly as he came through from the bedroom. 'I was just coming through to see you,' Donald croaked, having pulled on faded denims and a navy blue sweater after his shower.

He looked much better than he had an hour ago, when Rosie had taken him a cup of coffee in bed, and although it was clear that he was nowhere near well yet, he was obviously feeling brighter this morning. He had resisted all Rosie's efforts to keep him in bed, insisting he had to go and talk to Hawk this morning.

The probability that their talk was going to be about her wasn't in the least reassuring!

She easily pulled away from Hawk's hand as he relaxed his grip on her wrist, turning to face her father. 'I'm sure you shouldn't be out of bed yet—'

'Don't fuss, Rosie.' Donald smiled, taking any sting out of his words, moving slowly across the room to place his arm lightly about her shoulders. He turned away to cough, then prompted, 'So, what do you think of my daughter, Hawk?' He looked down at her proudly.

Rosie winced. Her dad probably didn't want to know what Hawk really thought of his daughter at this moment!

Hawk studied father and daughter, realising that Donald's prematurely white hair had probably once been as red as his daughter's. He could see a similarity in their facial structure too, now that he knew of their relationship, although Donald's eyes were hazel where Rosie's were that vivid green.

But he also knew this similarity to Donald was *not* the reason she had seemed so familiar to him yesterday!

He turned to the older man. 'She's very beautiful.' He stated the obvious.

'I didn't mean the way she looks!' Donald grinned. 'Although you're right—she is very beautiful,' he agreed, with a proud beam. 'But I was actually referring to—'

'I'm sure Hawk is far too busy to be bothered with all of this just now, Fa—Dad,' Rosie cut in hastily.

'I'm not busy at all,' Hawk assured her tightly.

Donald gave him a merry smile. 'Don't you recognise the music, Hawk?'

Hawk had never particularly been into classical music, although he did recognise certain pieces when he heard them being played. The piece he could hear at the moment wasn't familiar to him, though. Only the player...

'It's very—evocative,' he acknowledged, looking challengingly at Rosie as the violin rose to a crescendo of aching loneliness that was almost painful to listen to.

Rosie, he could easily see, looked distinctively uncomfortable. And so she damn well ought to after the way she had deceived him!

Rosie turned abruptly away from Hawk's piercing gaze. She had wanted to talk to her father alone this morning. Before she left.

Because she *was* leaving. She had realised that as she lay awake last night thinking of Hawk, of the emotions that were never far below the surface whenever they were together—even when they *weren't* together, she had pondered, as she'd fought the need she still felt for him!

Now she realised that she couldn't run away any more.

Her days of running were over. And all the evasion and prevarication between herself and Hawk had to be over too.

And then she had to go back to England and face whatever needed to be faced...

But first it seemed she had to face Hawk.

And if his guarded remarks about the newspaper

article she hadn't yet seen were anything to go by, then she needed to get reading.

If his sarcasm was anything to go by, something had alerted Hawk to more than who she really was...

CHAPTER TWELVE

'Dad, Hawk doesn't—didn't know about any of that,' she amended. Warily, she shot Hawk a nervous glance.

Donald gave him a beaming smile. 'Nevertheless, I'm sure that he's heard of the violinist La Bella Rosa…'

'Dad—'

'The beautiful rose?' Hawk translated dryly.

A teenage protégée. A musical phenomenon who had performed all over the world for seven, eight years to sell-out audiences, her beauty as renowned as her incredible talent.

The violinist on the CD Donald was playing.

A woman who, it was well-known, always wore black.

For Rosie Harrison read Rosemary Harris.

Because Rosie was definitely La Bella Rosa!

Making a complete nonsense of Hawk's suspicions that she might be here to wheedle money out of Donald. Hawk might not know a lot about classical music, but he did know that Rosemary Harris was one of the highest-paid classical musicians in the world!

Hawk was still waiting for the friend he had called in England to get back to him with any information he could find on Rosie Harrison. But after seeing her photograph in the newspaper this morning, and the article that went with it, Hawk had realised that he didn't need his friend—because he already knew exactly who and what she was!

If he had expected to see Rosemary Harris, world-famous violinist, in his Canadian home... But all he had seen yesterday morning was a hauntingly beautiful woman who had claimed—eventually!—to be Donald's long-lost daughter, Rosie.

Damn it, Hawk had been determined to know the truth about her—he just hadn't expected to find it out by reading in a newspaper!

He looked at her coldly. 'You certainly had me fooled, Rosie—or should I call you Rosemary?' he enquired harshly.

'Rosie will do,' she assured him quietly, inwardly wincing at the anger she could hear in his voice. She wanted to explain, to tell him everything now, but she knew from the coldness of his gaze as he looked at her so scathingly that he no longer wanted to hear it. That whatever he had read in the newspaper this morning about Rosemary Harris made it too late for explanations.

He stood up, appearing very tall and powerful in the confines of Donald's flat. And even more remote. 'I think I should leave the two of you to talk—'

'Hawk, please—' The coldness of his gaze silenced

her as she would have protested. She swallowed hard. 'I really would like you to stay,' she told him, almost pleadingly.

He had to listen—had to understand—

No, she realised heavily. Hawk didn't have to listen or understand anything if he chose not to.

And why should he choose to?

Because he had kissed her? Because she had kissed him? Because they had shared a time of such exquisite passion that she hadn't been able to think of anything else all night?

Because she believed she was falling in love with him? If she hadn't already done so!

But that was only how *she* felt, not Hawk. What had happened between them yesterday might have been nothing out of the ordinary to him…

That didn't alter the fact that she owed him an explanation.

'Did I miss something…?' Her father looked confused by the obvious tension between Rosie and Hawk.

Only ten years of her life, Rosie choked inwardly to herself as she moved away from the warmth of her father's arm. Ten years that stretched between them like a yawning chasm.

'Nothing at all,' Hawk assured the older man tautly, his blue eyes glacial as he gave Rosie a hard glance. 'Rosie, why don't you start by telling us the reason for your unexpected visit?' he prompted hardly. 'I presume there has to *be* a reason you've just turned up like this…?'

Rosie looked at him searchingly, seeing only the implacability in his gaze and his set and unsmiling mouth.

'What…what did you read in the newspaper, Hawk?' she questioned slowly.

'What do you think?'

She didn't know. But she could guess. Oh, yes—knowing her mother as well as she did, Rosie could certainly guess.

Yes. It would be better if Hawk stayed and heard her explanations now, with her father present. Because it was obvious from Hawk's accusing expression that he had no interest in hearing anything she would like to say to him in private!

She straightened, tensing her shoulders even as she drew in a controlling breath, not looking at either man now, just wanting to have her say before leaving. 'Firstly, I think you should both know I'm already booked on a flight back to England later today—'

'No!' her father groaned protestingly, even as he sank down weakly into an armchair, his face pale as he stared up at her.

'Why?' Hawk probed abruptly. 'What's back in England that you have to leave before you and Donald have spent any time together?'

Rosie turned to give him a smile. Not that mischievous smile with the infectious laughter of yesterday, but a smile tinged with sadness.

That same haunting sadness he had heard in her music minutes ago…

'Or should I have asked *who*...?' he amended pointedly.

Rosie shook her head, her smile rueful now. 'Don't believe everything you read, Hawk!'

What the hell did *that* mean?

That he shouldn't believe the announcement he had seen in the newspaper? That it wasn't true that 'La Bella Rosa' Rosemary Harris—Rosie!—was to be married on Christmas Eve?

'Gloria!' Donald spoke with flat disgust. 'That's who you came here to get away from, Rosie, isn't it?' He looked up at his daughter searchingly.

Gloria. Donald's ex-partner. Rosie's mother...

Rosie gave her father a weary smile as she nodded. 'I should have made a complete break years ago.'

'Easier said than done,' Donald acknowledged. 'It took me almost fourteen years—until you were twelve years old, Rosie!—to realise I couldn't live with my own wife any more!'

Hawk tried to hide his surprise. Gloria had been Donald's *wife*? Donald had lived with Rosie and her mother for the first twelve years of Rosie's life?

And then what?

Donald had left, obviously. But what of Rosie? What had Donald done about his twelve-year-old daughter?

Hawk had a hollow feeling in the pit of his stomach—just as he had a feeling he already knew the answer to that question!

Rosie had told Hawk she hadn't seen her father for years. Ten years...?

Donald's next words confirmed that. 'I should have taken you with me when I left, shouldn't I, Rosie?' he said emotionally. 'You haven't been as happy and successful as I always imagined you were, have you?' he realised gruffly.

Hawk looked searchingly at Rosie, seeing the unhappiness in her face for what it was now. Those shadows in her eyes. Her unsmiling mouth. The music she played—still audible in the background—with such aching loneliness.

Rosie frowned across at her father. 'As you always imagined…?' she repeated slowly.

Hawk looked from daughter to father, remembering all those classical concerts that Donald had disappeared to so often over the years. The fact that he was playing one of Rosie's CDs now. The fact that he always played Rosemary Harris on the stereo in the car…

Donald might have left his wife and daughter ten years ago, but that didn't mean he hadn't kept in touch with Rosie's life in all that time—that he hadn't gone to one theatre venue or another all over the planet just to see and hear her play.

'I used to watch you, Rosie.' Donald softly confirmed Hawk's suspicions. 'I would just sit back in my seat, close my eyes and listen to the sweet music you produced so easily. And I would think *That's my daughter down there on that stage—my Rosie,*' he added proudly.

Hawk watched Rosie as she took in the full import of what Donald was saying.

She hadn't known!

She had never known of Donald's presence at any of her concerts over the years—hadn't realised that he'd sat in the darkness with hundreds of other people and watched his own daughter perform on the stage.

Until now...

CHAPTER THIRTEEN

ROSIE STARED AT her father disbelievingly. All those years… All that time when she had imagined… All that time when she had believed her father had forgotten her very existence…!

'You came to my concerts?' she finally managed to say.

'Five, six times a year,' Donald confirmed. 'As often as I could get away.'

She gave a dazed shake of her head. 'But why—? You never let me know you were there! You never came backstage and spoke to me…!' she cried emotionally. 'All these years I've thought—believed—'

'What did you believe, Rosie?' Hawk was the one to prompt softly.

Her eyes were so full of tears when she looked at him that she couldn't even see him. 'I thought he had left me. That he had abandoned me. Sometimes I used to lie awake at night—' She broke off as her voice failed her.

'It's okay, Rosie,' her father encouraged gruffly. 'Everything is going to be okay.'

She nodded. 'Sometimes I would lie awake at night,' she repeated firmly, once she had herself under control. 'I would imagine that you would somehow be at one of my concerts—that you would realise I was Rosemary Harris. Gloria decided on that shortened version of our name very early in my career!' she explained. 'I hoped and prayed that you would be there, that you would come and see me, that you would tell me it had all been a mistake, that—that you still loved me,' she ended shakily.

'I've never stopped loving you, Rosie!' her father protested, and he stood up, his face very pale.

She had wished for those things so much, so often, but they had never happened. And with time she had learnt to accept that her father had cut her out of his life as completely as he had her mother.

She had accepted it—but never understood it.

'Then why did you never come for me?' she cried. 'Why did you just leave me with—leave me like that?'

Leave her with her mother. Hawk knew what she had been going to say and then hadn't.

He had never thought—never guessed at the heartbreak behind this visit to her father. He had only looked at Rosie, unaware she was Rosemary Harris, and questioned why she had never been to see Donald before now, wondered why she was here now.

A part of Hawk so wanted to go to her, to put his arms around her and tell her it was going to be okay, that he would allow no one and nothing to ever hurt her again. But it wasn't his place to do that. Rosie had a fiancé back in England—the man she was due to marry in a matter of days…!

If anyone comforted her now then it had to be Donald.

'Gloria said— Your mother told me you didn't want to see me.' Donald spoke flatly now. 'For eighteen months after we separated I telephoned, I came to the house, but each time I did she told me you didn't want to speak to me. I finally gave up beating my head against that brick wall and took off for America.' He looked incredibly sad. 'Gloria was lying when she said you didn't want anything to do with me, wasn't she…?'

'Yes,' Rosie confirmed huskily, her hands clenched so tightly together her knuckles showed white. 'Is that why you never came backstage at any of my concerts? Because you thought I didn't want to see you?'

Donald closed his eyes. 'I've been such a fool, haven't I?' He shook his head self-disgustedly.

'We both have,' Rosie said huskily. 'I should have known—should have guessed when I found your current telephone number a couple of days ago, in the same box as she keeps our passports, that all of this was Gloria's doing…' She gave a shake of her head, her expression pained. 'She's known where you were all along, hasn't she?'

'I always made sure she knew where to contact me if—if you should ever change your mind and want to see me again,' her father confirmed grimly. 'I sent birthday and Christmas presents every year too.' He looked at her questioningly.

Rosie swallowed hard. 'I never received them.'

'I can't believe— All these years...!' Donald groaned, his eyes glittering angrily now at his ex-wife's machinations.

Hawk could well understand the older man's anger. He felt slightly murderous towards Gloria Harrison himself.

He could see the hurt and bewildered child inside Rosie now, the loneliness that was so apparent in her playing of the violin. Could understand the reason she had talked of Donald these last couple of days as if he were a stranger to her. He understood her reserve towards Donald, for that was what it was—a barrier against being hurt again, against being rejected by her father again, as she had thought she had been rejected as a child.

His own anger towards Rosie for her deception wasn't important right now—at that moment he just wanted to strangle Gloria Harrison for the pain she had caused her ex-husband and her daughter!

Rosie gave a shaky smile. 'But we know the truth now...' She spoke almost questioningly.

'We certainly do,' her father responded tautly, his expression softening as he saw the way she looked at him so uncertainly. 'Is it too late, Rosie?' he questioned uncertainly. 'Do you—? Can we start again, do you think?' He looked at her anxiously.

She had believed it was too late, that too many

years had passed for her and her father ever to have a real relationship again. But as she looked at her dad he was once again the strong and loving man of her childhood—the man she had always looked up to and adored. The man who, despite believing she didn't want any more to do with him, had travelled the world just to see her perform…!

She gave a tremulous smile. 'No, it's not too late,' she assured him.

'Rosie…!' her father groaned emotionally, and he enfolded her into the strength of his arms.

Hawk felt decidedly out of place now. He knew he shouldn't be here—that this moment belonged to Rosie and Donald.

Neither Rosie nor Donald seemed to notice as he quietly let himself out of the apartment and went back downstairs, a perplexed expression on his face as he tried to work out how he really felt about Rosie's wedding on Christmas Eve…

'I came to say goodbye.' Rosie spoke gruffly when she found Hawk in the farmhouse kitchen, sitting at the breakfast bar, an hour or so later, drinking coffee.

It had been a very emotional hour. She and her father had talked and talked as they'd learnt how each of them had spent the last decade, coming to an acceptance that they had been kept apart by the selfish ambitions of a woman who had deliberately done so, using Rosie's talent to make a life for herself regardless of who else she was hurting.

They had a long way to go yet before they relaxed in their relationship as father and daughter, but Rosie had no doubts that they would get there.

In the meantime, she intended going through with her decision to return to the UK later today. She knew she had the emotional strength she had been searching for to confront her mother once and for all.

But first she had to say goodbye to Hawk...

And she didn't want to!

Twenty-four hours. A single day. That was how long she had known Hawk. But already she knew that she loved him. That saying goodbye to him was going to be harder than all those years of believing her father didn't care about her.

Because there would be no happy-ever-after between herself and Hawk. Rosie knew that the most she could ever be to him was the daughter of his employee and friend Donald Harrison.

Yes, saying goodbye to Hawk would be the hardest thing she had ever done in her life.

'I'll be leaving for the airport soon,' she told Hawk brightly as he looked up at her guardedly. 'I'm afraid I never did get around to helping you decorate the Christmas trees,' she added ruefully. 'But my father insists he's well enough to drive me to the airport, so perhaps he'll help you when he gets back.' She shrugged, Hawk's continued silence making her uncomfortable.

His eyes widened. 'Donald isn't coming to England with you?'

'No,' Rosie replied softly.

'Why the hell not?' Hawk rasped, not at all happy with the idea of her confronting her mother alone—he didn't like the sound of Gloria Harrison at all!

She grimaced. 'He wanted to—but I have to do this for myself, Hawk.'

He could understand that. He knew that there were things Rosie wanted to say to her mother that perhaps no one else should hear. He just didn't like the idea of her facing it alone.

Rosie raised her chin determinedly. 'As you already know—read in the newspaper—my returning to England is also a little more—complicated than just talking to my mother,' she explained awkwardly.

Hawk's gaze narrowed on the delicate beauty of her face. A face he knew was going to haunt his nights as well as his days!

'Because you're supposed to be getting married on Christmas Eve?' he grated harshly, knowing she must have finally got around to reading the article in the newspaper he had given her, that claimed 'La Bella Rosa'—violinist Rosemary Harris—wasn't available for comment at the moment, but that her wedding to the conductor Edmund Price would be taking place on Christmas Eve as expected!

Rosie turned away, unable to meet the condemnation in Hawk's gaze. 'I told you it was complicated,' she said.

'You also told me not to believe everything I read,' he reminded her directly.

She drew in a deep breath. 'Because I'm *not* get-ting married—on Christmas Eve or at any other time!'

'You just forgot to tell your fiancé that?'

'No, I—Look, I really do have to go now.' Rosie sighed wearily. 'I have to pack. I only came to say goodbye, and to—to thank you for your hospitality—'

'What hospitality would that be?' Hawk cut in. 'Un-less you're referring to the fact that I almost took you to bed yesterday?' he continued angrily. 'What was I, Rosie? A last fling before you accepted the bonds of matrimony?'

Her cheeks flamed fiery-red. 'Of course not—'

'Of course, *yes*!' Hawk contradicted furiously, standing up to move sharply away from her.

'I just told you I'm *not* getting married on Christ-mas Eve—'

'That isn't what the newspaper says—'

'The newspaper is wrong!' she insisted fiercely. 'Hawk—'

'Why all the fuss, Rosie?' Hawk cut in tauntingly. 'Do I really look as if I'm interested one way or the other?' he scorned.

Rosie stared at the uncompromising rigidness of Hawk's expression for several long, painful seconds before turning on her heel and hurrying back up to her father's flat.

Hawk was right. The two of them had nothing left to say to each other...

CHAPTER FOURTEEN

Three days later...

'YOUR FLIGHT SHOULD be ready for boarding in half an hour or so, Miss Harris,' the hostess in the executive lounge at Heathrow Airport told Rosie as she cleared away Rosie's used cup. 'Could I get you another drink while you're waiting?'

Rosie looked up to return the other woman's smile. 'A coffee would be lovely, thank you,' she accepted, not too bothered by the slight delay in her flight.

The last few days had been hectic, to say the least, and it was nice just to sit down in the airport lounge and relax, away from the barrage of reporters who seemed to have been dogging her every move since she'd arrived back in England. At least they couldn't follow her in here!

Rosie couldn't help smiling as she looked across the room at two small children standing gazing at the enormous Christmas tree that dominated one corner of the room, their faces glowing as they looked up at the multitude of coloured lights and the star shining at the top of the tree. The light snow falling outside on the airport runways was a perfect backdrop for their obvious excitement at the rapidly approaching time for Father Christmas to arrive.

The snow reminded her of Canada. Of Hawk…

'Could you make that two coffees, please?' a familiar voice drawled huskily from just behind Rosie.

She spun sharply round in her chair to look up at Hawk with dazed eyes. It was almost as if just thinking about him had brought him here!

But he really *was* here!

Not just in England, but *here*, in the executive lounge at Heathrow Airport, of all places!

'Of course, Mr Hawkley.' The hostess gave him a beaming smile, before disappearing back to her workstation.

Rosie barely noticed the other woman leaving, having eyes only for Hawk.

She had thought of him so often since they had parted three days ago—of how his dark overlong hair felt so silky to touch, of his eyes that deep, warm blue in his ruggedly handsome face, a face she loved so much!—that for a moment she remained speechless and just continued to stare at him.

Hawk tilted his head slightly sideways, smiling ruefully as he looked down at her. 'Can I sit down?' he prompted softly.

'I—of course,' she replied awkwardly. 'Please do.' She indicated the chair opposite hers—a gesture he ignored as he lowered his long length into the chair next to her. 'I didn't even know you were in Britain...?' She had spoken to her father several times over the last few days, and again only a few hours ago, and he hadn't mentioned that Hawk was in the UK...

Hawk gave a half-smile. 'I'm not. Well, I am—obviously—but only just.' He grimaced. 'Rosie, I got off the plane that just arrived from Calgary...'

The same flight she would be getting on to return to Canada...

Now she was thoroughly confused. If Hawk had only just *arrived*, what was he doing in the executive lounge...?

Where to begin? That was Hawk's problem. It had all seemed so much easier after he had seen the announcement of the cancellation of Rosie's wedding in the newspaper. He would fly over, see her, talk to her— see if he couldn't persuade her that there was now no reason why she couldn't come back to Canada to spend Christmas with her father. And him, of course...

Only it hadn't worked out that way!

'You telephoned Donald *when*, to tell him you were flying over for Christmas after all?' he asked.

'Just a couple of hours ago, when I managed to get booked on the flight,' Rosie said slowly.

Hawk nodded. 'And I was already on the incoming flight, coming to see you. Luckily Donald had the foresight to book me on the same flight back as you. Thanks.' He gave the hostess a warm smile as she brought them their coffee.

Only one thing in Hawk's statement really registered with Rosie. 'You flew over to see *me*…?'

Why had he flown over to see her? The two of them hadn't parted very well in Canada, or so much as spoken to each other on the telephone since she had arrived back in England, so why had Hawk flown over to see her now?

'Shouldn't you be at home with your family?' She knew from her father that Hawk's parents, sister and her family had already arrived to spend Christmas with him.

'Shouldn't you be somewhere else today too?' he came back pointedly.

Christmas Eve. Her wedding day. Except that both of them knew it wasn't.

Rosie shook her head. 'The only place I want to be for Christmas is Canada, with Donald.' *With you*, she added inwardly, still not sure what Hawk was doing here.

Hawk looked at her long and hard for several long seconds before answering. 'And the only person I want to be with for Christmas is sitting right here, next to me.' He spoke gruffly, that dark blue gaze never leaving her face.

'Hawk…?' she breathed raggedly, hardly daring to breathe at all, in case all of this was a dream and she woke up.

He shrugged powerful shoulders beneath the brown suede jacket he wore over a black silk shirt and black denims. 'I was an idiot three days ago. I should never have let you leave like that. At the very least I should have insisted on coming with you. But I thought you had only come to Canada because you'd had some sort of falling-out with the guy you were due to marry—that you would come back here and everything would be smoothed out again. Hell, Rosie,' he cried, 'you could have at least *told* me that Edmund Price is almost old enough to be your grandfather!'

'He isn't that old!' she exclaimed protestingly.

'Okay—your father, then.' Hawk scowled. 'I thought he was some young guy that— Never mind,' he dismissed impatiently, reaching out to take one of her hands in both of his. 'That relationship is definitely over?'

'As far as I was concerned it never began, really,' she admitted ruefully. 'My mother thought it would be a good idea for me to marry a prestigious conductor like Edmund—that it could only further my career. Having no backbone at the time, I went along with it.' She grimaced self-disgustedly.

'You have backbone, Rosie—'

'Now I do.' She nodded firmly. 'But no matter what you may have thought, what that newspaper article said, I had already broken my engagement before I went to Canada to see Donald,' she added determinedly, her hand feeling very warm inside Hawk's. 'My mother was the source of the article you read in that newspaper three days ago.' She sighed. 'She refused to accept that the wedding was off—simply couldn't bear to have anyone thwart her. But I've broken all my business ties with my mother since I returned. In future I intend managing my own career and my own life,' she told him decisively.

The scene with her mother wasn't very pleasant to recall, but Rosie had no regrets. She hoped that one day—in the distant future!—she and her mother might be able to find some sort of relationship again. Just not the unforgiving business partnership they'd had for the last ten years.

'So I heard,' Hawk drawled. 'The Canadian newspapers have been full of the story these last few days too. How you sacked your mother as your manager and cancelled all your wedding plans,' he finished admiringly.

Rosie really didn't want to talk about that. She wanted to move on with her life, not look back. 'Why did you want to see me, Hawk…?' she enquired guardedly.

If anything, these last three days away from Hawk had only confirmed what she had already known in Canada: she was in love with him. Deeply, madly, completely. She just had no idea how he felt about her.

But he was here, wasn't he? He had flown to Britain especially to see her. That had to mean something.

Hawk's gaze roamed over the beauty of her face. Her hair was loose today, flowing like flame over her shoulders and down her back. And she wasn't wearing black either, but a soft cashmere dress in the same shade of green as her eyes, her legs long and silky beneath its knee-length, her high-heeled boots the same colour as her dress.

'I see you've been out shopping,' he told her approvingly.

'For Christmas presents? Yes.' She held up the large bag beside her that was full of gaily wrapped parcels. 'My credit card wasn't maxed out after all.' She grinned.

Hawk shook his head. 'I meant the dress and boots. You look—wonderful,' he assured her huskily.

A delicate blush coloured her freckle-covered cheeks. 'The black clothing was another idea of my mother's—I've given it all away to a charity shop.' She smiled ruefully. 'Hawk, you didn't answer my question: why did you want to see me?'

She had grown in confidence the last three days, Hawk acknowledged. She seemed in control of her own life now, and obviously enjoying it.

Did he have the right to ask her to give up even a little of that freedom she had only just fought for, and won so determinedly?

He looked down at her hand as it rested in both of his, his thumb moving caressingly over her creamy skin. Just touching her like this, being with her again, made him feel weak at the knees, and he knew if they weren't in such a public place that he would have taken her in his arms and kissed her by now.

His gaze returned to her face, to find her looking at him anxiously. He reached up to smooth the frown from between her brows before moving his hand to cradle her cheek. 'You are so beautiful, Rosie,' he murmured tenderly. 'So absolutely, perfectly beautiful.' He gave a shake of his head. 'I came to England to ask you, beg you if necessary, to give me a chance—to marry me. But—'

'Yes!' Rosie spoke quickly, before he could complete his sentence. She didn't want to hear any buts. From now on there would be no second-bests in her life—no wishing, no dreaming, no negatives at all if she could prevent it.

Which was one of the reasons she was returning to Canada so soon. She wanted to spend Christmas with her father, of course, but she had wanted to see Hawk too—to see if they had any chance of a relationship together.

Though she had never thought that Hawk would come to her like this...!

Hawk became very still, his gaze moving searchingly over her face, lingering on the deep glow of her eyes and her softly parted lips. 'Yes...?' he repeated uncertainly.

She nodded. 'If that was a proposal of marriage, then I accept!'

He shook his head, his gaze unwavering. 'That wasn't a proposal of marriage, Rosie,' he breathed huskily.

Oh, God, had she just made a complete idiot—?

'*This* is a proposal of marriage!' Hawk assured her firmly, even as he moved out of the chair and got down on one knee in front of her, her hand still held tightly in his as he looked up at her. 'Rosie Harrison, will you marry me?'

She hadn't made a fool of herself! Hawk really *was* asking her to marry him!

They were surrounded by happy travellers on their way to spend Christmas with their loved ones, those two children still played happily beside the glowing Christmas tree, the snow was still falling softly outside, and Hawk had just asked her to marry him!

It was almost too magical to be true…!

'Do you think you could give me an answer soon, Rosie?' Hawk murmured ruefully when she hadn't spoken for some time. 'We're attracting quite a lot of attention,' he added self-derisively.

She glanced around them. Sure enough, the other travellers waiting in the lounge were all indulgently watching the drama taking place across the room, and the hostess was openly staring at the two of them too.

Rosie turned back to Hawk. 'Yes, yes, yes—I'll marry you!' she assured him ecstatically.

Hawk grinned triumphantly at the softly called congratulations from the crowd gathering around them, and he moved to take Rosie in his arms and kiss her with all the longing he had felt since she'd left him three days ago.

'I love you, Rosie Harrison,' he groaned when he finally came up for air. 'I had no idea it was possible to miss someone so much until you left Canada and came back to England. Since you left me!' He rested his forehead on hers, his arms still tightly wrapped about her.

'I love you too, Hawk,' Rosie breathed shakily. 'So very, very much.'

'Then that's all that matters,' he murmured. 'Loving each other, wanting to be together, is all that will ever matter.'

It was too, Rosie realised. No matter what happened in future, no matter where their individual careers took them—because she *was* going to play again, *wanted* to play again!—as long as they loved each other nothing else mattered.

'As Christmas presents go, this is quite something, Rosie,' Hawk told her gruffly exactly a year later, their baby daughter, born only a few minutes before, held carefully in his arms.

'She's our gift to each other.' Rosie smiled, gently touching the baby's hand, hardly able to believe this miracle herself.

It had been a year of smiles and laughter, of loving, of being loved, of juggling two careers and her pregnancy so that their partings weren't too often. And the birth of their daughter Sophie had only made their happiness all the richer.

'Donald and Mom and Dad will be along later this morning,' Hawk assured her as he tenderly placed their red-haired daughter into her arms, before sitting down on the hospital bed beside her. 'I telephoned Gloria and told her the good news,' he added with a grin. 'She sent her congratulations and hopes to see us all the next time we're in New York.'

Rosie's relationship with her mother was still fragile, to say the least. Her mother was now working for a PR company in Manhattan and the two women had only met twice in the last year—tense meetings, when they'd found they really had nothing to say to each other.

It didn't matter. Nothing else mattered but the happiness Rosie and Hawk had found together—a happiness that had spread to her father and to Hawk's family.

'Shall we try for a son next Christmas?' Rosie looked up at Hawk glowingly, more in love with her handsome husband than ever, as she knew he was deeply in love with her.

Hawk bent down to kiss her lingeringly on the lips. 'Glad to oblige, Mrs Hawkley,' he murmured lovingly.

Mrs Hawkley.

Not Rosemary Harris.

Not Rosie Harrison.

But Rosie Hawkley.

Hawk's wife.

That was all she ever wanted to be…

* * * * *

Silent Night Man

DIANA PALMER

The prolific author of more than a hundred books, **Diana Palmer** got her start as a newspaper reporter. A multi-*New York Times* bestselling author and one of the top ten romance writers in America, she has a gift for telling the most sensual tales with charm and humour. Diana lives with her family in Cornelia, Georgia.

Visit her website at www.DianaPalmer.com.

CHAPTER ONE

AT THE FUNERAL home the friend of the deceased was a big, richly dressed man who looked like a professional wrestler. He was wearing expensive clothing and a cashmere coat. He had olive skin, black eyes and wavy black hair that he wore in a long ponytail. He stood over the casket without saying a word. He looked aloof. He looked dangerous. He hadn't spoken to anyone since he entered the building.

Tony Danzetta stared down at John Hamilton's casket with an expression like stone, although he was raging inside. It was hard to look at the remains of a man he'd known and loved since high school. His best friend was dead. Dead, because of a woman.

Tony's friend, Frank Mariott, had phoned him at the home of the man he was working for temporarily in Jacobsville, Texas. Tony had planned to stay around for a little longer, take a few weeks off from work before he went back to his real job. But the news about John had sent him rushing home to San Antonio.

Of the three of them, John had been the weak link.

The other two were always forced to save him from himself. He fantasized about people and places that he considered were part of his life. Often the people were shocked to learn that he was telling his friends that he was on close terms with them.

Tony and Frank thought that John was harmless. He just wanted to be somebody. He was the son of people who worked for a local clothing manufacturing company. When the company moved outside the United States, they went to work at retail stores. Neither of them finished high school, but John often made up stories to tell classmates about his famous rich parents who had a yacht and their own airplane. Tony and Frank knew better, but they let him spin his yarns. They understood him.

But now John was dead, and that...woman was responsible! He could still see her face from the past, red with embarrassment when she'd asked him about one of their assignments at the adjunct college class they were both taking in criminal justice. That had been six years ago. She couldn't even talk to a man without stammering and shaking. Millie Evans had mousy-brown hair and green eyes. She wore glasses. She was thin and unremarkable. But Tony's adopted foster mother, who had been an archivist at the local library, was Millicent Evans's superior and she liked Millie. She was always talking about her to Tony, pushing her at him, right up until the day she died.

Tony couldn't have told his foster mother, but he knew too much about the girl to be interested in her.

John had become fixated on her a couple of years ago and during one of Tony's rare visits home, had told him about her alter ego. In private, he said, Millie was hot. Give her a couple of beers and she'd do anything a man wanted her to do. That prim, nervous pose was just that—a pose. She wasn't shy and retiring. She was a party girl. She'd even done a threesome with him and their friend Frank, he'd told Tony in confidence. Don't mention that to Frank, though, he'd added, because Frank was still embarrassed about it.

What Tony had learned about Millie Evans had turned him right off her. Not that he'd found her attractive before that. She was another in a long line of dull, staid spinsters who'd do anything to get a man. Poor John. He'd felt sorry for his friend, because John was obsessed with Millicent Evans. To John, Millie was the queen of Sheba, the ultimate female. Sometimes she loved him, John moaned, but other times she treated him like a complete stranger. Other times, she complained that he was stalking her. Ridiculous, John had told Tony. As if he had to stalk her, when she was often waiting for him at his apartment, when he got off from work as a night watchman, wearing nothing at all!

John's description of the spinster was incomprehensible to Tony, who'd had beautiful, intelligent, wealthy women after him. He'd never had to chase a woman. Millicent Evans had no looks, no personality and she seemed rather dull witted. He never had been able to understand what John saw in her.

Now John was dead. Millicent Evans had driven him

to suicide. Tony stared at the pale, lifeless face and rage built inside him. What sort of woman used a man like that, abused his love to the extent that she caused him to take his own life?

The funeral director had a phone call, which forced him to approach the silent man in the viewing room. He paused beside him. "Would you be Mr. Danzetta?" the man asked respectfully. The caller had identified him as tall and unconventional looking. That was an understatement. Up close, the man was enormous, and those black eyes cut like a diamond.

"I'm Tony Danzetta," he replied in a deep, gravelly voice.

"Your friend Mr. Mariott just phoned to tell us to expect you. He said you had a special request about the burial?"

"Yes," Tony told him. In his cashmere coat, that reached down to his ankles, he looked elegant. "I have two plots in a perpetual care cemetery just outside San Antonio, a short distance from where my foster mother is buried. I'd like you to put John in one of them." He was remembering a hill in Cherokee, North Carolina, where his mother was buried and a cemetery in Atlanta that held the remains of his father and his younger sister. He'd been in San Antonio since junior high school, with his foster mother. He described the plots, one of which he intended for John. "I have a plat of the location in my safe-deposit box. If I could drop it by in the morning?"

"Today would be better," the man replied apologetically. "We have to get our people to open the grave and prepare it for the service on the day after tomorrow, you understand."

He was juggling appointments, one of which was with his banker about a transfer of funds. But he smiled, as if it was of no consequence. He could get the plat out of the box while he was doing business at the bank. "No problem. I'll drop it by on my way to the hotel tonight."

"Thank you. That will save us a bit of bother."

Tony looked down at John. "You did a good job," he said quietly. "He looks...the way he used to look."

The man smiled broadly.

Tony looked at his watch. "I have to go. I'll be back when I've finished my business in town."

"Yes, sir."

"If Frank shows up before I get back, tell him that, will you? And tell him not to go out for food. I'll take him out to eat tonight."

"I will."

"Thanks."

The funeral director walked out of the viewing room, pausing to speak to someone. Tony, his eyes resting sadly on his friend's face, only half noticed the conversation.

He heard soft footsteps come toward the casket and pause beside him. He turned his head. And there she was. The culprit herself. She'd be twenty-six now, he judged, and she was no more attractive than she'd been all those years ago. She dressed better. She was wearing a neat gray suit with a pink blouse and a thick dark coat. Her dark brown hair was in a bun. She was wearing contacts in her green eyes, he imagined, because his foster mother had often mentioned how nearsighted she was. The lack of glasses didn't help her to look any prettier. She had a nice mouth and good skin, but she held no attraction for Tony. Especially after she'd been responsible for his best friend's death.

"I'm very sorry," she said quietly. She looked at John with no visible sign of emotion. "I never meant it to end like this."

"Didn't you?" He turned, his hands in the pockets of his coat, as he glared down at her with piercing dark eyes. "Teasing him for years, playing hard to get, then calling the police to have him arrested as a stalker? And you didn't mean it to end like this?"

She felt cold all over. She knew he'd worked in construction years ago, but there had been rumors about him since, whispers. Dark whispers. John had intimated that Tony was into illegal operations, that he'd killed men. Looking into his black eyes now, she could believe it. He wasn't the man she'd known. What had he said about her teasing John?

"Don't bother to lie," he said icily, cutting off her question even before it got out of her mouth. "John told me all about you."

Her eyebrows arched. What was there to tell, except that his friend John had almost destroyed her life? She drew herself up straighter. "Yes, he was quite good at telling people about me," she began.

"I never could understand what he saw in you," he continued, his voice as pleasant as his eyes were homicidal. "You're nothing to look at. I wouldn't give you a second look if you were dripping diamonds."

That hurt. She tried not to let it show, but it did. God knew what John had told him.

"I...have to go," she stammered. She was no good at confrontations. This big man was looking for a fight. Millie had no weapons against him. Long ago, the spirit had been beaten out of her.

"What, no urge to linger and gloat over your triumph?" He laughed coldly. "The man is dead. You drove him to suicide!"

She turned, her heart breaking, and met the tall man's eyes. "You and Frank could never see it," she replied. "You wouldn't see it. Other men have infatuations. John had obsessions. He was arrested other times for stalking women—"

"I imagine you put the women up to reporting him," he interrupted. "John said you'd accuse him of stalking and then be waiting for him at his apartment, wearing no clothes at all."

She didn't seem surprised at the comment. He couldn't know that she was used to John's accusations. Much too used to them for comfort.

She moved one shoulder helplessly. "I tried to make him get help. When I finally had him arrested, I spoke to the district attorney myself and requested that they give him a psychiatric evaluation. John refused it."

"Of course he refused it. There was nothing wrong

with his mind!" he shot back. "Unless you could call being infatuated with you a psychiatric problem." He raised both eyebrows. "Hell, I'd call it one!"

"Call it whatever you like," she said wearily. She glanced once more at John and turned away from the casket.

"Don't bother coming to the funeral," he said coldly. "You won't be welcome."

"Don't worry, I hadn't planned to," she replied.

He took a quick step toward her, infuriated by her lukewarm attitude, his dark eyes blazing with fury.

She gasped, dropped her purse and jumped back away from him. Her face was white.

Surprised, he stopped in his tracks.

She bent and scrambled for her purse, turned and ran out of the room.

There were murmurs outside the room. He glanced back at John, torn between anger and grief. "God, I'm sorry," he said softly to his friend. "I'm so sorry!"

He forced himself to leave. The funeral director was standing at the front door, looking worried.

"The young lady was very upset," he said uneasily. "White as a sheet and crying."

"I'm sure she was grieving for John," Tony said nonchalantly. "They knew each other a long time."

"Oh. That would explain it, then."

Tony walked to his car and felt better. At least he'd dragged some emotion out of her on behalf of his friend. He got behind the wheel of his expensive sports

car and revved it out of the funeral home parking lot,
his mind already on his appointment with the bank.

Millie Evans sat at the wheel of her little black VW
Beetle and watched Tony drive away, out of her life.
She was still crying. His coldness, his fury, had hurt
her. She'd had to deal with John's histrionics and threats
for two years, watching her life and career go down
the drain while he told lies about her to anyone gull-
ible enough to listen. He'd persecuted her, tormented
her, made a hell of her daily life. Now he was dead,
and Tony wanted to make her pay for driving his poor,
helpless friend to suicide.

She wiped at her eyes with a handkerchief. Poor
friend, the devil! Perhaps if he and Frank had realized
that John was mentally ill years ago, they might have
made him get help. He might have straightened out his
life and gone on.

Millie was secretly relieved that John hadn't carried
out his last, furious threat to end her life. He'd told her
that she wouldn't get away with rejecting him. He had
friends, he told her, who wouldn't hesitate to kill her
for the right amount of money. He had savings, he'd
raged; he'd use it all. He'd make sure she didn't live to
gloat about pushing him out of her life!

She'd worried about that threat. The news was full
of people who'd gone off the deep end and killed others they blamed for their problems, before killing
themselves. It was, sadly, a fact of modern life. But
she'd never dreamed that she—plain, prim little Millie

Evans—would ever have something like that happen to her. Most people never even noticed her.

She'd wanted to be noticed by Tony. She'd loved him forever, it seemed. While his foster mother was alive, she'd coaxed the older woman into talking about her adoptive son. Tony had come a long way from North Carolina. He and his sister, both Cherokee, had lived with their mother and her abusive husband—but not their biological father—in Atlanta just briefly, but the man drank to excess and was brutal to the children. Tony and his sister went into foster homes in Georgia. After his sister, also in foster care, died, Tony's nurturing foster mother moved him to San Antonio, where she had family, to get him away from the grief. She worked as an archivist at the public library in San Antonio, where Tony was a frequent patron; and where Millie worked after school and between classes while she went through college.

Millie had loved hearing stories of Tony as a boy, as a teenager, as a soldier. Sometimes his foster mother would bring letters to the library and show them to Millie, because they were like living history. Tony had a gift for putting episodes in his life down on paper. He made the countries where he was stationed come alive, and not only for his parent.

Millie had hoped that Tony might spend some time at the library when he came home on leave. But there were always pretty girls to take on dates. Frank Mariott worked as a bouncer in a nightclub and he knew cocktail waitresses and showgirls. He introduced them to Tony, who always had a night free for fun.

A library, Millie supposed, wasn't a good place to pick up girls. She looked in her rearview mirror and laughed. She saw a plain, sad-faced woman there, with no hopes of ever attracting a man who'd want to treasure her for the rest of her life. It was a good thing, she told herself, that she'd stockpiled so many romance novels to keep her nights occupied. If she couldn't experience love, at least she could read about it.

She wiped her eyes, closed up her purse and drove herself back to work. She'd forced herself to go and see John, out of guilt and shame. All she'd accomplished was to find a new enemy and hear more insults about herself. She knew that she'd never meet up with Tony again after this. Perhaps it was just as well. She'd spent enough time eating her heart out over a man who couldn't even see her.

Tony made his funds transfer, got the plat from the safe-deposit box, had the bank copy it for him and replaced the original before he went back to the funeral home.

All the way, in the back of his mind, he kept seeing the fear in Millie's face when he'd moved toward her. That reaction was odd. She might have been surprised by the speed of his movement—a lot of people had been, over the years. But she'd expected him to hit her. It was in her eyes, her face, her whole posture. He wondered what had happened to her in the past that made her so afraid.

Then he chided himself for that ridiculous compassion, when she'd caused John's death. At least he'd made sure that she wouldn't come to the funeral. That would have been the last straw.

He pulled up at the funeral home and locked his car. It was getting colder. Strange weather, he thought. First it was like summer then, in a matter of days, winter arrived. It was normal weather for Texas in late November, he mused.

As he walked into the funeral home, he saw some of John's family gathered, talking among themselves. Frank spotted Tony and came out into the hall. They shook hands.

"I just have to drop this off," he told Frank, lifting up the copy of the plat. "Then we'll spend a minute talking to John's people before we go out to eat."

The funeral director spotted them and came forward. He took the copy of the plat, smiled at Frank and went back to his office.

"You may get a shock," Frank murmured as they walked into the viewing room.

"What do you mean?" Tony asked, surprised.

John didn't have much family. His parents were long dead. He did have a sister, Ida. She was there, dry-eyed and irritable. She glanced at the doorway and put on a big smile.

"Tony! How nice to see you again!" She ran up to him and hugged him. "You look great!"

"Sorry we have to meet like this," Tony began.

"Yes, the idiot, what a stupid thing to do!" Ida muttered. "He had a life insurance policy worth fifty thousand dollars. I paid the premiums for him, me and Jack, and look what he does! Suicide! We won't get a penny!"

Tony looked as if he'd been hit in the eye.

"Oh, there's Merle. Sorry, honey, I have to talk to her about the flowers. She's giving me a good deal on a wreath..."

John's cousin Ben came forward to shake hands.

"What a mess," he told the two men. He shook his head. "I bailed him out of jail. He didn't exactly skip bond, but I'll forfeit what I put up," he added heavily. "Two thousand dollars," he grumbled. "He swore he'd pay me back." He wandered off, still shaking his head.

An elderly woman with dyed blond hair and wearing a hideous black dress, peered at Tony. She grinned up at him. "You must be that rich friend of Johnny's," she said. "He said you owned several islands out in the Atlantic and that you were going to give him one and a yacht, too, so he could get to and from this country."

"That's right, Blanche," Frank said, smiling. "Now, you'll have to excuse us, we've got an appointment. We'll see you at the funeral."

"I sure would like to see that yacht," Blanche added.

Frank took Tony by the arm and propelled him out into the lobby.

They were sitting in a good Italian restaurant fifteen minutes later, having given in their order.

"I can't believe it," Tony said furiously. "His own

family! Not one of them seems to be sad that he's dead!"

"He was nothing but trouble to them," Frank replied. "He didn't work, you know," he added, shocking Tony, who'd already had a few shocks. "He told the government people that he had a bad back and he fed liquor to two vagrants who signed sworn statements that they'd seen the accident that crippled him. He convinced his doctor and got a statement from him, too, and talked a lawyer into getting him onto partial disability." He shook his head. "But it was barely enough to live on. He pestered his relatives for handouts. When he got arrested for stalking, this last time, he talked Ben into posting his bond. I warned Ben, but he said John had promised that his rich friend would pay Ben back."

"I've known John since high school," he told Frank. "You've known him since junior high. He was a good man."

Frank paused while the waiter served them appetizers and ice water.

"He changed," Frank said quietly. "More than you know. You only saw him on holidays, while your foster mother was still alive, and hardly at all in the past couple of years. I saw him constantly."

"You're trying to say something," Tony murmured, eyeing the other man.

Frank toyed with his salad. "He made friends with some members of a gang a few months ago," he said. "It really thrilled him, that he could kick around with people who weren't afraid of the law. He hated cops,

you know," he added. "Ever since the arrest for stalking, when he went after—"

"Yes," Tony interrupted him. "That Millie creature!"

"Creature!" Frank sat back, shocked.

Tony was beginning to feel uncomfortable. "She
caused John to kill himself, remember?"

"Who told you that?"

"John did. He sent me a letter. Left me a letter."
He pulled it out of his pocket. It had arrived the day
he got the news that John was dead, obviously having
been mailed in advance of the suicide. "He said she
tormented him...hell, read it for yourself." He pushed
it across the table.

"I can imagine what's in it," Frank said. He ignored
the letter and finished chewing a bite of salad. "He accused women of teasing him when they were only trying to get him to leave them alone. Millie was more
kindhearted than most—she kept forgiving him. Then
when she refused dates, he started telling tales on her
to her coworkers." He glanced at Tony, sitting stiffly,
still unbelieving. "You've seen Millie. Now, you tell
me, does she really look like the sort of woman who'd
lie in wait at John's apartment wearing a French maid's
costume with a bottle of champagne in one hand and a
champagne flute in the other?"

"It would be tough to imagine," Tony had to admit.
"Still, mild-looking women have done crazier things."

"Yes, but Millie's not like that." Frank's face softened. "She sat with your foster mother when she was

dying in the hospital, before you could get home. She was there every night after work."

"Sure, you'd defend her, when you did a threesome with her and John!" he snapped.

Frank gaped at him. "I beg your pardon?"

The other man's reaction made Tony even more uncomfortable. He fiddled with his water glass. "John told me about it."

"Oh, for God's sake!" Frank burst out. "I've never done a threesome in my life, much less with Millie!"

"Maybe he made a mistake with the name," Tony mumbled.

"Maybe he made a mistake telling you lies about me," Frank shot back. "I'd give anything to have Millie notice me! Don't you think I know how little I have to give to a woman with her brains? She has a degree in library science. I barely got out of high school. I'm a bouncer," he added heavily. "A nobody."

"Stop that!" Tony said immediately. "You're not just a bouncer. It's a rough job. It takes a hell of a man to do it."

"I'm sure there are guys in New York City who place ads hoping to get hired as bouncers in bars," Frank said sarcastically. "Here in San Antonio, it's not exactly the dream job of most men."

"You're sweet on Millie Evans, so you're defending her."

"I'm sweet on her, all right. If the competition wasn't so stiff, I might even try my luck. That's what made John crazy. He couldn't stand the competition, either.

He knew he'd never replace that other guy Millie's been in love with for six years."

"What other guy?" Tony asked carelessly.

"You."

It was as if time stopped and everything went around in slow motion. Tony put his fork down and looked across at Frank as if he'd gone mad. "Excuse me?"

"Do you think Millie needed courses in criminal justice to be a librarian?" Frank asked drolly. "She took those courses because your foster mother had told her you were taking them, in addition to your regular college classes, so you could get your degree faster. It was an excuse to be around you."

Now, horribly, it made sense. He hadn't even questioned her presence in the classes.

"Great," Tony muttered. "The murderer of my best friend thinks I'm hot!"

"She didn't kill him. But no jury would have convicted her if she had," Frank persisted. "He got her fired, Tony. He went to her boss and told her that Millie was hanging out in bars to have sex with men for an audience. He told that to three of the library's richest patrons, one of whom sat on the board of directors for the library. They demanded that she be fired."

Tony watched the other man warily. "And how do you know it wasn't true?"

"Because I went to a friend of mine at the local precinct and got John's rap sheet and showed it to them."

Tony was feeling ill. "Rap sheet? John had a rap sheet?"

"Yes. For fraud, defamation of character, petty theft, three charges of stalking and a half dozen other charges. I got a statement from the last woman he'd stalked, a receptionist for one of the dentists John went to. She swore in court that John had threatened her life. He convinced a lawyer that she was lying and produced a witness who heard her bragging that she'd get John arrested."

Tony waited for the rest.

"The gang members testified in his favor and got the case thrown out of court. A couple of weeks later, the receptionist was raped. Nobody was ever caught or charged."

Tony leaned forward. "Don't tell me John was mixed up in that!"

"He never admitted it," Frank replied heavily. "But I knew he was. A few months later, one of the gang members was pulled in on a rape charge and he bragged to the arresting officer that he could get away with it anytime he liked. He had alibis, he said. Turned out they were also members of his gang. Sadly for him, on the second rape case, the new gang member he bragged to was wearing a wire. He's doing hard time now."

"But John wasn't like that," Tony protested. "He was a good man!"

"He was sick," Frank said flatly. "He utterly destroyed Millie's life because she didn't want him. Even his relatives apologized to her for what he'd done. There are still people who go to that library who are convinced that Millie has orgies down in the basement, because John told them she did."

"I can't believe it," Tony said to himself.

"Obviously. You didn't know the adult John became. You still saw the kid who played sandlot baseball with you in ninth grade."

"He had a rap sheet. I never knew."

"He was a troubled man. There's something else, too. My friend at the precinct said that when they searched John's room, they found an open bank book on the coffee table. It showed a withdrawal of five thousand dollars in cash—John had apparently sold everything of value that he had. The pawn slips were there, too, neatly arranged. There was a note, addressed to Millie, with only a threat: 'You'll be sorry.' The police haven't told her yet, and they warned me not to say anything. But I'm afraid for her."

"What do you think John did with the money?" Tony asked.

"I don't know."

Tony was frowning. "Any of those gang members ever been suspected of murdering anybody?"

"Yes," came the curt reply. "John had a vindictive nature. It wouldn't surprise me if he didn't put out a contract on Millie."

The John whom Tony knew as a teen wouldn't have been capable of such actions. The man he was only now coming to know might well have done it. He could hardly get his mind to function. He'd come home with clear-cut ideas of the good guy and the bad woman, and now his theories were worthless. He was remembering Millie's tragic expression when he accused her of murdering his friend. He was remembering, too, what Frank had just told him, that Millie had cared about him. It was a good bet that she didn't anymore, he thought cynically.

Frank checked his watch. "I have to get back to the funeral home. Millie said she was coming over to see John. I tried to talk her out of it, but she said that it was something she had to do, that she felt responsible. Even after all John had done to her, she still felt sorry for him."

Tony closed his eyes and groaned. He didn't know how to tell his friend that Millie had already come to see John, and that Tony had treated her like dirt and made her run out of the building in fear of him. It wasn't a revelation he was looking forward to.

CHAPTER TWO

FRANK ACTUALLY winced when Tony told him how he'd treated Millie when he'd seen her at the funeral home earlier.

"Good God," Frank said heavily. "That poor woman. How could you, Tony?" he asked accusingly.

Tony grimaced. "I didn't know any better," he defended himself. "All I had to go on was the letter John sent me and the memory of those visits I made home, when he'd cry on my shoulder about how bad she was treating him. I was sure that she'd killed my friend with her heartless behavior."

Frank sighed heavily. "I wish she hadn't gone to the funeral home early."

"Yeah. Me, too," Tony replied. He was never going to be able to forget Millie's mad dash out the door. It would haunt him. "Look, that friend of yours at the precinct," he said. "Could you get him to ask around and see if there's any word on the street about a potential hit?"

"I could do that," Frank said, and brightened a little.

"Maybe John just left a lot of money to an animal shelter and made the threat to scare her," Tony said.

Frank gave him a sour look.

Tony held up both hands. "Sorry."

"It won't matter what he finds out," Frank said. "There's no budget for protective custody on supposition, no matter how educated. They won't be able to assign anybody to protect her."

"I'm off until the new year," Tony said. "I can handle that."

Frank blinked. "I'm sure she'll welcome having you around, after the warm reception you gave her at the funeral home."

Tony flinched. "Yeah. Well, I'll have to apologize, I suppose."

Frank didn't say anything to that. Privately he thought Tony was going to find it difficult to bend enough to convince Millie that he was sorry. His friend had spent most of his life in violent surroundings. His social skills were a bit rusty, especially around women like Millie. Tony's taste was the brassy, forward sort of females he could find in bars. Millie was both refined and reserved. It would be a tough combination to crack for a hard nut like Tony.

The next morning, a penitent Tony joined Frank at the funeral home for John's last rites. There was a very small group of people there, mostly family. A couple of rough-looking men were sitting in the back, looking around constantly. Tony wondered if they might be John's gang friends.

After the brief service, Tony drove Frank and himself to the cemetery for the graveside service. It was equally brief.

Tony noted that the rough-looking men had also come to the cemetery. One of them was intent on Tony and Frank, as if he found their presence suspicious.

"We're being watched," Tony told his friend as they walked back toward Tony's sports car.

"I noticed," Frank replied. Working as a bouncer had given him a sixth sense about trouble. Tony, in his line of work, also had developed it. They pretended to talk casually, without making it obvious that they saw the two men.

When they got to the car, and were seated and ready to travel, Tony looked in the rearview mirror and noted that one of the men was unobtrusively writing down his license plate number. He started laughing as he pulled the car around two of the family's vehicles and exited the cemetery road.

"What's funny?" Frank asked.

"They're cops," he said.

"What?"

"They're cops," Tony repeated. "Gang members wouldn't give a hoot in hell about my plate number. They want to know who I am, and what my connection is to John." He glanced at his friend. "How about asking your contact in the police department what they want to know about me? I'll phone him with the details."

Frank chuckled. "Fair enough. I'll call him when I get home."

Tony grinned. It amused him to be viewed with suspicion. He mostly was these days. He kept a low profile and never talked about his job.

He dropped Frank off at his apartment, and promised to meet him the following day for lunch. Then he went back to his hotel.

He noted that he was being followed again. He gave his car keys to the valet who handled the parking, walked into the lobby and slowed his pace as he went toward the elevator. He felt eyes on his back. Someone was following him. This was amusing.

He got into the elevator and pretended to be disinterested in his surroundings. A man whom he recognized as one of the two strangers at the funeral got in with him and stood apart, also pretending unconcern.

When Tony got off, on the wrong floor, he noted that the man remained behind but jotted down a number.

He took the staircase down, and was waiting in the lobby when the man following him got off the elevator. He looked up into Tony's black eyes and actually jumped.

Tony gave him a worldly look. "If you want to know who I am and why I went to John's funeral, come on in the bar and I'll buy you a drink and give you the lowdown."

The man raised his eyebrows, and then started laughing.

"How did you figure it out?" he asked, when they were seated at the bar.

"I've worked with cops before," Tony told him, "in between jobs overseas."

"What sort of jobs overseas?"

Tony chuckled, reached into his pocket for his wallet, flipped it open and displayed his credentials.

The man whistled softly. "I thought about going with them, once, but after six months of being called, interrogated, lie-detected, background-checked and otherwise investigated to death, I gave up and joined the police force. The pay's lousy, but I've only been involved in one shoot-out in ten years." He grinned. "I'll bet you can't say that."

"You'd be right," Tony had to admit. "I'm carrying enough lead in me to fill a revolver. They can't take some of the slugs out because of where they lodged."

"You knew the deceased, I gather."

He nodded. "He was my best friend since high school." He grimaced. "But it turns out I didn't know him at all. He was stalking a woman we both knew and I thought she was lying about it."

The man pulled out a notepad. "That would be Miss Millicent Evans."

"Yes."

"She wasn't lying," the police detective told him. "She called us in on a 10-16 domestic, physical," he added, using the ten code for a domestic disturbance call. "He'd knocked her around pretty badly."

Tony felt two inches high as he remembered Millie's

unexpected reaction when he'd moved so abruptly in the funeral home. He couldn't speak.

"But when it was time to press charges, she wouldn't," the detective said flatly. "We were disappointed. We don't like women beaters. She said he was drinking heavily and had apologized, and it was the first time he'd hit her."

"Was it only the one time?" Tony had to know.

"I think so. She isn't the sort to take that kind of abuse on a routine basis. About a week later, he killed himself." He leaned closer. "We got word that a local gang boss took money to have her killed. That's why we were at the funeral. You got a friend named Frank?"

"Yes."

"He and my lieutenant are best friends," the man told him. "He's got us looking for people who might fit the description of a hit man."

Tony laughed. "And I fit the description."

"I've seen mob hit men who look just like you." He cocked his head. "You Italian?"

Tony grinned. "Cherokee," he said. "My mother's husband adopted me, but he wasn't my father."

"Goes to show," the detective said, "that you can't tell who people are by looking."

"Absolutely."

Tony went by the library the next morning, hoping to apologize to Millie and go from there. But the minute she spotted him in the lobby, she went through a door that had the sign Employees Only and vanished. He asked for her at the desk, as if he hadn't noticed. The clerk on duty went back through the door and reappeared a minute later, red-faced and stuttering.

"I'm sorry, I…couldn't find her," she finished.

Tony smiled sadly. He didn't blame Millie for hating his guts. "It's okay," he said. "Thanks."

He left. Apparently protecting her was going to be done at a distance, unless he could think of a way to get her to listen to him.

He tried calling her at the library when he got back to his hotel. The minute she heard his voice, she hung up. He sighed and called Frank.

"She ran the other way," he told his friend. "I expected it. But I can't convince her that she needs protection if I can't get within speaking distance of her. Any ideas?"

"Yeah," Frank said. "I'll go by her apartment and speak to her."

"Thanks. Tell her I'm sorry. It won't do much good, but I really mean it."

"I know you do."

"I bought one of our tails a drink," Tony told him. "He said they were looking for guys who fit the profile of a hit man. He thinks I do."

Frank burst out laughing. "If the shoe fits…"

"Thanks a lot," he muttered.

"I'll get back to you when I've seen Millie," he promised.

"Okay. I'll be here."

* * *

Frank called him the next morning. "She'll talk to you," he told Tony. "But it took a lot of persuading. And she won't believe that John would do anything so drastic as to hire someone to kill her. You're going to have a hard time selling her on the idea of protection," he added.

"Well, I'll work on my people skills," Tony replied.

There was a pause. "I heard a comedian say that you can get a lot more with a smile and a gun than you can with a smile. That about sums up your people skills."

Tony burst out laughing. "You do have a point," he conceded. "I'll try to mellow before I go to see her. Any news from your detective friend?"

"Not yet. He anticipated me, it seems." He chuckled. "He already had his men working on the gang angle, to see if anybody hired a shooter. Maybe he'll turn up something."

"Meanwhile, I'll do what I can to safeguard Millie," Tony replied. "See you."

"Yeah."

Tony dressed casually for the visit to the library, hoping he wouldn't attract too much attention if anyone was watching Millie. He wore jeans and a cotton shirt under a leather jacket. He looked outdoorsy, like a cowboy, but he refused to put on a wide-brimmed hat. He'd never liked to cover his black wavy hair, and he still wore it in a ponytail. He wasn't going to be conservative, no matter what the job called for. He was too much of a renegade.

He walked to the desk and asked for Millie, smiling at the clerk. She smiled back, obviously interested in him. She picked up the phone, pushed a button and told Millie she had a visitor out front.

As she spoke, she was sorting mail. "Oh, and you got a package," she added, still talking to Millie on the phone, her hand reaching toward a flat but lumpy-looking brown envelope with spiky writing on the front.

"Don't touch that," Tony said at once, whipping out his phone. He dialed the emergency services number and requested a squad car and the bomb squad.

The clerk looked at him as if she thought he'd gone nuts.

"Get everybody out of the building," he told her in a tone bristling with authority. "Don't waste time," he said when she hesitated. "There's enough explosive in there to blow up a city block. Hurry!"

She rushed into the back as Millie came out front. She stopped at the desk, where Tony was still arguing with the dispatcher about the bomb squad.

"Listen, I work for the government," he said in a deep, steady tone. "I've seen letter bombs before. I know what I'm talking about. Do you want to read in the newspapers tomorrow morning that a library blew up because you didn't take the threat seriously? They'll even spell your name right...yes, that's what I said, the bomb squad. And hurry!"

He glanced at Millie, his face hard, his eyes glittering. "We have to get out of here," he told her.

"Out? I've got a package there..."

He caught her hand as she reached for it. "If you like having two hands and a head, you'll do what I tell you. Come on!" he called to the clerk, who was hurrying several patrons and a couple of employees out the front door.

"You are out of your mind," Millie said primly. "I'm not leaving…!"

"Sorry," he said as he whipped her up in his arms and carried her right out the front door, which a grinning patron held open for him. "I don't have time to argue."

A squad car rolled up along with the bomb squad. Tony went to talk to the sergeant in charge.

"It's a letter bomb, on the counter in there," he told the man. "I worked a case in Nairobi with one that looked just like it, but I couldn't get anybody to listen to me. It killed two foreign workers when it went off."

The sergeant sighed. "Okay. We'll check it out. But if you're wrong, you're in a lot of trouble."

"I'm not wrong," Tony told him, and showed his credentials. The sergeant didn't say another word. He went straight to work.

The librarians were skeptical; so were Millie and the patrons. But they all stood patiently in the cold while the bomb squad went hesitantly into the building and looked for the brown envelope Tony had described.

The sergeant came back out, grim-faced. "I'm not completely convinced," he told Tony, "but we'll go by the book. It does look suspicious."

They had a robot with a gripping arm. They sent it into the building to retrieve the package. It took a long time, and many spectators gathered, kept back by two more units of police who arrived to help with crowd control.

There was a camera crew from a local television station on the scene now, and people with camera phones were snapping images to send to the media as well. Some of them were laughing. One man, a grumpy library patron, said he was going to catch cold while the police wasted their time on a bomb threat that would turn out to be a package of photographs or something equally stupid.

As he was speaking, the robot reached the containment bin in which the bomb squad collected suspicious packages. No sooner had it gone in than there was a terrific explosion which knocked the robot onto its back and had spectators screaming and running away.

Tony glanced at the bomb squad sergeant who grimaced. He turned to Millie. She was white-faced and sick at her stomach. If Tony hadn't come in when he did, if she'd opened that package…

He caught her as she slumped to the pavement.

When she came to, she was lying in the backseat of Tony's rented car. He was holding a cold soft drink at her lips, supporting her with one big arm.

"Come on. Take a sip. It will help," he said quietly.

She managed to swallow some of the fizzy liquid. She coughed. "I fainted. I never faint."

"If somebody sent me a bomb, I'd probably faint, too," he replied with a grin. "You're okay. So is everybody else."

She looked up at him quietly. "Why?"

The grin faded. "Some men take possession to the grave with them. John couldn't have you. He wanted to make sure that nobody else ever did. He paid somebody a lot of money to do this. And he almost pulled it off. Now we have to keep you alive while they find out who he hired."

She sat up, breathing heavily. "Surely they won't try again? They'll know that the police are watching now."

"The police don't have the sort of budget they'd need to give you round-the-clock protection. The bomber will know that. Of course he'll try again."

"He's already got the money," she faltered.

"I wouldn't bet on that. More than likely, John set it up so that he can't get it until you're dead and the bomber has proof that you're dead," he told her flatly. "If a gang leader is holding the money, it will be a point of honor with him. Don't look like that, they do have honor among themselves, of a sort. Especially if the leader was John's friend and felt an obligation to him for some reason."

"You knew it was a bomb without touching it," she recalled. "How?"

"It isn't my first bomb," he replied. "I don't do ordinance, but I know guys who do. I learned a lot by watching, the rest by experience."

She frowned. "In the Army? Or working on construction gangs?" she asked.

He hesitated. "I work for the government, in between freelance jobs," he said. "I'm an independent contractor."

"A what?"

"I'm a professional soldier," he told her. "I specialize in counterterrorism."

She was very still. Her pale eyes searched his dark ones. "Did your foster mother ever know?"

He shook his head. "She wouldn't have approved."

"I see."

His eyes narrowed on her averted face. "You don't approve, either, do you?"

She couldn't meet his eyes. She rubbed her cold arms. "My opinion wouldn't mean anything to you."

She climbed out of the car, still a little rocky on her feet. He steadied her.

"You need to get your coat and your purse and come with me," he told her. "We have things to talk about."

"But—" she began.

"Don't argue, Millie," he interrupted. "If you stay in there, you're endangering your coworkers."

That hadn't occurred to her. She looked horrified. "But I have to work," she protested. "I have bills to pay…!"

"You can ask for a leave of absence, can't you?" he persisted. "A few days off won't put you on the streets."

He was making sense, and she knew he was right, but she was afraid that if she asked for time off, she'd

lose her job. She'd been at the library all her working life, and she loved what she did. Her superior still
hadn't gotten over the gossip John had caused by insinuating that Millie had a wild lifestyle. God knew what
she'd say when she heard about the bomb.

"I may not have a job when my boss finds out what
happened here today. She's out of town until next Mon-
day," she added sadly.

"Come on. I'll go in with you."

He escorted her back into the building and insisted
on seeing her supervisor with her. He explained the
situation matter-of-factly, adding that he was certain
her colleagues wouldn't like to risk another such incident by insisting that she stay on the job until the culprit was apprehended.

"Certainly not," Barry Hinson said at once. "Millie,
we can manage without you for a few days. I'm sure
Mrs. Anderson would agree."

Millie sighed. "I don't suppose I have a choice. I'm
very sorry," she began.

"It isn't your fault," Barry said firmly. "None of us
ever blamed you for what that man did. He should have
been locked up," he added, unaware that Tony had been
John's friend.

Millie flushed. She didn't look at Tony. "Well, I'll
get my things and leave. I'll be back next week."

Barry smiled. "Of course." He glanced warily at
Tony. "You won't let anything happen to her?" he
asked, assuming that the big man worked for law enforcement.

"No," Tony assured him. "I won't."

Millie didn't want to feel that enveloping warmth that his words caused. She'd risked her heart on this man once before and had been crushed by his rejection. If only, she thought, you could banish feelings and make them leave you alone forever. She went to get her purse and coat and explain to the clerk what she'd been working on before the bomb disrupted their day.

"Now, what?" Millie asked as she paused by her little black VW in the parking lot. It was used, but clean and well looked after.

"Now, we go somewhere and talk and make decisions."

"There's a cafeteria down the street, where I usually have lunch," she said, naming it.

"I'll meet you there."

She nodded meekly and got into her car.

Ten minutes later, they were having sandwiches and coffee, a late lunch because disposing of the bomb had been a protracted business. Millie ate and drank automatically, but she didn't taste much. It was disconcerting to realize that John actually meant to kill her.

"Stop brooding," Tony said as he sipped coffee. "It won't help."

"I never thought John would want to kill me," she said.

His eyes narrowed. "He beat you up."

She gasped. "How did you know that?"

"Frank."

Her lips made a thin line. "He'd been drinking. He said it was all my fault that his life was falling apart, because I wouldn't marry him. I tried, for the twentieth time, to explain that I didn't love him in that way, but he wouldn't listen. He lost his temper and the next thing I knew, he was slamming me into a wall. Even when it happened, I could hardly believe it. I screamed and screamed, and when he let go of me, I locked myself in the bedroom and called the police."

"You didn't press charges," he muttered.

"He was in tears by the time the police got there. He swore it was the alcohol, that he didn't realize how much he'd had. He said he loved me, he couldn't believe he'd done such a thing. He begged me not to press charges." She shook her head. "I should have. But I felt sorry for him. I always felt sorry for him. He had mental issues, but he wouldn't face that, and he wouldn't get help. I thought I could do something for him."

"You can't fix a broken mind," Tony said heavily. "He was obsessed with you."

His tone intimated that he didn't understand why. She knew what Tony thought of her, because John had told her, time and again. Tony thought she was the most boring woman on earth, and he'd need to be drunk to want to touch her. Looking at his expression now, she was certain that John had been telling the truth. She was plain and prim and unexciting. It was a fact she'd faced long ago.

She pushed back her coffee cup. "After that night,

it got to the point that I couldn't walk out of my apartment without running into John. He said he was going to make sure that I didn't have any other man in my life, and he was going to watch me night and day. When he told those lies about me, and then started spending the day in the library, it began jeopardizing my job. I finally decided that I had no other choice than to file stalking charges against him." She ran a hand over the tight bun she kept her long brown hair in. "It was what pushed him over the edge. I even knew that it would—it's why I waited so long to do anything about the problem. He swore he'd get even, no matter what it took." She looked tired, drained of life. "When I knew that he was dead, I was so ashamed, but all I could feel was a sense of relief. I was finally free of him."

"But you came to the funeral home," he commented.

Her face tautened as she recalled Tony's attitude when he'd met her there. "Yes. It was the guilt. I had to see him. I thought it might make amends, somehow."

"And you found me, instead," he replied, grimacing at her expression. "You have to understand, all I had to go on was what John told me. And he told me a lot. He left me a letter, blaming you for his death. I had no reason to doubt him, at the time. Not until Frank told me the truth."

Of course he'd believed his friend, she thought. It wouldn't have occurred to him that Millie wasn't a wild girl. He didn't know Millie. He didn't want to know her. It hurt, realizing that.

"I'm sorry for the way I reacted," he said stiffly. "I didn't know."

She shook her head. "Nobody knew. I was harassed, blackmailed and slandered by him for years, and he made everybody think it was my own fault, that I encouraged him." Her gaze was flat, almost lifeless. "He was the most repulsive man I've ever known."

He frowned. "He was good-looking."

She glanced up at him. "You can't make people love you," she said in a subdued sort of tone. "No matter what you look like. He was coarse and crude, and ugly inside. That's where it counts, you know. The outside might have been attractive. The devil, they say, was beautiful."

"Point taken."

She finished her coffee. "Where do I go now?"

"Back to your apartment. I'm coming with you, to see what I'll need for surveillance."

She frowned. "Surveillance?"

He nodded. "I want cameras and microphones everywhere. It's the only way we can save your life."

And in that moment, she realized, for the first time, just how desperate her situation really was.

CHAPTER THREE

MILLIE'S APARTMENT was on the third floor of a building about ten blocks from the library. She had a small balcony, on which lived many plants during the warm months. Now, the pots contained nothing except dead remnants of the autumn foliage that she'd been too busy to clean out. The past few weeks had been hectic indeed.

Her walls were full of bookcases and books. She was a great reader. Tony noted the titles ranged from history to gardening to languages to true crime. He smiled when he noticed all the romance novels, including several that had to do with professional soldiers. He'd never told her what he did for a living until today, and she hadn't guessed. But apparently she had an adventurous nature that she kept tightly contained, like her hair in that bun.

He noted that she liked pastel colors, and used them in her decorating. The apartment's contents weren't expensive, but they suited the rooms in which she lived. She had good taste for a woman on a budget.

He poked his nose into every nook and cranny of the place, making notes in a small notebook, about entrance, exit and possible avenues of intrusion. Her balcony was a trouble spot. A man with an automatic rifle could see right into the apartment through the glass sliding doors, which had no curtains. The doors had the usual locks, but no dead bolts. The apartment was only feet away from an elevator and a staircase, which gave it easy access. There was no security for the building, and Tony had noticed two or three suspicious-looking men on his way up in the elevator.

He dug his hands into his pockets. It had seemed like a good plan at the time, but now that he'd seen where Millie lived, he knew he couldn't just move in with her and start waiting for an attack to come.

"This won't work," he said flatly.

She turned from the hall closet, where she'd been pulling out a coat and a sweater, and stared at him blankly. "What?"

"This place is a death trap," he said matter-of-factly. "Easy entrance and exit right outside the door, no dead bolts, a perfect line-of-sight aim for anybody with a high-powered rifle with a scope. Add to that a noticeable lack of security and a few shady characters who live in the building, and you've got an impossible situation. You can't stay here."

"But it's where I live," she said plaintively. "I can't just move because some crazy person is trying to kill me. Besides, wouldn't he just follow me?"

"Probably," he had to admit.

"Then what do I do, live out of my car and switch parking lots every night?" she wondered.

He burst out laughing. He hadn't credited her with a sense of humor. "You'd need a bigger car," he agreed.

She let out a long breath. "I guess I could do something illegal and get arrested," she thought aloud. "I'd be safe in jail."

"Not really," he replied. "Gangs operate in every prison in this country, and in other countries. They're like corporations now, Millie—they're international."

"You're kidding," she said, aghast.

"It's the truth. They have a hierarchy, even in prison, and some measure of control and exploitation. They can order hits inside or outside."

She sat down heavily on the arm of her sofa. "Call the U.S. Marshal's office," she said. "Tell them I qualify for the witness protection program. I can be renamed and transplanted."

"Not unless you testify against somebody really evil," he returned. "Sorry."

Her eyebrows arched. "Ouch."

He lifted a huge shoulder. "So we have to look for a different solution. I'll take you back to the hotel with me—"

She flushed and stood up. "I'm not moving in with you."

"Okay. Which one of your coworkers would you like to put into the line of fire?" he asked. "Because that's your choice right now."

She looked worried. "I don't know any of my co-

workers that well, and I wouldn't ask them to risk being
killed on my account even if I did."

His eyes were curious. "You've worked there for
years, and you don't know any of your colleagues well?"

She bit her lower lip. "I don't mix well. I live in another world from most modern people."

"I don't understand."

She laughed. It had a hollow sound. "I go to church,
pay my bills on time, obey the law and go to bed with
the chickens, alone. I don't fit into a society that re-
wards permissiveness and degrades virtue. I don't go
around with people who think cheating is the best way
to get ahead, and money doesn't mean much to me, beyond having enough to get by. Making money seems to
be the driving force in the world these days, regardless
of what you have to do to get it."

She made him feel uncomfortable. She was describ-
ing his own world, into which he fit quite well.

She saw that and sighed. "Sorry. I told you I wasn't
normal."

"I haven't said a word," he said defensively.

She searched his dark eyes. "Frank mentioned that
you think women are a permissible pleasure, and that
the brassier they are, the better you like them."

His jaw tautened. "What's wrong with that?" he
asked. "I'm a bachelor and I don't want to settle down."

She lifted her hands. "I didn't mean it as an insult.
I'm just pointing out that our views of life are very different. I'm not going to be happy staying in the room,
overnight, with a man I barely know."

He could have debated her take on their relationship. They'd known each other for years, even if distantly. But he didn't pursue it. He cocked an eyebrow. "I haven't offered you half my bed," he said curtly. "And I never would. You aren't my type."

"I thought I just said that," she replied.

He made a sound deep in his throat. She made him feel small. He looked around the apartment. "I've got a suite," he said after a minute. "You'll have your own bedroom. The door has a lock." He looked straight into her eyes. "Not that you'll need it."

That was meant as an insult. She understood it. But she'd had years of practice at hiding her feelings from him. She didn't react. She didn't have much of a choice, either. Thinking of her close call at the library was still unsettling. John's criminal friends would see her dead, if they could. Tony was the only thing standing between herself and a funeral parlor, and she was arguing. She pushed back a wisp of brown hair and turned away from him. She was running out of choices.

"Well, I can't stay here," she said to herself.

"No, you can't. And local law enforcement doesn't have the sort of budget they'd need to house and feed you indefinitely. This could go on for weeks, Millie."

"Weeks?" She was staring at him with pure horror. "Surely not! The bomb…"

"May have been a test," he interrupted, "to give your assassin a dry run, show him how quickly local law enforcement reacts to an emergency call."

"I hadn't considered that," she confessed.

"You should. This isn't some petty criminal," he added. "He's a professional. He may not be the best—that plastic explosive he used for the bomb wasn't well concealed or particularly well made. But he knows how to get to you, and that makes him—or her—dangerous. We have to put you someplace where he doesn't have easy access, lure him in and help him make a mistake, so we can nab him."

"How do we do that?" she asked.

"You move in with me," he said simply. "We let the word get around. Then we wait for developments."

"Wait." She tugged at a lock of loose hair. "I can't wait a long time," she worried. "I have to work. I have to support myself."

"You have to be alive in order to do those things," he reminded her. "I'll call Frank. He can get his contact in the police department to help us out."

"That might be wise," she agreed. She was still debating her options, but she didn't seem to have any left. She wished she could go back in time, to a period in her life when she hadn't known Tony Danzetta. She'd eaten her heart out over him for so many years that it had become a habit. Now here he was, protecting her from danger, for reasons he still hadn't disclosed. He was honest to the point of brutality about his lack of interest in her as a woman. Was it guilt, she wondered, that drove him to help her? Perhaps she'd have the opportunity in the days ahead to learn the answer to that question.

* * *

His hotel suite was huge. Millie was fascinated by the glimpse of how the other half lived. She knew what a suite cost in this luxury hotel, and she wondered how Tony's government job made it affordable to him. Maybe, she considered, his father, the contractor, had left him a lot of money. He was obviously used to having the very best of everything.

"Hungry?" he asked when he'd put her suitcase inside what was to be her bedroom.

"Actually, I am," she said. "Could we go somewhere and get a salad?"

He pursed his lips, smiling. "What sort of salad?"

"A Caesar salad would be nice," she said.

"How about a steak to go with it, and a baked potato with real butter and chives and sour cream?"

Her eyes widened. "That sounds wonderful. Coffee, too."

He nodded. He picked up the phone, punched in a number, waited a minute and then proceeded to give an order to someone on the other end of the line. It must be room service, she thought. It fascinated her that he could just pick up the phone and order food. The only time she'd ever done that was when she ordered pizza, and small ones, at that.

"Thirty minutes," he said when he hung up.

"I've never stayed in a hotel and had room service," she confided. "I went on a trip for the library one time, to a conference up in Dallas and stayed in a hotel. It was small, though, and I ate at a McDonald's nearby."

He chuckled. "I couldn't live without room service. I flew in from Iraq late one night, starving to death. I ordered a steak and salad and this huge ice cream split at two o'clock in the morning."

"There's room service then?" she exclaimed.

He didn't mention that he paid a big price for having those items sent up, because room service didn't operate in the wee hours of the morning. He was also friends with the general manager of that particular hotel. "There is in New York City," he told her.

She sat down in one of the big armchairs and he took off his jacket and sprawled over the sofa.

"I guess you've been a lot of places," she said.

He closed his eyes, put his hands under his head and smiled. "A lot."

"I'd like to go to Japan," she said dreamily. "We have this nice old couple who came from Osaka. I love to hear them talk about their home country."

"Japan is beautiful." He rolled over, facing her, tugging a pillow under his head. "I spent a few days in Osaka on a case, and made time to take the bullet train over to Kyoto. There's a samurai fortress there with huge wooden gates. It was built in 1600 and something. They had nightingale floors…"

"What?"

"Nightingale floors. They put nails under the flooring and pieces of metal that would come in contact with the nails if anyone walked on the floor. It made a sound like a nightingale, a pretty sound, but it alerted the samurai inside instantly if ninja assassins were about to attack them. Ninjas were known for their stealth abilities, but the nightingale floors defeated them."

"That's so cool!" she exclaimed.

He studied her with new interest. When she was excited, her face flushed and her eyes shimmered. She looked radiant.

"I've read about Japan for years," he continued. "But little details like that don't usually get into travel books. You have to actually go to a place to learn about it."

"I watch those travel documentaries on TV," she confessed. "I especially like the ones where just plain people go traipsing into the back country of exotic places. I saw one where this guy lived with the Mongols and ate roasted rat."

He chuckled. "I've had my share of those. Not to mention snake and, once, a very old and tough cat."

"A cat?" she asked, horrified. "You *ate* a cat?"

He scowled. "Now, listen, when you're starving to death, you can't be selective! We were in a jungle, hiding from insurgents, and we'd already eaten all the snakes and bugs we could find!"

"But, a cat!" she wailed.

He grimaced. "It was an old cat. It was on its last legs, honest. We used it for stew." He brightened. "We threw up because it tasted so bad!"

"Good!" she exclaimed, outraged.

He rolled onto his back. "Well, the only other thing on offer was a monkey that kept pelting us with coconuts, and I'm not eating any monkeys! Even if they do taste like chicken." He thought about that and laughed out loud.

"What's funny?" she wanted to know.

He glanced at her. "Every time somebody eats something exotic, they always say, 'It tastes just like chicken!'"

She made a face. "I'll bet the cat didn't."

"You got that right. It tasted like…" He got half the word out, flushed and backtracked. "I'd rather have had pemmican, but it's in short supply in the rest of the world. My great-grandmother used to make it. We visited her a couple of times when my stepfather was working in Atlanta and we lived with him. She lived in North Carolina, near the reservation," he recalled thoughtfully. "She was amazing. She knew how to treat all sorts of physical complaints with herbs. She went out every morning, gathering leaves and roots. I wish I'd paid more attention."

"She was Cherokee?" she asked, even though she knew the answer.

He nodded. "Full blooded," he added. His expression grew dark. "Like me. My mother married an Italian contractor. They didn't like it. He was an outsider. They disowned her, everyone except my great-grandmother. She died when I was a kid, and I haven't been back since."

"That's sad. You still have family there, don't you?"

"Yes. An uncle and a few cousins. I heard from my uncle a couple of years ago. He said I should come home and make peace with them."

"But you didn't."

"My mother had a hard life," he said. "When my sister and I went into foster care, it was like the end of the world. Especially when they separated us." His face went taut. "She killed herself."

"Your sister?" she asked, sad for him.

"Yes." He glanced at her. "Didn't my foster mother tell you any of this?"

Millie flushed. The woman had told her quite a lot about Tony, but nothing really personal. She wasn't going to admit that she'd tried to worm things out of her. She averted her eyes. "It must have been hard on you, losing your sister."

"Yeah." He stared at the ceiling. "Some boy in foster care got her pregnant and tried to force her to have an abortion. She wouldn't. She was deeply religious and she saw it as a sin if she went for a termination. She told the boy. So he made threats and she felt that she had nowhere to turn." He sighed, his eyes sad. "She would never have done that if she hadn't been half out of her mind. She thought of suicide as a sin, too. But in the end, she took the only way out she could find."

"I hope he ended up in prison," she muttered. "That boy, I mean."

He made a deep sound. "He did. And shortly afterward, he died mysteriously. Strange things happen to bad people."

She wondered if Tony had any hand in the boy's demise, but she didn't want to ask.

There was a knock at the door. Tony sprang to his feet, grinning. "Food," he guessed.

He peered out the keyhole and saw the trolley, and the waiter. He opened the door and let him in.

Lunch was delicious. Millie had never had food served on a white linen cloth, with heavy utensils and dishes under metal covers. It was a revelation. She munched her salad with obvious enjoyment and went into ecstasies about the tenderness of the steak and the delicious baked potato. Even the coffee was wonderful.

Tony found her obvious delight in the meal humbling. He took fancy food and fancy hotels for granted. He'd long since become blasé about such things. But Millie came from a poor background, and lived on a meager budget. He imagined she'd never stepped into the lobby of a luxury hotel, much less been a guest in one. He pictured taking her out for a spin in his convertible, or taking her sailing on his yacht down in the Bahamas and lying with her in the sun. She had a delightful body. He wondered how it would feel to make love to her on a sandy tropical beach. Then he wondered what the hell he was thinking of. She wasn't his sort of woman. Millie would never go to bed with a man she hadn't married, no matter what her feelings for him were.

That brought back a comment of Frank's, that Millie had once been in love with Tony. He recalled her shy presence at his foster mother's house from time to time as an invited guest, her radiance when he dropped

in at the library to see his parent and Millie happened
to be around. He must have been blind, he decided,
not to have noticed how his presence illuminated the
quiet, introverted woman across from him at the table.

Millie stopped eating and stared at him, discon-
certed by his unsmiling, level stare. "Am I...doing
something wrong?" she asked at once, her attention
diverted to the silverware. "I don't know about fancy
place settings—"

"It's just lunch, Millie," he interrupted. "I wasn't
studying your eating habits. I was thinking about something, in the past."

"Oh." She was watchful, unconvinced.

He sipped coffee. "Why didn't you tell me what John
was doing to you when I came home two years ago?"
he asked.

She felt the question keenly. "I knew you wouldn't
believe me. You've never liked me."

He frowned. "I didn't know you."

"And didn't want to, either." She laughed hollowly.
"I was the invisible woman whenever you came home
to visit your foster mother. She'd invite me over sometimes, because she knew I had no life to speak of. You
never even noticed that I was around. You only stayed
long enough to say a few words and then you were off
on some hot date that Frank had fixed up for you, from
the bar where he was a bouncer."

That made him feel worse. "I didn't want to get serious about anyone," he said after a minute. "Those glit-

tery women are fine for a good time. You don't plan a future around them."

He was insinuating that they were fine for a one-night stand. The thought embarrassed her, made her uncomfortable. It was one more reminder of the distance between her world and his. She picked at her baked potato and lifted a forkful to her mouth. She wasn't really tasting it now. It was something to do.

"Why didn't you tell John to get a life and get off your back?" he asked suddenly.

She seemed to draw into herself. "It wouldn't have done any good," she told him. "I did try that, repeatedly. It just made him mad."

"Maybe it would have helped drive the point home if you'd stopped forgiving him," he continued doggedly. "Especially after he beat you up. No self-respecting woman would take that sort of behavior from a man."

Her face flushed. She put down her fork and glared at him across the table. "That's so easy for a man to say," she began in a low, angry tone. "You've never been beaten to your knees by an enraged man bent on making you pay for not loving him. I had bruises all over my body and I was terrified that he was actually going to kill me! He yelled at me and called me names and said he'd beat me to death if I didn't give in and agree to marry him." She wrapped her arms around her body, as if she felt a sudden chill. Her eyes went blank. "I believed him. I was sure that he was going to kill me. In the end, I just screamed and screamed. I expected to die. It was a miracle that I got a locked bedroom door between us in time to call for help. The sound of police car sirens was the most beautiful music I'd ever heard," she added in a soft undertone that made Tony feel even worse. "The policewoman who came in first gave John a furious look and when he started toward her, she drew her service pistol and pointed it right at his nose. I knew she'd shoot if he came any closer, and I guess he knew it, too, because he stopped. He sat down on the sofa and started crying. He said it was all my fault because I wouldn't marry him."

"Had he been drinking?"

"Yes. But not enough to make him out of control," she said bitterly. "The policewoman told me that. She asked me to press charges, but John came on his knees to beg me to forgive him. He was sobbing. I felt embarrassed and guilty and I agreed not to have him arrested. It didn't win me any points with the police," she added. "But I don't know that having him arrested again would have done any good. It certainly hadn't stopped him from stalking me, or spreading lies about me. He'd been arrested before, but he was always out in a few days, starting all over again. I got over the beating, but I would never go to his apartment again or let him in if he came to mine. I made sure there were always people around when he came to the library."

Tony felt very small. "Frank said he spread lies about you to your boss."

"Yes. And to the patrons." Her eyes closed in bitter memory. "I thought I'd lose my job forever. I would have, if Frank hadn't talked to a few people. He's been the best friend to me through all this. I don't know what I would have done without him."

"He's sweet on you," he said deliberately. "But he thinks you wouldn't give him the time of day because he works in a low class of job."

"The job wouldn't matter if I could feel that way about him. I wish I could," she added quietly. "But I can't."

The confession made him feel good. He didn't want to know why. He finished his coffee. "Want dessert?" he asked.

She laughed. "I'd have to put it in my pocket," she said. "I'm stuffed."

"So am I. They have a good kitchen staff here."

"I'll say." She finished her own coffee. "Do we push the trolley back down to the kitchen?" she asked.

"Good heavens, no," he exclaimed. "They come and get it."

She flushed. He made her feel like an idiot.

He noticed that and grimaced. "Millie, I wasn't always rich," he said gently. "I had to learn about things like proper table settings and etiquette, too."

She shrugged. "I'm just a country hick, you know," she said with a faint smile. "I live frugally. This—" she waved her hand around "—is like another planet to me."

"Learning new things doesn't hurt," he said. He chuckled. "The first time Jared and I ate in a five-star restaurant, we had to ask the waiter about the utensils and all the courses. Fortunately he was a nice person.

He could have made us feel small, but he didn't. Jared tipped him a hundred dollars."

She gasped. That was almost a week's salary for her.

"I know. It was a lot of money to me, at the time," he said. "I'd been a soldier, and before that, a common laborer, working in a construction crew."

"How did you make so much money?" she asked, genuinely curious.

"Hiring out to governments as an independent contractor," he said simply. "Including our own. Jared and I learned counterterrorism skills and for a while, he ran a security company that I worked for. Counterterrorism skills are a valuable commodity in some circles. It's a specialized job and it pays very well."

"Do you go into combat?" she asked.

"If the job calls for it," he replied. "You can't teach in a classroom in a combat zone," he added with a smile. "We teach small forces about incursions and stealth tactics, about IEDs and organizing local militia—stuff like that."

"What's an—" she felt for the word "—IED?"

"You could answer that now." He chuckled. "It's an improvised explosive device. You had one sent to you." The smile faded as he remembered how dangerous her introduction to the world of terror had been. The device, as clumsily built as it was, could have killed her in a heartbeat.

"You said it wasn't well made," she recalled.

"It wasn't. The good ones would pass for a small manuscript," he said. "It's a cowardly way to kill somebody."

She sighed, staring at the carpet. "I can't believe John was this desperate," she said, shaking her head. "To kill somebody, just because they couldn't love you. It's…" She searched for a word.

"Insane," he said through his teeth. "John had mental problems. I'm still shocked that Frank and I didn't see it and you did." It made him uncomfortable for another reason, too, but he wasn't telling her any secrets about his past. Not yet.

She laughed hollowly as she looked up at him. "That's because he wasn't trying to force you to marry him."

He drew in a long breath and looked at his watch. "I've got to meet a man in the lobby about a job," he said. "You stay put, okay?"

She nodded. "Thanks for lunch."

"My pleasure."

He left her sitting on the sofa and went downstairs to see a government agent from his department. There had been a string of kidnappings of rich persons along the Texas border, and Tony's skills might come in handy, they thought. He put Millie out of his mind before he exited the elevator.

She wandered around the suite while he was gone, straying into his bedroom out of curiosity. His suitcase was open on the bed. She picked up a shirt on the carpet that had been hastily discarded, probably when he changed early this morning. She held it to her nostrils and drew in the smell. She smiled, with her eyes closed. People had a personal fragrance, she thought, every one different. She'd know Tony's in a dark room. He smelled of the outdoors, of spice and fir. She loved the smell. She recalled the feeling it gave her to be carried, when he'd taken her out of the library protesting. His arms had been warm and strong and she'd never wanted to leave them. But she was going to have to move on.

She put the shirt down. After a minute she realized that he'd know it had been moved, a man as sharp as Tony. She dropped it back onto the carpet, went out of the bedroom and closed the door.

CHAPTER FOUR

IT WAS LATE when Tony came back. She was watching a movie on television, curled up on the sofa in slacks and a soft yellow knit shirt, with her bare feet under her. He smiled at the picture she made. He thought of a small kitten, cuddly and sweet, and snapped that thought right out of his mind.

"Found something to watch, I gather?" he teased.

She fumbled for the remote control. "Just a movie on regular television," she said quickly, flushing.

He frowned. "You can watch pay-per-view if you want to," he said. "Listen, kid, three or four bucks for a movie isn't going to break the bank."

She flushed even more. "Thanks."

Her embarrassment made him uncomfortable. He was used to women who didn't mind ordering the most expensive items on the menu, who asked for trips to the most expensive concerts, who wanted jewelry for presents. This one was nervous because he might think she'd watched a movie on the pay channels. He felt odd.

She sat up and worked her feet back into her loafers.

"You want to take in a show or something?" he asked.

She stared at him. "A show?"

"There's a good theater company here. They have a ballet, an orchestra. Somebody's probably doing something Christmasy, even though it isn't quite the holiday season."

She would have loved to go. But she recalled that she didn't have a dress that would do to wear to something fancy. Her clothes closet was bare, except for a few mix and match outfits suitable for work. She didn't even have the sort of shoes she'd need for an evening on the town. Tony probably had a dinner jacket or even a tuxedo packed away in that hanging bag she'd seen on the door to his bathroom.

"Mmm...no," she drawled. "I don't think so. Thank you."

Unaware of her wardrobe difficulties, he took the refusal in stride, thinking she probably didn't care for highbrow entertainment.

"Do you play cards?" he asked.

She shook her head. "Sorry."

He shrugged and sighed. "It's going to be a long week," he murmured. He studied her curiously. "Okay, then. When you're home, what do you do at night?"

She looked uncomfortable. "I read books, mostly, if there's nothing interesting on the military history channel."

His eyelids flickered. "You like military history?"

"I love it," she replied, smiling.

"Which period?"

"Any period," she told him. "I've read everything I could find about Alexander the Great, Julius Caesar, Napoleon, cavalry and Native American battles of the nineteenth century, generals of the Second World War," she rattled off. "I never met a battle I didn't want to read about."

He sat down across from her. "I took my degree in criminal justice," he said. "But I minored in history. My favorite period was World War II, European theater."

She smiled. "I remember. Your foster mother said you were always outlining battle plans to her over dinner."

He chuckled. "She didn't understand a thing I talked about, but she was always patient and kind." The smile faded. He looked down at his shoes. "She convinced me that not all foster parents are bad. I went through several after we moved from the reservation in North Carolina down to Georgia."

This was an experience that had left scars in him. She'd heard his foster mother talk about it. "You said once that your mother died when you were young."

He looked up. His eyes were flat, lifeless. "That's not quite true. I haven't really talked about her in years. About him, either. My stepfather, I mean." His broad shoulders rose and fell. "I tell different stories about them to anybody who asks. I guess I've been running away from the truth all my life."

She didn't speak. She just listened. Waited. Hoped.

He noticed and smiled. "My real father was my mother's second cousin. He lived on the Cherokee reservation in North Carolina where she grew up. But he was married. She got pregnant and she didn't have any money for a termination. So there was this big, loud Italian construction worker doing a project near the res. She started going out with him and by the time she told him she was pregnant, he thought it was his. Then she gave birth to a full-term baby in what he thought was her sixth month, and the jig was up. He hated her. But they stayed together for three more years, until my sister was born. He took a powder and left her with the kids."

"That must have been rough. Was she young?"

"She was nineteen when she had me," he said. "Not terribly young. But my sister was half Cherokee and half white, and my mother couldn't take the constant criticism from her family. When I was seven, she left the reservation and took us on a bus to Atlanta. We didn't know it, but her husband was working there. He found out from her kin where she was. He moved back in with us. She might have tried to run, but he told her that he had legal rights to take the kids if she ran away. So she stayed. And I ended up with an Italian name that has nothing to do with my ancestry." He laughed. "The only good thing about it is that it saved a few soldiers' lives when I got teased. They didn't make Indian jokes around me, because they thought I was Italian." His eyes glimmered. "I'm proud of my ancestry. Cherokees are still a proud people, even after all the hell the government put us through when they marched us out to Oklahoma in the dead of winter, walking, in 1838."

"I know about that," she said. "It was a tragic episode."

"One of many," he agreed.

She saw the pain on his face. He was talking around his childhood, trying not to remember. She wanted him to deal with it. She might be the only person alive that he'd ever really talked to about it. It would help him. "Your parents didn't have a happy marriage," she prompted.

He shook his head. He traced the back of a big fingernail absently. "My so-called father drank. A lot. And when he drank, he remembered that I wasn't his kid and made me pay for it. I was in the emergency room every few months with bruises and cuts. Once, with a broken bone."

She winced, thinking how hard it must have been for him, at that age, to be so badly treated by a man he considered to be his father. "Didn't your mother do anything to protect you?" she asked, aghast.

"She couldn't. She was a little woman. He knocked her around all the time. He was a big man. She was scared to death of him. She had no place to go. He knew it. He liked that." His face tautened. "But then he started doing things to my little sister, when she was about eight." His whole body seemed to contract. "My mother caught him at it, late one night. She was very calm. She went into the kitchen, got the biggest butcher knife she could find and hid it behind her. She went back into the living room, smiling. She said it was all right, she wouldn't make a fuss. He smirked. He knew she wouldn't do anything. He said so. I can still see her, smiling at him. She went to him like somebody sleepwalking. She stabbed that knife up to the hilt in his stomach, all the way to the heart. He never saw it coming. She was still smiling when he fell down on the floor." His eyes closed. "I never saw so much blood. She didn't move. She stood there, holding the knife, while the life drained out of him. She never stopped smiling, not even when they took her away in the police car."

Millie was horrified. No wonder he wasn't eager to get married and settle down. "What happened to her?" she asked gently.

He drew in a long breath. "They committed her. They said she was insane."

Her heart jumped. "Was she?"

He met her eyes. "I've never been sure, Millie," he said gently. His expression was tormented. "She died long before they had tests that could have backed up their theories." He shifted a little. "Our first set of foster parents told us very little, but they did mention that the psychiatrist said it was schizophrenia. There's a hereditary tendency toward it, I've read."

No wonder he wouldn't reveal his background. He was ashamed. Perhaps he was afraid, too. Maybe he thought he'd go mad himself.

She got up from the sofa and knelt down in front of him, balancing herself with a hand on one big knee. "I've read about mental illness. Some disease processes have a genetic tendency. That doesn't guarantee that anybody else in the family will ever develop the same illness," she said firmly. "You're as sane as I am," she added. "If you'd had mental deficiencies, believe me, they'd have shown up early. Very early."

He looked down at her, scowling. "You think so?" he asked.

"I know so. Did you ever torture an animal for fun? Set fires in your house? Wet the bed when you were in your teens?"

He laughed. "None of those."

"I'm no psychologist," she told him. "But I'm a great reader. Children show signs of mental illness in childhood. Since you were in the child welfare system, I'm sure the caseworkers paid close attention to you, considering your mother's illness. They would have put you in therapy immediately if they'd even suspected you had problems."

He cocked his head and laughed hollowly. "I can tell that you've had no contact with the system," he said with a sigh. "There are people who do their best for foster kids. The woman you knew, who brought me to San Antonio and got me through high school was certainly one of the best foster parents. But I lived with one family in Atlanta who had seven foster kids. They used the money the state gave them to gamble. They went up to Cherokee every month and blew it on the slot machines, hoping to get rich. Meanwhile, the kids went without school clothes, food, attention, you name it. No caseworker ever set foot in the house. Nobody investigated when we went to school dirty. The state did finally get wise, when one of our teachers started asking questions. We were removed from that house. But, you see, there wasn't another family willing to take me and my sister together. That's when we got separated, just before I was fostered to the woman who adopted me and eventually brought me to Texas."

"I'm sorry," she said.

He drew her hands up to his mouth and kissed them. "You always did have the softest heart," he said gently, surprising her. "I remember how you loved kids. You'd tell stories in the library during summer vacation, and they'd gather around you like flies around honey." He laughed softly. "I loved watching your face when you told those stories. You lit up like a Christmas tree."

She was surprised. "When did you see me doing that?"

"Many times," he said surprisingly. The smile faded. "I thought a lot of you. I was in a dangerous profession and a long way from wanting to settle down. But I used to think that if I ever did, you'd be high on my list of prospects." His face darkened. "And then John started feeding me lies about you. And I listened."

She started to draw away, but he caught her wrists and held her there, his black eyes steady and probing.

"I wish I could take it back," he said. "But I can't. I'm really sorry for the way I treated you. Especially at the funeral home."

The feel of his big, warm hands around her wrists wasn't threatening to her. They were comforting. "You didn't know me," she said.

"I didn't want to know you." He grimaced. "Maybe I won't ever go off the deep end like my mother did. But I've got a past that's going to make it hard for any woman to live with me on a permanent basis. I make my living with guns, Millie," he added, watching her face. "I work for a government agency that sends me in when every other option fails. It's dangerous work. I can't afford any sort of distraction. That's why I don't get involved with nice girls. Girls like you."

It began to make sense. Good time girls didn't expect happy endings. They, like Tony, lived for the moment. He liked his job, had no thought of ever quitting it, and he was telling Millie to back off. In a nice way, but definitely the same message.

She forced a smile. "You're warning me off," she said, trying to sound nonchalant. "Should I be flattered?"

He let go of her wrists. "I don't want to hurt you," he said solemnly. "I could. You're not worldly."

She got to her feet and went back to the sofa and sat down. "I guess I'm not. I'm a librarian," she said philosophically. "Library work isn't Indiana Jones stuff."

"No. But if you read military history, you're an armchair adventurer, at least," he teased.

She smiled, hiding her misery. "What do you like to read?"

"The classics," he said. "But I'm partial to military history myself."

"Do you have a hobby?" she asked, fascinated with what she was learning about him.

He grinned. "I like to cook," he told her. "I can make almost anything, even French pastries."

She laughed. "So can I."

He pursed his lips. "Pity we don't have a kitchen here."

"Isn't it, just?"

He stood up and stretched, powerful muscles rippling in his chest and arms. "It's been a long day. I usually stay up late, but I'm pretty tired. Watch another movie, if you like. It won't disturb me."

She nodded, but she looked uncomfortable.

"What is it?" he asked.

She grimaced. "I was so upset that I forgot to pack anything to sleep in…"

"Now that's a problem I can solve," he told her. He went into his bedroom, rummaged in his suitcase and came back with a round-necked white T-shirt in pristine condition. "It will swallow you whole. As good as a gown, I'd say." He grinned.

She laughed and fought a blush. He really was huge. It would come down to her knees and wrap around her three times. "Thanks."

"Hey. We're bunkmates. We have to share, right?" He winked at her. "Sleep tight."

"You, too."

He went into his room and closed the door. She turned off the television and withdrew into her own room. After she'd put out the light, she lay in the darkness, loving the feel and smell of the T-shirt against her skin. She wondered if she could find some excuse for not giving it back.

She was delighted that he'd told her the true story of his background. She understood him much better. He had good reasons for wanting to stay uninvolved with women. But she wondered if he was beginning to feel the need for companionship, more than just a night's worth. And he'd mentioned watching Millie read to the kids, as if he'd cherished the memory. She felt warm all over at the idea that he'd felt something for her, until John killed it with his lies.

Her heart grew heavy. It was very well to think that she'd touched that cold heart, but he wasn't saying that he loved her or wanted to live with her. He was just looking after her, probably out of guilt because of the way he'd treated her. This wasn't a prelude to a life of happy togetherness. To Tony, it was just another job. She was a job. She'd do well to remember that and get her priorities straight. When the danger was over, she'd go back to her library and Tony would leave and never look back.

She closed her eyes and tried to sleep. It was almost morning by the time she finally managed it.

Two more days passed with no sign of any hired killer. Tony was in contact with both Frank and his detective friend. There was no gossip on the streets about the hit. That bothered Tony. He knew that the killer probably knew where Millie was, and he was biding his time until he saw an opening. This could drag on for weeks.

Millie couldn't stay out of work forever, and Tony had a commitment coming up overseas. But there didn't seem to be any way to draw the hired killer out into the open.

Millie was wearing on him. He found himself watching her. She was pretty, in a way, and her figure was tantalizing. He was aroused by her. She didn't dress in a provocative manner, but she had pert little tip-tilted breasts that weren't disguised by her bra or the knit blouses she wore. He spent more and more time thinking how they might feel in his mouth.

It made him ill-tempered. He was used to women who gave out without reservations. Millie was attracted to him, too. He could see it. Frank had said that she was in love with him. He was tempted to see how far she'd let him go, but he wasn't certain about his own ability to stop in time. He hadn't had a woman in months, and he wasn't a man who could abstain for long periods of time.

Millie noticed his growing irritability and guessed that he didn't like having her cramp his style. Obviously he couldn't cavort with another woman while he was protecting her. She felt guilty. She would have liked to have gone home, and have him smile at her again, even if it meant giving him up to some flashy woman. She was resigned to the fact that he was never going to want her. He'd said several times that she really wasn't his type.

The next night, he paced the floor until he made her uncomfortable enough to go to bed.

"Don't rush off on my account," he said curtly. "I'm just not used to this much inactivity."

"No, I'm really sleepy," she assured him. "Good night."

"Yeah. Good night." He said it with pure sarcasm.

She put on his T-shirt and stretched out on the bed with the lights still on. She was as restless as he was, and probably just as uncomfortable. She ached for something, for kisses, for caresses, for human contact. He hadn't touched her since he'd held her hands while he was talking about his mother. But he'd watched her. His eyes were narrow and covetous. She might be innocent, but she recognized that heat in him. It was in her, too, and she didn't know what to do about it. She'd never felt it so strongly before.

She stretched again, moaning softly as she thought how sweet it would be to lie in Tony's arms and let him kiss her until the aching stopped.

She heard the phone ring. A couple of minutes later, he rapped on her door and opened it without asking if she was decent.

He froze in the doorway, his eyes homing to the sharp peaks of her breasts and the long, uncovered length of her pretty legs. His teeth clenched. "A shark must feel like this, just before he bites," he said in a harsh tone, and he laughed.

"What?" she asked, breathless.

He closed the door behind him, tossed the cell phone he'd been using onto the dresser and made a beeline for the bed.

While she was conferring with herself about what to do next, he moved onto the bed, slid his big, warm hands under the T-shirt, and started kissing her as if he were starved. The combination of the heated, urgent kiss and his warm, enormous hands on her taut breasts was more than her prim scruples could overcome. She arched up into his hands and moaned so hungrily that he swept between her long legs without a second's hesitation, letting her feel what she already knew—that he wanted her.

It was every dream of passion she'd ever had, coming true. He smelled of rich spice and soap. His long, wavy black hair was unbound, around his shoulders. She gathered it into her hands and savored the silky feel of it, loving its length. She looked down through a heated mist at his mouth on her soft skin, completely covering one small breast. It was so erotic that she arched up off the bed to force his mouth closer. She closed her eyes, shivering with tension that built and built until she thought she might die of the ache.

The T-shirt was on the floor somewhere, along with his pajama bottoms. His mouth was all over her, on her throat, her mouth, her breasts, sliding down with expert cunning to her flat belly and lingering there while his hands teased at the edge of her briefs. He felt her trembling, heard her breathing catch. Just a few more seconds, he thought with pure lust, and she wouldn't be able to stop him. He was on fire, so far gone that his head was spinning with the sweetness of her skin under his mouth.

She felt his hand go under her briefs and when he touched her, instead of completing the arousal, it shocked her into the realization of what they were about to start. He would leave town and go back to work and never even remember what had happened. She would be left with a tarnished dream and a possible pregnancy, because she had nothing to use for birth control.

But when she pushed at his shoulders, he didn't realize she was trying to stop him. He was working the briefs off and she was almost too hungry to argue. But she had to. He'd never forgive her…

"I can't!" she burst out. "Tony, I can't! You have to stop!"

He lifted his head. His eyes were glazed. He was breathing like a distance runner. His broad, muscular, hair-covered chest was heaving with every breath. "What?" he choked.

"I…I can't!" she repeated.

The breathing didn't slow, and his hand was still moving. "Why not?"

"I'm not on the pill!" she burst out.

"Not on the pill." He blinked. "Not on the pill."

"I could get pregnant!" she insisted.

Sanity came back in a cold rush. He took slow breaths until he could control himself. That only made it worse, because he'd been totally helpless and she'd seen it. His eyes grew hot with anger, with condemnation.

With one smooth motion, he bounded away from her and rolled off the bed to his feet. He jerked on his

pajama bottoms and turned to face her, still condemn-
ing as she scrambled under the bedcover.

"Well, if that doesn't beat all!" he muttered furiously.
"You give me a come-hither look, open your arms to
me and give it back like a professional. Then at the
last minute, when I'm out of my mind, you jerk back
and say I have to stop because you could get pregnant!
That's just priceless! Priceless!"

"I didn't realize…!" She tried to defend herself.

"Of all the dirty, mean tricks to play on a man, that's
the worst," he said in a tone that could have taken rust
off. "You were getting even, weren't you? I treated
you badly at John's funeral and you wanted payback?"

She flushed and dropped her gaze. She wouldn't cry.
She wouldn't cry! She bit her lower lip, hard, as she
fought for control. "I didn't do it to get even."

"The hell you didn't!"

"I didn't have anything to use," she protested shakily. "I've never…I haven't…I don't know…"

"You knew all that when I came in here," he said
coldly. "You could have said so then."

He was right, of course. She could have. But she'd
never been in Tony's arms, held close by him kissed
by him, and she'd have died for the experience. It had
been like paradise, for those few heated minutes before
she came to her senses. She couldn't defend herself. He
was probably hurting. She gritted her teeth. She didn't
even know how to apologize.

He glared at the picture she made, wrapped up in
the cover, only her head showing, her eyes hidden, her

face white. If he hadn't been hurting so badly, he might have been less volatile in his treatment of her. But the pain was bad.

He turned and slammed out of the room, leaving the door ajar, fuming and cursing under his breath. His cell phone rang and rang. He finally realized it was on the dresser in Millie's room. She hadn't moved an inch when he scooped it up and opened it.

"Hello," he said furiously.

"Hi, stranger," came a purring, sexy tone. "I heard from Frank that you were in town. How about a little action? I don't have a thing to do tonight."

"Nothing to do?" His voice changed. The tone dropped. He sounded seductive, aware that he was still standing in the doorway of Millie's room and that she could hear every word. "We can't have that. Tell you what, baby, why don't you come over here and we'll have a couple of drinks and see what develops."

"What a nice idea!" she enthused. "Since I already know the name of the hotel, and the room number," she said, "I'll see you in about, ten minutes?"

"Ten minutes will be fine. Just enough time for me to have a shower and get into something comfortable. See you, sweetheart."

He didn't look back. He could imagine Millie's expression, and it made him feel good. She'd given him a nasty surprise, it was fair play for him to give her one. He went right into his own room, swiped up some clean clothes and walked right into the bathroom to shower without a single regret.

CHAPTER FIVE

MILLIE HEARD TONY'S brazen invitation to the other woman with pure anguish. He didn't bother to look her way as he headed toward his own room. Maybe she'd frustrated him, maybe he was angry, but that was no excuse for bringing one of his glittery women over here to seduce her in earshot of Millie.

She might be a disappointment to him, as a woman, but she wasn't a doormat. No way was she staying in here to listen to him cavorting with his girlfriend! No way!

Furious, now, she threw on her clothes and her overcoat, fighting back tears, grabbed her purse, closed the bedroom door and walked right out of the suite. The last thing she heard on the way was the sound of the shower running.

Tony had on slacks and a blue shirt that flattered his dark complexion. He greeted Angel with a smile and invited her in. She was wearing a sexy pair of black slacks with a lacy blouse, and her long black hair was swinging free. Her black eyes teased him as she walked in front of him to the living room.

"Long time no see." She laughed. "You look good."

"So do you." He bent and kissed her, not passionately, but nicely. He went to pour drinks. "How've you been?"

She told him. He seemed to be listening, but his mind was on what had happened with Millie. Now that he was less stimulated, he recalled that it hadn't been Millie who started things rolling. It had been him. He'd dived on her like a starving shark. She, with her obvious inexperience, hadn't stood a chance. If she'd kept quiet, there wasn't a chance in hell that he'd have stopped in time. By now, they'd be having a conversation about blood tests and babies. His face flushed at just the thought.

"What's wrong?" Angel asked.

"Nothing," he said quickly, pasting on a smile. "Seen Frank lately?"

She let out a loud breath. "Tony, I've just been telling you about Frank. There's a job opening in Dallas and he wants to take it. The manager of the club's offering him advancement into security work, and he'll train him. It pays well."

"You don't say. He didn't tell me anything about it," he added.

"He's been in Dallas, interviewing. He just got back. I saw him at the club when I went off duty tonight. He's going to tell you tomorrow." She sipped her drink, put it down and brazenly slid into Tony's lap. "Don't let's talk about Frank. I'm lonely." She put her mouth against his with a little moan.

In the old days, that would have set the fires burning. But not tonight. Tony was remembering Millie's wretched expression. She'd be sitting in the bedroom hearing him with Angel and probably crying her eyes out over his insensitivity.

He drew away. "We're going to have to put anything past the drinks and conversation on hold," he said gently. "I'm working a job. There's a woman I'm protecting," he added, jerking his head toward the bedroom. "She's asleep, but she might wake up."

"Is she your girl?" Angel asked.

"She's a librarian," he replied flatly.

"Oh, good Lord, you poor man!" She laughed. "A librarian! How did you ever get talked into a job like this?"

He was offended by her attitude toward Millie. "It's not exactly easy to get those jobs," he said, his eyes narrowing. "My foster mother was a research librarian. She went through college to get the job, and even then she had to beat out the competition for it. So did the woman I'm guarding. It takes a good education," he added.

"Well, excuse me." Angel laughed. "Here I am with my little high school diploma making fun of a college graduate!"

He felt uncomfortable. He pushed her away and got to his feet. "It's just a job."

She got up, too. She gave him an amused smile as

she picked up her purse. She stopped just in front of him. "Just how old is this bookworm you're taking care of?"

"I don't know. Somewhere in her twenties."

"Pretty?"

He frowned. "Inside, she's pretty," he replied.

"Poor man," she sighed. She reached up and kissed his cheek. "I guess we all meet our Waterloo someday. Looks like this is yours." She chuckled. "Good luck."

That same thought was only beginning to form in his own mind. He smiled sheepishly. "Yeah. Thanks." He bent and kissed her cheek. "It was fun while it lasted."

"Same here. See you around," she added, and winked as she let herself out.

Tony stood, staring at the closed door, with his hands in his slacks pockets and his heart even with his shoes. He'd made a terrible mess of things. Millie was going to hate his guts.

He paused outside her door. He wanted to apologize, to tell her that inviting Angel over was mean-spirited and he was sorry about it. He was sorry for pushing her into a corner and making her feel guilty and cheap, when it was his own fault. He was the one who'd caused the problem and he'd blamed her. It was going to hurt, this apology. With a wistful smile, he knocked gently on the door.

"Millie?" he called.

There was no answer. He tried again, with the same result. She might be in the bathroom and couldn't hear him. Gently he opened the door and peered inside. The bed was empty. Millie's coat and purse were gone. He ran to the bathroom. It was empty, too. She'd gone! She'd walked out, probably while he was in the shower gloating about having Angel come over to show Millie he couldn't care less what she thought of him. Now she was walking into danger. If the contract killer was keeping an eye on her, he'd see her leave the hotel, in the dark, all by herself. He'd have a prime opportunity to kill her, and Tony would be responsible.

He grabbed his cell phone and punched the speed dial for Frank's number. God, he hoped Frank had it turned on!

Sure enough, he had his cell phone on. He answered on the second ring.

"Frank!" Tony said at once. "I need you to call your detective friend and tell him that Millie's on her way back to her apartment, alone. I have to get my car out of the parking garage and it will take precious time. He needs to send somebody to her address right now!"

"She's gone home alone?" Frank was all at sea. "But how did she get out past you? And why did she leave in the middle of the night?"

Tony ground his teeth together. "Tell you later," he gritted. "Do what you can about getting somebody to her apartment, will you? She may be perfectly safe, but I've got a feeling… Never mind. Thanks." He hung up before Frank had the chance to ask any more embarrassing questions. Then he ran down the stairs, foregoing the elevator, on his way to the parking garage. He prayed every step of the way that he wouldn't be too late. That sweet, gentle woman wouldn't stand a chance if the contract killer was anywhere nearby!

He broke speed limits and ran red lights across the city getting to Millie's apartment building, and had the good luck not to be seen by a squad car in the process. He parked in the first spot he came to, got out and ran toward the building. He didn't see another car, or another person, on the way in. Maybe, he thought, just maybe he'd get lucky.

He took the staircase up to the fourth floor and walked cautiously down the hall. He stopped in front of Millie's apartment, looking around carefully. He was relieved not to see any activity. He'd just relaxed and was about to knock on the door when he heard voices inside the apartment. One was male.

Tony almost threw his weight against the door to force it in a moment's panic, but that way would get her killed if the voice he heard was the killer's. So he slipped out of his shoes, picked the lock with ridiculous ease—thanking God that she didn't have a dead bolt lock—and slid his sidearm out of its holster as he silently opened the door.

"...never thought it would be this easy." A male voice chuckled. "So much for your boyfriend's skills."

"Could you just shoot me," Millie asked in a world-weary tone, "and not talk me to death?"

"Well, you've got grit," the man said with reluctant admiration. He raised a pistol with a makeshift

DIANA PALMER

silencer—an empty two liter soft drink bottle—duct-taped to the muzzle. "Goodbye from John."

"No. Goodbye from me." Tony had the pistol leveled at the man even as he spoke, his hands steady, his voice calm and cool.

As the hit man turned, shocked, and then lifted his gun again, Tony pulled the trigger. The killer fell to the floor and didn't move.

Tony put away his pistol, checked to make sure the hit man wasn't going to get up again and knelt beside Millie, who was sitting frozen on the edge of her bed. Her face was white. Her eyes were blank with shock. She looked at Tony, but she didn't even see him.

There was an urgent knock at the door. "Miss Evans?" a voice called with deep concern.

"Stay put," Tony said gently. "I'll answer it."

He opened the door, and Frank's detective friend was standing there with a patrol officer.

"We heard a gunshot when we got off the elevator. Is Miss Evans...?" the lieutenant began.

"She's fine," Tony said. "But, sadly for him, the hit man didn't hear me come in."

The lieutenant noted the pistol in its holster. Tony reached for his ID, but the lieutenant waved it away. "No need," he said. "I was on the phone with your boss just this afternoon. Where's the deceased?"

"In here." Tony led them into Millie's bedroom. She was sitting, staring into space. "She's pretty shaken," he told the other men.

"Miss Evans, wouldn't you like to sit in the living room while we process the scene?" the lieutenant asked her.

She looked at him blankly. He grimaced.

Tony bent and lifted her into his arms, cradling her a little too close to his massive chest in the aftermath of fear, and carried her tenderly into the living room. He brushed his mouth over her forehead as he put her on the couch. "It will be all right," he said softly. "I promise."

She didn't make a sound. In the space of minutes, her whole life had been turned upside down. The night had gone from a fulfilled dream to a nightmare. Tony, kissing her. Tony, furious and insulting her. Tony, bringing his girlfriend to the apartment to humiliate her. And now, Tony shooting another man in a space of seconds without hesitation, with eyes so cold they didn't even seem alive. She looked down and saw tiny droplets of blood on her overcoat. The killer's blood.

She took it off, with jerky motions, and dropped it quickly on the floor. She shivered. Tony's job had seemed otherworldly to her until tonight. Now she understood how deadly he was, how dangerous he was. Her eyes went involuntarily to the crumpled human figure on the floor of her bedroom, with dark stains growing around it. She shivered again. She'd only ever seen dead people in caskets. This was sickening. Terrifying. She realized that it could be her own body lying on the floor like that, except for Tony's dark skills.

Tony drew in a quiet breath. "I'm so sorry," he said. He pulled a crocheted afghan off her easy chair and draped it around her. "I never meant tonight to end like this."

She shivered again. She didn't answer Tony, or even look at him.

People came and went. A team of crime scene investigators tramped over the apartment in funny blue pull-on boots, wearing masks and gloves, taking samples of everything, lifting fingerprints, bagging evidence. If Millie hadn't been so shell-shocked, she would have enjoyed watching the process that she'd only ever seen in television dramas.

Through it all, Tony stood with the detective, watching and commenting. At one point, Tony came back in with statement forms and asked if she felt up to writing down what had happened when she got home. She nodded zombielike, took a pen and started writing. Tony filled out his own form from across the room, just to make sure the lieutenant knew he wasn't collaborating on stories with Millie.

Hours later, many hours later, the police and the medical examiner's crew left with the body.

"You can't stay here," Tony told her quietly. "Not after what happened."

There was a tap on the door. Tony opened it and Frank came in. "I just got off work," he said, hesitating when Millie jumped up from the sofa and threw herself into his arms. She cried as if all the tears in the world were suddenly pouring out of her. She clung to Frank, sobbing incoherently. He held her, patting her back, while Tony looked on with anguish. He didn't need to ask why she was suddenly so animated with another man. She'd seen Tony shoot a man. His profession had suddenly become crystal clear to her, and she was afraid of him now. It was a miserable feeling.

"You can't stay here," Frank told her gently. "You can stay with my mother. I already talked to her about it."

"That's so…so kind of her," Millie choked, wiping at her eyes with the back of her hand.

"She likes you. Don't worry about packing anything," he added quickly when she looked, horrified, at her crime-scene-taped bedroom door. "She'll lend you a gown. Come on."

"Okay." She held on to his sleeve. She didn't quite meet Tony's searching eyes. "Thank you for saving my life," she said, like a child reciting a line her parents has prompted her to say.

"You're welcome," he replied in a cool tone. He was more shaken than he let on. He'd just killed a man. It wasn't the first time. But then he'd never seen himself through the eyes of an innocent. Millie couldn't even look at him anymore. He felt less than human.

Frank saw that. "I'll call you later," he told his friend, knowing that Tony would still be awake however long that was.

Tony drew in a long breath. "Sure."

Frank drew Millie out the door with him. He left it open. Tony stood there watching them until they were out of sight.

* * *

He went back to the hotel, but he didn't sleep. He was still awake late in the morning, so he ordered breakfast and sat down to eat it when it came. He called Frank as he made inroads into his second cup of strong black coffee.

"How is she?" he asked his friend.

"Shaken," he replied. "She couldn't stop talking about the way the man got into her apartment so easily, even before she had time to take off her overcoat. She figured he was watching and followed her home."

"That would be my guess, too."

Something in Tony's tone was familiar to the man who'd known him for so many years. "You never really get used to shooting people, do you?" he asked.

Tony sighed. "No. It goes with the job description, I guess, but in recent years I've been more of a planner than a participant. It's been a long time since I had to throw down on an assailant."

"You've got too much heart, and too much conscience, for the line of work you're in," Frank said flatly. "You need to consider a change, before you get so old that they retire you. Imagine having to live on a government pension," he added, and chuckled softly.

Tony laughed, too, but his heart wasn't in it. "Your friend the lieutenant have anything more to say about last night?" he asked.

"About the killer, you mean? He knew the guy, actually. He'd weaseled out of two homicide charges, just in the past year. In one of them, he shot a pregnant woman, killing her and the child. Funny thing, the two witnesses died in strange accidents, about a week before they were going to testify against him. He said the guy would do anything for money, and it's no loss."

"He was still a human being," Tony said in a dull, quiet tone. "He had family that must have loved him, at least when he was little. He had a mother…"

"He pushed her down a flight of stairs and killed her when he was eight," Frank mused. "It was in his juvy record. The psychiatrist figured it was a terrible accident and shouldn't be held against the poor orphan."

"You're kidding me!"

"The psychiatrist was later sued by the victim's family."

"No wonder."

"So stop beating your conscience to death," Frank counseled. "I'd like to tell you about my new job."

"In Dallas, I guess. Angel was over here—" He stopped dead. That had been a slip he shouldn't have made.

There was a long pause. "So that's why Millie went home alone, huh?" Frank asked, and in a different tone of voice. "Don't tell me—you made a heavy pass at Millie, she ran, you called Angel to come over and soothe you so that Millie could hear it all and see what she'd missed."

"Damn!" Tony muttered. Frank knew him right down to his bones, and he didn't like it.

"She's a virgin, you idiot!" Frank grumbled. "That

sort of woman isn't going to go running headlong into a one-night stand. She believes it's a sin."

"Yeah, well, I wasn't exactly thinking clearly at the time!" Tony shot back.

"Now you are, and you've blown it," Frank advised him. "She doesn't want to see you again, ever."

Tony's heart felt as if it were weighed down with bricks. "Yeah. I sort of figured that's how she'd feel."

"Someday, you're going to fall for a woman. I hope for your sake that she doesn't treat you the way you've treated Millie," Frank replied. "She's special."

"I guess she'll marry you and live happily ever after, huh?" Tony asked sarcastically.

"Don't I wish," Frank sighed. "Why do you think I'm moving to Dallas? I'm sick of eating my heart out over Millie."

"You might try candy and flowers and soft music," Tony replied, trying to sound lighthearted.

"I've tried everything. She told me once that you can't make people love you," he added bitterly. "She was right. So I'm cutting my losses."

"She'll have nobody left to talk to," Tony said quietly. "She doesn't mix well. She's never had a real girl-friend that she could confide in. She won't let people get close to her."

"You don't know much about her, do you?" Frank asked.

Tony hesitated. "Not really, no."

"Her father was a roughneck, worked on oil rigs. When he came home, he drank. Excessively. Millie's mother tried to leave him, but he kept Millie with him and threatened to cut her up if her mother didn't come back. She was too scared of him not to do what he said. Millie's whole childhood was one of stark terror, of being afraid to trust anyone. It was almost a relief, she told me, when he died of a heart attack. She and her mother finally had some peace, but it was too late for Millie to reform her character. She doesn't trust anybody these days. And especially not after what John did to her. It was her father all over again, only worse."

Tony felt even smaller. "She never told me."

"Why would she? I'm sure she knew that you weren't interested in her."

"Yeah."

There was another long pause. "What's next on your agenda?" Frank asked.

"What? Oh. I've got an assignment over the border. Very hush-hush."

"Most of them are." Frank chuckled. "Well, I'll leave my forwarding address with Angel. You can come see me up in Dallas after the first of the year."

"I'll do that. I won't have any reason left to come back to San Antonio, once you're gone."

They were both talking around the fact that Millie would still live there.

"Can you tell her I'm sorry?" Tony asked after a minute. "I mean, really sorry. I tried to tell her just after I got the hit man, but she was too scared of me to listen."

"Is that surprising? Most people are scared of you."

"I don't mind it with most people," Tony said gruffly. "She's gone through a lot. More than she should have had to. If I hadn't listened to John, maybe I could have spared her some of it."

"If."

"Yeah. Your lieutenant thinks she's out of the woods, then?"

"He does. One of his men's confidential informants said that the gang boss who was holding the money for the contract killer decided he needed a nice new car, so he wasn't passing the contract along. Good news for Millie."

"Very good." Tony was relieved. At least she'd be safe now, from John and his postmortem attempts on her life.

"So you can get on with your life now."

"I can."

"Keep in touch," Frank said.

"You know I'll do that. See you around, pal."

"You, too."

Tony leaned back and stared blankly at a painting of Japanese flowers and characters in the frame on the wall. It was all over. He'd go back to his assignments, Millie would go back to work, Frank would take up his new job in Dallas, and nothing would draw the men back to San Antonio ever again. Well, Frank's mother still lived there, so he'd go to see her, probably. But he was willing to bet that Frank wouldn't contact Millie again. Anyway, he consoled himself, he wasn't emotionally attached to Millie. It had been a physical need, brought on by abstinence and proximity. He'd be over it in no time.

He got up and started packing.

Millie was back in her own apartment. Frank had called in a marker and had the people who cleaned the night-club come over and scrub Millie's apartment. He'd paid them out of his own pocket, but he hadn't told her.

When she left Frank's mother's house, Millie was still getting over the trauma. She wasn't looking forward to having to live where a man had died. But when she got inside, she was surprised. The bedroom had been rearranged. It was spotlessly clean. There were new curtains, a new bedspread. It looked brand-new.

"Oh, you shouldn't have done this!" she exclaimed, smiling up at Frank.

He shrugged and grinned. "We're friends. It's for old times' sake. I won't be around for much longer."

"I know." She looked sad. "You'll like Dallas. My mother was from there. We used to go visit my grand-mother, until she died."

"I'll like it," he agreed.

"This is great." She looked around, touching the curtains, smoothing the bed. Her eyes were sad. "Tony saved my life, and I barely thanked him," she said in a subdued tone. She looked at Frank, worried. "You know, he never blinked an eye. Tony was ice-cold. He never needed a second shot." She wrapped her arms around herself. "I've never seen anybody shot before."

"It's upsetting, the first time," Frank, a combat veteran, replied.

She cocked her head. "You've shot people."

He nodded. "I was in Iraq, in the early nineties," he reminded her.

She managed a smile. "It's not like they show it on TV and in the movies," she said. "Or in those spy films, either. This guy didn't have a metal silencer. He'd made one from a soft drink bottle and duct tape."

"Homemade ones still do the job," Frank told her. "He didn't want to attract attention."

"That gun of Tony's sounded like a cannon," she recalled. "The hall was full of people when we left, all trying to get in to see the crime-scene examiners work. I wish I'd paid attention. I was too shaken."

"So was Tony," Frank replied. "Regardless of the contract killer's background, he's still a human being. Tony used to go through some sort of purification thing. He won't go near the res in North Carolina, but he has cousins from his clan in Oklahoma. He hangs out with a couple of them. They build a sweat lodge and help him get through the emotional pangs."

She was fascinated. "I never knew that. Neither did his foster mother, I guess, because she didn't say anything about it."

"She didn't know," he said simply. "He didn't want her to know what his job actually involved. He told her he worked for the government, and she figured that meant he was a desk jockey."

"He protected her," she said.

"Exactly."

She went back into the living room silently, her eyes on the sofa where Tony had placed her so gently after the shooting. He'd been supportive, nurturing, and she'd backed away from him. That must have hurt, especially when he'd shot a man to save her life.

"He said to tell you he was sorry," Frank told her.

She glanced at him. "He didn't need to be."

"About Angel," he emphasized.

She flushed. "Oh. The glittery woman."

He scowled. "Excuse me?"

She drew in a long, resigned breath. "You were always introducing him to girls who worked at the club," she recalled with a sad smile. "Those were his sort of women. He told me so. He didn't want ties, ever."

"He may want them someday."

"Not my business," she said quietly. "He brought her to his room to show me how little I meant to him. It wasn't necessary. I already knew that." She turned to Frank and laughed shortly. "I'm a librarian. Doesn't that just say it all?"

He scowled. "If you'll recall, that girl in the mummy movie was a librarian. She was a two-fisted heroine as well."

"Not me," Millie sighed. "Thanks for everything, Frank," she added, tiptoeing to kiss his tanned cheek. "I'll miss you."

He looked at her with anguished longing that he quickly concealed. He grinned. "I'll miss you, too, kid."

CHAPTER SIX

WEEKS PASSED. Thanksgiving went by in a flash, and suddenly it was almost Christmas. Millie stopped by the window of a department store when she got off the city bus at her stop. It was beautifully decorated in an old-fashioned sort of way, with artificial snow and trees and mountains, and a classic Lionel train set running through the scenery. Millie loved electric trains. One day, if she could ever afford a bigger apartment, she promised herself she was going to buy one and run it every Christmas.

It was cold, even in San Antonio. She tugged her coat closer. It was a new coat, an extravagance, but she couldn't bear to wear the old one ever again, even with the blood spatters removed. She'd given the coat to a charity drive.

She wondered how Frank was doing. He'd already moved up to Dallas. He phoned her and said he liked his new colleagues, and thought he was going to enjoy the job. He did miss San Antonio, though, he added. Dallas was brassy and cosmopolitan, a sprawling city with odd, futuristic architecture. San Antonio still retained its historic charm. It was also smaller. But what he really meant was that he missed Millie. She was sorry she couldn't care for him as he cared for her. Despite everything, even after his cruel behavior, it was still Tony who lived in her heart.

Tony. She pulled the coat closer as she walked down the sidewalk toward her apartment building. She imagined he was off in some exotic place with some new glittery woman, having a ball. It was a modern sort of life for most women these days, rushing around from one sex partner to the next with no feeling of obligation or permanence. The movies reflected it. So did television and books. But Millie was a romantic. She lived in a past where men and women both abstained before marriage, where family mattered, where two people got to know each other as individual human beings long before they got to know each other physically. In that world, Millie lived. She devoured romance novels with characters who shared her old-fashioned views on life and society. So what if it was only make-believe. The carnal quality of relationships in real life was as empty as an office trash can on Sunday. Empty and sad. Like Tony's life.

For all his adventures, he would never know the joy of holding a baby in his arms and reading to his child at bedtime; watching him grow and learn and laugh. Millie wanted children so badly that it was almost painful to see them with their parents in stores and know that she would never experience that singular delight. She thought back often to the night in Tony's hotel room when she'd chosen virtue over experience, and she wondered what might have been if she hadn't stopped him. Perhaps there would have been a child, and she could have had it in secret and he'd never have known. It made her sad to think about that. She could have loved the child, even if Tony wouldn't let her love him.

She did enjoy her job. She got to read to children there. In fact, on Christmas Eve the library opened up for an orphan's home. Volunteers gathered to give presents to the children. The volunteers also read stories to the children. It was a new program that the library had only just instituted, and they were hoping that it would be a success. Millie was looking forward to it. She'd wear her red Santa Claus hat and a red dress, and for one night she could pretend that she was a mother. It was the only way, she thought wistfully, that she'd ever be one.

A newspaper reporter had shown up with a camera and a notebook computer to cover the event. Several other people were snapping photos with their cell phone cameras and movie cameras, probably to post on the Web. Millie was having the time of her life with two little girls in her lap. She was reading the story of *The Littlest Angel* to them. It had been her favorite as a child. Judging by the expressions on their faces of these small children, it was becoming a favorite of theirs as well.

She wasn't aware of a movement in the entrance of the library. A big man in a tan cashmere coat and a suit was standing there, watching the activity. The sight of Millie with those little girls only reinforced a thought he'd been harboring for some time now—that she would be a wonderful mother.

"Is it okay for me to be here?" he asked a woman wearing a name tag who was standing next to him.

She looked way up into large black eyes in a darkly tanned face, surrounded by wavy black hair in a ponytail. She smiled. "Of course," she said. "Do you know one of the children?"

He shook his head. "I know the lady who's reading to them," he corrected. "We've been friends for a long time."

"Miss Evans, you mean." She nodded. She smiled sadly. "She's had a very bad time in recent years, you know, especially when that man tried to kill her. She's much better now, though."

"Yes."

"You can go in, if you like," she added. "We've invited the public to participate. Actually," she added, "we're hoping that the children may form some attachments here that will benefit them. Donors are always welcomed. And there might be an opportunity for adoptions as well."

He frowned. "I hope you've screened the men."

She grimaced. "I know what you mean," she said softly. "No, that wouldn't have been possible, I'm afraid. But there are two undercover police officers in there," she added with a chuckle. "So if anybody has uncomfortable intentions, they'll be in for a big surprise."

He smiled broadly. "Nice thinking!"

She laughed. He was a very pleasant man. "Why don't you go and speak to Miss Evans? She's been very sad the past few weeks. I found her crying in the ladies' room, just after she came back to work. After the shooting, you know. She said she'd been so wrapped up in herself that she'd failed someone who was very close to her." She looked up at his expression. "That wouldn't be you, would it?"

His broad chest rose and fell. "I failed her," he said quietly.

She patted his big arm. "Life is all about redemption," she said softly. "Go make up."

He grinned at her. "You wouldn't be in the market for a husband, I guess?" he teased.

She laughed merrily. She was seventy if she was a day. Her white hair sparkled in the overhead light. "Get out of here, you varmint."

"Yes, ma'am."

He reached Millie just as she ended the story and kissed little cheeks.

"Go get some cake and punch now," she told them, easing them back on their feet.

They laughed and kissed her back. They were pretty little girls. One had jet-black hair and eyes, the other was a redhead. They held hands on the way to the treat table.

Millie was smiling after them when a shadow fell

over her. She looked up into Tony's face and caught her breath.

He knelt in front of her chair. "Yeah," he said deeply, searching her green eyes through the lenses of her glasses. She wasn't wearing contacts tonight. "That's how I feel when I see you, too. It takes my breath away."

She didn't have enough time to guard her response. She was so happy to see him that she began to glow. "I didn't expect to see you," she said.

"Didn't you?" His dark eyes smiled. "I stayed away until I thought I'd given you enough time to get over what I did."

"You saved my life," she protested. "I barely thanked you for it."

"You look good with little kids in your lap," he said quietly. "Natural."

"I like children."

"Me, too."

She searched for something to say. "Why are you here?"

"Because you're here, and it's Christmas Eve," he said.

She didn't understand. "But how did you find me?"

"I work for the government," he pointed out. "I know how to find anybody."

That reminded her of the shooting, which brought back disturbing images.

"I'm mostly administrative these days," he said quickly. "I don't have to use a gun. That night..." He looked tormented. "I didn't have a choice," he began.

She put her hand over his mouth. "I'm sorry!" she said huskily. "I'm so sorry. I didn't mean to make you feel guilty over what you did. If you'd hesitated, we wouldn't even be having this conversation!"

He caught her wrist and kissed the palm hungrily.

Her breath caught again at the hunger his touch ignited in her.

He saw it. His dark eyes began to glow.

For long seconds, they just stared at each other, blind to amused looks and muffled conversation.

"Can you come outside and sit in the car with me for a minute?" he asked, clearing his throat.

"I guess so."

He got up and pulled her up with him. He waited while she got into her coat and spoke to the white-haired lady Tony had been flirting with. The elderly woman gave Tony a thumbs-up sign behind Millie's back and he laughed.

"What was that all about?" Millie asked as they went out the front door.

"I'm thinking of having an affair with that lady you were just talking to," he said with a blatant grin. "She's a hoot."

"Mrs. Mims, you mean?" She laughed. "Isn't she, just! She's president of our 'friends of the library.' Before she retired, she was an investigative reporter."

"Well!" He saw something in Millie's face that made him curious. "What does she do now?"

"She writes mystery novels," she told him. "Very successful ones."

"I should talk to her. I know a lot of mysteries." He frowned. "Well, most of them are classified. But I could give her a few hints."

"She'd love that."

He unlocked the door of his rental car, a luxury one, and helped Millie into the passenger seat. She was smoothing the wooden dash when he got in on the other side.

"You do travel in style," she mused.

"I can afford to." He turned on the dome light and pulled something out of his pocket. "I've been doing a lot of thinking, about my life," he said as he faced her, with one arm over the back of her bucket seat. "I've been alone and I've enjoyed it. I've had brief liaisons, and I've enjoyed those, too. But I'm getting older. I'm tired of living alone."

She was hardly breathing as she sat, entranced, staring into his black eyes with breathless hope.

He reached out and touched her soft mouth with his fingertips, loving the way her eyes closed and her breath jerked out when he did it.

"Oh, hell, the rest can wait a minute. Come here!"

He dragged her over the console into his big arms and kissed her so hungrily that she actually whimpered with smoldering desire.

His breath caught at the sound. His arms contracted. His mouth opened on her lips, his tongue penetrating, his own moan overwhelming hers in the hot, urgent silence that followed.

After a minute, he shuddered and caught her arms.

He put her back into her own seat with visible reluctance. He was almost shaking with the force of his need. She was so unsteady that she fell back against the door, her mouth swollen, her eyes wild and soft, all at once.

"My foster mother was like you," he managed. "Old-fashioned and bristling with principles that seem to be a joke in the modern world. But I happen to like it." He fumbled in his pocket for a gray jeweler's box. He put it into Millie's hands and closed them around it. "Open it."

She fumbled trying to get the spring lid to work. Finally he had to help her—not that his hands were much steadier.

There, in the box, was a set of rings. There was a yellow-gold emerald solitaire with diamond accents, and a gold wedding band with alternating diamonds and emeralds.

"They're beautiful," she whispered. Maybe she was dreaming. Yes. That was probably it. She pinched her own arm and jumped.

"You're not dreaming," he said, amused. "But I've done my share of that, since I messed up things in my hotel room." He made a whistling sound. "That was a closer call than you'll ever know, girl. If you hadn't started protesting, I couldn't have stopped. I'd never lost control like that in my whole life, even when I was in my teens."

Everything went over her head except the last sentence. "Really?"

"Really. You are one hot experience."

"Me?" she asked, surprised. "But I don't know any-thing."

He grinned slowly. "Yeah. That's the exciting thing."

She blushed. He laughed when he saw the color in her cheeks. He was thinking how rare a thing that was. He couldn't stop thinking about how it had been with her, on that hotel bed. Even in memory, it made his blood run hot.

"I've done bad things in my life," he said then, very solemnly. "I like to think I did them in the service of my country, to protect our way of life. It was exciting work, and profitable. But I've put a lot of money away, and I've gotten the wild streak in me tamed somewhat." He hesitated. It was hard work, putting this into words. "What I'm trying to say…I mean, what I'm trying to ask…"

"I'd marry you if we had to live in a mud hut in a swamp with ten million mosquitos!" she interrupted.

He caught his breath. "Millie!"

He scooped her up again and kissed her so long, and so hard, that the windows all fogged up. Which was probably a good thing. Because when the tap at the window came, they weren't in any condition to be seen.

They scrambled apart, rearranging clothing, trying to look normal.

Tony buzzed the window down, with a carefully calm expression that didn't go well at all with the smear of lipstick across his mouth and face, and his hopelessly stained white shirt and half-undone tie and unbuttoned shirt. "Yes?" he said politely.

The white-haired woman doubled up laughing.

He scowled, trying to neaten himself up. In future years, the story would be told and retold by both partners.

"I just wanted to say…" she choked, trying to stop laughing long enough to be coherent, "that we're opening the presents, and the little girls…would like Millie to help them open theirs."

"We'll be right in. We were just getting rings out of boxes and stuff," he said, ruffled.

She murmured that it looked to her that it was a good idea to get the rings on and the words said in some legal fashion, and pretty quickly. Then she laughed some more and left.

Tony slid the engagement ring onto Millie's finger and kissed her. "So much for surprising your colleagues," he mused. "I imagine Ms. Perry Mason there will have tipped off the whole bunch by the time we get back inside."

"I don't mind," she said shyly.

He was lost in her smile. "Me, neither," he said.

Then he had to kiss her again. But they managed to get back into the library before all the presents were opened, to an unconcealed round of laughter that only the adults in the group truly understood.

They spent Christmas Day together talking about the future in between kisses. Tony offered her a church wedding, but they both decided that it could probably wait until they had more than one friend to ask to attend it. Meanwhile the local probate judge's office did nicely, with an attorney who was looking for a birth certificate and a judge's clerk for witnesses.

It had been Tony who refused to go past some energetic petting before the wedding. He wanted Millie to have things just the way she wanted them, he explained. So they'd wait.

However, the minute they reached Millie's apartment, which was closer than his hotel room, they were undressing even as Tony locked her door. They didn't even make it to the bedroom. Millie had her first intensely intimate experience on the carpeted floor of her apartment, and she never felt the carpet burns until she and Tony were lying in a tangled, sweaty heap under the soft hall-ceiling light.

"Wow," he managed.

"Oh, yes," she whispered while her heartbeat threatened to pound her into the floor.

He stretched his tired muscles, laughing when they cramped. "Hell!" he muttered. "I really tried to make it to the bedroom…"

"I don't care," she said in a tone that almost purred with satisfaction. "On a floor, standing up, in the bathroom…I never dreamed it would feel like that!"

He rolled over, so that he could look down into her soft green eyes. Her glasses and her clothing were strewn around them. "It hurt, at first."

"Did it?" she asked, surprised. "I didn't even notice."

"You flinched," he mused, brushing his warm mouth over her swollen lips. He chuckled softly. "But I knew what to do about that."

She blushed as she recalled exactly what he'd done about that.

His mouth smoothed down over soft, smooth, warm flesh. "I'm still vibrating," he murmured. "It was like swallowing fireworks!"

"Yes." She reached up and pulled him down to her, loving the feel of his muscular, hairy chest over her bare breasts. The contact electrified her. She arched up, catching his legs with hers, curling them around, tugging hopefully.

"It may hurt," he whispered.

"It may not," she whispered back, touching him shyly, but boldly.

He groaned. After that, he wasn't in any condition to protest.

She had to sit down very carefully. He noticed and his pursed lips smiled, reminding her of the restraint he'd tried to exercise.

"You insisted," he charged.

She grimaced. "Yes, but now I know better." She grinned at him anyway. "It was worth it."

He laughed out loud. "Yes, it was. Are you hungry?"

Her eyebrows arched. "I am."

He went into the kitchen and started looking through cabinets and the refrigerator. He laughed. "I can see that you're not impartial to Italian cooking."

"I love it. But you're not Italian."

"Not hardly. I just have that last name, since my mother married the devil." He frowned. "I should have had it changed, I guess. But that SOB who got her pregnant would never have let her use his name, and I don't want it, either." He shrugged. "Nothing wrong with an Italian name. It confuses people who think they know my background." He glanced at her. "I like confusing people," he said.

She got up and went to him, sliding her arms around his middle, pressing her cheek against all that warm strength. "I love you so much," she whispered. "I thought I'd die of it."

His own arms contracted. He kissed her hair. "I didn't say the words," he whispered. "But you must know that I feel them, right to my soul. These past few weeks without you have been pure hell!" He bent and kissed her soft mouth with something like anguish. "God, I love you!"

Tears welled up in her eyes and overflowed. Afterward, he stood just holding her, rocking her in his big arms, while they savored the belonging.

"It's a few days too late, now, but I just remembered that I didn't get you anything for Christmas," he said suddenly, disturbed.

"Yes, you did," she argued. She looked up at him with clear green eyes. "I got you for Christmas." She kissed his chin and grinned. "You're the best belated present I ever had! My very own Silent Night Man."

She cuddled close and added impishly, "My very own CIA agent! But I promise not to tell a soul."

He laughed wholeheartedly and wrapped her up close with a sigh. "You're the best present I ever had, too, precious. Merry Christmas."

"Merry Christmas, my darling," she whispered. She closed her eyes. Under her ear she heard the deep, steady beat of his heart. She remembered the instant she'd looked up into his eyes on Christmas Eve, and the glorious happiness she'd felt. It had only gotten better in the days that followed. This had been, she decided, the best Christmas of her whole life. She was holding her happiness in her arms.

* * * * *

A Man in her Stocking

LEANNE
BANKS

Leanne Banks is a *New York Times* and *USA TODAY* bestselling author who is surprised every time she realises how many books she has written. Leanne loves chocolate, the beach and new adventures. To name a few, Leanne has ridden an elephant, stood on an ostrich egg (no, it didn't break), gone parasailing and indoor skydiving. Leanne loves writing romance, because she believes in the power and magic of love. She lives in Virginia with her family and a four-and-a-half-pound Pomeranian named Bijou. Visit her website, www.leannebanks.com.

CHAPTER ONE

CHRISTMAS GAVE HIM heartburn.

Lucas took a deep swig directly from the bottle of antacid as he stood in the darkened kitchen of his ranch. It was midnight here in Kent, Missouri, and he'd just driven one hundred miles to finalize the sale of several hundred head of cattle to a rancher who wore a Stetson that played "Jingle Bells" every time the man touched it—and he touched it a lot. Lucas usually enjoyed talking with Ben Ericson, but the constant reminder of the holiday season had made his gut knot and burn.

Lucas had a legitimate reason for disliking Christmas, but he didn't want to stop the holidays for anyone else. He just wanted to be left alone.

He heard a sound from the stairs and figured he must have awakened his longtime housekeeper, Flora. Screwing the lid on the medicine bottle, he strode into the hallway, ready to reassure Flora.

From the side of the steps, he watched a pair of slim, silky legs descend the stairs, and his words stopped in his throat. Lucas took in bare feet, trim ankles, shapely calves and flashing glimpses of creamy thighs as a short silk robe caressed ivory skin.

No disrespect intended to his housekeeper, Lucas thought, but Flora sure as heck didn't have legs like that!

He craned his neck to get a better look. His gaze skimmed up the curve of the mystery woman's hips and waist, lingered on the swell of her breasts, then wandered higher to a face that somehow managed to combine the look of a wide-eyed elf with a full mouth designed to fuel a man's most forbidden fantasies. The fact that her auburn hair stuck out in no less than eight different directions didn't stop a surge of unbidden heat inside him. Lucas cleared his throat.

The woman gasped and jerked her head toward him, clutching her robe to her throat. "Who…oh…are you Debra's brother? Are you Lucas Bennet?"

Lucas pulled his brain out of his jeans. Debra was his sister. So she was behind this. "Yes, I'm Lucas. And you are…?"

The woman bit her lip as she descended the rest of the way down the stairs. Her face wasn't classically beautiful in the same way as his former wife's. This woman was more well, *cute,* he guessed, but her rapid-fire change of facial expressions was compelling. "You didn't get the message she left on your cell phone, did you?"

Lucas shook his head. After hearing "Jingle Bells" until he was gritting his teeth, he hadn't wanted any noise. He'd turned off the radio in his truck, as well as his cell phone and cherished blessed silence.

The woman winced. "Oops. Well, I had a problem with my house and uh—"

"Problem?"

"There was a fire," she said, a trace of sadness darkening her eyes. "It will take some time to figure out what's salvageable and what isn't."

"Sorry," he murmured, immediately wanting to know more. Lucas was a volunteer fireman for the community. "Do you know what caused it?"

She lifted her shoulder in a gesture of uncertainty. "They mentioned something about faulty wiring."

"Were you there at the time?"

She shook her head. "It happened while I was at school. I'm Amy Winslow, the new elementary schoolteacher. Your sister Debra wanted me to stay with her, but her house is crowded since her mother-in-law is visiting, so she assured me that you had plenty of room and wouldn't mind my staying here temporarily."

He felt her green gaze search his face and swallowed an oath. His sister knew damn well that all he wanted during the holidays was to be left alone.

"If I had family, I could go home, but…"

Lucas could have sworn he felt the weight of a noose around his neck. "No family?"

She shook her head, her auburn hair fluttering around her face. "My parents have been gone a long time. If my staying here is a problem…" she began, her voice trailing off uncertainly.

Lucas stifled a groan. It definitely was a problem, but Lucas knew how hard the small rural community had worked to attract a schoolteacher. Most teachers fresh out of school couldn't be less interested in accepting a position in a small community deep in the ranch country of Missouri, where a hot time in town was defined as the monthly dance at the community center. Now that the small community of Kent had a teacher, folks would do everything they could to keep her, and Debra would expect him to do his part. Plus it would be flat out cruel to turn the woman away.

She looked as if she were determined to remain calm, but Lucas had seen enough people rendered homeless from fires to know that shock would follow. Amy technically had no one.

He shelved his own needs. "It's not a problem. I've got plenty of room."

"It's just until I find another place to live," she promised, and Lucas blinked as a plump calico cat scampered down the steps and rubbed against Amy's ankles. Her gaze locked with his, guilt glinting from her eyes. She bit her lip and quickly picked up the cat. "Oops. Debra told me you don't like cats. I'll try to keep Cleo in my room."

"Cleo," he echoed, still staring at the cat. Lucas had never understood the appeal of cats. Felines reminded him of fickle women. He was a dog fan through and through.

"I'll just be here through Christmas," Amy reassured him earnestly. "I'm a big believer in Christmas, so I'll make sure it looks, sounds and smells like the holiday season."

Lucas's gut twisted. "That's not necessary."

Amy shook her head emphatically. "Oh, I absolutely insist." She tilted her lips in a lopsided smile, and her entire face lit up. "I love Christmas. It's my favorite time of the year."

Lucas sighed. *Oh, goody,* he thought. He was stuck with a Christmas nut whose body could rewind the clock of every man in town. Maybe he should sleep in the barn.

The following morning, Lucas rose earlier than usual and wandered into the kitchen for his first cup of coffee. Amy stood by the counter sipping a cup of coffee and nibbling on a piece of toast. Her hair damp waving from a recent shower and face scrubbed clean of makeup, she wore a pair of low-slung jeans and a chunky celery-green sweater. She looked like she was thirteen years old.

Except for her mouth, he thought, watching as she pursed her lips to blow, cooling her coffee. She turned to look at him. "Good morning."

He nodded. "Mornin'," he said. "You're up early."

"I'm going to my house. A fireman told me I would probably be able to get a few things today."

"I'll go with you," he said, pouring himself a cup of coffee. His training made safety a priority.

"That's not necessary. I don't want to interrupt your schedule."

"You'll have to interrupt someone's schedule if you're going to go prowling around a house that was on fire yesterday. I'm a volunteer fireman. It may as well be me."

She blinked. "Oh."

"You look surprised," he said, curious despite himself. He took a gulp of the hot black liquid, and felt it burn all the way down.

"I was told that you own the biggest ranch in the county. I wouldn't think you would have time for fire fighting."

"Luckily, there aren't that many fires to put out. We're a small community, and we try to look after each other, so a lot of us cover more than one base."

Amy smiled. "I keep being surprised by the differences between living in the city and the country."

"You miss the city?"

"Not much so far. Every once in a while, I crave a little retail therapy or would like to see a movie before it's two months' old."

He gave her an assessing glance. "Our winters can get a little tough."

Amy heard a combination of doubt and challenge in his deep voice. She wasn't quite sure what to make of Lucas. So far, he seemed the polar opposite of his friendly, outgoing sister. He hadn't cracked a smile since she'd met him; however, he emanated strength, both in his imposing, muscular frame and rock solid character. Here was a man who wouldn't be easily shaken, but something about the way he looked at her made her feel jumpy.

Amy ignored the sensation, met his gaze and was momentarily distracted by the thick fringe of his eyelashes. For such a hard man, he had killer eyelashes. She shook off the thought and answered his doubt. "I can handle a tough winter. I've got a good winter coat, a sturdy pair of boats, lots of warm socks and a humdinger of a recipe for hot chocolate."

Taking another drink of coffee, he gave a nod, but she could tell he wasn't convinced. If Missouri needed a poster boy for the state slogan *Show Me,* then Lucas was their man.

Amy stiffened her already hard resolve. She would *show him* and everyone else who doubted her. "Just curious. Do you have a stainless-steel throat, or is there some secret to how you can swallow scalding coffee?"

His hard mouth twitched, and his eyes glinted with a hint of humor. "Practice." As if to prove his point, he finished the cup. "We can leave as soon as you dry your hair."

"I never dry my hair in the morning," she said. "I can leave now."

"Didn't your mother ever tell you going out in cold weather with a wet head is a great way to get sick?"

"No," she said. "My mother relinquished care of me to the state when I was four years old, and I lived in a children's home until I left for college."

He was quiet for a long moment and studied her.

"Well, you're on my time now. So dry your hair and we'll leave."

"Your time?"

He nodded. "My sister put you in my care. I'll make sure nothing happens to you while you're in my home."

Amy felt a burst of feminist outrage at the same time she was utterly confident that if any man could keep a woman safe, it was Lucas. Irritated, she lifted her chin. "I've been taking care of myself for a long time."

"Every mother in this community will have my head if I let anything happen to the new teacher they're all raving about. If you've been taking care of yourself for a long time, just look on this as a little break," he said with a shrug.

Amy didn't know whether to be flattered by his sideways compliment of her teaching skills or frustrated by his stubbornness regarding her *care*. She sighed, then took one last sip of her coffee. "Give me two minutes," she said, unwilling to expend any more of her energy on an argument. This was temporary, she told herself as she strode upstairs, and it was Christmas. The supposed season of peace...even if Lucas generated anything but peace.

On the way to Amy's house, Lucas called the volunteer fire chief so he would know what to expect. As soon as they walked through the front door, he was bombarded with the scent of smoke and the sight of charred Christmas decorations. Sooty packages sat beneath a small scorched Christmas tree, a nativity on the fireplace mantel, and the staircase rail was lined with red ribbon and greenery limp from water sprayed from a firefighter's hose. The decorations were tasteful, but Lucas still felt the burn of pain beneath his ribs.

Amy stood perfectly still as she took in her flame-ravaged home. He almost reminded her to breathe, but she shook herself and fled past him. "I just want to check on a few things," she said, rushing up the stairs.

He followed her up the staircase into a bedroom where half the room had been blackened by the blaze. Amy skipped the jewelry box on the dresser, the clothes closet, and fell to her knees beside her bed, digging out two boxes. She opened one and gave a sigh of relief. "Photos survived." She peeked in the other box, which was dark around the edges and smiled. "All okay." Snapping the top on the box before he could get a look at what it held, she looked up at him. "If I can get the gifts downstairs, I should be set."

"What about some clothes or your jewelry?"

"Oh," she said with a blank expression, as if she'd been so intent on rescuing other items that clothing hadn't occurred to her. She rose to her feet and turned to the closet. "I should get a suitcase," she mumbled to herself, pulling out a piece of luggage from inside. She covered her nose. "The smoke smell is so strong."

Lucas nodded, opening the suitcase for her. "You might want to choose wash-and-wear now. The insurance company will help cover smoke damage for everything. You should probably go ahead and schedule a professional cleaning."

"I'd love to schedule the cleaning, but I imagine a lot of people are taking off for the holidays," Amy muttered as she pulled a few pieces of clothing from the hangers, then turned to her dresser. With both hands, she scooped up a couple of nighties and silky underwear and bras.

Lucas felt an odd twist in his gut at the sight of the sensual intimate clothing that she would wear next to her naked skin. A forbidden, *unbidden* image of her dressed in ivory satin panties and bra slithered across his mind, raising his body temperature.

She dumped the lingerie into the suitcase, then quickly grabbed her photo album and the mystery box. As if she were on autopilot, she reached for the suitcase, but Lucas shook his head. "I'll carry it."

He followed her down the stairs and watched as she gathered the charred gifts from beneath the tree. Biting her lip, she tried to stack them to carry them outside and Lucas saw an accident waiting to happen.

"Stop."

At the sound of his voice, Amy immediately halted and met his gaze. Lucas saw a world of vulnerability in her eyes. "You'll be okay," he told her, reading her need for reassurance.

She nodded, but her eyes looked far less certain. "Of course I will. It's just unsettling to be—" Her voice wavered and she gave a weak smile. "Unsettled."

Lucas could tell Amy was no wuss. Her back was ramrod straight, but he couldn't help wondering how much weight her slim shoulders should bear. Her chin was set with determination, but her eyes showed a storm of emotions he suspected she would never confess. The urge to embrace her hit him in the stomach like a knockout punch.

He walked closer and stopped a mere step away from her. "It's normal to feel unsettled, even a little afraid," he told her.

Amy took a deep breath, her gaze surveying the damage to her home. "I just want a safe place of my own. My own home. Now it's such a mess, and I don't even know if I'll be able to move back in." She closed her eyes for a few timeless seconds, then opened them and met his gaze. "But it's Christmas, and I refuse to whine."

She whirled around and Lucas felt a rumbling suspicion that he'd just encountered something a hell of a lot stronger than a house fire. That something was the indomitable will of Amy Winslow.

After Lucas dropped Amy off at the ranch, he drove his truck out to check the livestock. Pulling to a stop, he got out and inhaled the cold winter air. Lucas liked the cold at Christmas. It numbed him, and blunted the pain. His marriage to Jennifer hadn't been perfect, but he'd made promises, and Lucas believed in keeping promises. She hadn't been happy living on the ranch. Four days before Christmas, she'd left a note telling him she'd made the two-hour drive to St. Louis and would return late that night.

But there'd been an ice storm, and a semi had

crushed her car, killing her. He'd buried her on Christmas Eve. He'd also officially buried his interest in celebrating Christmas.

Hearing a car slowly move toward him, he turned his head and spotted his sister's SUV. His sister, Debra, was the bane of his existence, but he would die for her. After all, she was his youngest sister. She'd bugged the devil out of him when he was a teenager, tagging after him, horning in on phone conversations. Even though Debra was younger, once their parents died, she acted as if it were her place to watch over his social life. After Jennifer died, Debra had relentlessly tried to lure him into enjoying the season when all he wanted was to be left alone.

Debra, six months pregnant with her third child, stopped the car, got out and walked toward him. She had that busybody glint in her eyes, but her face was slightly pale. She didn't get enough rest for a woman in her condition. When Lucas looked at her, he still saw his little sister in pigtails instead of a grown mother of three. "So when will you be speaking to me again?"

"Never," he said. "You need to get more rest."

"Yeah," she said, standing next to him. "Easier said than done. I think I'm suffering from overexposure to my mother-in-law. Two women in the same kitchen is like—"

"Like having two dictators with different strategies make battle plans. War or détente?" he asked, looping his arm around her shoulder.

"Détente if it kills me."

"I would never wish you pain, but you deserve a truckload of discomfort for sending me Kent's answer to the unsinkable Molly Brown. You know that all I want for Christmas is to be left alone."

Debra sighed. "Left alone so you can punish yourself for Jennifer's death. When are you going to stop blaming yourself?

"She was my wife, my responsibility."

"She was an adult, too."

Lucas shrugged and moved away. He couldn't explain his harsh sense of failure and disappointment in himself to his sister, and he wasn't going to try.

"Well, your overdeveloped sense of responsibility is one of the reasons you were chosen to house Amy Winslow," she said. "That, and the fact that everyone knows you've turned into a monk."

Lucas gave her a double take. "What are you talking about?"

Debra crossed her arms over her bulky coat and arched her eyebrows. "You weren't the only volunteer to have her as a guest."

Lucas looked toward the heaven for help. "*I* didn't volunteer. I was *drafted!*"

"Well, there were plenty of volunteers. Men, some single, a few, married, wanted to have Amy in their houses for Christmas. Every single one of them was wearing a wolfy gleam in their eyes, champing at the bit to get their paws on her. I could tell what they wanted, and I knew Amy needed to be protected. That's why I volunteered your house. She'll be as safe with you as she would be with a monk, since you've obviously decided you're never going to have sex again."

CHAPTER TWO

THE WREATH ON his front door was the next sign that Lucas's home had been invaded. It was a cheerful combination of greenery, holly berries and bells, topped off with a bright-red bow. Lucas frowned.

He would allow the wreath, but drew the line at a tree. No Christmas tree allowed.

Lucas felt the familiar twist in his gut and opened the door to the sound of children's voices and Christmas music on the stereo. "What the he—" He walked toward the kitchen and entered the doorway.

Five little kids, faces smeared with various colors of frosting and big smiles, crowded around his kitchen table as Amy helped them decorate cookies and his housekeeper removed a pan of cookies from the oven. Lucas's gaze automatically swung back to Amy. She wore a red apron, and one cheek was smudged with red and green frosting.

A little girl spotted him first. "Who's he?" she asked.

Flora, his housekeeper, whipped around, and her eyes grew wide with surprise. "You're early!"

"He's big," another little girl said.

"He looks mean," a little boy said.

Amy winced at the little boy's words and shot Lucas a wary glance. "He's not mean, Ryan. He's just surprised. This is Mr. Bennet's home," she said, then turned directly toward Lucas. "Before the fire, I had promised my special readers that if they met the goals we'd set then we would celebrate with a cookie-decorating party. I didn't want to disappoint them, and Flora said you probably wouldn't mind."

She did? Lucas threw Flora a sharp glance, but his housekeeper just busied herself at the kitchen counter.

"Wanna cookie?" a little girl asked, holding up a cookie decorated with a large blob of green frosting.

Every eye in the room gazed at him expectantly. Lucas withheld a sigh. "Sure," he said, and was rewarded with bright smiles from both the little girl and Amy.

Eating the too-sweet cookie, he felt a tug on his jacket. Ryan, the little boy who had said he looked *mean,* looked up at him. "Can you draw a reindeer? I wanna put a reindeer on my cookie."

With that, Lucas washed his hands and got sucked into decorating cookies with Amy's special readers for the next thirty minutes. Amy helped the little rascals clean up, and sent each of them home with a dozen cookies and a smile on their face.

As soon as they left, she turned to Lucas. "Thank you. I get the impression Flora thought you wouldn't mind the invasion as long as you didn't know about it, but you did. The kids loved having you there."

"It's no big deal," he said gruffly, uncomfortable with the gratitude in her eyes.

"Yes, it was," she insisted. "It takes a real man to be willing to draw reindeers on cookies for first graders."

The husky sound in her voice did strange things to his stomach. It was probably those damn cookies, he told himself. Although Amy was attractive, Lucas wasn't open for business. Besides, as his sister pointed out, he was supposed to be protecting her... instead of thinking about licking the tiny smudge of frosting off the corner of her lips or wondering what kind of sounds she made while making love.

Feeling an unwelcome rush of heat, Lucas bit back an oath and shrugged. "I have some numbers to crunch in my office," he said, and walked away from temptation.

That night Amy dreamed she settled into a new home, only to see it devoured again and again by flames. The dream upset her so much she woke up, her heart pounding and filled with dread. She inhaled several deep breaths before she realized she was in Lucas Bennet's house and she was safe.

The irrational threat of the dream, however, hung over her, just as it had last night. Glancing at the clock, she made a face at the hour: 2:00 a.m. Wide-awake, she knew she wouldn't go back to sleep anytime soon, so she tossed back the covers and slid out of bed. Maybe hot chocolate would help. She pushed her arms through her robe and quietly crept downstairs to the kitchen.

She mixed the ingredients to her special recipe into a saucepan, thinking she could stand an extra shot of Kahlúa. As much as she was determined to pretend otherwise, being displaced by the fire dug up painful childhood memories.

Amy found routine and longtime possessions comforting. Unlike many of her friends, she didn't yearn for the excitement of travel and new experiences. She longed for a home of her own, and six months ago, she had decided to make her home in Kent, Missouri. She couldn't remember a time when she hadn't wished for her own family and a safe place.

Her friends and colleagues in Baltimore had thought Amy was nuts to accept a position in nowhere, Missouri, but in the warm, rural community of Kent, Amy had seen the seductive possibility of at least part of the life she'd envisioned for herself.

She hadn't, however, envisioned a fire destroying her home during the Christmas season. Amy had spent her entire life battling the knot of apprehension in her chest that she shouldn't count on much of anything. The fire had brought back that familiar knot of apprehension. She absently rubbed her chest and took a deep breath. Pouring the hot chocolate into a mug, she tossed in a few marshmallows and wandered toward the picture window in the large den. The moon gleamed over the frost-covered ground.

Cold outside. Cold inside, Amy thought and shivered.

"It's either a little early or a little late, isn't it?" a male voice said from behind her.

Surprised, she turned to see Lucas walking toward her in a pair of jeans and an unbuttoned shirt that revealed his muscular chest, the shadow of chest hair, and his washboard flat abdomen. His brown hair was attractively sleep-mussed and his eyelids lowered in a sexy half-mast. With his thumbs hooked through the loops of weathered jeans, his casual gate belied the masculine power he oozed. A complex, intriguing man, he operated the largest, most successful ranch in the area, pitched into the community by serving as an on-call volunteer fireman, guarded his solitude, yet wouldn't turn his back on a first grader asking for help. If he weren't so remote, Amy could be entirely too susceptible to his strength and... Her gaze took in the length of him and felt her heart hammer at his rugged appeal.

Dismayed by her involuntary response, she took a quick sip of her chocolate and immediately singed her tongue. A tiny yelp escaped her throat, and she fanned her tongue.

The corner of his mouth tilted upward. "Too hot?"

Amy's gaze lingered on the smooth bare skin of his chest that his shirt didn't cover. He had no idea. "Yes. I forgot to pick up that stainless-steel lining for my mouth and throat in town today. Which store carries it?"

His half grin grew. "There are only five stores within the town limits."

He moved closer, and Amy felt a flutter of nerves. "I'm sorry I woke you. I tried to be quiet."

He pushed his hand through his hair. "I think I smelled chocolate."

"There's still some left in the pot if you want a mug."

"Thanks. Maybe in a few minutes," he said with a shrug of his impressive shoulders. "Why're you up?"

Amy lifted the mug to her lips and took a tiny, careful sip. "I woke up and couldn't go back to sleep."

"What woke you?"

Amy resisted the urge to squirm beneath his intent gaze. "Nothing important," she muttered.

"What woke you?" he repeated.

Amy sighed. "It was just a silly dream."

"But it bothered you enough to keep you awake," he concluded. "What was it?"

"I dreamed my new home kept catching on fire, again and again. Just as I relaxed and started to think everything was going to be okay, the fire would start again."

He nodded slowly and gave her a considering glance. A strange silence hung between them for a few seconds. "You wanna go for a walk?"

Amy did a double take. "Excuse me? A walk at this time of night?"

He nodded again and gave her that almost smile. "Might as well. We're both awake. A walk in the cold will—"

"Wake us up even more," she interjected.

"Then maybe returning to the warm house will make us sleepy."

She stared at him, wondering why his suggestion appealed to her. "I'll need to change," she said.

"Not on my account," he drawled. "But you might be more comfortable."

Amy's heart tripped over itself and she did another double take. *Was he flirting with her?* No, she immediately answered herself. Absolutely not. She didn't think Lucas was capable of flirting, and his sister had insisted that since he wasn't interested in romance, Amy would be perfectly safe with him. Her gaze encompassing his partly bare chest, she took a careful breath. "I'll go change."

Three and a half minutes later, she scurried down the steps as she shoved her arms into her coat sleeves and pulled on a hat. Lucas waited for her at the front door wearing a Stetson, jacket and boots, in addition to his jeans and shirt. He opened the door and dipped his head for her to proceed.

The cold air hit her face like a wall of ice. She breathed in quickly and her lungs felt frozen. Her expression must have revealed her shock.

"A little nippy?" he asked with a sexy edge of humor in his voice that surprised her.

"A little," she said, then corrected herself. "A lot."

"You're just not used to going out in the middle of the night in Missouri," he said, walking beside her down the steps to the front walkway.

"Why are you?" she asked.

"Because farm animals and ranch problems have their own timetable. It's not like school. The bell doesn't really ever ring for recess here."

"How long has the ranch been in your family?"

"Five generations," he said, leading her down a pathway along a pasture where the ground glistened with frost.

"Now, that's cool. Having all that history must feel great."

"Sometimes," he said. "It depends if you want to follow the family plan."

Although she didn't know Lucas very well, she couldn't imagine him doing anything but ranching. "Did you ever want to do something else?"

"I thought about it a few times when I was in college and after my wi—" He broke off suddenly and turned quiet.

"After your wife died," she said quietly. "Debbie told me that was rough for you."

"Yeah," he said, narrowing his eyes as a dozen emotions passed through them.

"I'm sorry."

He shoved his hands in his pockets. "What made you come to Kent?"

"Because the community really needed me. I received other offers, but I could tell Kent really needed me. I could see myself belonging, and that's something I've wanted my entire life."

"But what about the lack of entertainment?"

She smiled. "Entertainment is a matter of taste. I

couldn't walk along a path at 2:00 a.m. and see this kind of view in Baltimore."

"True," he said. "But there aren't a lot of singles' bars in town, either."

"I don't think I'll find what I want in a singles' bar," she said wryly.

He stopped. "What do you want?"

"Not that much. To feel needed and wanted. To make a place for myself."

"I bet you'll get bored as hell after you've lived here awhile."

His doubt in her pinched. She frowned. "You don't know me well enough to make that judgment."

"I know the winters here are long, and you're a city girl used to creature comforts."

"It all depends on what creature comforts are important to me."

He adjusted his hat but still wore a doubtful expression on his face. "Okay, I'll bite. What creature comforts are important to you?"

"A warm fire. A safe home of my own. People calling my name when I walk down the street. Friends who stay in my life for a long time."

"What about family?"

The question cut at a tender place she tried to keep hidden. She crossed her arms over her chest. "My friends will be my family," she said. "And Cleo."

"Your cat?" he queried, raising an eyebrow in disbelief. "Why don't you just get married? You're attractive. You should be able to find a guy to marry you."

Amy tilted her head at his backhanded compliment. "Thank you—I think. I don't want to be married unless it's to the right person. It looks like a lot more pain is caused by being married to the wrong person than by being single. But I could say the same to you. You may be grouchy and remote, but you're attractive. You should be able to find a woman to marry you," she said with the sweetest smile she could muster.

He frowned. "I didn't say I wanted to get married."

"Neither did I."

The vapor from her breath mingled with his as she met his gaze. She noticed that they had stopped walking and he was standing entirely too close to her. She told herself to pull away, but her feet refused.

"Are you ready to go to bed now?" he asked in a low voice.

Her heart hiccuped in her chest. *Bed.* In a flash, an unwelcome visual flitted through her mind of Lucas, naked, hot and anything but grouchy and remote. Amy found the image too appealing, too tempting. After his cool reception of her, she liked the idea of getting him hot and bothered. A distant mental warning bell sounded. Bad idea, she told herself. This was not a man to taunt.

He gently chucked her chin with his forefinger. "Cleo got your tongue? You think you can go back to sleep now?"

Fat chance. "Sure," she said, even though she was certain she was awake enough to paint the house. "I'll probably drift right off as soon as I get warm again."

"Good," he said, and they made the return walk in silence.

As soon as they entered the house, she was compelled by politeness to thank him. "It was nice of you to suggest a walk when you probably could have gone back to sleep with no problem."

His eyes glinted with mischief. "I guess I'm just a nice, grouchy, remote, but attractive man."

Amy bit her lip to keep from smiling. He was throwing her description of him right back at her. "I guess you are," she returned and reached out to squeeze his arm. "Thanks."

He glanced down at her hand on his arm, and when his gaze met hers, she could almost swear she saw the barest hint of sexual intent. She moved her hand away as if she'd touched a hot stove.

Lucas didn't sleep well the rest of the night. It was almost as if someone had stuck a splinter in his side since Amy had shown up. His peace and solitude had been completely disrupted, and her assessment of him got under his skin. He wasn't all that grouchy, he thought. He just didn't like Christmas.

Every time he closed his eyes, he saw her face. Changeable green eyes wanting to trust and that full mouth of hers that could produce an innocent smile one moment, and remind him what he'd been missing the last few years the next. This woman, he concluded, got on his nerves.

The next morning, he rose early and threw himself into work. The natural rhythm of caring for the animals and repairing a stretch of fence calmed him, and he didn't return to the house until evening.

The wreath on the door greeted him, then as soon as he entered, he heard Christmas music playing on the stereo, and the cat appeared, rubbing against his ankles.

His housekeeper, Flora, met him wearing a wary expression. "I couldn't say no to her."

His gut knotted. "What do you mean?"

Flora shrugged helplessly and pointed toward the den.

Carefully stepping over the cat, Lucas strode to the den, fully prepared to do what Flora had been unable to do. He stopped midway into the room at the sight that beheld him. Perched on a ladder, Amy strung lights around a large Christmas tree. The scent of pine filled the air.

The tree felt like a knife between his ribs. He remembered all too well taking down the tree his wife had decorated before she'd died. He swore under his breath.

Amy must have heard or felt him. Her gaze shot to his, her eyes rounding at his presence. Startled, she wobbled on the ladder, losing her balance. "Oh, no!"

Lucas's heart stopped, and he rushed toward her, grabbing her and falling backward at the same time. He landed on the floor bottom first with her cradled on top of him. They lay in silence for a few breath-shattering seconds.

Amy lifted her head and looked down at him, her bangs falling over one eye. "Are you okay?"

Lucas felt a twinge in his backside. "As long as I don't sit down for the next month."

She winced. "I'm sorry."

His heart still hammered in his chest, but his other senses began to engage. He inhaled her sweet, sultry scent and felt the soft pressure of her breasts against his chest. The weight of her lower body rested intimately against his.

Her gaze locked with his, and he watched her eyes darken with gradual feminine, sensual awareness. She licked her lips.

"I should move," she murmured.

"Uh-huh," he said, but neither of them did.

CHAPTER THREE

AMY FOUGHT THE delicious, seductive sensation that urged her toward Lucas. He was so solid, so strong, so... She wondered how he kissed and stared at his mouth for a long moment. Glancing back into his eyes, she saw that he'd caught her. Her cheeks heated. Hoping he couldn't read her mind, she began to carefully back away, the same way she might back away from a lion.

Holding her with his gaze, he followed her up on his elbows.

A dozen tingly, odd sensations coursed through her, and she cleared her throat to break the silence. "You move fast for such a tall man."

"I didn't want you to hurt yourself," he said.

His intent expression made her knees unsteady, but she forced them to work anyway, standing. "There you go with that overdeveloped protective streak again," she joked.

He didn't smile. His face was dead serious. "No falling," he said. "I don't want you on the ladder unless someone is right beside you."

"But—" she protested.

"But nothing," he said, pulling off his suede jacket. "I'll put the rest of the lights on the tree, then you can decorate up to the ladder level and stop."

"But—"

He leaned his head so that he was two breaths away from her. "This is nonnegotiable."

Amy's throat went dry at the sensual combination of velvet and steel in his voice. Confused, she gave a tiny nod, wondering what was wrong with her. She'd never been attracted to domineering men.

He didn't appear satisfied. "Repeat after me. Lucas, I will not climb the ladder unless another person is helping me."

"Are you always this bossy?"

"When it's important," he said, without one iota of apology. "I'm waiting."

She sighed and rolled her eyes. "Okay, I won't climb the ladder unless I have help. There. Are you satisfied?"

"It'll be one less thing to give me heartburn," he muttered turning toward the ladder. As he climbed it, Amy couldn't help observing that Lucas had an incredible backside. He quickly strung the rest of the lights, and descended the ladder. "All yours."

She plugged in the lights. The tree lit up, and she nodded in approval as a wave of bittersweet nostalgia passed over her. "Thank you. Ever since I lived at the children's home I've always had a Christmas tree. Even when I went to college, I had one of those little tabletop artificial ones in my dorm room. I think of Christmas as the time of year when most everyone is a little nicer. I think the season brings out the best in people. A little light in the darkness, kinda like the lights on the tree."

She looked at Lucas and suddenly felt self-conscious at her disclosure. "Sorry. Didn't mean to get all soppy on you."

He looked at her thoughtfully. "No apology necessary," he said, then a glint of pain sliced through his eyes.

His expression tugged at something tender inside her. She was filled with the odd longing to wipe away his grief. She balled her fists to keep from reaching out to embrace him. He wouldn't appreciate it, she told herself. He didn't want a hug, even if she wanted to give one.

"Enjoy the tree, Amy," he said, and left her staring after him, her hands feeling strangely itchy and empty.

Lucas successfully avoided his on-site Christmas fairy during the next twenty-four hours by sticking to outside work. The cold weather suited him, numbing him to the pain that sneaked up on him at odd moments. It was dark when he returned to the house. The first thing he noticed was a cluster of about ten cars spilling from his driveway. Even before he opened the front door, he heard a chorus of voices singing a Christmas carol.

Lucas sighed, pushed the door open, and the sound of the season assaulted him. There was no way he could escape Christmas with Amy in his house. Amy's cat,

Cleo, scampered out of the den and rubbed against his legs.

The music ended and laughter filled the air.

Amy appeared in the doorway with an uncertain expression on her face. "I asked Flora if you would mind if some Christmas carolers met here for a little practice. Everyone was originally supposed to meet at my house, but you know what happened." She glanced down at his feet and her lips twitched. "Look at Cleo marking you. She likes you."

Lucas glanced down in consternation as the cat continued to wind around his ankles. "Marking me?"

She nodded. "Cats rub against you and mark you to show they like you."

Lucas had no idea how to respond. Why in the world did he feel vaguely pleased that Amy's cat liked him? This was insane. He removed his hat and slapped it against his thigh in frustration.

"Flora shouldn't have said the Christmas carol practice would be okay with you, should she?" Amy asked in a low voice as she stepped closer. "I can get everyone to leave."

Lucas sighed and shook his head. He couldn't say no to Amy any better than Flora could. "I'll grab a sandwich and eat it in my room."

"Hey, Amy," a male voice called from the den. "Where'd you go?"

"Are you sure?" she asked, ignoring the man's call. Her gaze tangled with Lucas's for a long moment, and the look in her eyes made his heart thud with a rough, edgy rhythm.

A man strode into the doorway, breaking the odd moment stretching between Lucas and Amy. Lucas immediately recognized him—Dan Arthur, a local attorney. And he was looking at Amy the same way a cat looked at a canary.

"You disappeared," Dan chided her, looping his arm over her shoulders. He glanced up at Lucas and nodded. "Seasons greetings, Lucas. Nice of you to give our favorite teacher a place to stay after the fire. I bet you've enjoyed her Christmas decorations. The only thing missing is mistletoe," he said, with a pointed grin for Amy.

Lucas's gaze hung on the man's arm around Amy's shoulders. His stomach knotted with an unwelcome feeling he couldn't quite identify. *Mistletoe.* Dan clearly wanted to do a heck of a lot more than kiss her. Lucas resisted the urge to push Dan away.

Annoyed at the territorial instinct roiling inside him, he swallowed an oath. "Give her time," Lucas muttered darkly, and left the couple in the foyer. He had two words for Dan Arthur, and they weren't *Merry Christmas.*

Hours later, Lucas sat in bed and read an article on ranch management instead of sleeping. The holiday season always unsettled him, but tonight he was equally unsettled by thoughts of Amy.

It was bad enough that the woman had the fervor of Santa's elves when it came to the holiday season, but

Amy bothered him in other ways. She wasn't classically pretty, he kept telling himself, but that didn't stop
him from studying her face every chance he got. He
shouldn't find her sexy, but she projected an earthiness
that made him want to strip off those baggy jeans and
chunky sweaters and slide deep inside her.

After Jennifer died, he'd ruthlessly pushed aside his
sexual needs. His wife had died, so denying himself
pleasure seemed just and right. He had failed to protect her, so why should he be happy?

Sighing, he tossed aside the journal and rose from
the bed. He wandered to his window and raked his
hand through his hair.

A muffled whimper from down the hall penetrated
his brooding isolation.

The nightmare had returned. Desperation seeped
through her like acid. Her heart hammering, Amy
shook her head. "No, no, no." She saw her new home.
She was finally settled, surrounded by furnishings
she'd chosen that made her feel as if she had at last
found home. Then, the flames kicked up, destroying
everything. Over and over again, she walked into her
home, hopeful, only to see the flames burn her precious dreams to ashes.

"No, no!" she said, watching her photos melt from
the relentless fire.

She felt strong hands on her arms, shaking her. The
visual of the fire faded.

"Amy."

The male voice immediately diminished her panic.

She blinked and sat up, finding herself in Lucas's arms. Disoriented, she sucked in several deep breaths. "It was the dream. The fire," she murmured, trying to steady herself. "The dream. I'm okay."

"You're safe. There's no fire."

I'm here. He didn't say it, but she felt it, and his presence made all the difference in the world. Amy instinctively sank against him. She couldn't refuse his reassurance. Here was unadulterated strength. At times Lucas might be cranky, but he was solid through and through. His complete reliability got under her skin and touched her where she was most vulnerable. In Lucas's arms, she was a lonely little girl again, wanting to feel safe, believing it was possible.

The feelings sent her equilibrium spinning.

His fingers slid through her hair in a comforting caress, and she closed her eyes. She inhaled his clean, masculine scent. Her palms rested on his chest, and his skin was smooth over the steel of his muscles. His strength again seduced, and she couldn't resist the urge to touch.

The air was cool, but he was warm.

"What was your dream?" he asked in a low voice that sent a delicious shiver through her.

"I keep making a home for myself, but every time I think I'm safe, the fire comes back."

"You hide your fear very well," he said.

She looked up, searching his face in the darkness. "What do you mean?"

"You sing your Christmas carols. You bake your cookies. But your dream tells that you're afraid."

She stiffened in defense. "I'm not—"

He placed his thumb over her lips. "It's normal," he told her. "I've watched a lot of people fall apart when they lose their homes. You haven't."

"I don't want to fall apart. I'm not going to fall apart."

"I believe you," he said. "You're tough."

She sighed and dropped her head against his chest. "I don't feel tough," she whispered.

"You are," he said, sifting his fingers through her hair again.

"But the dream keeps coming back."

"You're expecting too much of yourself. Give yourself some time."

"How come you're so smart about this?"

He chuckled, and the sound rippled through her nerve endings. "I'm just naturally smart."

She smiled at his masculine humor and lifted her head to look at him. "Sorry I interrupted your sleep again."

"I wasn't asleep."

Surprise skipped through her. "Kinda late for a rancher who gets up early every morning. Or do you have special powers? Like your stainless-steel throat. You don't need sleep?"

"No," he said, and his gaze held banked heat. "Contrary to popular belief, I'm very human."

Amy stared into his eyes, and felt a bone deep-connection with him resonate inside her. Her breath hitched, and an electric anticipation sizzled in the air.

His gaze drifted to her mouth as if he were struggling with an inner demon, and Amy's heart hammered against her rib cage. She was acutely aware of his naked chest beneath her palms, skin against skin, the whisper of a chance for more. For a millisecond she wondered if she should move away, but couldn't imagine moving from his warmth.

Lucas lowered his head slightly and Amy gave in to the drugging wanting sensation inside her. She lifted her mouth, and he took it.

His mouth was warm and supple as he rubbed hers. She parted her lips and giving a low sound of approval, he slid his tongue just inside her mouth, tasting and teasing. He coaxed her response with a subtle seductiveness that made her want more. He ran his tongue around the inner perimeter of her lips and she grew hot from the inside out. Her fingers instinctively massaged his well-developed pecs.

He rubbed his tongue with hers, slid his thumb down her neck to finger the tiny strap of her nightgown. Cocking his head to one side, he sought deeper, more intimate access as he continued to toy with the strap. Amy felt her breasts grow heavy with arousal, and she shifted as her blood pooled in all her sensitive places.

Lucas thrust his tongue inside her mouth, simulating how his body would take hers. She suckled his tongue, and Lucas pushed the strap off her shoulder, and skimmed his finger down her breast. At the same time he made love to her mouth, he rubbed his finger over her nipple.

She gasped at the electric sensations that coursed through her.

Pulling his mouth away, Lucas stared at her with fire in his eyes, his nostrils flaring. He nudged her down and replaced his finger with his mouth on her nipple. His tongue laved the turgid tip, and passion roared through her head. He slid his hands to her nightgown and between her thighs.

His hands and mouth were persuasive, but the raw need he emanated made her weak. Sinking her fingers into his crisp hair, she wriggled against him. Giving a low growl, he moved up her body. "So responsive," he murmured, sliding his fingers just inside her panties.

Amy bit her lip. Her body clamored to go further, to sink deeper into him, but some buried instinct of self-protection clanged like a loud bell inside her head. She covered his hand with hers. "Fast," she managed to say breathlessly.

His gaze, full of need and want, wrapped around her for a full moment. He swore under his breath, then shook his head. Pulling away, he moved from the bed in one smooth moment that left her feeling cold and exposed. She pulled her nightgown into place and lifted the covers to her shoulders.

"Crazy," he muttered, raking his hand through the same hair she'd touched just moments before. "Insane. I don't know what got into me," he said, looking at her. "I heard you when you were having your nightmare, but I didn't intend to—" He broke off. "Put it down to sexual deprivation and forget it happened," he said, and left her staring after him.

Stunned and insulted, Amy lay in bed for a half moment. *Crazy, insane.* She could buy that, but the notion that any woman could have aroused him raised her blood pressure. Tossing back the bedcovers, she jumped out of bed and stalked after him. He'd already closed the door on his room, but that didn't stop her. She rapped smartly on it, then pushed it open.

He stood by the window, the moon spilling over his tall, powerful form. Her heart dipped, but she tried to ignore the sensation. "Sexual deprivation," she said, moving toward him. "Are you telling me that the reason you kissed me had no emotional basis? That you're not attracted to me in the least?"

"Yes, to the first question. No to the second," he said bluntly. "It's been a long time since I've had sex."

"With your sparkling personality, I can understand why."

"I gave up sex after my wife died."

Amy suddenly felt two inches tall. "Oh," she said.

"Don't expect anything emotional from me," he warned. "I have nothing to give."

Amy felt a wave of pain emanate from him. The depth of his wound and his remote attitude grabbed at something inside her. He was so different from the man who had held her and kissed her with such passion just moments ago. "I'm not sure I can agree with that," she said, forcing herself to move toward him even though he couldn't be less welcoming. "If you had nothing to give, then you wouldn't have come to me when you heard me having a nightmare."

"It wasn't personal," he told her in a quiet voice.

A sharp stab slowed her pace toward him. "So you would have comforted anyone having a nightmare. That's okay. Does that mean you would have kissed anyone, too?"

He gave a heavy sigh. "Don't take any of it personally. I'm not used to having a woman like you around the house all the time." He raked his hand through his hair and looked over her shoulder. "I'm sorry it happened."

I'm sorry it happened. I'm sorry I held you. Nothing personal. Nothing personal was her worst nightmare. If there was one thing Amy didn't want with a man, it was a temporary burst of passion. She wanted a relationship that would last, something worth keeping. A knot formed in her throat and she followed his gaze to his dresser where a photo sat. She walked toward the photograph to better see it. A beautiful blond woman wearing a lace wedding dress smiled with happiness and confidence. Perfect smile, perfect features.

"Your wife?" Amy asked even though she already knew.

"Yeah," he said, keeping his distance.

"She's beautiful."

"Yeah," he said, and a silence full of grief and heavy emotions filled the room.

Confused, Amy didn't want to face Lucas at the moment. She didn't want to look at him, nor did she want him looking at her. She wanted to hide. "I'll go now," she said quietly, and left the room. Lucas was a good man. He just wasn't good for her.

Lucas didn't see Amy at all the next day. Long after nightfall, she was nowhere to be seen. That was good, he told himself as he looked outside the window. He didn't need her around messing with hormones he'd thought were dead. He didn't need her constant reminders of the Christmas season. Christmas might be a favorite time of the year for others, but for him it meant loss. He didn't need her around upsetting his routine and making him feel...alive.

Lucas swore under his breath. The phone rang, distracting him from his dark thoughts. He picked it up, and his sister was on the other end of the line.

"You need to go into town to Lucky's," Debra said without preamble.

Lucas glanced at the clock. It was after 10:00 p.m. Lucky's was the only bar in town. "Why?"

"Because the Christmas carolers went there after they finished singing, and Dan Arthur is after Amy. I just know he's going to have too much to drink, and he'll end up doing something lewd and insulting."

Small-town gossip spread faster than a five-alarm fire. "Deb, you're being a busybody," Lucas said.

"I'm protecting my children's education. Amy is the best teacher we've ever had here, and nobody wants to lose her."

"Then why don't you go to Lucky's?" Lucas asked.

"Because I'm not big or hairy enough to be threatening to Dan. A man needs to do this."

Lucas rolled his eyes. "Don't you think Amy can handle this kind of thing herself?"

"Maybe," Debra conceded. "But just in case she can't, I think you should be there."

"And what exactly am I supposed to do?"

"Look big and threatening to Dan and give Amy a ride home."

Lucas shook his head. "I'm settled in for the night. I'm not going to Lucky's because *you* are afraid Dan Arthur is going to turn into a raging bull in rut with poor little Amy."

"Lucas Bennet, if we lose Amy because you wouldn't do your part in taking care of her, then I promise you I will send all of my children to *your* house every day for you to teach them. Goodbye," she said, and hung up.

Amy wasn't feeling very Christmasy. The cold wind whipped through her as if she weren't dressed in layer on top of layer. Trudging down the lane from town, she adjusted her knit cap and wondered if she should be walking toward Lucas's house or not.

She had thought the outing tonight would take the sting out of his *apology* for kissing her. She snarled in distaste. The Christmas carol part had helped, but sharing a hot toddy with Dan Arthur afterward to fortify her feminine ego hadn't been one of her better choices. Dan had already been pushy, and after a few drinks, he'd become grabby. She'd felt as if she'd been fighting off an octopus, and when she'd decided to leave, he'd protested loudly. He insisted on driving her to his house for them to talk, but Amy knew he didn't want to talk, so she'd left the bar.

Lucas lived too far from town for her to walk the entire way, but Amy thought she might be able to stop at one of her fellow carolers' homes and get a ride. There were no cars on the road because, with the exception of Lucky's, the town had closed.

Fighting her horrid mood, she belted out "Rudolph the Red-nosed Reindeer," as she continued walking against the brisk winter wind.

Thirty minutes later, her voice grew raspy, her jaw shivered, and she couldn't feel her toes. Her nose was running.

A truck, the first vehicle she'd seen since leaving Lucky's, pulled alongside her. Amy was so cold she would consider accepting a ride from her worst nightmare.

The driver-side window whirred downward and Lucas looked out at her.

Her worst nightmare, she thought. Close. She didn't want any more favors from him, even a ride, but the seductive promise of warmth won over pride.

"Want a ride?" he asked.

She nodded and strode to the other side of his truck. He pushed the door open for her and she climbed in. Heat roared from the vents and warmth immediately enveloped her.

"Want to tell me what happened?" he asked.

"Not really," she said, rubbing her hands together and looking away from him. "Mind if I change the heat vents?"

"No."

As soon as he muttered the word, she flipped the controls so that heat flowed from the lower and upper vents. She stuck her face in front of one of them, relishing the warm air.

"Problem with Dan Arthur?" he ventured.

"Yes," she said, feeling she owed him a limited explanation since he'd rescued her from the cold. "He had too much to drink at Lucky's and got a little—" She broke off, searching for the right word. "Pushy." She pulled off her glove and wiggled her hand in front of the vent. "Oh, that's wonderful."

"Dan was wonderful?" he asked.

She shook her head. "No. The heat is wonderful. I don't want to talk about Dan. He's not going to be very happy with me when he finds out I took his keys."

"Why did you take his keys?"

She pulled off her other glove and wiggled her other hand in front of the vent. "You have no idea how good this feels."

The near-sexual purr in her voice slid under Lucas's skin. "Dan's keys," he prompted.

She sighed, pulled off her hat and poked her face in front of one of the vents again. "I couldn't let him drive, so I took his keys when he went to the bar to buy a drink for me."

"If you took his keys, why didn't you just drive his car home?"

She made a face. "He's an attorney and he'd probably sue me or call the sheriff if I took his car. He'd have a tougher time going after me just for keys. I'll return them tomorrow."

"I'll take them back for you," Lucas said, anger burning in his gut. "What kind of man lets a woman walk miles in the freezing cold at night?"

"Since I sneaked out of the bar, he didn't really know I would be walking in the freezing cold. In fact," she added dryly, "he invited me to stay overnight at his house."

Lucas scowled. His sister had been right. He felt Amy's gaze on him.

"I was lucky you drove by," she said. "What brought you out tonight?"

"Neighbor called. Asked me to check on something," he hedged, then pulled into his driveway. He turned the corner of the drive and stopped in front of the house. "Let's get you inside."

She shot him a gaze full of reluctance. "I don't want to."

He arched a dark eyebrow. "Why?"

"Your house is cold. It's warm here."

He heard a tinge of feminine pique in her voice. Watching her wrap her arms around herself, he suspected she was talking about more than room temperature. She was probably talking about him. "I'll turn the heat up."

When she said nothing, he sighed. He shouldn't care squat if she wanted to camp in his truck the rest of the night. "C'mon. I'll build a fire."

She threw him a look of skepticism laced with a sexual dare that hit him like an unexpected undercut. "Are you sure you know how to build a fire and keep it burning?"

CHAPTER FOUR

STOP BEING NICE to me, Amy wanted to say to Lucas after he quickly built a fire in the wood stove insert, then situated her in front of it. *I don't want to like you.* He gave her a blanket, disappeared for a few minutes, then returned to offer her a mug of hot chocolate.

"I used your mix in the glass canister on the counter," he said, leaning next to the mantel.

Amy took a sip and the liquid kicked and burned all the way down. She cleared her throat. "I think you added something."

His mouth lifted in a lazy half grin. "A couple shots of bourbon. I figured you could use it. You've had a rough night."

His hair slightly tousled, he stood in casual attention-getting ease, wearing a flannel shirt and jeans that molded to his powerful thighs. She sighed and took a deep gulp of her cocoa. If he were uglier or meaner, she wouldn't find him so utterly compelling. Maybe if she didn't look at him, that would help keep her defenses in place. "Thank you," she said, closing her eyes and leaning her head back against the chair.

"You're welcome," he said quietly. "Warm enough?"

"Yes," she said, even though she knew he could make her a lot warmer. She took another sip. She'd never been a big drinker, but the sweet cocoa countered the bitterness of the alcohol. She took another sip and felt some of the tension leave her body.

"I walked past your room and noticed you hung some kind of ball over your door."

Amy immediately stiffened and opened her eyes to meet his gaze. "It's not a hint," she told him. "It's not personal."

Confusion wrinkled his brow. "What is it?"

"It's one of my most treasured possessions and, no matter where I've been, I have hung it every Christmas since I was six."

"You still haven't told me what it is," he said.

She paused a moment, reluctance holding her tongue. "It's a holiday kissing ball," she finally admitted in a low voice. "I've been working on it since I was six years old. A lady came to the children's home where I lived and helped us make them." A wave of nostalgia passed through her. "She told me she wanted to keep me, but she couldn't."

"Why not?"

"She was sick. She visited me several times, but then she died that next year."

"That must have been tough."

"Yeah," she agreed. "But she was one of those people that I was lucky to meet even if it was only going to be for a short time. She knew that Christmas was going to be her last, but she was determined to make the best of it. Even though she knew her time was running out, she made sure it counted. I was young, but old enough to be impressed, and I wanted to be like her." She closed her eyes, remembering that wonderful feeling of being wanted. "I felt so special that she could want me."

Amy felt the silence stretch between them and took a long sip from her hot chocolate. "Oops. I'm getting all sentimental and I'm probably making you very uncomfortable, so I'll stop. Tell the truth, that kissing ball is the gaudiest thing you've ever seen, isn't it?"

He looked at her in consternation, then chuckled and shook his head. "It's vivid," he said, as if he were straining to find the right description.

"Don't be kind about my kissing ball," she said. "Martha Stewart would need a tranquilizer if she took one look at it. There's something on that kissing ball from just about every stage of my growing up years."

"Really," he said, looking at her, then leaving the room.

"Where are you—" She broke off and shrugged, then took one last swallow of her hot cocoa.

He returned to the room with the kissing ball dangling from his hand. "Inquiring minds want to know. Why the black ribbon and skull and crossbones?"

Surprised by his interest, but too relaxed by the

cocoa-with-kick to be overly self-conscious, she smiled. "My very brief Goth period."

"Goth," he echoed in disbelief.

"Yeah, it's when I died my hair black, wore all black clothes and a black leather choker and bracelets."

He wrinkled his nose in distaste.

"Mercifully brief," she said, and pointed to the tiny pony charms. "That was my pony period. I asked Santa for a pony for Christmas. He said I was a little too young to care for one by myself, but perhaps when I was older, I could have one. Shrewd guy. Knew how to cover his posterior without totally mashing my dreams."

Lucas nodded. "What about the sparkles?"

"Magic phase. I wanted to change the world," she said with deadpan seriousness. "By being a fairy."

Lucas cleared his throat to cover a chuckle.

She narrowed her eyes at him. "You're not laughing, are you?"

Lucas took in the sight of her hair sticking out in at least four different directions, smudged mascara beneath one eye, and her bad-girl mouth trying to be stern but not succeeding. She wasn't pretty, but she was fascinating. Her Christmas Pollyanna attitude got on his nerves, but he understood it a little better now. And she was right about the kissing ball. It was the most gosh-awful conglomeration of color, fabric, and doohickeys he'd ever seen, but through her stories it, too, became oddly fascinating.

He'd hated the lost look he'd seen in her eyes when

he'd picked her up on the side of the road. That was why he'd started the fire and fixed the cocoa. That was why he'd asked her about the kissing ball—to distract her. For himself, he couldn't be less interested.

"What about the lace?"

She winced. "Bride stage. I wore a veil for about three months."

"When did that stage end?"

"When I found out that boys pay more attention to football games than they do to girls. Tommy Vincent kissed me in the coatroom at school, but when I asked him to come to my birthday party, he said he would rather play ball with his friends than eat cake and ice cream with mine."

"Kissed you in the coatroom," he repeated, filled with the unsettling image of kissing the grown-up Amy in a coatroom.

She nodded. "I have never had a face that would launch a thousand ships," she said, referring to the legendary beauty of Helen of Troy, "but when Tommy Vincent kissed me, I felt like the bomb. A good kisser can knock a girl off her feet."

It irritated him for her to think less of herself. She wasn't classically pretty. She was more, better in some strange indefinable way. "Don't you remember that beauty's in the eye of the beholder?"

"Or in the case of my situation tonight, beauty's in the eye of the beer holder," she wisecracked with a gamine grin, then met his gaze and sighed. Her smile fell and hints of seductive emotion glinted in her eyes. "You should go to bed, now."

"Oh, really," he returned, surprised at her abrupt suggestion. "Why?"

"It's late and you have to get up early because you are a Type A rancher, and…" Her voice dipped and faded. She caught her upper lip with the edge of her teeth and Lucas was distracted once again by hot visuals involving her mouth and his body.

"And?" he prompted.

"For a man who I'm sure is distantly related to Ebenezer Scrooge, you are very hot," she said with a feminine frankness that was so sexy he felt an immediate surge of arousal. "You've been very kind, but I shouldn't take it personally."

For one intense visceral moment, even though he'd warned her off him, he wanted her to take it personally. He wanted to wipe out the memory of Tommy Vincent's kiss. He wanted to sink inside her and devour her honest need.

He wanted. And that wasn't good. That now-familiar edgy feeling of deprivation ate at him again. Steeling himself against it, he pushed it aside, but it was getting more difficult.

He handed her the kissing ball and stood. "G'night," he said, taking in the inviting sight of her wrapped in a blanket relaxing in front of the fire. As he climbed the steps, his mind taunted him with a picture of stripping off her clothes and warming her all the way through.

* * *

Over the next two days, Lucas vacillated between his usual seasonal brooding and his reluctant attraction to Amy. She was like a bad virus that affected all his senses. When he entered the house, he listened for her throaty laughter. He stood closer to her than he should just so he could inhale her sweet, sexy scent. He didn't know what soap she used, but it reminded him of clean, bare, feminine skin. Every once in a while, she accidentally rubbed against him as she walked past, putting his nerve endings on high alert. When she brushed her tongue over her lips, he remembered how she'd tasted, how she'd felt during that forbidden night when he'd allowed himself to taste and touch her. The trouble with sampling Amy was that a sample hadn't been enough. He wanted to make an entire meal of her.

After Flora set out a dinner he ate by himself in his office, Lucas took his dishes into the kitchen and walked into the den as he flipped through his mail. Although the room was quiet, the tree screamed holiday memories at him, so he quickly headed back to his office.

Amy whipped around the corner with a laundry basket in her arms and slammed right into him.

"Oh!" The laundry flew out of the basket onto the floor.

Lucas instinctively shot out his hands to steady her.

Jolted, she looked at him with chagrin. "Sorry, I didn't see you coming." She met his gaze and stood perfectly still, sensual awareness gradually seeping into her eyes. Glancing down at his hands on her waist, she cleared her throat and stepped backward. "Sorry," she said, glancing down. "I've made a mess."

"No harm. Nobody got hurt," he said, bending down to help her collect her clothing. He picked up a wild striped sock and a shirt.

Amy shook her head as she scooped up part of the clothing. "I'm glad I hadn't folded yet. It looks like a laundry bomb went off. Are you going to your sister's house tomorrow night?"

Distracted by the black bra he found in his hands, he tossed it into the basket. He couldn't help remembering how responsive her breasts had been to his touch. "Why would I go to my sister's house?"

Amy looked at him in disbelief. "It's her Christmas party. She said she holds a big bash with food and dancing every year. Don't you usually go?"

Uncomfortable, Lucas shrugged. "It depends on what else I have going on. I'm not a party animal."

"But this is *your sister's* party," she said as if she couldn't imagine him not attending.

Lucas absently picked up a silky garment and glanced down at it. A black thong. His mouth went bone dry. Despite her usual casual attire of jeans and big sweaters, he could easily visualize Amy dressed in the black bra, thong, heels and nothing else. He ran his thumb over the skimpy thong, imagining the way her skin would feel as he slipped the garment from her hips, down her silky thighs.

After a moment, he realized she had turned silent.

He glanced up and saw her watching him as he held the garment that touched her where he wanted to. She bit her lip and her eyes darkened with banked desire.

"Do you really wear these?" he had to ask.

She cleared her throat. "They don't cause panty lines when I wear something that fits."

"So the idea is to make you look like you're wearing nothing underneath," he said, feeling a surge of heat. Lord help him, he hadn't thought about women's undergarments in years.

"I guess," she said, pulling the thong from his hands and putting it in the basket. "Debra tells me the party is dressy."

He nodded, rising with her as she stood. "She likes giving everybody an excuse to dress up at Christmas time. The women like it."

"The men don't," Amy concluded with a grin.

"The men don't mind looking at the women," he said.

"Hmm," she said with a nod. "Well, I'll let you get back to what you were doing while I go fold my laundry. And maybe I'll see you tomorrow night at your sister's party."

Or not, he thought as he watched her climb the stairs, her shapely bottom swaying from side to side, conjuring an erotic image with that black thong.

His distraction with her irritated him. After a cold shower late at night, he wondered how to get her out of his system. A rebellious part of him asked him why he shouldn't take what he wanted. They were both adults.

It didn't help that he often caught her looking at him with sensual curiosity just before she glanced away.

Lucas told himself that just because he took her to bed didn't mean he had to take her down the aisle.

He didn't want to hurt her or lead her on, though, and he knew she wasn't the kind of woman who separated her body from her feelings. That knowledge, however, was part of the attraction. If a man was able to tap Amy's passion, what kind of lover would she be? The possibilities taunted him like a forbidden fantasy in the midnight hour, luring him, irritating him, frustrating the living daylights out of him.

Reading the newspaper the following evening, he caught sight of Amy as she fluffed her hair and stuck her arms in the sleeves of a winter coat. Her long slim legs were encased in black stockings, and the hem of her little black velvet dress stopped three inches above her knees. He wondered if she was wearing the black bra and thong he'd held in his fingers the night before. Surreptitiously searching for panty lines beneath her dress, he saw none and felt a slow heat build from the inside out.

Her eyes sparkled, and she'd emphasized her full lips with red lipstick. It occurred to him that he couldn't imagine any man in the community of Kent who wouldn't be angling for a kiss from Amy under his sister's mistletoe. The notion irritated him.

She glanced up at him and smiled. "Still undecided about the party?"

"I may go over later," he said, still not willing to

commit himself. He hadn't gone to a Christmas party since his wife died.

"You should," she said as she pulled on her gloves. "It'll be fun. Bye." She whirled out of the foyer, leaving her feminine scent in her wake.

Fun, Lucas thought. Christmas hadn't been fun for him for years. Why should it be now?

Debra's face fell when she looked past Amy standing in the doorway to her lovely home. "I'm so glad you came, but I was hoping…"

"That Lucas would come, too," Amy finished for her as she stepped into Debra's beautifully decorated, large home. "He said he might, but I wouldn't put money on it. I've never met a man less inclined to celebrate Christmas than your brother."

Debra squeezed Amy's shoulders and gave a sad smile. "It's true. Ever since his wife died a few days before Christmas, he hasn't—"

"At Christmas," Amy interjected, giving Debra a double take. Her heart squeezed tight in her chest. No wonder Lucas acted like a grinch. Every year represented a painful reminder. "I knew his wife had died a few years ago, but not during Christmas."

Debra nodded as she took Amy's coat. "Lucas has a Superman complex. Even though his wife was miles away when her car crashed, he somehow thinks he should have done something to protect her."

Amy remembered the photograph of Lucas's wife on his dresser and felt her stomach twist. "They must have had a wonderful relationship for him to still be in love with her."

Debra wore a neutral look on her face. "I don't know. Some people suffer from survivor guilt more strongly than others. But I can't solve this for Lucas, although heaven knows I've tried." She gave Amy a once-over. "I'm envious. You wear that tiny black dress so easily, and I look like a model for a dancing Christmas tree ornament."

Amy laughed and shook her head. "You look beautiful. You have the pregnant glow."

"New makeup," she confided and ushered her into the large formal living room filled with the citizens of Kent. "Let me introduce you to a few local bachelors. It'll be fun for me to watch them salivate over you."

"You're exaggerating, but it's nice to hear," Amy said, thinking again of how her appearance couldn't ever compare to the beauty of Lucas's former wife. She frowned at the thought. Comparing appearances had never gotten her anywhere, so she wasn't going to start that again. "Lead on," she said, determined to forget about Lucas.

Within a half hour, three men had asked for her phone number. Unfortunately, since she was temporarily living at Lucas's house, she didn't really have a number except her cell phone. All three men solved the problem by giving her their business cards with home phone numbers scrawled on the back.

Along with several other couples, Debra shooed Amy and Mr. Business Card number three, Frank

Ginter, into the center of the room to dance to the sounds of Harry Connick Jr.

Amy looked into Frank's friendly eyes and couldn't help noticing his fair, spare eyelashes. He wasn't as tall as Lucas, and his shoulders weren't—

Stifling a groan, Amy stopped her useless comparisons. She'd told herself not to think about Lucas tonight. She'd told herself to flirt, to focus her undivided attention on whatever was happening at this very moment.

This very moment, over Frank's shoulder she spotted Lucas entering the room dressed in a crisp white shirt, a dark burgundy tie, black slacks and suspenders.

Weeooo. Amy had a thing about a man in suspenders.

She felt his gaze collide with hers and wrap around her like a hot encircling flame.

She stumbled. "Oops."

Frank steadied her with a smile. "No problem. Song's over. Would you like a drink?"

"Good idea," she said, determined to keep her gaze fixed on Frank's kind face. Her ornery peripheral vision caught a half glimpse of Lucas. The man was entirely too watchable. Out of the corner of her eye, she saw Debra give her brother an enthusiastic embrace, which he returned.

Her attention divided, Amy blindly allowed Frank to guide her toward one of the refreshment tables. He whirled around and smiled. "Merry Christmas, Amy." Then he lowered his head and quickly kissed her.

Confused, she stared at him.

"Mistletoe," he said, pointing upward.

She looked up and saw the familiar greenery. "Oh, Merry Christmas," she said because she could think of nothing else to say and turned to get her punch.

Although it took some effort, she managed to escape intense attention by ducking into the kitchen. She spotted Debra ruffling the hair of one of her children as she looked out the window.

"One more treat, then off to bed," Debra said, then met Amy's gaze. "Teacher, please tell this little elf she'll get sick if she eats too many more Christmas cookies."

"Miss Winslow!" the little girl said, her happy face covered with crumbs.

Amy recognized her student and smiled. "Hilary, you look like you're having a wonderful Christmas."

Hilary gave a big nod. "That was our assignment, Mom."

"But if you get a tummy ache from eating too many goodies, it's going to be hard to complete your assignment," Amy reminded the little girl.

"Okay," Hilary said reluctantly. "Did you see that my mom is gonna have a baby?"

"Sure did," Amy said. "Are you excited?"

"I want a sister since I already have a brother."

Debra ruffled Hilary's hair again. "We'll see what we can do. Bedtime in fifteen minutes," she said.

"Oh, *Mom*," Hilary protested.

"Or now," Debra said.

"Fifteen minutes," Hilary said and ran out of the kitchen.

"She's great in class. Whenever I ask questions, her hand shoots up first," Amy said.

"Well, she absolutely loves Miss Winslow. I think you gave a good holiday assignment. I just wish everyone would follow your instructions," Debra said, tilting her head meaningfully toward the window.

Amy stepped closer and saw Lucas standing outside on the patio decorated with tiny white lights. The strong solitary image tugged at her heart. "Tough time of year for him," she murmured.

"Yeah. I keep hoping for a change," Debra said with a sigh. "I should return to the party." She hugged Amy. "I'm glad you came."

"Me, too," Amy said, then her attention returned to Lucas as Debra left the kitchen with a platter. He probably preferred his solitude, she thought, unbidden instinct nudging her to reach out to him.

Go, a soft insistent voice inside her said.

Don't go, the loud, self-protective, practical voice ordered.

Go. She couldn't bear his loneliness.

Don't go. He wouldn't want her intrusion.

Torn, Amy bit her lip. She closed her eyes, but his image remained, stamped in her mind. No escape. Warning bells clanging loudly inside her, she walked out to join him.

CHAPTER FIVE

"Hi," she said breathlessly, the winter air freezing her lungs. She had hoped to muster something more original or clever, but she felt edgy approaching him.

Lucas immediately turned to meet her gaze. "Hi," he said. The music playing in the den was piped outside.

No conversational help from Lucas, she thought, wrapping her arms around herself. "Beautiful night," she said, nodding toward the stars. "Freezing, but beautiful."

He nodded. "Why'd you come outside?"

Because you looked lonely and I couldn't bear it. She bit her tongue, then forced herself to smile. "Because I had escaped to the kitchen and saw you out here so I wanted to say hi."

"I saw you with Frank. He made good use of the mistletoe."

"He took me by surprise," she said, and moved closer. "I wasn't sure you would come."

"I wasn't, either. Not a party animal."

"You dress the part well."

He raised an eyebrow and almost smiled. "Is that so?"

Amy rolled her eyes. "As if you didn't know every woman was drooling over you."

He chuckled in disbelief. "The only female I saw drooling was a teething six-month-old baby." He paused. "*Every* woman was drooling," he repeated, studying her intently. "Does that include you?"

Amy felt a rush of discomfort. Her cheeks heated, and she prayed the darkness hid her telltale sign of embarrassment. Keep it casual, she told herself. "I'm not blind. For a cranky rancher, you're pretty amazing eye candy."

He blinked and dipped his head as if he didn't understand. "Eye candy. No one has ever called me eye candy."

She lifted her chin. "Maybe not to your face."

He chuckled again. "Wanna dance?"

Amy's jaw dropped. Shock ran through her. "Pardon me?"

"Dance," he said, moving closer, his eyes full of things that made her heart bump. "Wanna dance?"

"Uh, sure," she said and stood there like a post.

Lucas extended his arms and drew her against him. The sounds of another Harry Connick Jr. song drifted through the outdoor speaker as Amy swayed in rhythm with Lucas. His shoulder was strong beneath her hand, and her head fit just beneath his chin. She inhaled deeply and was convinced the scent of his aftershave was formulated to inspire a woman to strip off her clothes and throw herself at him.

Amy closed her eyes and allowed herself a moment

to play a game of pretend. What would it be like to be the woman Lucas wanted more than anything? How would it feel to be the object of his affection?

Bittersweet longing slid through her and twisted her heart. To be wanted by him. To see passion and love in his eyes for her. To hear words of love from his mouth. To be the woman who made him smile.

She wondered if he had danced this way with his wife. She wondered if he longed for his wife tonight. The ache inside Amy spread to her throat and stomach.

As his thighs rubbed against hers, she wanted to lean forward to kiss his throat, to taste his skin. She shouldn't be thinking these things. If she did what was good and safe, she would wipe all these crazy, impossible thoughts from her head. When it came to Lucas, even a few moments of the game of pretend was dangerous.

Yet Amy couldn't find it in herself to walk away. Deep down, she knew he was hurting and lonely.

Following an impulse, she pulled back. "I think we should leave and try to find some moose tracks ice cream."

He looked down at her as if she were crazy. "Ice cream? I thought you said it was cold."

"It is," she said. "But sometimes you just need some moose tracks ice cream."

"There's nothing rational in that statement," he said, clearly not convinced.

"That's the beauty of it. Irrational, impulsive enjoyment." She paused. "Or we could always rejoin the party."

He frowned. "Wild-goose chase for ice cream or a party. Great options," he muttered, then shook his head. "We might as well try to find this deer droppings ice cream."

"Moose tracks," she corrected with a chuckle. "We brought separate cars, so—"

"Let's take mine. We can pick yours up in the morning."

"Okay, I need to get my coat."

He shook his head. "If you go back in there, you'll never get out before midnight. Frank will grab you and hold you hostage by the mistletoe."

"I'll freeze," she complained as he led her around the perimeter of the house.

"I'll turn the heater on high."

Lucas figured he had covered about eighty-seven miles and visited seven backwater convenience stores before they'd hit pay dirt. So now they sat in his truck with the heater blasting in the parking lot of Rob's Hop-In. He was so hot he'd tossed his tie and unbuttoned his shirt down to his waist and wanted to ditch the rest of his clothes. His body temperature wasn't exclusively the result of his truck's roaring heater.

Just across from him, Amy sat on the seat in her black stocking feet with her legs splayed to the side, making her little velvet dress ride up her thighs. That was bad enough, but if he watched her lick the spoon from her carton of ice cream one more time, he thought he might explode.

She dipped the plastic utensil into the carton and lifted a heaping spoonful of ice cream. Lucas felt a trickle of sweat roll down his back. He prayed she wouldn't eat it. He prayed she wouldn't lick that spoon with her wicked pleasure-promising tongue.

She smiled and extended the spoon. "Wanna bite?"

He let out a hiss of breath. "Of moose droppings," he muttered, still unable to believe that he'd run all over two counties to get ice cream. He had lost his mind, and it was all because of Christmas. He never should have gone to his sister's party.

"Moose tracks," Amy corrected and lifted the spoon closer to his lips. "Better hurry or it'll drip."

He covered her hand with his and lifted it to his mouth. The creamy combination of vanilla, chocolate fudge, and peanut butter filled his mouth while Amy licked her own lips. He stifled a growl. "Not bad," he said.

"Moose tracks ice cream has magical restorative powers. I discovered it in college," she said, lifting another spoonful of ice cream to his lips.

He guided the spoon into his mouth and a nudge of curiosity. "Who introduced you?"

She furrowed her eyebrow in confusion. "Who introduced me to whom?"

"Who introduced you to Moose Droppings?"

"Tracks," she said again with a mock-glare. "A group of girls in the dorm introduced me."

Lucas relaxed slightly. "Hen party," he said with a wry grin.

She looked affronted. "We were a group of intelligent, liberated women discussing—"

"Men and PMS," he finished and took the spoon from her when she gaped at him. He dipped a spoonful and rubbed the bottom of the spoon on her lower lip. She sucked the ice cream into her mouth and he felt a visceral tug in his gut. He wanted to see her mouth on his flesh.

She lifted her chin. "We were discussing British Literature."

"And?"

"Men," she reluctantly admitted.

"And?"

"Women's issues," she said in a snooty voice.

Lucas threw back his head and roared with laughter. Amy stared at him.

"What?" he asked.

"You should do that more often," she said.

"Do what?"

"Laugh," she said. "It makes you look so— It's so wow— You look—" She broke off and shook her head. "Then again, maybe you shouldn't."

"I look what?" he demanded, curious about the look in her eyes.

"Never mind," she said, eating another bite of ice cream.

He covered her hand. "You started the sentence. Now finish it."

"I don't want to."

"Tough. You owe me. I went all over the place to get you ice cream."

"I thought this was a gift from the heart," she said with a mock-lovelorn expression.

"It wasn't. Finish the sentence," he said, refusing to be dissuaded.

She rolled her eyes. "Okay. If you answer one of my questions first, I'll answer your question."

He nodded. "Ask your question."

"Name three things you want for Christmas," she said.

Drawing a complete blank, Lucas groaned and wiped his hand over his face. "All I want for Christmas is for it to be over."

"Sorry, Ebenezer, that's not an answer."

Lucas swore. He couldn't remember the last time someone had asked him what he wanted for Christmas. Even his sister knew better than to ask him such a question. Racking his brain, he threw out the first things that came to mind. "Socks, a new rack for my truck, and… a Maserati."

Amy stared blankly at him. "Socks," she echoed. "You want socks and a new rack for your truck for Christmas. That's the lousiest Christmas wish list I've ever heard."

He grinned. "Don't forget the Maserati. Your turn."

She took another bite of ice cream and slowly licked the spoon clean, torturing Lucas with her tongue so much he nearly jerked the plastic utensil out of her hand.

"When you laughed," she finally said in a low voice, "you looked very, very sexy. Satisfied?"

"Not nearly," he said and gave in to what he'd wanted to do all evening. He took her impudent, sassy, drive-him-crazy mouth with his.

With Lucas's lips on hers, Amy felt herself melt into the leather seat. The texture of his mouth was both firm and supple, irresistibly sensual. He nibbled at her with his lips as if he wanted to consume her. His tongue slid over hers, invading, inviting. He tasted like ice cream, felt like sin, and she drew his tongue more deeply into her mouth.

She was peripherally aware that Lucas moved the nearly empty carton of ice cream from her hand and pushed back his seat. Before she knew it, he pulled her onto his lap. One of his hands slid up her thighs, and her head began to spin.

The kiss turned carnal, cranking up her internal heat. He shifted so that his hardness intimately rubbed where she grew damp and swollen. He guided her bottom in a primitive mind-robbing rhythm that snatched her breath and good sense.

"This is crazy," she breathed, but opened her mouth for his kiss.

"Damn, you get me hot." He squeezed her bottom and groaned again, this time in frustration. "Panty hose should be outlawed."

Pulling back, he stared into her with eyes nearly black with arousal. "I want you," he said, his rough bluntness sending a shocking but euphoric adrenaline through her veins.

He lowered his lids, and his outrageous eyelashes concealed his expression. "I want you naked in my bed. Under me. I want inside you."

His raw need echoed inside her. She moaned as he took her mouth again for a quick, illicit caress.

"If it weren't the dead of winter, I would take you right now in this damn truck," he muttered.

The urgency coursing through her turned her equilibrium upside down. Lucas had no idea how much his agreement to find moose tracks ice cream had weakened her defenses. It was a small thing, but his determination to please her filled her head with crazy thoughts. Thoughts like maybe, just maybe, if Lucas wanted her, maybe he could grow to love her. Maybe he could grow to need her.

Dangerous thoughts, but now, in his arms with matching need pulsing from him to her, Amy couldn't turn him away. "Maybe we should go back to the house," she said.

His gaze met hers. "You need to know that I'll do everything I can to get you in my bed. No-holds-barred."

Her stomach danced at the possibilities. She inhaled deeply. "You make me curious what no-holds-barred means."

"Hang around and you'll find out," he promised, reluctantly returning her to her seat. "Nothing will stop me except you."

He put the car in gear and drove toward his house. They said little, the air in the truck heavy with anticipation. He slid his hand behind her nape and caressed her with his fingers while he drove. Stopping the vehicle just before he turned onto his driveway, he tilted her chin upward while he lowered his mouth to hers for a scorching kiss that left no doubt of his need and intent.

A trickle of nerves skittered through Amy. "What about Flora?"

"She sleeps through everything."

Except a call from the emergency room, Amy learned within three minutes. Dressed in her robe, Flora greeted them at the door with the telephone in her hand.

"My niece has gone to the emergency room. She was in terrible pain. They don't know what's wrong with her."

"Which niece?" Lucas asked.

"Valerie. She has five children and—"

"Lives on the other side of St. Louis," Lucas recalled.

Flora nodded. "Her mother died a few years ago, and I don't have any children, so Valerie and I have become much closer. I realize I'll never take my sister's place, but if she needs me, then I will have to go."

Lucas squeezed Flora's shoulder. "If Valerie and her family need you, then I'll understand. I know you're upset, but you don't have all the information yet. You may get another call telling you she's fine."

Flora gave a long sigh. "You're right. I'm still worried, but you're right. You have to be the most rational, levelheaded man in the state."

Lucas looked at Amy, his gaze filled with irony, and she could see that he was thinking about how both of them had been anything but levelheaded just an hour ago when he'd wanted to make love in his truck. With Flora's crisis, Amy knew she and Lucas wouldn't be sharing a bed tonight. His gaze, however, promised the time would come.

Flora wrinkled her brown. "Where's your coat?" she asked Amy.

Heat rising to her cheeks, Amy didn't dare look at Lucas. She shrugged. "Crazy, but I walked right out of Debra's house without it." Diverting attention away from herself, Amy motioned toward the kitchen. "Let me fix you something to drink while you wait for your call."

"Oh, no," Flora protested, but allowed Amy to fix her a cup of herbal tea. Lucas and Amy kept Flora company until early morning. When both of them urged her to get some rest, Flora shook her head, insisting she couldn't sleep until she received word on her niece's condition.

Amy climbed the stairs to her guest room and pushed open the door. Lucas snagged her wrist and gently whirled her around to face him. He lowered his head and gave her a French kiss that made her dizzy.

Or maybe her dizziness was due to the lateness of the hour. *Wishful thinking.*

"This was just a temporary delay," he told her in a velvet voice that stroked her secret places.

"Or an opportunity to gain a little sanity," she said.

"Can you honestly say you don't want me?" he dared her.

"No, but—" She inhaled deeply and the scent of his aftershave slid past her protests. "But I can't honestly say it would be rational or levelheaded, either."

"You're right. It wouldn't," he said, running his finger over her bottom lip.

Amy barely resisted the urge to slide her tongue over his finger. She'd like to see him at least half as off-kilter as she felt.

"It sure as hell won't be sensible. It will just be unforgettable." He dropped his finger from her mouth, but his gaze lingered on her lips. "'Night, Amy."

She swallowed over her dry throat. "G'night," she said, and wondered how she could say no to this man. Especially when everything inside her wanted to say yes.

The following morning, Flora learned her niece had suffered appendicitis. The emergency surgery was a success, but her niece would still need help for a few days, so Flora left and assured Lucas she would return as soon as she could.

Not long after Lucas left to tend to the stock and Flora left for her niece's house, the snow began to fall.

Amy put a pot of homemade chowder on the burner and did some last-minute shopping on the Internet. Since moving to the community of Kent, she'd learned the value of Internet shopping.

The day wore on, and the snow continued to fall. Amy checked the weather forecast and heard the weatherman admit he had missed the mark with his prediction for a light winter snow. Kent, Missouri, was being hit with a blizzard.

As the hours passed, Amy told herself not to worry about Lucas. If any man could handle himself in a crisis, it was Lucas. When she looked out the window at the whiteout conditions, though, a knot formed in her stomach. What if he had hurt himself and couldn't get back?

Day turned to night, and Amy watched and worried. She ate a bowl of chicken corn chowder. Taking comfort in Cleo, she rubbed her cat and listened for the door. When the clock struck eight o'clock, she couldn't stand the images in her mind of Lucas hurt and freezing. Putting on so many layers of clothing she could barely walk, she grabbed a lantern and stomped through the fresh-fallen snow.

Lucas finished securing the horse barn for the harsh weather and stretched his back. He always kept a skeleton crew in the winter, and during Christmas most of his ranch hands visited their families. Ordinarily Lucas welcomed the distraction of long hours during the holidays, so he didn't mind the lack of help. This year, a different distraction burned inside him. This year, a warm woman waited for him in his home. He'd slept alone too long.

The door to the barn swung open, making him jump. Someone wrapped up like a mummy appeared in the doorway. A hat covered the head, a scarf shielded the face.

"What the hell—"

"I was worried about you," Amy said in a voice muffled by the scarf. She lowered the scarf slightly. "You were gone a long time and the snow kept falling, and I was afraid you were hurt and freezing to death."

His heart swelled at her concern. "I've been through plenty of these winters. I know how to handle myself."

She lifted a shoulder uncertainly. "I know, but just in case."

He shook his head. "You're not exactly Amazon Woman. What did you think you could do?"

"Rescue you?" she ventured doubtfully.

He turned his head and looked up at the barn ceiling for help from on high. This woman was the physical equivalent of an elf. "You shouldn't have come out. You could have gotten lost. It's not like you could carry me."

"I might could drag you," she said, lifting her chin a millimeter. "What was I supposed to do—leave you hurt and freezing to death?"

"I wasn't hurt or freezing."

"How was I supposed to know that?"

Unaccustomed to having anyone check on him, he

opened his mouth, then closed it. "You were supposed to trust that I can handle myself."

"That thought did occur to me."

"That's good to know," Lucas said dryly as he pulled on his gloves.

"But I just couldn't stand the idea of you hurt and freezing to death."

She was so wrong, but so earnest. Feeling an odd tug in his chest, he chuckled despite his frustration. "Next time just sit tight. I'll be okay. Now let's get back to the house."

As they walked through the windy, snowy night, his houselights shined like a beacon in the darkness. Lucas noticed Amy seemed to struggle with her progress through the snow. "You need me to carry you?"

In mummy mode again, she shook her head. "I'm okay, just slow. I put on a couple extra layers, and it's a little bulky," she said in a muffled voice. "Isn't your face freezing?"

"Nah. I haven't been out in the snow for a while."

"You don't look like you have on many clothes for a blizzard."

He chuckled to himself. "Looks like I can borrow from you if I need anything."

Slowing, she lowered her scarf a tad and glared at him. "You don't have to be smug."

"I'm warm-natured."

Her gaze darkened in feminine mystery. "Must be nice."

"Comes in handy in the winter."

"I'm sure you do," she said, and the husky tone in her voice affected his anatomy in a way that he'd previously considered impossible in a blizzard.

He helped her make a stiff-legged climb up the front porch steps. "You cleared the steps," he said, surprised.

"I kept coming out to sweep with the broom, so it didn't have a chance to accumulate."

He opened the door and immediately caught a whiff of something mouthwatering. "What do I smell?"

"Chicken corn chowder."

His stomach growled in protest of his hunger.

Amy stomped the snow off her boots, stepped inside the door and began to peel off her clothes. First the gloves and scarf, then the hat, then the jacket. She pulled her wool sweater over her head and her red hair crackled with electricity. Next she ditched her wind pants, sweatpants, and tugged off her turtleneck. She stood before him in a long sleeve black silk T-shirt and a pair of black stretch pants.

Lucas glanced down at the pile of clothes in amazement. "No wonder you couldn't walk," he muttered. "Well?" he said expectantly.

"Well what?"

"Don't stop now."

CHAPTER SIX

A MY'S HEART somersaulted at the predatory look in Lucas's eyes. This man was hungry for more than food. She pulled off two of three pairs of socks and regarded him carefully. "I'll get your bowl of chowder," she said and hightailed it to the kitchen, fanning her face as she stepped out of his sight.

She bit her lip as she ladled the chowder into a bowl. She poured a cup of coffee and turned around to find him less than a foot away from her. She jumped in surprise, barely saving the chowder from a spill. "I didn't hear you." Her heart was beating too freakin' loudly. "Here," she said, extending the steaming bowl to him. "Eat this."

He gave her a considering glance. "Okay, thanks."

He gobbled two helpings of chowder in the den while she sat gingerly on the edge of a chair. Lucas built a fire, then took his bowl to the kitchen. Amy's nerves stretched tight when he was gone longer than a minute. Rising from the chair, she walked to the tree and stared at it, anticipation zipping through her. She heard his footsteps behind her, but didn't turn. She felt the warmth of his body when he stopped inches from her.

"You're nervous, aren't you?"

"Not really," she said, turning to face him.

"You have reason to be."

Her stomach dipped. "Why?"

"Because I'm gonna get you."

She gulped and tried to hide it by tossing her head. "In order for you to get me, I have to choose to be gotten."

"And are you?" he asked in a velvet voice that slid through her like rum.

She took a deep breath.

He pulled his hand from his back and lifted her homemade kissing ball above her head. Amy knew she was sunk.

He lowered his mouth to hers. "Gotcha," he muttered against her lips, and kissed her. Scooping her up in his arms, he carried her to the rug in front of the fireplace. "I want to see the firelight on your hair and skin."

He made her feel beautiful when she knew she wasn't beautiful. "I'm not pretty," she said.

"You're the bomb," he told her. "And I'm not stopping until you say it."

"Say what?"

"You're the bomb."

"You're the bomb," she said. "But you already knew that."

He groaned and slid his hands under her silk T-shirt.

"I'm not stopping until you say the following words: *I am the bomb.*"

She gaped at him. "I don't know about that."

"You will soon enough," he promised, and pulled her T-shirt over her head. He didn't pause a beat before he unfastened her bra and slid his hands down to her stretch pants.

Amy had stopped breathing two minutes ago…her head was spinning. She wanted him to slow down and hurry up at the same time. He lowered his mouth to hers and dipped his tongue inside as he pushed both her leggings and panties down her legs. The combination of his warm hands on her body and his lips luring and seducing made her shiver.

"Cold?" he asked, pulling her against him.

She shook her head.

"Tell me what you like," he urged her, moving his lips down her throat.

Her heart rate jumped into overdrive. "Everything," she said breathlessly as his mouth slid to her breast. "Everything you do."

He met her gaze, and her secret wish that he could want her, even love her, seemed possible. In his arms, everything wonderful was possible. Following her heart, she unfastened his buttons with unsteady fingers. He took her mouth in an erotic kiss that distracted her.

"Don't stop," he muttered against her mouth, and she lowered her hands to his jeans and unbuttoned them. The whir of the zipper as she pulled it down kicked up the anticipation permeating the air between them.

He was going to take her. What he didn't know was that *she* also planned to take *him*. She slid her hand beneath his briefs and caressed his hard masculinity.

His breath came out in a hiss. "Careful."

"Why?" she asked, helping him push his jeans from his body.

"It's been a while, and it's going to be hard for me to go slow." She touched him again, and he shook his head. "Not yet," he insisted, and gently pushed her back on the floor. His mouth trailed a blazing path over her tight nipples and lower, while his fingers sought and found her hot spot.

Shocked at the power of the pleasure coursing through her, she arched upward, her body clamoring for more.

"You feel so good," he murmured, fondling her, turning her to liquid. "I can't wait to feel you wrapped around me," he said, plunging his finger inside her.

Amy shuddered and felt the waves of sensation take her over the edge. Gasping, she clung to the hard muscles of his shoulders. Just when she was ready to come down, he lowered his mouth and kissed her intimately. His wonderful, wicked tongue brought her to one climax, then another.

Twitching from the outrageous pleasure, she begged him to pause. "Stop," she managed to say. "Just for a minute. I can't—"

He moved up her body, his eyes nearly black with desire. "I love the sounds you make."

Amy reveled in the sensation of his delicious chest

hair against her sensitized nipples. She slid her hands over his powerful back, down to his hard buttocks.

He kissed her again, and she wiggled beneath him, wanting more. Shifting to her side, she lowered her hand to touch his hardness and found the first few drops of honeyed arousal. She spread the sensual lubricant over him, stroking him until he groaned, then she took her own trip down his body, running her tongue over his flat male nipples, pressing open-mouth kisses on his abdomen and lower.

"What are you doing?" he asked, his voice strained with need. "What—"

Amy boldly took him into her mouth and made love to him with her mouth.

He began to swear, and the sound was deliciously seductive to her ears. He turned her upside down so easily. She wanted to weave a fraction of the same magic over him.

"Amy," he said, his voice a combination of earthy huskiness and passion.

She swirled her tongue over him, and he swore again.

"That's it," he said, pulling her up his body and rolling them both over. Grabbing a packet of protection from his discarded jeans, he put it on and parted her thighs.

His eyes were so fierce with passion that she felt a twinge of fear. She needed just a little tenderness. She lifted her hand to his, and he paused. His gaze gentled a hair, and he twined his fingers through hers.

"You look afraid," he said.

"A little," she whispered. "You look like you're going to eat me alive."

He lowered his mouth to hers and gave her a kiss that combined an irresistible combination of compassion and desire. "I am. But I'll do my damnedest to make sure you like it," he said, and thrust inside her.

Her eyes widened at the sensual invasion, and she sucked in a quick breath.

"Problem?" He paused, studying her.

The way he looked at her made her feel as if he weren't just invading her body, but also her mind and heart. "You're big."

"Is that bad?" he asked, and she could feel his need to move permeating her.

"Kiss me again, and it won't be bad."

He took her mouth in an achingly slow sensual kiss, but didn't move a millimeter. His tongue dallied and seduced, his lips nipped at hers, he sucked her tongue into her mouth. Her body began to hum again, and she shifted restlessly beneath his.

As if he read her body like a book, he began to move in a hypnotic rhythm that made her crave more and more of him. Amy moaned and squeezed him intimately.

He groaned. "Those sounds you make," he muttered. "They're driving me—" He broke off, increasing the pumping rhythm.

She looked in his eyes and saw his primitive need mixed with something deeper, more powerful. With each thrust, she felt herself bound to him. She wanted everything with this man.

"You—are—so—beautiful," he said in a rough voice.

In that moment she believed him, and they both went soaring over the edge.

Moments passed before she caught her breath. Lucas moved to his side and she rolled over, curling against him. His naked skin pressed against hers, and with her hand on his chest, she could feel his heart pounding. She was so close, she almost felt as if she could climb inside him. Amy sighed at the emotions overflowing inside her.

"Is that a good sigh or a tired sigh?" he asked.

She pressed her face against his throat. "It's a *you're amazing* sigh."

"I could say the same about you."

Her heart turned over and she couldn't contain her secret smile. "You inspire me."

He slid his arms around her. "I didn't hear you say I am the bomb."

"You are the bomb."

He chuckled. "No. I didn't hear you say these words: *I am the bomb.*"

"Oh, well, you made me feel the bomb."

"Close but no cigar."

She pulled back slightly and met his warm gaze. "Maybe you can try again."

His eyes lit like twin flames. "I can do that," he said.

And he did. They eventually made it upstairs to his

bedroom, where they made love until early morning. While she slept, Lucas took care of the animals, then returned. She fixed breakfast, and with a foot of snow calling a halt to most outside activity, they spent the day in an isolated cocoon of conversation and lovemaking. Amy fell completely under his spell and wanted it to never end.

That night, they danced naked in the firelight, and he made love to her with a fervor that shook her soul. In the dark of the middle of the night, she clung to him. "You make me feel the bomb," she whispered in his ear as he held her tight.

The following morning Amy awakened to the sight of Lucas standing in front of his dresser, staring at the photograph of his former wife. Her heart twisted. During the last two days, she'd tried to push the beautiful woman's image from her mind. She could never compete with the woman's beauty, and Lucas clearly still had deep feelings for her.

Amy wondered if even now he was comparing her with his late wife. A knot formed in her throat. She wanted to wipe Lucas's pain away. She wanted to be the one who helped make him happy.

Drawing her covers with her, she sat up in bed and bit her lip. It was as if he was in another world. Far, far away. The notion hurt, especially after they'd been so close. It had been more than sex, she thought. She hoped she wasn't fooling herself.

"You still miss her," Amy said quietly.

As if she'd invaded a private moment he hadn't

wanted to share, he whipped his head around in surprise. His eyes full of conflicting emotions, he met her gaze, then looked away. "This is always a tough time of year."

"I'd like to make it easier for you."

He inhaled, then let out a long breath. "I don't think you can."

Amy felt another stab just behind her ribs. "But I care about you, and these last few days have been amazing. I haven't ever been happier, and you've seemed happy, too."

He shrugged. "I don't know. Let's not make this bigger than it is. We're both adults, and we haven't made any promises or big declarations."

Her heart felt as if it stopped. Her worst fear climbed from her stomach to form a knot in her throat. "The last few days were not just about sex," she said, fighting tears and praying he would say what she needed to hear. "There's more between us than sex."

His silence was damning, and she hated the distance between them. Just hours ago, they'd been as close as two humans could possibly be. "I've got work to do," he said finally, and left her alone in his bed.

Shell-shocked by Lucas's retreat, Amy took a shower to wash his scent off of her. Although she knew Lucas still suffered over the loss of his wife, she couldn't believe he would throw away what he and Amy had found in each other. Mostly hurt but angry, too, she searched for a distraction, something she could do to make herself feel better.

Interrupting Amy's thoughts, Debra called and told her that since the roads had been cleared, Debra's husband, Craig, would be returning Amy's car in a few minutes. Debra prodded Amy for information about why she and Lucas had left the party early, but Amy changed the subject by asking about Debra's pregnancy.

While Amy stewed and waited for her car, she checked through her date book in search of any tentative plans she might have made. The nursing home had canceled Christmas Bingo yesterday due to the snow. Amy made a quick call and learned the residents would be thrilled to reschedule today. She hung up resolved to get back at least a smidgen of her Christmas spirit.

Six hours later, after calling countless games of Christmas Bingo, she left the nursing home with a smile on her face. The residents' laughter and gratitude reminded her of all the good things about the holiday season. She tried not to think about Lucas and how much his retreat had devastated her. Deliberately humming a carol, she noticed the temperature had dropped again, and she nearly fell as she walked toward her car.

"Oops, icy," she muttered to herself, carefully stepping into her little coupe. She sank into her seat, started the engine and turned the heater on high even though the air it blew would take a while to warm up.

Thoughts of Lucas slipped across her mind again, making her heart hurt. For a moment she toyed with the idea of not returning to his house. When she realized she was thinking about him, she turned up the volume on her radio in an attempt to drown out her unhappy thoughts.

Driving down the narrow county road, she calculated that it should take her about an hour to get home. Home. The thought was so seductive, so alluring. So dangerous. Not *her* home, she quickly reminded herself. *Lucas's* home.

Approaching a sharp, steep curve, she pressed down her brake. Her car swerved wildly, sending panic racing through her. Ice. She desperately turned the steering wheel first one way, then the other, to gain control. She mashed on the brakes again, to no avail. As if her car had a will of its own, it raced off the side of the road and smashed into a tree.

A scream of horror vibrated from her toes. The air bag slammed into her, banging her face and chest with its force, knocking the breath out of her.

While Lucas sat in front of the fire with the newspaper, trying not to think about Amy, her cat, Cleo, sat just across from him, staring at him. She regarded him with a disdainful, accusing expression, as if to tell Lucas that he had treated her mistress like a jerk this morning.

If that cat could talk, she would have said, "You are lower than snail spit."

Lucas scowled at Cleo, but she merely turned her head and licked her paw.

The phone rang. He glanced in the direction of the kitchen and considered not answering it. He preferred to brood in silence. Cleo eyed him expectantly. The phone rang again.

Sighing, he rose and picked up the receiver, hoping it was a telephone solicitor so he could hang up abruptly. "Hello," he growled.

"Lucas?" Amy said in a wobbly, high-pitched voice.

His heart contracted. "Amy, what—where—"

"My car hit a patch of ice and ran off the road. I ran into a tree," she said in a breathless rush. "I probably should have dialed 911, but I automatically thought of you."

She sounded disoriented. Alarm rushed through him like a cold shower. "Are you hurt?"

"I, uh, I don't think so," she said vaguely. "I might be sore from the air bag."

His gut knotted. "Amy, where are you?"

She sighed. "I'm beside a field."

Lucas gritted his teeth in frustration. *Everywhere* in Kent was beside a field. "Where did you go this afternoon?"

"Christmas Bingo at the Kent Friendship Manor. There was one little old man who was so sweet. He—"

"Route 7. Keep your cell on and hang on. I'll be there as fast as I can," he said, and grabbed his hat and coat on the way to the door.

His heart pounded against his rib cage as he ran to his truck and turned on the ignition before he closed his door. He had to make sure Amy was okay. He couldn't lose her today. He couldn't. Sucking in a cold, quick breath, he narrowed his eyes as he gunned his truck down his driveway. December 20. Was it destined always to be the worst day of his life? He'd lost his wife on this day years ago. He damn well didn't want anything to happen to Amy today.

The drive seemed interminable. As soon as he turned on Route 7, he flicked on his high beams and continually scanned both sides of the road. He didn't blink for miles. His gut was churning.

Where was she?

Just as he reached for his cell to call her, he spotted her car in a field on the left side. Turning off the road, he saw the deployed bag. The front side of her sedan resembled an accordion. Squinting his eyes, he caught sight of her hunched over in the back seat with the door open.

His stomach clenched again. She was hurt, and he hurt from looking at her. He rushed from his truck to her car and bent down. Her eyes were closed and her arms wrapped around her waist.

"Amy," he said, carefully touching her arm.

She opened her eyes and looked at him, pain shimmering in her gaze. "You're here," she said.

"Yeah," he said, a sliver of relief rolling through him. At least she was conscious. He didn't see any blood, although there could be internal injuries. The thought made him nauseous.

"Thanks for coming. I feel stupid. I must have taken that curve too—" She stopped and winced.

"You're hurt," he said.

"A little, I guess," she said. "I—"

"I'm taking you to the E.R.," he interjected, reaching for her. "Let me help you to the truck."

She winced as he picked her up. "Sorry," he muttered, and settled her into the truck. He spent the entire drive to the E.R. swearing and praying. The intake nurse hustled her into an examination room as soon as they arrived.

Twenty minutes later, Debra walked into the E.R. with her husband in tow. Craig waved at him and wandered to a different area in the waiting room.

"How is she?" Debra asked, reaching out to hug him.

Lucas returned the embrace from his baby sister, who was round with her pregnancy. "I don't know. Nobody has told me anything. She was hurting when I brought her in."

Debra shook her head and gave a murmur of sympathy. "First the fire, now this. She's had a rough time."

He pulled his hat off his head and sighed. "Yeah, and she hasn't let any of it get her down. Even me," he muttered ruefully.

"Even you," Debra echoed with a frown. "What do you mean? What have you done?"

He waved his hand and turned away. He struggled to separate his feelings about his wife's death and Amy's accident. If he were superstitious, he'd swear he was cursed.

"Well I'm going to ask the nurse about her," Debra said, and marched toward the nurses' station. Lucas watched the nurse take her toward the examination room. He walked closer to his brother-in-law and glanced at the basketball game Craig watched on the television.

"Rough night," Craig said.

Lucas nodded, not taking in anything on the television. Hearing his sister's voice, Lucas turned. Debra walked toward him. "Three broken ribs and the doctor says she'll have some colorful bruises on her face."

He felt a load of weight lifted from his chest. "Good," he said.

"Come over here for a minute," she said, pulling Lucas to the side. "Are you okay?" she asked in a low voice. "You don't look so good."

"I'm okay," he insisted.

She surveyed his face and after a long silent moment, then the light of recognition dawned on her face. "It's the anniversary of Jennifer's death."

He nodded but said nothing.

"Are you over her?"

"I've been over her," he admitted. "I've just had a hard time getting over the fact that I wasn't there to save her."

Debra's gaze gentled. "Superman complex."

"Whatever."

"You've gone and fallen for Amy."

His heart squeezed tight. He wanted to deny it, but he couldn't. "What makes you say that?"

"You came to my party. You haven't been to my parties since Jennifer died." She paused. "So what are you gonna do about it?"

"Nothing," he said without hesitation.

Debra frowned. "Why?"

"Because I have nothing to offer her. She's everything I'm not."

"Opposites attract."

"And eventually drive each other crazy."

"So you've hated having her in your house," she concluded.

"I didn't say that."

"And you're perfectly willing to let her get away?"

He needed to be perfectly willing, but he damn well wasn't.

"It's okay to want someone, Lucas. It's even okay to need someone."

"Not if they die."

"You're going to lead a very empty life if you don't do something. For heaven's sake, Lucas. You saved Amy. Now save yourself."

"What do you mean?"

"Replace your sad memories with happy ones. You've found something worth keeping. I dare you to go into that examination room and tell Amy that you love her."

"This is none of your damn business, Debra."

She was unimpressed. "You only swear at me when I'm right. I'm going home. If you don't want to look after Amy, I'm sure I can find any number of male volunteers."

"Forget the volunteers. I'm taking care of her. Now get your pregnant self home," he told her gruffly.

She gave him a quick kiss on his cheek. "I love you."

"I love you, too."

"See how easy that was," she said, moving toward her husband. "Just three little words."

Lucas watched her waddle out the door, then turned toward the nurses' station. His sister's words echoed in his brain. *You saved her. Now save yourself.* He slowly approached the intake nurse and asked if he could go into Amy's exam room. The woman nodded and escorted him.

Inside the room, he found Amy with a blanket wrapped around her. She was singing a slightly off-key rendition of "Rudolph the Red-nosed Reindeer." He remembered how just a week ago Christmas music had made him feel grumpy and melancholy. Now the sweetness of her voice lifted his heart.

"Hi," he said.

She glanced at him, her face coloring with embarrassment. "Oops. You caught me."

He walked closer to her. "I hear you've got some bum ribs."

She nodded. "I'm all taped up, but no snowball fights for me for a while. Thanks for coming to get me. I should have called 911, but I thought of you."

"I'm glad you did," he said and paused a moment. He felt as if he were jumping off a cliff. "I want you to always think of me."

Her gaze searched his. "What about this morning?"

"I'll tell you about that another time. Now, I have a confession to make."

She looked at him warily. "You don't have to confess anything to me. I think you confessed enough this morning."

He shook his head, frustrated and nervous. "This morning was all wrong. I want to tell you that I lied about what I want for Christmas."

She blinked and studied him with a confused expression. "Uh, okay."

He moved directly in front of her and took the biggest step of his life. "What I really want for Christmas is for you to stay with me," he said. "Always."

She went perfectly still.

"You've given me back Christmas, Amy. You've given me back my life. I love you. I want you to marry me."

Her eyes rounded in shock. She opened her mouth, but no sound came out. She lifted her arms, and winced at the movement.

The gesture was enough invitation for Lucas. He gently swept her into his arms and inhaled the sweet scent of her head tucked under his chin. His heart felt so full and alive, he thought it might burst.

"You really love me?" she asked in disbelief.

Her doubt pinched at him. He would make that doubt go away. "Yeah, I really love you."

She glanced at him. "Gosh, I hope I'm not delirious. I hope this is true."

"It is," he promised. "And I'll tell you again tomorrow if you forget."

Her eyes welled with tears. "Oh, Lucas, I tried very hard not to love you, and I failed miserably."

"Thank God," he said, looking into the most precious, beautiful face on earth. "Will you marry me?"

"Yes, yes, yes," she said, and smiled through her tears. "I am the bomb."

EPILOGUE

DESPITE THE SHORT notice, the little white church in the center of town was packed for Lucas and Amy's wedding on Christmas Day.

Amy still wasn't sure how all the preparations had been accomplished so quickly except for the fact that everyone seemed thrilled that Lucas, the favored town son, was to be married. Debra had even found a beautiful white lace dress for Amy.

The brief ceremony was made even sweeter by a song sung by Amy's students. Every minute Amy felt Lucas's gaze on her. The joy and love in his eyes took her breath.

At the casual reception held at the Community Center, raspberry-sherbet punch and good wishes flowed freely. A local guitar trio even volunteered to play music.

Lucas took her in his arms for the opening number. Her ribs still sore, Amy tried to hide her wince.

"You're hurting," he said, sliding her arms down to his waist to lessen the pain. "We don't have to dance."

"Oh, yes, we do. I'm going to remember this for the rest of my life." She looked up at him and saw an incredible future for herself. "You've given me something I've only dreamed of."

"What's that?"

"A home," she said. "It's more than a house. I belong to a person I love more than anything." She covered his heart with her hand. "I belong with you."

Amy could see the emotion brimming from his eyes. He was nearly overcome, and the knowledge that she could be so necessary to such a strong man humbled her. "And I belong to you," he said, lifting her hand to his lips and making promises that would fill her for a lifetime. "Forever."

* * * * *

The Tycoon's Christmas Engagement

REBECCA
WINTERS

Rebecca Winters, whose family of four children has now swelled to include five beautiful grandchildren, lives in Salt Lake City, Utah, in the land of the Rocky Mountains. With canyons and high alpine meadows full of wild flowers, she never runs out of places to explore. They, plus her favourite vacation spots in Europe, often end up as backgrounds for her romance novels, because writing is her passion, along with her family and church. Rebecca loves to hear from readers. If you wish to email her, please visit her website, www.cleanromances.com.

CHAPTER ONE

"THE ROBERTS RESIDENCE."

"Ms Roberts? It's Mitch Reynolds."

Immediately Annie's hand tightened on the receiver. She would know his deep, almost grating voice anywhere. It had a sensuous quality that had always unnerved her. Whenever she dropped in to see her mother, who worked at the Hastings Corporation, he inevitably appeared, as if he had radar and knew when she was in the building.

According to her mom, most women thought him the most attractive man alive.

Annie had thought the same thing when she'd first met him at seventeen. There was a dangerous quality about him that had drawn her to him, but of course he'd been too mature and sophisticated for her to even consider getting to know.

David Hastings, on the other hand, was younger and more like the boy next door. He didn't challenge her with every look. He was...safer, and darling.

Six years later, Annie hadn't changed her opinion

of either man. Except that now she was a woman she recognized that a type like Mitch Reynolds was more dangerous than ever. Her awareness of him had grown even stronger, if that was at all possible.

Whenever she felt those Arctic blue eyes assessing her, she would tremble for no good reason.

She was trembling now, which was absurd.

Why would the thirty-two-year-old vice president of Hastings be calling here this early in the morning? Surely he knew today was her mother's wedding day?

"I'm sorry, but I'm afraid she and Roger left for San Pedro Port an hour ago."

"Actually, it's you I wanted to reach. Roger told me you would be delivering invitations for the office Christmas party later this morning. I wondered if you needed any help."

A thrill of alarm caused her pulse to race. Why would he be concerned over such a trivial matter?

The temptation to put the receiver back on the hook almost won the day. But out of respect for Roger, who was about to become her new stepfather, she refrained.

Roger, the CEO and owner of Hastings, thought Mitch walked on water, so she didn't dare offend his right arm.

"I appreciate your offer, Mr Reynolds, but I have everything under control."

There was a pregnant pause.

"Obviously I'm keeping you from something pressing."

She tensed. It seemed her response hadn't satisfied him. "If I sound out of breath it's because you caught me as I was walking out the door."

She hated feeling this breathless around him, even over the phone.

"Then I won't delay you any longer. Just remember my door is always open if you need anything."

Annie bit her lip. "Thank you. I'll remember that." But she wouldn't act on his offer. She didn't dare. Instinct told her a man like that could sweep you away until you were no longer in control of anything. Mitch Reynolds was an unknown quantity she knew to avoid at all costs.

Stimulated by anticipation of today's events, Mitchell Reynolds, who preferred to be called Mitch, hung up the phone and levered himself from the bed to get ready for work. The old adage about the early bird getting the worm was definitely in play.

There was nothing Mitch loved more than a presumably impossible challenge. And Annie Roberts rated right up there at the top.

There were reasons why he'd been waiting for the right time to capture her full attention. But, after her cool reaction on the phone, maybe he'd waited too long, and she was too emotionally distanced to respond to him. If he hoped to develop a real relationship with her, then where she was concerned unorthodox measures were called for.

So far their association had been superficial, because he hadn't wanted to invade David Hastings's space if anything was going to develop between him and Annie. Mitch revered Roger too much to create problems with his son.

But, since he hadn't seen signs of things heating up in that department, Mitch had given himself permission to make her take notice of him.

Not since Hannah had he wanted a woman this badly. In case this was his last chance, he wasn't beyond using everything in his arsenal to win a war she wasn't aware had begun.

A half-hour later he left his Beverly Hills condo, jumped in his car and joined the mainstream of traffic headed into downtown L.A.

The new Hastings complex sat on a prime piece of real estate, well manicured, with leafy ground cover and palm trees. He pulled into his parking space. The white Nissan he was looking for hadn't arrived yet. So far so good.

He left his car and walked into the building, waving to the gardener, who was putting fresh bark under one of the newly planted ornamental trees.

Mitch's office suite was located in the east wing of the ground floor, next to Roger's. Roger's son David's was across the hall.

Since Mitch's secretary hadn't arrived yet, he made coffee for both of them, then planted himself at his desk to read the rest of yesterday's *Wall Street Journal*.

Soon he heard activity in the outer office and buzzed his secretary.

"Mr Reynolds— I didn't realize you were already here. Can I make you some coffee?"

"I already fixed it for us, so come on in and help yourself."

"I will later. Thank you."

He took another sip. "Would you do me a favor and contact Olympia Cruise Lines? I'd like a magnum of champagne sent to the stateroom of Mr and Mrs Roger Hastings aboard the *Olympia Princess*, with my compliments."

"Yes, sir. Anything else?"

"Yes. Let me know as soon as David Hastings comes in."

"He might already be in the building. Hold on and I'll check with Susan."

Mitch drank the rest of his coffee while he waited.

"She says he just walked in."

"Thank you. I'm headed there now. If anything comes up, you know where to find me."

He'd already delivered Christmas presents to the main staff, but still had one more to go. Reaching for David's gift, he exited the private entrance of his suite. David's office was further on down the hall.

"Good morning, Susan."

She lifted her head. "Hi, Mr Reynolds! It *is* a good morning, isn't it?" she exclaimed. "Last day of work until after New Year's."

"Amen," he said, before rapping on David's door.

"Not so loud!" the blond twenty-seven-year-old complained.

Mitch moved inside and closed it.

After assessing the situation, he poured coffee from the cafetière on the sideboard and handed the mug to David. "Too much celebrating with your dad last night?"

"You could say that." He tested the hot liquid, then drank most of it. "What brings you in here? With Dad and Marion off on their honeymoon, nobody's going to get a lick of work done today. I'm calling it quits in about five minutes."

Mitch smiled at the younger man. "Then I'm glad I got here in time to wish you a Merry Christmas." He put the gift on his desk. "You never know what can happen when everyone else starts to let down. Kingdoms can rise or fall in the blink of an eye."

"You sound like Dad," he muttered testily.

"Where do you think I learned that piece of wisdom?"

Roger Hastings was one of Southern California's most renowned and successful commercial developers. Mitch felt privileged to work for him.

David struggled to remove the ribbons from the package. "Golf balls. I can always use these. Thanks, Mitch. I'm afraid I haven't done any shopping yet."

"Don't worry about it."

Just then Susan buzzed David. Mitch could hear her clearly through the speaker.

"Sorry to interrupt, Mr Hastings, but one of Santa's helpers is here, giving out official invitations to the office Christmas party. She has one for you and would like to deliver it in person. Shall I send her in?"

David swore under his breath. "That's all I need. Dad probably told somebody on the committee to make certain I show up."

Mitch could have told him it was a self-appointed committee of one who'd been trying to get David's attention for the last year—without success. Whether it was still a crush on Annie's part, left over from her teenage years, or something more, Mitch was determined to find out.

"Mr Hastings?" Susan called to him again.

"Go ahead and send her in."

As soon as Mitch moved away from the door it opened, and Annie Roberts walked in.

She was a taller, more slender version of her mother, Marion, who was probably Roger's wife by now. Roger had arranged for a minister to marry them aboard ship. Both women were natural dark-haired beauties. But not even Mitch was prepared for the sight of a gorgeous elf in a thigh-length green tunic whose shapely legs went on forever. It was hard to know where to look first.

The second she saw Mitch, the mischievous smile on her face beneath the fetching red elf hat with the bell disappeared, as if she'd just received a shock. At least she wasn't indifferent to him.

Silence filled the room, prompting Mitch to say, "Good morning again, Ms Roberts. May I offer you and David my congratulations on your parents' wedding? That makes you two official stepbrother and sister today."

By her stunned expression, he'd caught her totally off guard. That was good. It helped him to read between the lines.

"Thank you," she finally said in a tremulous voice. He was curious to understand why she sounded so emotional.

"You make a charming elf, by the way. Doesn't she, David?"

"I hardly recognized you in your costume, Annie."

That didn't surprise Mitch. David could hardly keep his eyes open. Though he was trying hard because Annie was a breathtaking sight. But as far as Mitch was concerned David was a year too late on the uptake. He'd had his chance without encountering any interference. Now Mitch was going to make his move...

"After your parents get back from their cruise, we'll have to arrange a party for them. But one party at a time, right?"

When she didn't say anything, he turned to David. "Did you know Annie's in charge of this year's Christmas party?"

David shook his head. "I had no idea."

"It makes sense, since she has always helped her mother plan it. At least for as long as I've been here anyway."

Mitch's gaze switched back to Annie. "I'm looking forward to seeing the invitation. May I have mine now?"

She was only holding one, of course. He could tell she was upset to find him in here. A flush had seeped into her already colorful cheeks. Was it because she'd been caught red-handed? Or was there some other element at work, too? He'd sell his soul to know.

"Someone else is delivering yours, to your office."

If that was a hint for Mitch to leave, he had news for her.

"I'm sorry to have missed them. Since I'm not in there, do you mind if I look at yours, David?"

"Be my guest. I'm not sure I could read the writing anyway."

Mitch put out his hand, forcing her to give him the scroll tied with red ribbon. If he wasn't mistaken, she trembled at his touch.

He undid it and studied the contents. It was in poetic form. He read it aloud. "'Twas the night before Christmas and all through L.A., the deserving employees at the Hastings Corporation were ready to play. The Roof Garden at the St Regis was decorated with care, in hopes that Mr and Mrs Claus soon would be there. While the children were nestled, all snug in their beds, their parents had visions of a champagne gala running

through their heads. With Dasher and Dancer taking
a turn around the floor, Santa would give out fabulous
surprises galore. So away to the Roof and witness his
flight, after he wishes one and all Merry Christmas
and goodnight.'"

David squinted at her. "Cute."

It was a lot more than cute. Judging by what Mitch
had gleaned from Roger, since working so closely with
him, he knew how hard Annie had been hit by the death
of her father. All the wonderful memories of her childhood were wrapped up in that poem. His thoughts were
verified when their gazes collided. He felt the vulnerability in those troubled gray orbs, and possibly her
resentment of him because he'd been the one to read
what was in her soul.

"Everyone will love your invitation," he murmured.
"Especially Roger. This is the one Christmas Eve party
he'll wish he hadn't missed. I know I'm going to enjoy
attending. In fact, I can't wait."

He put the scroll on David's desk, then turned to her.

"As long as you have other invitations to deliver,
I'll walk out with you. It'll be worth the effort just to
see the look on the others' faces when they read your
amazing and clever rendering. See you at the party,
David," he called over his shoulder.

"I'll make it there at some point."

Noting the deflation on Annie's face, Mitch cupped
her elbow and escorted her past Susan's desk. He hadn't

wanted to give her time to feel worse over David's less than enthusiastic response.

"It's evident you've outdone yourself on this party. Since I have no more business, let me help you finish delivering the rest of the scrolls."

By the time she'd removed her arm from his grasp, her classic features had closed up.

"Thank you, but I've had other people helping me and it's all done. Now I'm going home."

A home with no one there…

"That's a coincidence. So am I. I'll walk with you to the parking lot."

She shook her head so the little bell tinkled. "You go ahead. I have to change in Mother's office."

"No problem. I'll wait for you."

Her mobile mouth had tightened. "I get the feeling something's wrong, Mr Reynolds."

"Please call me Mitch."

"Mitch, then," she amended, taking an extra breath. "Mother didn't tell me I needed to work with you on this. If I should have done that, then I apologize."

"You've misunderstood, Annie. I only wanted to be of help if you needed a hand. Why don't we talk about it after you remove your very attractive costume?"

CHAPTER TWO

ANNIE LOCKED HERSELF in the bathroom, unable to credit that Mitch Reynolds had been in David's office, standing there larger than life, at the precise moment she'd walked in.

There had been something intimidating about his tall, lean build, and the slightly cruel smile as he'd spoken. A little scar stood out along his hard jaw. Couple that with his unruly black hair and she had hardly been able to think for the adrenaline rush that had assailed her body. She was still shaken remembering how he'd assessed her so intimately with those cobalt blue eyes.

David might as well have not been in the room.

After all the trouble she'd gone to, hoping to garner his interest just this once, it had been Mitch who'd praised her silly poem and offered to walk around distributing the rest of the invitations for her. She didn't want to give him any credit. It was churlish of her, but for some reason she couldn't help it.

Feeling distinctly out of sorts, she changed into designer jeans and a white hooded pullover. After brushing her hair, she put the costume in an old airline bag and left the suite.

The second Mitch saw her, he stopped talking to one of the accountants who'd just received his invitation. In a few swift strides he'd joined her at the main doors to the complex.

She'd never seen him in anything but a suit and tie. Still, that civilized veneer of sophistication couldn't hide his inscrutable side, the one that had made her increasingly aware of him over the last year.

Though he'd never stepped out of line, never said or done anything she could criticize, she couldn't shrug off her uneasy feelings.

Since his early-morning phone call she'd felt a new energy coming from him. Whether it was a comment or a look, he'd managed to set her nerves on edge.

Maybe he didn't think her capable of handling the Christmas party without her mother. Maybe he resented the fact that Roger had given her *carte blanche* now that she was an insider by virtue of his marriage to her mom.

If so, that was too bad, because it was Roger's company, and he was her stepfather now.

As for David, she'd been hoping to have more than a platonic relationship with him one day. The office party had seemed a likely place to make him notice her as an intelligent, desirable woman in her own right. But his half-hearted assurance that he'd "show up at some point" had filled her with yet another disappointment.

David should have been the one to say he couldn't wait for the party.

"Are you all right?" Mitch asked as he held the door open for her.

"Of course."

The cold air felt good against her hot face. Once she'd walked a few yards, she turned to him, brushing some strands of hair off her cheeks. It was time to deal with him head-on.

"I can tell there's something on your mind. If you've any objection to any of my plans for the Christmas party, I'll fix them if I can."

"You seem intent on misunderstanding me, Annie. I only wanted to commend your choice of location for the party."

"Mother reserved it six months ago—"

"On your suggestion," he interjected. "I overheard you talking to her about it at last year's party."

That didn't surprise Annie. Mitch Reynolds had a brilliant mind, and was the eyes and ears of the company.

"It's a wonderful choice of place," he assured her. "You have no idea how much Roger values his employees. A celebration with this kind of elaborate planning and attention to detail reflects his feelings and shows how much he cares. He'll be particularly appreciative of your hard work during this time while he's away with your mother."

"Thank you," she murmured, not knowing what

else to say. If David had been saying these things to her, she would have been thrilled. The fact that it was Mitch made her less trusting, which she admitted really wasn't fair to him.

"You're a woman of hidden talents. After you receive your MBA in the spring, I'd like to be the first person you come to see. I know of a position in the corporation that needs a person like you." After a pause he added, "See you at the party."

He headed for his car, which was parked in the VIP section.

Annie stared after him, her feelings ambivalent—because he was so different from the man she'd thought she'd known all these years. To be told she could have a job at Hastings after graduation had been a dream of hers. But she hadn't expected the opening to come through Mitch Reynolds.

Nothing had gone the way she'd planned it this morning. It should have been David who'd walked her out to the car and said all those things to her.

Having been thrown totally off balance, she turned in the opposite direction and rushed to her Nissan. Unable to deal with her conflicting feelings where Mitch was concerned, she was determined to put him out of her mind.

But when he drove by her car and flashed her another penetrating glance, it brought back that moment in David's office, when Mitch's gaze had swept over her, missing virtually nothing. She was still reacting to the weakness that had attacked her.

Maybe this was the way the competition felt when he was about to swoop in for the kill.

Needing to channel her frenzied emotions toward something constructive, Annie took a deep breath and headed for the beauty salon, where she'd made an appointment.

Twenty minutes later she walked in the shop, ready to undergo a drastic change. The receptionist motioned to a guy with spiky blue hair. He examined her with a critical eye.

"Hi, love. What can I do for you today?"

"On Christmas Eve I have to look perfect. I'd like my hair cut short, but not too short, if you know what I mean."

He nodded. "Soft and feminine."

"Exactly."

"Come on back to my chair."

Annie followed the stylist, who was rumored to be one of the best in Hollywood.

Once he'd put the drape around her neck, he said, "I know exactly what you need."

The man was a wizard, and prophetic, too. Within the hour he handed her a mirror. "Long hair is for teenagers. Now you look like a woman."

He was right! His hands had worked magic.

"What color dress are you wearing for the big night?"

"Flaming red chiffon with spaghetti straps."

He winked. "Nice. Whoever you're trying to impress won't be able to look anywhere else."

She shivered, because she was still reeling from Mitch Reynolds's all-encompassing scrutiny. Somehow she had to put the incident behind her and keep her emotions in check.

After paying the stylist a big tip, she left the salon, loving the feel and style of her new cap of soft, gleaming curls. More black than brown, they framed her oval face to her jawline. The change gave her an elegance that had been missing. Surely David would be aware of the difference and find himself intrigued?

Since Mitch had ruined her moment in David's office, she was resolute that nothing would go wrong the night of the party.

Once again she got in her car and headed to her mom's seventies-style home to grab a late lunch. She needed to make a few phone calls to the guys in her study group from UCLA. The presentation for their university marketing class was due after the holidays.

But trying to get four grad students together to divide up the work was difficult, at best. Two of them held jobs, which made it tricky to arrange schedules, but it had to be done.

Annie was thankful for the grant that was allowing her to finish up her MBA without having to deal with a part-time job. The result being that she'd maintained a good grade point average.

The companies that came on campus to recruit new graduates might claim to look at the total student, but it still held true that the top academic achievers got picked first.

She could hardly credit that Mitch had already approached her to come to work at Hastings. His offer would have pleased Annie's father. Before he'd died, he'd made her promise she would distinguish herself in some kind of college pursuit. He hadn't cared which profession she went into. If she so chose, it could even be patent law, the kind he'd practiced. The important thing for her was to focus all her energy on getting that coveted degree. Then her path would be set before her and she would always be able to take care of herself.

Her mom had been in full agreement. She'd pointed out that if she hadn't received her bachelor's degree the Hastings Corporation wouldn't have even considered her application for employment.

As a result, Annie hadn't played as much as she'd studied. While she'd seen friends drop out of college to get married and have babies, she'd avoided heavy romantic involvement to stay the course.

The crush she had on David had helped her remain emotionally unattached from any guys she'd dated. If she went to work for his father's company after graduation they'd see each other on a daily basis. Maybe that was what it would take for him to ask her out. But after today she wasn't sure of anything. Mitch had driven home the point that she and David were now stepbrother and sister. She hoped it wouldn't change David's view of her. It wasn't as if they were related by blood.

As she reached in her purse for her cellphone, it rang. The caller ID said "out of area." Maybe one of the guys in the study group was calling.

"Hello?"

"Annie, honey? I promised I'd call when I became Mrs Roger Hastings."

"Mom—" Tears spurted from Annie's eyes. "I'm so happy for you."

She was, of course. Her mother had been in love with the dynamic owner and head of the Los Angeles–based Hastings Corporation for a long time.

The attractive widower had built a multimillion-dollar business that bought and developed commercial real estate. He'd first hired Marion Roberts as his secretary. In eight years she'd gone from private secretary to being his wife. They were perfect for each other.

Annie could feel her mother's joy. No one deserved it more than she did. After all they'd been through together, after the death of her father, Annie was thrilled her mother had found happiness again.

"To take you on a cruise is so romantic. He loves you, Mom. I'm so excited he finally realized and did something about it."

"Me, too, honey. But I hate leaving you alone at Christmas."

"I won't be alone. Roz and her boyfriend are having

me over for dinner. Don't you know your marriage has *made* my Christmas?"

"Annie..."

"It's true, Mom. Some women never get the chance to be married once, let alone twice. Before Daddy died, he begged you to find someone else and be happy. I've always thought Roger was that person."

"He *is* wonderful."

"Then forget everything except making each other happy!"

"God bless you, my darling girl."

Annie clicked off and had a good cry. Afterward she left messages for the guys in her class to phone her.

With that accomplished she ate a sandwich, then left the house to pick up the coupons for the hams they were giving as gifts. She'd already printed off the bonus checks and could start stuffing the Christmas cards. Roz and her boyfriend had agreed to help Annie, and would be coming over for pizza later in the evening.

As long as she kept busy she wouldn't have time to think about the vice president of Hastings, or the way he made her feel no matter how hard she tried to erase all thoughts of him from her consciousness.

CHAPTER THREE

BY THREE O'CLOCK Christmas Eve afternoon, Annie had dressed to kill and left for the St Regis Hotel in downtown Los Angeles.

Before this year the party had always been held at the Alhambra House. It was time for a change.

The famous Roof Garden atop the St Regis had a black-and-white-striped canopy fanning out from the ceiling that gave it a garden feel. From the windows you could see all of L.A.

Everyone would love the new, exciting change of venue.

Annie had plans to meet the florist there. Though the hotel had already put up a Christmas tree, and had strung Christmas lights to adorn the canopy, she'd ordered pots of red azaleas and poinsettias for the centerpieces, which would be given away as prizes.

The Roof Garden was circular in design, with four evenly spaced exits.

She'd ordered garlands of evergreens to be draped

in each one, with a large bunch of mistletoe holding up the centers.

When she arrived, she noted with satisfaction that most of the decorating had already been done, right down to the individual colorful elves poking their faces out of the flowering plants.

A bank of poinsettia trees had been set in place where the dance band would sit.

She checked in with Mrs Lawson, the hotel restaurant manager, who showed her a back room where she could leave the Santa and Mrs Claus outfits until it was time for the entertainment.

Everyone would be getting a box of chocolate truffles, with a card, a five-hundred-dollar bonus and a gift coupon for a honey-baked ham. Roger was always generous. This year he'd okayed a larger budget than usual to pay for everything.

Annie had decided there would be no head table or placecards. For a change people could sit where they wanted at tables surrounding the dance floor. Better yet, they could order anything they wanted from the menu.

Annie had already worked out a special price with Mrs Lawson to keep the cost of the party down. Buying champagne from a Napa Valley distributor she knew had helped to get a better price in that department as well.

Before she knew it, the hotel dining room staff had

started to put condiments on the tables and do the general set-up.

The band arrived with their instruments and settled in. One of them wheeled in a piano and set up the mike.

Hoping David would show up soon, she decided she would ask him to be the master of ceremonies. But deep down she wasn't sure she could count on him. She would have thought he'd phone her, if only to talk about their parents for a few minutes. But no such call had come. Maybe *he* wouldn't come, either.

For the first time since knowing him she wondered if she'd made the mistake of endowing him with qualities he didn't possess. That was the problem with never having gone out with him. They'd flirted a lot, but she was beginning to wonder if she really knew him at all. Odd how her thoughts kept flicking back to Mitch, who'd made all the overtures she would have expected to come from David.

Bemused, she looked around the Roof Garden, knowing all the employees, including David, would be blown away by the setting and decorations.

There was nothing she'd love more than to blow *him* away. But she couldn't do that if he decided to give the party a miss.

Haunted by the fact that Mitch Reynolds *would* come, she started to get nervous and began pacing.

Little by little the guests started to trickle in. While she stood there, wondering what the night would bring, she saw a blond head at the far exit. It was David. He was built like his father. Both of them were six feet with trim builds.

He entered the room from the other side. To her relief he'd come without a date. Things couldn't be working out better. But with his good-looking face and expressive brown eyes, she wouldn't be the only woman in the room who noticed him.

She knew the moment he saw her, because he paused, then started walking across the dance floor toward her.

Just then the photographer she'd hired appeared out of nowhere. "You look good enough to eat." He grinned, and took her picture. The flash went off, startling her.

"My sentiments exactly." A familiar male voice sounded directly behind her. Suddenly a strong pair of hands grasped her slender waist and spun her around.

She discovered herself staring up into the hot blue eyes of Mitch Reynolds. He was smiling at her with a devilish gleam that set off alarm bells.

"Merry Christmas, Annie. It is you, isn't it? The dress is stunning. So is your new hairstyle. May I be the first at the party to try out the mistletoe? Which I confess is tempting me beyond my power to resist."

Her escape was barred as Mitch lowered that cruel mouth to hers, acting like he'd done this many times before and knew exactly how to satisfy her.

The first touch of his lips wasn't the invasion she'd expected, but rather a persistent coaxing of her own lips to respond. His touch created enough heat to send fingers of awareness through her body. Without knowing how it happened, her mouth opened to the growing pressure of his. Soon they were drinking from each other's mouths as if they were parched and couldn't get enough.

What was supposed to be a holiday kiss, given in fun, had turned out to be something incredibly different. Annie's heart pounded too hard. She could scarcely breathe.

Another flash went off, bringing her out of her dazed state.

She tore her lips from his, trembling so violently it was humiliating.

"Can anyone get in line?" she heard David ask, but by now she'd sneaked into the hall, where she could attempt to recover without an audience.

Both men followed her. Mitch's eyes held an enigmatic glitter.

"That's up to your stepsister."

She was already shaken by what had just happened, and Mitch's needling remark caused her to turn blindly to David. She pressed her lips to his, wanting desperately to wipe out the memory of Mitch's kiss, which had been like an assault on her senses.

David kissed her warmly, the way she'd been dreaming about for years. But something was wrong. And it wasn't because she could smell alcohol on his breath.

Though he was putting real feeling into it, she felt... nothing.

Absolutely nothing!

"The band leader is motioning to you, Annie. Shall I see what he wants while you're otherwise occupied?"

Mitch Reynolds was like a specter she couldn't get away from fast enough.

Summoning all the self-control she could muster, she backed away from David, who seemed reluctant to let her go. The knowledge should have thrilled her.

Practically incoherent, she said, "Excuse me for a minute, David."

"I will—on the condition that you hurry back and sit at my table."

"Let me see what's going on first."

It wasn't until she reached the band that she realized she'd forgotten to ask David to take charge. For those moments in Mitch's arms she'd forgotten everything. It was like she'd always believed. He had the power to sweep you away to a place you'd never been before. That was what had just happened, and she'd gone right along with him—as she'd feared.

Mitch trailed the feminine woman in red who had unconsciously sashayed her way through the tables to talk to the band leader. He couldn't take his eyes off her legs, flirting with him as the red material floated back and forth in a tantalizing rhythm.

While the band leader and Annie had their heads together, discussing the Christmas music repertoire,

Mitch took advantage of the time to reach for the mike. Ignoring Annie's vexed expression when she noted his actions, he looked out over the crowd of coworkers and said, "Merry Christmas, everyone! On behalf of Roger Hastings, who's away on his honeymoon with none other than our own Marion, may I welcome you to the Roof Garden for the annual company Christmas party? As you can tell, a certain lovely elf has been busy creating this magical wonderland. Though words can't adequately express our appreciation, let's give Annie Roberts a big round of applause for all her hard work. She's really outdone herself."

The dinner guests burst into enthusiastic applause that lasted such a long time she blushed.

After the din had finally subsided, he grasped her cold hand. She looked so poised, who would have guessed?

"If the band will play their rendition of 'I Saw Mommy Kissing Santa Claus,' Annie and I will start the dancing with the hope that the rest of you will join in."

To anyone else, she looked serene and impossibly beautiful as he pulled her into his arms. But he could feel her bristling from the tips of her toes to the last shiny black curl tumbling over her forehead.

"Relax," he whispered against her warm temple. "The evening has barely begun. Just go with the flow."

CHAPTER FOUR

ANNIE HELD HERSELF rigid. "There's nothing I'd like more, but I have things to see about, Mr Reynolds."

"After that kiss you gave me a few minutes ago, I think we've graduated permanently to first names, don't you?"

He felt her breath catch. "How much have you had to drink tonight?"

"If you knew me better, you'd know I don't drink alcohol. What else do you want to know about me?"

"Right now, I have this party on my mind. The entertainment needs to happen on time, so those with children can leave and get home to them."

"I'm sure they'll appreciate that. So, what can I do for you?"

After a slight hesitation she said, "Mingle with the crowd and make certain everyone is having a good time."

"We'll do it after a few more dances. I haven't done this for so long I'm rusty."

"In case you hadn't noticed, there are quite a few

female employees here without partners. I'm sure any one of them would be thrilled to dance with you."

He pulled her closer, burying his lips in her glossy hair. She smelled like a field of wildflowers.

"I'd rather be dancing with you. I wanted to dance with you at last year's party, but I thought your card was all filled up. In case you can't tell, you're making me look good out here."

He felt every shocked breath she took. "I can't do this much longer."

"I could do this all night. Just stay with me until the music ends. They're playing 'White Christmas' now. It's my favorite song. Reminds me of Minnesota, where my grandparents raised me. Christmas doesn't seem the same without snow."

"I'm sure it doesn't. Now, if you'll excuse me, there are things to be done."

"I agree. Let's do them together, shall we?" Since that kiss there was no way he was letting her get away from him now.

He swung her around to the edge of the dance floor. Tightening his hold on her hand, so she couldn't run off, he began walking around the tables with her, saying hello to everyone. She tried to pull away from him, then gave up in favor of not creating a scene.

Mitch took a circuitous route, nodding and chatting with people until they'd covered the room. When David saw them coming, he stood up.

"At last! Your dinner's getting cold, Annie."

"There's work to be done, David. She'll have to eat later," Mitch explained, forestalling anything she'd planned to say to the other man. "If you want to be useful, you could rove for a while, to ensure everything's going smoothly."

Whisking her away once more, Mitch headed for the exit that led to the room where he'd seen the Santa suits.

Once inside, he walked over and held up the Mr Claus outfit. "You picked out the perfect size for me."

Annie glared at him from beneath her lashes.

The fact that it *was* the right size infuriated her. So did his wolfish white smile that had worked its way under her skin.

Hot-faced, she said, "If you had given me time a few minutes ago, you would have heard me ask David if he would play Santa."

Mitch already knew she'd responded to his kiss, but she didn't want him to think she was craving more.

One dark eyebrow quirked. "This costume would drown him. Besides, he's already had a little too much holiday cheer. But if you want me to get him, I will."

Annie averted her eyes. If she hadn't kissed David, and discovered for herself he'd been drinking before the party, she wouldn't have believed Mitch. As it stood, she couldn't allow a flushed Santa with glazed eyes to help hand out the company gifts—especially not when it was Roger's son.

And her stepbrother, as Mitch had reminded her the other day under no uncertain terms.

He flashed her a mysterious glance. "Need help with your Mrs Claus costume?"

She swallowed hard. "No, thank you." Being crushed against his hard body for those few minutes had been all the closeness she could handle.

Right in front of her, he slipped off his shoes. Next he removed his suit jacket. To her shock, he pulled off his trousers before putting on the bottom half of his costume, which was already padded. Then came the red velvet jacket and the big black belt with bells.

Mesmerized by the transformation taking place, she had a hard time believing it was Mitch under the hat and beard.

Realizing she was staring, she slipped the red granny gown over her head, then pulled on the wig with the bedcap. After putting on a large pair of spectacles, she was ready.

Mitch had put on the black Santa boots, making him a good six-four. "Where's my sack, darling?"

Drawing in a fortifying breath, she said, "Behind the Christmas tree, dearest."

He made a "ho-ho" sound, then bent over and kissed her hotly on the mouth. Though his beard scratched her skin, she found herself lost again in the build-up of heat he created with a mere touch.

"That's to keep us warm while we spread Christmas cheer to kith and kin. Then we'll go home for a long winter's nap."

He left the room ahead of her, not giving her time to

ponder his remarks, or the way that last kiss had shot through her like wildfire.

He was turning out to be such an unknown quantity, and she didn't know what he would do next. Anxious and fascinated at the same time, she hurried after him, to tell him what she'd planned for this portion of the program.

But it was too late. He'd already found the big bag that held the gifts, and had dragged it out in front of the tree in plain sight of the crowd, jingling his bells and saying "ho-ho-ho" in a booming voice.

If Annie didn't know better, she would think he played Santa Claus for a living. Mitch could put his mind to anything. It amazed her. A few days ago she couldn't have imagined him in this role, let alone enjoying it. Now that he was performing so brilliantly, she couldn't imagine David carrying it off. In fact, she was beginning to realize it would never have occurred to him to help her.

As Mitch reached in the sack, he lifted his head to their audience. "In case you didn't notice, I brought my bride along tonight to keep me company. It gets mighty cold up there in that sleigh. If truth be known, she gives out more heat than our fireplace at the North Pole."

The crowd roared with laughter, causing Annie's cheeks to burn a fiery red.

"Come closer, darling. I'm going to need your help giving out the gifts our industrious little elves have made."

He filled her arms with as many boxes as she could carry. Then he loaded his own arms and they worked the room while the band played "Santa Claus is Coming to Town."

He'd stepped into the part like he'd been born to it, putting all the dinner guests in the spirit of Christmas. At every opportunity they whispered to Annie that it was the best party the Hastings Corporation had ever put on.

Annie appreciated the compliments, but she had to admit it wouldn't have been the same without the audacious Mitch Reynolds running away with the show.

He'd told her she was a woman of many talents, but she couldn't hold a candle to *his* performance—on or off the stage.

When she'd delivered the last gift, she joined him at the bandstand and took over the mike.

"An elf has put a Christmas sticker on the back of one of the chairs at each table. Whoever is sitting there can take home the centerpiece."

There were more cheers before everyone checked their chairs.

Mitch took the mike back. All she could see of his face were his dark blue eyes, studying her with a look that made her panic. He was going to do something outrageous again, and there was no place to hide.

Once more he turned to the crowd. "My bride has worn herself out, working so hard. Her poor little feet need a rest, don't you think?"

Their captivated audience responded with a resounding, "Yes!" and started clapping.

"No, Mitch— Please—" she cried. It did no good. He picked her up in his strong arms without missing a breath.

Carrying her toward the nearest exit, he called out, "Merry Christmas to all, and to all a goodnight."

When he paused beneath the mistletoe, she had an idea what was going to happen. Before her groan could escape his mouth had descended on hers once more, blocking out the light, the noise, the music—everything except the frantic pounding of her heart.

Furious with herself, because she'd discovered she wanted the kiss to go on and on, she found the strength to break it. On a burst of inspiration she turned her head toward the audience and called out, "Can't you at least wait until we're back in the sleigh, Mr Claus?"

The room exploded with laughter. The applause seemed to crescendo.

Chuckling out loud, Mitch carried her all the way to the back room. He slowly let her down until her high heels touched the floor.

"That was the perfect exit line, Mrs Claus. Remind me to do this with you again next year."

The moment made her feel close to him in a way she would never have dreamed. Weaving in place from the contact, she pulled off her spectacles. "Next year Mother will be back in charge."

She removed the wig and her granny gown, taking as much time as possible in an effort to recover.

"I had a lot of fun tonight, Annie."

"So did I," she answered honestly, and kept busy putting everything in the garment bag.

"But—?" he prodded.

In order to let him finish getting changed, she kept her back turned to him.

"No buts. With your help, it was a smashing success. I can understand what my mother meant when she said Roger stole you away from the competition. No one can match you at what you do best. It's no wonder he has already made you vice president."

"Rather than David, you mean?"

Annie wheeled around angrily, noting that Mitch was back in his formal navy suit jacket and striped tie, looking dark and aloof and...undeniably gorgeous.

"I didn't say that."

"You didn't have to. You forget I've seen you coming and going from the office for years now. Not much escapes you when you're a bystander there, or at other company parties."

The mention of other parties caused Annie to shudder. Last year she'd tried so hard to get David's exclusive attention when they'd been seated at the head table. But he'd only stayed by her side for a little while before excusing himself to go to another party. Crushed by his departure, she'd been left to face her nemesis, Mitch

Reynolds, who had been seated across from her, evidently observing her pain through those all-seeing eyes.

"If you want to join David now, feel free. I'll take care of the costumes." He plucked the garment bag from her arm. "The shop's address is right here on the label. I'll make certain they're returned after Christmas."

Her lips tightened. "The clean-up is part of my job."

"Nevertheless, after everything you've put in to this party, it's the least I can do."

The *least* he could do?

On the verge of hysteria, she muttered a thank you, reached for her purse and rushed toward the dining room, almost colliding with David in the hall.

"There you are." But when he put his hands on her arms, she felt she should be the one steadying him.

"How about I take you home in a cab and we'll celebrate our parents' marriage over a bottle of champagne?"

This was exactly how she'd hoped the evening would end.

"I have a few more things to do here. Why don't you meet me at Mom's in a half-hour."

"She lives on Canyon Drive, right?"

"Yes. 1094."

"I'll be there, waiting for you."

He brushed his lips against her cheek just as Mrs Lawson came to find her.

After signing for the party, Annie hurried into the dining room to pay the band.

All the guests had left. The only people who remained were the dining room staff, quietly going about straightening the room.

The second Mitch emerged from the hall, carrying the garment bags, she noticed a waitress approach him with a poinsettia and an azalea. He managed to juggle everything without problem.

Annie couldn't help but wonder if the flowers were for a woman he was planning to meet now that the party was over. It was Christmas Eve, after all, and the night was still young. He'd had his fun with Annie to ratchet up the excitement for their guests. But now he was going home to some woman who no doubt couldn't wait to be in his arms.

Until tonight she'd never given a thought to his personal life, beyond the probability that he had some beautiful woman in tow all the time. She could tell herself she wasn't really interested in what he did outside of office hours, but that would be a lie. She'd had a taste of him tonight. In her heart of hearts she knew she wanted more...

The photographer waved and let her know he'd send the bill and the prints to the office.

After one last walk around, Annie realized her job was done. With a curious mixture of satisfaction and let-down, because Mitch had gone, she left through the far exit and hurried to catch the next elevator going down.

Tonight she wouldn't have to go home to an empty house. David was going to be there. Her plan to spend Christmas Eve with him had actually worked. Yet the thought of being alone with him at last didn't make her heart race, or anything close to it.

"You," she gasped quietly, when she saw that Mitch was already inside the elevator.

He lounged against the wall, watching her through hooded eyes.

"You were expecting David?"

"I—I wasn't expecting anyone," she muttered crossly. "David has already gone ahead."

The door closed and the elevator began its descent to the lobby, fourteen stories below. Halfway down, it came to a stop without fanfare. At the same time the light went out, entombing them in total darkness.

She bit her lip. "The show is over, Mitch. We don't have an audience to play to right now."

She heard a strange sound come from his throat.

"You're the one standing next to the control panel, not me. If I didn't know better, I would think *you'd* staged this to get me alone," he murmured, in that wry, mocking tone of his.

She blinked. "You mean we're really stuck in here?"

CHAPTER FIVE

"So it seems. Don't worry. Some transformer probably overloaded because of all the Christmas lights. The power company will get it fixed before we know it."

She fought to control her panic. "I don't believe it." She moaned the words.

"Things could be worse. It might have happened during dinner. I'd say it's a good thing you got everybody out in time. Thanks to your party going off with precision, only you and I have to go down with the ship."

"That's a horrible thing to say!"

"I'm sorry, Annie. I didn't mean to upset you." His apology sounded genuine.

"I know, and I didn't mean to snap. It's just that I don't do well in enclosed spaces."

"Few people do."

"You seem to be handling it."

"That's because I have Mrs Claus with me. She keeps me steadied."

"Is everything a game to you?" She hated his condescension.

"Sometimes real life can be too painful."

His admission stunned her. "I'm sorry I said anything. Don't mind me. I'm not at my best right now. If we don't get out of here soon, you're going to find yourself locked up with a raving lunatic."

"In that case, I believe in making the most of a situation. If we're stuck here for the night, indulge me while I pad the floor with our costumes. Then we can sit or lie down and be comfortable."

She could hardly swallow. "Do you really think we could be in here till morning?"

"Maybe."

"I'm supposed to be home by now!"

"I know. I heard you making plans with David. When he learns the power is out, he'll realize you got caught somewhere and come to rescue you."

She sucked in her breath. "That was an unkind thing to say."

"What do you mean?"

She expelled a tortured sigh. "We both know he's had too much to drink. He'll probably fall asleep waiting for me."

"All's not lost. When we're freed from our prison, you'll be able to drive home and wake him up."

She hugged her arms to her waist.

"I've never seen him like that before."

"Neither have I. But, given the fact that his father

just got married, and his own engagement didn't work out, he's probably feeling a little isolated right now. Probably the same way you're feeling, with your mother gone."

"You certainly assume a lot."

"Roger has confided in me from time to time. He told me how much you loved your father, how hard it's been to lose him. Maybe it's because I've known loss, too, that I can relate. When my fiancée got killed in a skiing accident in college, I think I drowned my sorrows for a solid month. After I finally pulled out of the worst of it, I vowed never to drink again. It didn't solve anything—only displaced the pain which came anyway."

Maybe it was the darkness, but she could feel his remembered pain. To know he'd loved a special woman gave her new insight into his psyche.

"What was her name?"

"Hannah."

"I'm so sorry, Mitch." Her voice shook. "Were you skiing with her? Is that how you got that scar?"

"No to both questions. She was on the ski team. There was an icy track. She skidded off course into a tree. I was at the library, studying."

Annie closed her eyes tightly, but tears trickled out between the lashes anyway. She knew what it felt like to lose someone you loved.

"It's history, Annie. Don't waste any tears on me."

She wiped the moisture off her cheeks. "I'm not."

"And I got the scar in high school, playing basketball. Some spectator threw a beer bottle on the floor, and I fell on a jagged piece of it. Right. I've got everything ready now. If I sit first, then I can help you down."

"Thank you, but I'll stand for a little while longer."

After a silence, he said, "In order to avoid a fate worse than death, I make it a rule never to take advantage of a woman in a dark elevator."

She laughed gently, helpless to do otherwise. How could she ever have thought she couldn't trust him?

"I'm not worried about that."

Annie knew a lot of things about him she hadn't known before. And when you knew certain things about a person you started to care.

The last thing she wanted to do was care about Mitch Reynolds.

"Well, at least let me help you stay warm. It may not be a white Christmas in L.A., but it's cold out."

In the next instant she felt him put his suit jacket around her shoulders.

Her body immediately absorbed the warmth from his.

"Thank you."

"You're welcome."

"Now you're going to freeze to death."

"Not after those kisses you gave me." He squeezed her arms before letting her go.

It was a good thing, or he would have known she was trembling for another reason than the cold.

He sat down next to her legs. "You don't seem as frightened as before."

"That's because you've helped me get my mind off myself. In fact, without your assistance tonight, the party wouldn't have been such a huge hit with everyone. I owe you a lot."

"Don't give me any credit, Ms Roberts. It had your signature written all over it. Whatever part I played, my motives were strictly dishonorable."

"You mean Roger decided I couldn't be trusted to handle the party on my own, so he put you in charge of me?"

"Roger had nothing to do with my involvement," he bit out.

Like quicksilver he'd changed into the man who could be uncomfortably remote on occasion. But at least now she thought she knew some of the reasons why.

"Are you going to leave me hanging?"

"That's right. You're an intelligent woman. Maybe one day you'll figure it out."

She blinked. "Did you think I was going to fall apart because my mother got married, and so you decided to be there to pick up the pieces?"

"Well, you must admit the two of you are exceptionally close."

"Of course we are. After Daddy died of heart failure we had to pull together. But it doesn't mean we haven't lived our own lives since then. To be honest, I was hoping Roger would propose to Mother last year, but it didn't happen."

"That's because he knew you worshipped your father and might not be able to accept him in your lives."

"Not accept Roger?" she cried out, aghast. "I'm crazy about him! I always have been."

"Then he's a lucky man, in more ways than one."

Still trembling, she said, "If anything it was Mom who was worried David might not be able to accept her. Before Mrs Hastings died of cancer I understand their family was very close-knit, too. Mom thought maybe that was the reason it took Roger so long to get around to proposing."

"Well, with David waiting for you at your house, it looks like everyone's been worrying for absolutely nothing."

It was shocking how they could be talking seriously for a few minutes—really communicating—then suddenly she heard that mocking tone in his voice once more.

"You still haven't told me why you volunteered yourself as co-chairman of the Christmas party. The truth now."

"Have you considered I might not have had anyone to take to the party with me, and didn't want to sit there alone?"

"No," she blurted. "That possibility would never have occurred to me."

"Why not? David came by himself."

"Because you're nothing like David."

Not anything like him...

Disturbed by her train of thought, she pulled the edges of his suit jacket closer together to keep out the cold.

"You mean I'm not confident enough to show up on my own the way David did?" he drawled.

She rested her head against the wall. "There's no one with more confidence than you on this planet."

"Is that so?"

She shifted her weight, getting tired of standing. But she couldn't bring herself to sit down next to him, never mind the reason why.

"I meant it as a compliment."

"I took it as one."

Before she could say something she might regret, there was a strange whirring sound, then the light came back on. Once again they were continuing their downward journey.

Oddly enough, Annie wasn't quite ready for the experience to be over. Mitch still needed to explain himself.

With unconscious male agility, he got to his feet and checked his watch.

"It's five after midnight. The magic hour. Merry Christmas, Annie."

Impaling her with his dark blue gaze, he placed his hands on the wall, trapping her between them.

"You wouldn't begrudge a lonely man one last Christmas kiss before we part company, would you?"

Beneath the banter she sensed a hunger in him that matched her own. His lips brushed provocatively against her neck and throat, producing a moan from her before he did a takeover of her mouth. The sensuality of his deep kiss was so erotic she molded herself to him without being aware of it.

They kissed many times. Each one brought greater pleasure, until she thought she couldn't contain all her feelings.

"Mitch," she cried helplessly, before he devoured her mouth once more.

In the morning she knew she would regret her loss of control, but for the life of her she could deny him nothing tonight. His mouth had become the center of her universe. She wanted this conflagration to go on and on.

Out of her mind with desire, she slid her arms around his neck, making it easier to kiss every part of his masculine face. What a gorgeous man he was…

"Annie?" Mitch whispered against her swollen lips. His breathing sounded ragged.

"What?" she asked, close to being delirious. She'd lost track of time and place.

"We've reached the underground car park. People are waiting to get in the elevator."

She was dazed by sensations she'd never experienced in her life, and her eyelids were slow to flutter open.

Over Mitch's broad shoulder she saw two couples, watching them with amused interest.

She let out a cry of embarrassment before disentangling herself from his arms.

Her cheeks had to be as flaming red as her dress.

She helped him gather up the costumes and the flowers.

On their way out she heard Mitch wish their small audience a Merry Christmas.

The whole situation was humiliating, but she had to tough it out in front of this man who'd taught her what could happen when desire went unleashed.

"Annie?"

To her surprise, David came running up to them. She groaned in displeasure. Her first thought was, *Not here, not now, David.*

How incredibly ironic it was to think there'd been a time when she'd *wanted* David to be there.

"When I heard there was a power outage downtown I came here by taxi and waited by your car. Are you all right?"

"I—we're fine."

She didn't dare look at Mitch.

David's brown gaze eyed her with concern. "Thank heaven they got the main transformer repaired. Where were you when the lights went out?"

"In the elevator," Mitch declared. "I'm happy to say

Ms Roberts was able to calm my hysteria while we were trapped in there. She's worth her weight in gold."

With that remark, Annie's legs almost buckled. She could feel David's curious gaze studying both of them. He seemed to have sobered up some.

Her hands shaking, she rummaged in her purse for the remote to unlock her car. The two men took charge. Between them they put the costumes inside.

"Not the flowers," she cautioned, when Mitch started to place them on the back seat.

"Why not? They're yours."

She darted him a searching glance. "But I thought you were tak—"

"I asked the waitress to save them for you," he interrupted her. "A souvenir of the most fabulous party the Hastings Corporation has ever seen." He shut the back door and opened the driver's door for her.

"I'll second that," David said. "It *was* terrific. Everyone raved to me about it."

"Thank you."

"I'll follow you in a taxi. You don't want me to sit on the costumes," David murmured.

Mitch must have heard him, because he said, "Merry Christmas, you two. Drive safely, Annie."

After what had transpired in the elevator, it came as a shock to watch his tall, lean physique walk away from them. A hollow feeling enveloped her as she realized Mitch was actually leaving her there so David could see her home.

For him to leave her this bereft, she could hardly stand it.

"Annie? Are you okay? Would you rather I got a lift with you?"

Once, not too long ago—like as recently as the day her mother had left with Roger—Annie would have been euphoric to hear David say something like that to her.

"No— I—I mean, I'm fine," she stammered.

She hurriedly got in behind the wheel. "I'll see you at the house."

Then she backed out of her parking spot and headed for the exit. Without giving David another thought, she looked for Mitch's car. But it seemed he'd disappeared already.

Now that he'd given her the thrill of her life, along with helping Marion's twenty-three-year-old daughter with the party, it appeared he couldn't wait to spend Christmas with a woman of his own age and taste.

Annie might be young and inexperienced where intimacy was concerned, but even she recognized that Mitch was too virile a man to lead a monk's life. But for the tragic accident that had killed his fiancée he'd be married by now, and would probably have several children.

While she drove, reliving those moments of ecstasy in his arms, she heard a honk. It jerked her back to reality.

Looking around, she realized David was letting her know she'd driven past her mom's house.

Dismayed by her emotions, which were in utter chaos and had caused her mind to blank out for the twenty-minute drive, she made a U-turn and barreled into the driveway. She left the garment bags in the back, but reached for the flowers.

David paid the cab driver and joined her at the front door of the house.

"Let me help you with those." He took the plants from her so she could let them inside.

She walked through the foyer to the living room and turned on the Christmas tree lights.

"Just put the flowers on the coffee table. I'll make us some coffee. I'm afraid it will have to be instant."

"Sounds good to me." In the kitchen, he said, "It's nice and warm in here. Don't you want to take off Mitch's jacket?"

"Oh— I forgot I was wearing it."

She'd grown accustomed to its warmth. Mitch should have said something, instead of striding away without looking back. How could he have just left like that?

"A minute ago you almost forgot where your mom lived. What's going on, Annie?"

CHAPTER SIX

DAVID WATCHED AS she removed the coat and hung it over the back of one of the kitchen chairs.

"I guess I'm tired."

"It's no wonder. You knocked yourself out for the party. Dad's going to be doubly grateful to you."

"Doubly?"

He nodded. "For your hard work, and for letting him marry your mom. He's been in love with her for a long time."

She filled mugs with hot water and added the coffee granules.

"Don't tell anyone, but Mom wanted to marry him last year. Mitch said it was because of me that he didn't propose sooner."

David's eyes grew serious. "Mitch has a point. From the beginning it was your father this, and your father that. Dad didn't think he could win either of you over."

Annie smiled. "Mom had the same problem where you were concerned. Everyone in the company knew you and your father worshipped your mother. My mom wouldn't have dared try to compete, but somehow love won out in the end."

He grinned. "It sure did."

She passed him his coffee. They both started to sip the hot liquid.

"So, what's up with you and Mitch? He's a dark horse if ever there was one."

His comment startled her. "I'm sure I don't know what you mean."

"Come on, Annie. Except for one other time, I've never known the great Mitch Reynolds to act so out of character."

She put down her mug. "In what way? What other time?"

He cocked his head. "The weekend after I broke up with Barb, he cornered me in the parking lot and told me to leave you alone because Dad was ready to propose to your mom and didn't need that complication to foul things up."

Her pulse quickened. "I don't know why he'd say something like that when you've never even asked me out."

He eyed her speculatively. "Barb accused me of always flirting with you when you came around the office. I couldn't deny it. Mitch's lecture was considerably stronger. He told me I was a bastard for toying with your emotions when I wasn't ready for a serious relationship with anybody. He managed to make me feel selfish and guilty as hell for even thinking of it when you were about to become my stepsister."

An explosion of excitement filled Annie's body.

She averted her eyes. "I had no idea. How embarrassing—for you and for me."

"Mitch has this sixth sense about things. I think he's suspicious by nature. It's no secret my father brought him into the company because Mitch's powers of observation are uncanny. He's aware of everything going on, and can troubleshoot any problems—and that makes him an invaluable asset. Since then he's been protective of Dad, and he came on so heavy with me I knew I'd have to watch myself when you came into the building. For the last few months he's been like my personal watchdog. The second you show up, it's as if he's fine tuned, or something."

A shiver ran through her, because she knew what he meant.

"Take, for instance, the other morning when you arrived with the party invitations."

She darted David a questioning glance. "I have to admit I was surprised to see Mitch in your office that early."

"You weren't the only one. In the first place he barged in without asking me if I was busy. He's never done that before. I thought I'd made a mistake on one of my reports and he'd come in to ream me out. To my surprise he wished me Merry Christmas and gave me a present. Then you made your entrance.

"For a minute I thought he was going to give me another lecture about you. But for once I wasn't worried, because I figured there'd be no reason for you to be at the office party—not when the folks were away on their honeymoon and you don't even work there. For all I knew you had a heavy Christmas Eve date with some lucky college guy. But from the moment you walked in I felt like I was at a play where you and Mitch were the actors and I was the spectator. Under other circumstances I would be jealous."

"Jealous of what?" she cried.

"Of the way you two feel about each other."

"You're crazy, David Hastings! Mitch doesn't feel *anything* for me."

What had gone on between them was a purely physical thing on his part.

"He doesn't even know me."

Correction. He now knew she melted whenever he touched her. It was the most dangerous piece of knowledge for him to have.

"I'm sure your father asked him to make certain the party didn't fall flat. As you said, he was acting a part to put some pizzazz into the festivities. Don't take anything he said or did seriously."

Annie needed to listen to her own advice or she was in terrible trouble.

"You mean you weren't affected when he kissed you?"

"Of course I was. What woman doesn't like a surprise kiss under the mistletoe?"

"So my kiss left you in that same breathless condition, too?"

She eyed him curiously. It was truth time. But she didn't want to hurt his feelings, or at least not hurt his masculine pride, so she said, "You couldn't tell?"

His brows lifted. "I wasn't sure if it was your reaction to Mitch or not. I'd been drinking beforehand, and I'm no expert on the subject of his effect on women. He keeps his private life to himself. Still, something has been going on inside him over the last few days. The crowd at my table kept asking me if the two of you had a thing going."

"That's preposterous," she exclaimed. "I'm afraid the only woman he ever loved was his fiancée, Hannah. She was killed while they were in college."

David looked taken back. "I never knew about that. When did he tell you?"

"In the elevator."

"How did she die?"

After she'd related the details, he shook his head. "That's tough. I had no idea."

"I guess no one did."

"If you're convinced his strange behavior has nothing to do with you, then I have to believe you. I guess it doesn't really matter. It isn't as if you're an employee and have to work with him on a day-to-day basis."

"Heavens, no."

"Well, enough said about him, then. Why don't we

go in the living room? If you'd like to start planning the party for our parents, we could do that."

Annie could hear everything he was saying, but her mind was fixated on something Mitch had said to her a few days ago.

After you receive your MBA in the spring, I'd like to be the first person you come to see. I know of a position in the corporation that needs a person like you.

"Y-You know what, David? It's late, and I'm too exhausted to think clearly. Would you like to come over some time during the holidays and we'll put our heads together?"

"Sure. I'm not good for much right now, either. I'll call you in a day or two and we'll go from there." He kissed her forehead. "Merry Christmas, Annie. I never had a sibling and I love the idea. Welcome to the family."

Tears smarted in her eyes. "I like the idea of a brother, too. Merry Christmas, David."

She walked him to the front door and watched him walk away and hail a cab home.

The kiss he'd just given her felt the way she imagined a brother's kiss would feel if she'd grown up with one. That had to be the reason she'd felt nothing when he'd kissed her beneath the mistletoe.

You could try to make something happen. You could want it with all your heart. But if it wasn't meant to be, all the planning in the world couldn't change the outcome.

But another person could…

Annie suddenly had a suffocating feeling in her chest, because she was very much afraid that person's suit jacket was hanging on the kitchen chair.

What was it Mitch had said to her about being an intelligent woman?

Maybe one day you'll figure it out.

Had it been the alcohol talking, or had David hit upon something Annie wouldn't have guessed in a thousand years?

Filled with a different kind of energy, she walked back in the kitchen. Without conscious thought she slid her arms into the jacket and pressed the lapels to her chin. A faint trace of the soap Mitch used in the shower assailed her.

She drew in a shaky breath, recalling the different ways his mouth had seduced her throughout the evening. Every time he came near or touched her, her body turned to liquid. Whatever else might be imagined, the chemistry between them was explosive.

Something told her that the strange vibes she'd sensed around him all year long were the other side of the most primitive emotion known to man. It was called desire. Something you never got over once you felt it.

Filled with questions only he could answer, she strolled into the living room and lay down on the couch to look at the Christmas tree.

She and her mom had decorated it the other day— their private ritual in remembrance of Michael Roberts, beloved husband and father.

Her thoughts drifted to Mitch. Were his grandparents still alive? Did he have brothers and sisters to share Christmas with?

He'd been right about the snow. She was a Californian through and through, but how she'd love to wake up to a white Christmas.

Why had he moved here if he missed Minnesota so much?

When she couldn't stand not having answers to any of her questions, she went to bed. Tomorrow she would open the few presents sitting under the tree, then go into the office and do the paperwork she'd put off in order to plan the party.

When she got to the end of her mother's list of things to do, she'd get busy reading ahead for next semester's coursework.

After that, Roz and Larry were expecting her for a cheese fondue dinner at their apartment.

It was a far cry from the Christmas she'd planned when David had still been the object of her desire.

Her desire...

Until the Christmas party she hadn't known its true meaning. Thanks to Mitch Reynolds, she'd come alive and would never be the same again.

Mitch had barely entered his condo when his cellphone rang. Who in the hell was calling him at one-thirty Christmas morning?

His mood already black at the thought of Annie and David alone in her house, where more experimenting was probably going on, he checked the caller ID. When he saw who it was, his mind leaped to several conclusions—all of which filled him with dread. The last time he'd had such an unorthodox call, it had been the police, giving him news no one should ever have to hear.

He clicked on. "David?" His body broke out in a cold sweat while he held his breath, waiting to hear that he or Annie had been in an accident.

"Sorry, Mitch, but I figured you weren't asleep yet."

David's voice didn't sound like this was an emergency. Mitch exhaled in exquisite relief.

"I just got in. Are you and Annie all right?"

"She's fine, but I'm not. If Dad were available, I'd talk to him. But since he isn't, and this concerns Annie, I hope you don't mind if I dump this on you for a minute?"

Mitch stopped pacing. "Dump away. I'm not going to bed yet."

"Thanks. Let me explain first that you've been right all along about me. I've treated Annie like a jerk. To be honest, I never thought Dad would actually marry Marion. Now that he has, and Annie and I are related, I really feel like a louse for leading her on. It's weird, you know?"

Mitch relaxed. "I can only imagine."

"After I helped her into the house, I decided to take your advice and just be honest with her. The way I did it was to welcome her to the family and tell her it was nice to finally have a sister."

Mitch rubbed his scar, which was throbbing. "How did she take it?"

"On the surface she seemed okay. But I felt like a worse heel just leaving after that, when I knew she was alone. Here's my dilemma. It isn't as if she's someone I'll never see again. We're going to be part of each other's lives from here on out."

Mitch sucked in his breath. "If you called to ask me if you did the right thing, the answer is yes. You handled it with as much finesse as anyone could have."

"Thanks. Coming from you, that means a lot. But it doesn't take away the bad taste in my mouth for not having dealt with her sooner. And here's my other problem. She wants to plan a party for the folks. I told her I'd call her in a few days and we'd talk about it, but—"

"Not a good idea," Mitch broke in.

"I agree. That's why I'm calling you—to get advice from someone outside the problem. Sorry you have to be the one I picked on, but since you know the whole situation, I trust your judgment."

At this point Mitch's brain switched to overdrive. "Since the three of us were in your office when I offered to help plan a party for them, let *me* run with the ball. That leaves you free to fly to Sacramento this week and get a head start on the bidding for that property we were talking about."

"You'd do that?"

David sounded relieved. Mitch had the grace to feel

ashamed for some of the thoughts he'd harbored about him over the past year.

"You're not in an enviable position at the moment. Not with Annie needing a cooling-off period. I'll be glad to help out."

Annie's breathtaking response earlier tonight had started a fire he intended to make hotter.

"I owe you, Mitch. Would you believe there was a time a few months ago when I wanted to punch you out for interfering?"

David didn't know the half of it. But Mitch kept his thoughts to himself.

"But that's water under the bridge now." David went on talking. "I'm sure Annie will work with you. She knows how close you are to Dad. And she respects you—otherwise she wouldn't have asked you to take charge at the party tonight."

Mitch let that false assumption pass. All was fair in love and war.

"For what it's worth, Mitch, you're a good man to have around. Even though Dad's been saying that about you for years, I want you to know those are *my* words. I think maybe I can get some sleep now. Merry Christmas."

"The same to you, David." He hung up the phone. *"The same to you,"* he whispered.

For the first time in ages he felt like he had when he'd been a boy, on the verge of opening the one Christmas present he'd been dying for.

CHAPTER SEVEN

Since Roger had moved the company into the new facility, he'd added more security. Annie's mother had had to get Annie her own security pass so she could come and go from the building.

Once she'd flashed it to the security guard at the main doors, she entered the complex.

It seemed a shame the security men had to work on Christmas Day, but then that was the whole point.

It didn't matter about her, of course. She didn't have anyone at home. But those men had families.

Oh, well, Roger probably paid them time and a half and gave them extra perks for protecting the premises.

When the night watchman saw her through the window, he came out of his cubicle.

"Merry Christmas, Annie. What are you doing over here, today of all days?"

She smiled. "I have some work to do, and I wanted to return this suit coat to Mr Reynolds. He lent it to me after the party last night. Would you mind opening his office so I can leave it for him?"

"I'll do it right now."

They walked down the hall together. He undid the lock and waited while she put it over the chair in his secretary's office. As soon as she came out and shut the door he asked if she wanted her mother's door opened.

"No. I have her key. Thanks, Mel."

He nodded. "Have a good one."

"You, too."

Once seated at her mom's desk, she opened the pile of mail that had accrued over the last few days. A lot of it was Christmas cards sent to the firm. Some of them had personal messages intended for Roger. One in particular was Mitch's.

Helplessly fascinated by anything to do with him, she undid the envelope. He'd sent a large card with a beautiful picture. Inside, Mitch had written in his own dynamic cursive, "Do you have any idea how great it is to work for a boss who's the kindest man I've ever known? All the best to you, Roger."

He'd signed it with a simple "M."

Annie unconsciously pressed the card to her chest.

Where Roger was concerned, it was as if Mitch had taken the words out of her mouth.

Before the office party she would never have guessed he could have written something so heartfelt. In fact at times his slightly forbidding vice presidential persona ruled out the possibility that he even had a heart. Now she knew differently.

But that first kiss under the mistletoe had proved

he was all too human. From that point on he'd methodically exposed the woman in her until she'd been a pulsating mass of need. As for the wicked, outrageous antics he'd pulled all evening—they'd revealed the type of man he really was. A remarkable man, when she gave herself permission to admit it.

"I thought I might find you here."

Annie's head flew back in shock, while her insides vibrated at the sound of his male voice.

Except for his eyes, that burned like blue flames, she almost didn't recognize him in jeans and a well-worn leather bomber jacket.

Good heavens…

He moved closer. "What's got you so interested you didn't even hear me knock?"

She slid his card back in the opened stack, but it didn't prevent him from picking up the envelope he'd stamped and sealed a few days earlier.

His compelling mouth curved at one end. How had she ever thought it had a cruel twist?

"Mom asked me to open the mail for her."

"Did you like my card?"

Since she'd been caught in the act anyway, she said, "As a matter of fact I loved it."

His eyes narrowed on her upturned features. "I just opened *my* mail, but I didn't get what I was hoping for."

She'd give anything to know what he'd been looking for.

"Maybe next year," he murmured. "Thanks for returning my suit coat." It dangled from his hand. "The second I saw it, I knew that a certain charming elf was in the building somewhere."

She lowered her eyes to the desk. "I'm afraid that elf has retreated to the North Pole, never to be seen or heard of again."

"What a shame. I took a fancy to her."

Afraid to take him seriously, because she wanted to believe it too much, she said, "The latest company gossip says that you took a fancy to Mrs Claus, too."

He grinned, causing her heart to slam against her ribs. "That same rumor mill is spreading fiction that you and I are a couple. And though *we* know it isn't true, it might be wise to perpetuate the myth for a while."

The word "myth" shattered her fragile heart to tiny shards.

"Why would we want to do that?" She congratulated herself for keeping her voice steady.

He pursed his lips. "So David will get the message that you're over him. After all the years that you had a crush on him, it's hard for him to realize you've outgrown it. He's a little confused at the moment."

Annie's hand tightened around the letter opener. "What do you mean?"

"Your breathless response to my kiss, when you and I have only been acquaintances up to now, has done some damage to him. It's just as well that he'd had too much to drink and only got a vague impression that he might not be the only man in your life."

"But you're *not* in my life."

"For his sake let's be glad that for the moment he believes I am. The problem is, he could be hurt if this isn't handled carefully. Take it from me, a man is vulnerable after a broken engagement. In your case it's more complicated, because he's your stepbrother now."

She froze. "So what is it you're trying to say?"

"Maybe the best way to handle it would be for him to think you're interested in me—or at least open to the possibility. For the rest of the holiday you're welcome to use me."

The knife just kept driving deeper. "To do what?"

"To help you plan the party for your parents. I'd already decided to give them one. Under the circumstances we might as well do it together."

She clutched the sides of her chair so hard it cut off the circulation. "David said he was going to call me about it."

"I know. He just phoned me to talk shop and mentioned it in passing. That's because he's unsure of what to do about you now that he assumes you and I are an item."

After last night, everyone at the party would be assuming the same thing. She needed to fight her way through this so Mitch would never know how devastated she was. She'd actually begun to believe he wanted to get to know her better. Not just on a physical level, but in other ways. The job offer—the revelations about his fiancée—it had all been a starting point. Or so she'd fantasized.

"I thought it the perfect opportunity to tell him *I* would help you take care of the party if he wanted to leave on business in the morning."

"What business?"

"He's bidding on a project for us in Sacramento. By the time he gets back on New Year's and discovers we're together, he'll accept the fact that you've moved on and will only ever be his stepsister. Then, after you go back to school, it will have all blown over and he'll settle down to find the right woman. That will relieve Roger more than you know."

She gritted her teeth so tightly it was a miracle they didn't all crack.

Finally she'd figured out what secret mission had brought Mitch into the office.

He'd lost his true love, but he wasn't above using David as an excuse to have a little fun with her. And why not? She'd lit up like spontaneous fire with every kiss and caress he'd given her, and it was the holiday after all.

So what was to prevent her from giving him what he wanted for a little while longer? Slowly lead him on, then break it off as brutally as he'd just broken her heart.

All she really had to do was continue on the way things had been going. Let him keep coming on to her.

Let him keep taking over. Never realizing she was on to him big-time until it was too late.

Her first impression of him hadn't been wrong after all. He was a dangerous man. But she could be dangerous, too. Just how dangerous he was about to find out.

"I—I'm not sure if your idea will work, but the last thing either David or I want is to create problems for Mom and Roger. They've suffered enough pain and deserve some joy."

She eyed him solemnly. "I've already made plans with friends for this evening, but if you want to talk ideas tomorrow, we can."

"Good. I'll come by your house at noon. We can go to lunch and decide where to have the party."

"I have a better idea," she reasoned. "Why don't you come to the house at two and I'll treat you to the Christmas meal Mom always made for our family? If I don't fix it, it won't seem like Christmas even came this year. I didn't feel like making it for one person—but, since you're offering to help smooth the waters with David, it'll be worth the trouble."

For once he didn't have an instant comeback. She waited until he finally said, "Do you want any help?"

"Not this time. I'm not the greatest cook in the world and I need the practice without anyone looking over my shoulder."

"Understood. I'll be there at two."

She didn't miss the glimmer of satisfaction in his

eyes before he left the office, closing the door quietly behind him.

This is all-out war, Mitchell Reynolds. I've let you win the first few rounds. But the mother of battles is coming. Then the tide is going to turn, and I can't wait...

Mitch let out a groan of pleasure and put down his fork. "That was the best Christmas feast I've had in years."

"Thank my mom. They're her recipes, but I must admit it tasted better than I thought it was going to."

"When Roger finds out she's a marvel in the kitchen, he'll probably want her to stay home."

"If he takes early retirement, that's exactly what she'll do. Deep down she's a homebody."

His intelligent eyes assessed her from his place across the dining room table. "What about you?"

"I'm not sure what I am yet. As you reminded me yesterday, I've just started to spread my wings—and I like the feeling."

Her remark could be taken several ways. She wondered which way he'd chosen to take it.

He sat back in the chair, drinking the rest of his coffee. "Speaking of homes, how would you feel if we give the party at my beach house?"

She stirred in her chair. "I didn't know you had one."

He put down his cup. "It's in San Clemente. I bought it six months ago and have been remodeling it in my spare time."

Hmm. A condo in Beverly Hills and a house on the ocean. That had to be the best-kept secret at the Hastings Corporation.

There was no question Mitch was a millionaire in his own right. It proved what hard work and brains could do when your heart had died.

Annie was impressed. And she'd bet he knew she was so impressed she would agree to drive down and see it with him.

He'd be right. She was going to fall in with all his wishes…except for the one she planned to refuse him at the last minute.

"I would imagine Mom and Roger will love it."

"Good. Tomorrow I'll drive us down during the day, so you can get an idea of the layout for yourself."

He was as transparent as the crystal she'd put on the table.

"In that case I'll have to get an early start at Mom's office in the morning."

He nodded. "I have business, too, so I'll pick you up at eight-thirty and we'll go in together before we leave for the beach."

She lowered her eyes, afraid he would read the excitement in them and figure out she had an agenda of her own.

"Let me help you with the dishes." He got up from the table and started clearing it.

She knew exactly what was going to happen. Once they were at the kitchen sink he'd slip his arms around her waist, kiss her neck and continue the softening-up process until he had her where he wanted her. The way she'd been last night—biddable in his arms.

Deciding to let him suffer a little longer, she remained seated. He was going to have to work harder than that for what he had in mind.

When he came back in the dining room for more dishes she said, "I make it a rule never to allow a dinner guest to slave in my kitchen."

He put his hands on the back of one of the chairs. "You sound like you mean that."

She smiled up at him. "It's called saving you from a fate worse than death."

His lips twitched. "I like the way your mind thinks, Ms Roberts."

He stretched, drawing her gaze to the play of muscle across his back and shoulders beneath his green polo shirt.

"Under the circumstances, I take it you won't mind if I go back to the office now. I'm in the middle of some delicate negotiations that could take me into the night to work out. With a turkey dinner like the one you've just fed me I'm good for hours, and I'll be able to concentrate with no one else around."

Her heart lurched, but she managed to keep munching on the last of her pumpkin pie. How could she have forgotten for one second that she was dealing with a pro who didn't follow the normal rules of engagement?

"You have an amazing work ethic, Mitch. The guys I

date could learn a lot from a successful man like your-self. I'll walk you to the door."

His eyes were shuttered. "Don't bother to get up. I know my way out. I'll see you in the morning. Be sure to bring a parka and a pair of good walking shoes."

So he was planning to take her for a romantic walk along the surf? She wouldn't disappoint him.

"I won't forget. At least let me thank you again for the Christmas present. I'm sorry I didn't have one for you."

"What do you call the superb meal you went to all the trouble to fix me?" With those words, he disap-peared.

Clever as a fox. That was Mitch Reynolds.

She wandered into the living room to inspect the little Christmas ornaments he'd given her.

After she'd opened her package, he'd hung them on the tree. Mr and Mrs Claus.

If she weren't on to him, she would have been com-pletely taken in by his ruse.

She flicked Mr Claus with her finger. He swung back and forth, catching the light. Her eyelids squeezed tightly together as she remembered the thrilling taste and feel of his mouth beneath his Santa beard.

Years from now, if she was lucky enough to be mar-ried to the right man and had a daughter, she'd warn her about tall, dark, gorgeous men with piercing navy blue eyes and a scar on their jaw. They could tempt a saint, but could never be tamed by one.

Except that Hannah had brought him to his knees.

Annie felt shame for envying the dead woman who'd stolen his heart to the point that he'd wanted her for his wife.

CHAPTER EIGHT

SAN CLEMENTE WAS a Spanish-styled coastal town south of L.A. It had been founded in a romantic setting where there was some of the best surfing in Southern California. Inside and out, Mitch's home reflected the local flavor, preserving the integrity of the original architecture. It was a jewel of a find only someone in his exclusive circle of friends would have known had come on the market.

No doubt he'd brought other women down here, but all that had been kept secret. He was a dark horse, all right.

After he'd given Annie a tour, they'd walked along the surf for several hours.

He'd found them a charming spot overlooking the ocean to eat crab legs. For once they'd just made conversation, which had almost convinced her they were a normal couple out on a date. But nothing could be further from the truth.

Finally they returned to his beautiful beach house.

"What do you think?" he asked, as she looked up at the windows from the sand.

"You already know what I think. It's fabulous. The perfect place for a party."

"What about a place to live in year-round?"

She put her hands in her coat pockets, wondering what he was driving at. "If you're talking about yourself, I can see it would require a lot of driving back and forth from L.A. But it would be worth it to come home to this every night."

She turned her head in his direction. "Are you planning to sell your condo?"

His eyes held a faraway look. "Not until my grandparents have passed away. I'm thinking of moving them out here. They're already old, and getting older by the minute. Would you believe they've never seen the Pacific Ocean?"

Just when Annie thought she had him all figured out, he said or did something to change her perspective in a totally different way.

"Have you told them you'd like them to come?"

"Yes. But they don't want to be a burden and are fighting me. You don't know stubborn until you've met them. If I can't get them to consider it, then I'll have to tell Roger I'm moving back to Minnesota. They need me, even if they pretend they don't."

She tried to breathe normally but couldn't. The thought of him moving so far away was anathema to her.

"You don't have brothers or sisters to help share in their care?"

Though she'd promised herself she wouldn't get more involved with him, she couldn't help wanting to know anything and everything about his life.

"No. My parents died in a freak car accident when I was three."

"How awful," she murmured.

"I don't remember it. My grandparents raised me with high expectations. When I got a scholarship to Stanford they insisted I go and make them proud. But it's a pretty empty world without them in it—except for the times when I fly back to see them, of course. I went to see them just before the Christmas break."

Every revelation caused her to rethink her assessment of him. "Can't you get them to come for a visit, if nothing else?"

"With the right incentive it might be possible," he murmured.

"I should think a party at your own home to celebrate your boss's marriage would be a good enough reason. I would imagine they'd love to meet the man whose faith in you has been repaid a hundred fold."

"A hundred fold?" he queried, with a heavy dash of irony.

"Those are my mother's words. She was just repeating to me what Roger said about you."

"That's very gratifying to hear, but I'm afraid it's a big exaggeration."

No. If anything it was an understatement.

"If you'd like, I'll extend the invitation myself," she offered. His grandparents probably didn't know how important a man Mitch was. "When I let them know how much it will mean to my new stepfather to meet them, maybe they'll think twice before saying no."

His gaze trapped hers. If she wasn't mistaken, she thought she saw something flicker in those dark blue depths.

"You'd do that for me?"

If he only knew...

"Of course. The trick is to get them here. Once they arrive in San Clemente, and see what a heavenly spot this is, maybe they'll consider moving here. It's certainly worth a try. Otherwise—" Her voice trembled.

"Otherwise what?" he prodded, as if he really wanted to know.

"I'm afraid Roger's going to be in for a horrible shock when you tell him you have to leave the company. It won't be the same without you."

I won't be the same. There was no kidding herself about that.

"You're forgetting David."

She shook her head. "He could never take your place. In fact I have a hunch he'll end up doing something else one day. He isn't like you."

Mitch eyed her so intently she was afraid he could see through to her soul.

"You mean he doesn't have fire in his belly?"

It was unnerving the way he could read her mind.

"He has other fine qualities."

"I agree. He's a much nicer person than I am."

At one time Annie might have thought that, but no longer. She'd learned too much about him over the last few days. But she needed to keep her thoughts to herself—unless she wanted him to know how she really felt about him.

She pulled her hands back out of her pockets. "Since we've set a date for the party, why don't we go up to the house and phone your grandparents right now?"

She heard him take a deep breath. "I was just going to suggest it."

He cupped her elbow and they began climbing the stairs from the beach. It was the first time since the night of the office party that he'd touched her.

She hoped he couldn't tell how sensitive she was to the contact, how much she craved it.

In the face of his concern over his grandparents, she dismissed the idea that he'd brought her here because he'd been playing a game of seduction.

Judging from the tone in his voice, it was vital to him that his family be taken care of—if not here, then back in Minnesota.

Should that happen, he would disappear from her life. She was starting to panic over the possibility.

Crazy as it sounded, she knew she'd fallen in love with him. For a year or more she'd been intensely aware of him. In fact she had to admit to the strange thrill she'd always felt when she had visited her mother and found him following her with his searching gaze.

Roger had sung his praises for so long, she'd known he was a different breed of man—one who commanded the respect of other men. And he was a man her own mother admitted was so attractive that he drew women without even trying.

For a long time Annie had feared her adult feelings for him, not recognizing what was going on inside her. Now she knew why. Her newly awakened heart was quaking with the knowledge that she'd met the man she wanted to marry.

But, much as she ached for his love in return, she refused to be his plaything.

He'd said something about coming to see him in the spring after she graduated. But that would be pure torture if he only wanted her around for professional reasons.

How her mom had continued to work for Roger when she'd had little hope he would ever love her was beyond Annie's comprehension. She could never handle that kind of pain.

To be in the same building with Mitch and never be able to express her love would be tantamount to being handed a sentence of perpetual agony.

Already feeling the pain, she raced up the last few stairs ahead of him.

The sooner Mitch made this phone call, the sooner

she could ask him to take her home. It was time to get out of the fire.

When they reached the house and went inside, she'd already removed her parka, afraid he would help and she would let him. That would lead to more temptation, and ultimately more regrets.

While she found a seat on the couch facing the ocean, Mitch put another log on the fire, then pulled out his cellphone to ring the people who'd raised him.

Once he began to talk, she heard a tenderness in his tone that bespoke a lifetime of loving.

The more she listened, the more critical it became that she get them to say yes.

"Annie?" he whispered.

She jerked around and took the phone from him. The look in his eyes told her he didn't hold out much hope.

Crossing her fingers figuratively, she said, "Hello? Mr and Mrs Reynolds?"

"We're on the line." His grandfather spoke up.

"Good. It's Annie Roberts. I just wanted to urge you to come out for this party Mitch and I are planning. Your grandson is like a son to Roger Hastings, and I know Roger has wanted to meet you for a long time. It would mean the world to my mother, too. She's worked at the Hastings Corporation even longer than Mitch, and is very fond of him. Please say you'll think about it."

The silence on the other end prompted her to get up

from the couch and walk to the other side of the living room, out of earshot.

"I can't tell you how much it would mean to everyone. Your grandson is a legend around here." Her voice shook. "You'd be so proud of him. He's a credit to the way you raised him." They had to be remarkable people.

She heard someone clear their throat before Mitch's grandfather said, "What do you think, Martha?"

"I'd like to go, if you would."

"Well, then, young woman, I guess it's settled."

Annie had to hold back her tears. "That's wonderful. Why don't you tell Mitch? Here he is."

She found him over by the fireplace and handed him the phone without looking at him. If he could see her eyes, he'd divine her deepest feelings.

She moved over to the windows, waiting for him to finish talking to them. Soon the room grew quiet. She sensed his presence behind her.

"I thought you told me a certain Christmas elf had retreated to the North Pole." He sounded happy.

"I guess she made a small detour on the way."

"I guess she did. Do you have a suggestion how I can thank this elf?"

"Elves don't want or need thanks."

She heard his sharp intake of breath. "Why is that?"

"Because they're not human," she teased, and slowly turned to face him with a smile. "The important thing is that your grandparents said they'd come. I'm thrilled for you. Now, if you don't mind, it's getting late and I need to go home."

He studied her for a moment. "What's your hurry? We still have to decide on a caterer and work on a menu."

Maybe they'd get around to that, but the way she was feeling right now she would crawl into his lap at the slightest invitation. Then heaven help her.

"Could we discuss it on the way home? I'm meeting with my study group later tonight. We've got to finish a project and turn it in after the holidays."

It was a half-truth. Her group *had* decided to get together one night this week, but they hadn't finalized which night. Of course Mitch didn't know that—which was for the best, because she was in a precarious emotional state right now. Since the conversation with his grandparents, the situation had changed. She no longer trusted herself to be around him.

He flashed her an enigmatic glance. "I'll get your coat."

In a few minutes they were traveling back to L.A. on I-5. It had already grown dark and felt like ten at night instead of six-thirty.

By the time they reached her mom's house, all the party details had been worked out.

"Tell me about your project," he said, after shutting off the motor.

She'd been afraid he'd bring that up.

"It's for a marketing class."

"What's the precise assignment?"

He *knew* she'd lied to him about the group coming over.

"We have to plan an ad campaign for a fake product," she said, before bolting from his car.

He was right behind her when she reached her front door. "Have you thought of one yet?"

"Yes, but nothing's been decided."

Wishing he would leave, she pulled out her keys and unlocked the front door. "Thank you for lunch, and the tour of your beautiful home." She was praying he wouldn't touch her or she'd be lost.

"Thank *you* for talking to my grandparents. It made all the difference."

"I'm glad, Mitch. It will be wonderful to meet them." She had to clear her throat. "Well, goodnight…"

He didn't budge. "Before I go anywhere, I'll see you inside to make sure you're safe."

She panicked. "Of course I'm safe."

"Humor me," he said, in an authoritative voice. "A woman on her own, coming home to an empty house in the dark, is taking a risk."

Annie moaned. Letting him come inside would be a much bigger risk, but he'd left her no choice.

With her heart thumping in her chest, they entered the house. She ran ahead to turn on lights, then returned to the living room.

"As you can see, you worried for nothing. But I appreciate your concern." She took the lid off a box of chocolate orange sticks sitting on the coffee table. "Please take as many as you like before you go."

After a day of wind and salt spray, most women Mitch knew would have excused themselves to freshen up. Not Annie, who didn't need any artifice. He loved her disheveled hair. He loved the curve of her mouth that hadn't seen a coat of lipstick for hours. The lights from the tree illuminated the sheen of her dark curls. He had an overpowering desire to run his fingers through them.

His gaze took in her khakis and the black cashmere sweater she wore, providing a perfect foil for those luminescent gray eyes fringed with sooty lashes. They lightened or darkened according to her emotions.

His eyes didn't miss the curious throb at the base of her throat. Its incessant movement revealed a heightened state of nervousness that meant she was frightened.

Of him? Or herself? It was time to find out.

"What is it about me that threatens you so much you had to pretend to get home to study?"

Even with the few feet separating them he felt her body tauten.

"I admit I used that as an excuse to come home, but it isn't because I feel threatened. If that were true I wouldn't have driven to San Clemente with you in the first place."

"So why are you poised like a deer in the forest, sensing a hunter close by?"

She put the candy back on the coffee table. "I don't think of you as a hunter."

"Then why is your heart racing? I can hear it from here."

"David isn't the only one confused," she admitted.

"Meaning?"

She tossed her head back. "Meaning I got the shock of my life Christmas Eve, and I'm not proud of it. You would think that a woman almost twenty-four years old would have the emotional maturity to recognize a one-sided crush for what it was. The kiss you gave me was like a glass of ice water thrown in my face to wake me up."

"Didn't you like it?"

She stared at him with accusing eyes. "You know I did. My problem is, I was so fixated on capturing David's interest I didn't do enough experimenting over the years. Then an experienced man several years my senior comes along and opens up a whole new world of enjoyment to me."

Mitch would take that for openers. "I'll admit I enjoyed kissing you, too."

"But that's the problem, isn't it? I've discovered how easily I could be swept away by sheer physical pleasure. I don't know whether to thank you or curse you. Under the circumstances, I'm going to chalk it up to my coming of age and leave it at that."

She could leave it at that all she wanted. *He* intended to deal with the rest on his own terms.

"Thank you for your honesty, Annie. It's another of your qualities I admire. I'll see you in the morning. Goodnight."

CHAPTER NINE

ANNIE TRIED NOT to think too much about it when she didn't see Mitch in the building the next day. After two days with no sign of him, she decided he must have flown out to Minnesota.

At the end of the third day she left the building to get together with her study group. On the way to the parking lot she happened to see Elaine, getting into her car. Her husband and children were with her.

Mitch's secretary wouldn't have come by unless there was an important reason.

"Hi, Elaine!"

The other woman turned around. She held a stack of files in her arms.

"Annie! How are you?"

Since Mitch's departure from Annie's mom's house earlier in the week, she'd been suffering withdrawal. But that wasn't news she wanted anyone to know, least of all Elaine.

"I'm well. How are you?"

"Terrific. That was the best office party I've ever

been to in my life. You and Mitch brought the house down."

Her hands formed fists in reaction. He'd done a lot more than that to Annie.

"Chuck couldn't believe the bonus. It made our Christmas."

"Roger will be glad to hear it." She took another breath before asking, "What are you doing here? This is supposed to be your vacation."

"I know, but Mitch is sick and asked if I'd bring a couple of files to him. He says he needs to go over some figures that weren't scanned into the computer."

It had been so unlike Mitch not to make an appearance at the office, Annie had driven herself crazy wondering what was going on with him. Of all the reasons she'd considered, illness hadn't been one of them. The knowledge was almost as unsettling as the fact that he hadn't called Annie for help. He knew she was working at the office all week, to cover for her mother, yet he'd phoned Elaine and forced *her* to come in.

Apparently Annie's honesty the other night had produced the desired effect, because he'd left her strictly alone.

It appeared Mitch didn't need her help, or David's, until the night of the party. The invitations had already gone out.

It proved Annie's theory about men and their pleasure. They took it where and when they could find it.

Now that she was out of sight, she was no longer on his mind.

How unfair that he filled her thoughts until she couldn't eat or sleep anymore.

Elaine's children called out the window for her to hurry.

"I'm sorry, Annie. We're taking the kids to a movie, and they're not happy that we have to drive to San Clemente first."

After a slight hesitation, Annie said, "I'm headed in that direction for a study group session. I'll take those for you if you want."

"You're not making that up just to help me out? It's something you would do."

Annie crossed her heart. "We're meeting at one of the guys' houses at Dana Point. My backpack's in the car. I know where Mitch lives. It won't be more than five minutes out of my way."

"You're an angel." Elaine handed the files to her.

Annie waved the family off, then hurried over to her car and got in to start up the motor.

On the way to San Clemente she rehearsed what she would say when Mitch opened the door, but nothing sounded right.

Maybe a better idea would be to phone him and tell him she was leaving the files between the screen and his front door. That way she and Mitch wouldn't have to see each other.

Before long she arrived in his neighborhood and

pulled out her cell to call him. Unfortunately she was told to leave a message.

She could do that. But if by a horrible stroke of fate something happened to the files before he knew they were outside, she might live to regret it.

The only thing to do was ring his doorbell.

She pulled into the latticework carport covered in bougainvillea and shut off the motor.

Grabbing the files, she got out and rushed to the door.

Her whole body tensed as she pushed the button. It took a while before she heard a click. Then the door opened and she discovered Mitch, standing there in a white T-shirt and gray sweats. He was in his stocking feet, and his hair looked more disheveled than usual. With a five o'clock shadow, he had a raw male appeal that kindled the ache inside her.

"Hello," he said, in that low, husky voice she'd been missing.

"Hi, Mitch. Elaine came by the office as I was leaving. Since I was on my way to Dana Point anyway, I told her I'd drop these off."

He took them from her. "What's in Dana Point?"

"Mike Teale lives there. The study group is getting together at his house tonight. In case you were wondering, that's the truth."

"I'm sure it is," came the bleak response.

Somehow it made her feel guilty rather than defensive.

He gazed at her through veiled eyes. "Elaine must have been relieved."

"I believe so. They were leaving to go to a movie." Feeling more awkward and uncertain by the minute, she turned to leave, then paused. "She said you'd been ill. Are you all right?"

"I haven't been sick in the way you mean. I was up on the roof the other day and hurt my Achilles' tendon, so I've been nursing it."

"What were you doing up there?"

"Checking a vent, but the tiles were slippery."

"Why didn't you get a roofer to come out?"

A half-smile broke the corner of his sensuous mouth.

"My grandfather was a building contractor. By the time I graduated from high school I'd learned the business from him, and I never once hurt myself until now."

"That's why this house is so beautiful! You've been remodeling it yourself! Now I'm *really* impressed."

But a band had constricted her lungs. For someone as strong and tough as Mitch to stay home, his injury had to be more serious than he was letting on.

"I'm sure it's painful. Don't let me keep you."

She had the impression he was so miserable he couldn't wait for her to leave.

"Mitch? As long as I'm here, is there anything I can do for you?"

He rubbed the back of his neck. "I was going to ask Elaine if she had any painkillers with her. Is it possible you carry a bottle around?"

"No, but I'll run to the store for you right now."

"That isn't necessary. I don't need any more until I go to bed. If you wouldn't mind, maybe you could stop by with some after your study session and just leave it in that potted plant?" He motioned to the large terra-cotta jar by the door.

He didn't want to see her again. She reeled, before recovering enough to say, "I'd be happy to do that for you."

"Then this old man thanks you."

He slowly shut the door in her face.

Message received, Mr Reynolds.

By the time she'd backed out of his driveway she had dissolved into tears. No way would she make it through the study session.

The drive to Mike's house didn't take long. After giving him the ad campaign she'd printed out she begged off, saying something important had come up. If the guys needed to talk, they could call her on her cell.

With that accomplished, she went to the nearest store for medicine. She also picked up a can of soda and two gel-packs, already chilled, so he could ice his injury.

A few minutes later she drove back to his house and marched straight to the door. This time she had to ring twice before he answered.

The second the door opened she said, "Don't you think asking me to leave your medicine in a plant out-side your house in the dark is a little absurd?"

A stillness surrounded him. "I was only attempting to obey your rules, so you wouldn't think I'm out for what you hold most dear."

She swept past him, red-faced, and went into the kitchen to put the sack on the counter. He came in, limping.

While she opened the soda she said, "I'm breaking the rules this once in the hope that you'll still be able to host the party."

She undid the cap on the pills. "Here. Take some."

He did her bidding without remonstration.

"I brought you some ice packs. The pharmacist said to apply for twenty minutes, then wait twenty and apply again." She put one of them in the fridge.

"Let's get you in bed with this one, then I'll leave."

He followed her down the hall. "What happened to your study group session?"

His bedroom was a mess. Evidently he'd been living in it for the last three days.

She set out to make his bed with clean sheets and made sure he could get in it without lying on a magazine or newspaper.

"I dropped off my proposal. They'll get back to me later."

He lay down like an obedient child.

Avoiding his eyes, she said, "Which leg is it?"

"My right one."

She propped it with pillows, then he told her where to put the ice pack.

"That's cold."

"It's supposed to be."

He darted her a searching glance. "Are you sure you're not a nursing student?"

"Positive. So don't get any ideas that I'm going to give you round-the-clock care."

"You made that clear the other night."

"Then we understand each other." She got up from the bed.

"Could I ask you one more favor?"

"What is it?"

"Will you look for the remote to the TV? I think it fell under the bed."

Annie got down on the floor. "Found it." She stood up and handed it to him. "Anything else before I go?"

"Can you put those files where I can reach them?"

She placed them next to the pillow he was lying on. As she stood up, their eyes met. Something flickered in the recesses of his. She almost stopped breathing.

"Do you know what?" he whispered in a husky tone.

"No, and I don't want to know."

"I'm going to say it anyway. I'm glad you're not an elf."

For no good reason her heart began to thud. "Why is that?"

"As you reminded me the other day, they're not human—but you are." He pulled her down so she was half lying on top of him. "I don't give a damn if there's no mistletoe. I need to kiss you again whether you come willing or not."

"No—" she begged. But her cry for mercy went unheeded. He buried his mouth in hers and began kissing her. Over and over again. Long, hungry kisses that called up her desire until she matched him kiss for soul-destroying kiss.

With a groan he rolled her over, crushing her so close against his hard frame it felt like they were one pulsating body of need.

"You were right to be frightened of me, Annie. I want you so badly I'm losing control." He pressed his face to her curls. "It's the reason I told you to leave the medicine outside. I knew that if I got you in my arms again I'd never want to let you go. Do you hear what I'm saying?"

He kissed her with increasing passion, stirring up flames that licked through her body. The pleasure-pain he created was so intoxicating she was in danger of losing every inhibition.

"You're a beautiful woman. I want to hold you, look at you. I want to make love to you for hours. But if you're not prepared to stay the night with me, then you need to leave now."

His powerful body trembled, communicating the strength of his desire for her, but he was giving her a choice.

She could stay with him and experience a night of

ecstasy. He would be her first lover. But she wouldn't be his.

Naturally there'd been other women who'd known rapture with him, including his fiancée. How did they stand it when he grew tired of them and moved on?

How would *she* stand it?

After covering his face and mouth with kisses one more time, because she couldn't help herself, she found the strength to ease away from him and get to her feet.

While she swayed in place, he lay there, looking up at her through smoldering eyes.

"This isn't a game we're playing now, so you'll have to let me think about it. To go to bed with you would be the biggest step I've ever taken in my life—"

"Take all the time you need," his gravelly voice broke in. "But a word of caution. Don't come near me again unless you mean it."

His warning succeeded as nothing else could have to make her face reality.

"In other words, it's up to me whether we have a relationship or not?"

"That's right. Except for the night of the party, I'll be leaving you strictly alone."

When it came to the bottom line, he gave no quarter.

She shivered, because the corporate side of him had taken over.

All she had to do was get into bed with him and he'd know she meant it.

And because she was in love with him, nothing would be easier. *Until one day it wasn't.*

Annie might not have many answers to life's questions yet, but there was one thing she did know. She didn't want a future with him or any man that had an "until" in it…unless it was "until death and beyond."

To love a man like him would bring suffering and joy in unequal measure.

Annie wasn't willing to endure a lifetime of one for a fleeting moment of the other.

"Stay where you are, Mitch. I'll let myself out."

She left the room before racing through the house to her car.

CHAPTER TEN

ONCE Roger had left the house, Annie followed her mother into the bedroom. It was so good to have her home. She hugged her again before letting her go.

"I don't have to ask how the honeymoon went."

Her mom blushed—something she didn't do very often. "I'm so happy, Annie, and I want you to be happy, too. I have a present for you."

"I already opened it, on Christmas morning."

"Yes, well, this one's a little different."

She walked over to her dresser and drew an eight-by-ten envelope from the drawer.

Annie took it from her. "You've got me curious." She opened the flap and pulled out a deed to the house made out in her name.

Tears welled in her eyes. She stared at her mother through the blur. "I can't take this, Mom."

"It's yours now, rather than having to wait to inherit it. For the time being Roger and I will stay at his house. But we're planning to buy one we can make our own."

"That's the way it should be. Two newlyweds start-ing out fresh."

Her mom put an arm around her. "Roger won't come by for me until tonight. Let's go in the living room and talk. I want to hear about what you've been doing, and how the office party went."

"Everything was great. When you go back to work you'll discover a ton of thank-you cards for Roger. He's the most generous man I've ever known."

"It's certainly one of the reasons I love him so much. Did David help you?"

"Yes." Thanks to Mitch's goading. "He floated around to make sure everyone was enjoying them-selves."

"Did he bring someone with him?"

"No. As a matter of fact he came back to the house after. We've planned a party for you the day after to-morrow."

"I know! Since David's still in Sacramento, Mitch Reynolds met us at the ship to welcome us back. I un-derstand it's going to be held at his beach house?"

Mitch had met them at the dock? Her heartbeat sped up.

"Was he limping?"

"A little. I understand he hurt his foot while he was up on his roof, but he still took care of everything and wouldn't let me carry my bag. Why do you ask?"

Annie patted one of the sofa pillows. "I took him

some files right after he hurt himself. I'm glad to hear he's doing well enough to be up and around."

"Me, too. He raved about you, honey. Apparently he's had a flood of e-mails telling him it was the best party the company has ever had, bar none. Mitch also added that you made a very fetching elf who delighted everyone. He gave us one of the invitations you created. After Roger read it he was all choked up, and he said, 'That's our Annie.' Roger has grown to really love you."

"I love him, too."

Her mom reached out to squeeze her hand.

"I knew you'd do a wonderful job. I'm so proud of you, honey."

"Thanks," Annie whispered.

She could feel her mother's eyes studying her. "What's wrong? And I'm not talking about the fact that my marriage to Roger has changed things for all of us. You're not yourself. Did David say or do something to hurt you?"

She shook her head. "This has nothing to do with David. It's true I had a crush on him for years. I guess everyone in the office knew it. But, believe me, that's all over. We're both very happy to be stepbrother and sister."

"Roger will be relieved to hear it. He wants so much for the four of us to be a family."

"That's no problem, Mom. David's easy to love."

"Then let's talk about Mitch Reynolds."

She felt a stab of pain. "Why would you bring *him* up?"

Unable to sit still, Annie slid off the couch and reached for an orange stick.

"According to Mitch, you spent every second of your spare time working on the party or at the office. Since the two of you have had to be closely associated throughout this whole holiday, I have to conclude your weight loss has something to do with him."

Marion Roberts hadn't made it to be Roger's private secretary for nothing.

"My diet must be working."

Her mother continued to look at her speculatively. "All right. I'll leave it alone. But if you ever want to get something off your chest, I'm here."

"I know you are, and I appreciate the offer, but there's nothing to discuss."

Her mom stood up and wandered over to the tree. "These little Santa ornaments are darling. Did Roz give them to you?"

Her first instinct was to lie. But she couldn't do that to her mother.

"No. They're from Mitch. He helped me pass out the party gifts in the Santa costume I rented."

Her mother winked. "I'd have almost missed my wedding to see that."

"He really was something."

Her mom nodded. "He really *is* something. Speaking of presents, Mitch asked me to give you this when

I got home." She reached for her purse, lying on the coffee table.

Annie's adrenaline kicked in. "What is it?"

"Photos from the office Christmas party." She put the packet in Annie's hands. "He's had several sets of prints made up, so you can keep yours as a souvenir."

Annie frowned. "But the photographer was supposed to send the bill and the pictures to *your* office. I've been watching for them so I could mail the pertinent ones out to employees."

Her mother hunched her slender shoulders. "Mitch said you'd done enough work for ten people, so he was happy to take care of it. They're wonderful pictures!"

"You've seen them already?" Her overworked heart plunged to her feet.

"He gave Roger and me a similar packet. We looked at them on our way home in the limo. Your new haircut suits you. It's gorgeous. As for the party, it looked sensational. Roger couldn't believe all the trouble you went to. It erased the guilt he's been feeling for deserting everyo— Oh!" she cried, mid-sentence. "There's the phone! It might be Roger. Excuse me for a minute, honey."

Her mother ran to the kitchen as if she were a teenager who'd been waiting for her boyfriend to call.

Annie looked down at the packet. Her hands shook as she reached inside.

The first one showed her staring wide-eyed into the camera.

The second one was so shocking she almost fainted.

The photographer had caught her and Mitch in a clinch not meant for anyone else's eyes.

They looked like two people madly, desperately in love.

Not by any stretch of the imagination could she pretend to her mother that it had been a simple kiss beneath the mistletoe, meant in fun and nothing more.

And that had been *before* she'd known she was in love with him.

If the photographer had been in Mitch's bedroom last week—

Afraid to look at any more pieces of incriminating evidence, she rushed through the house to her bedroom and shoved the packet in a drawer, out of sight.

The photos would give Mitch every reason to believe she'd meant it at the time.

They would certainly have convinced her mother and Roger that she was over David. If ever they'd needed proof, then the way she was hungrily kissing Mitch would have removed all doubt.

"Annie?"

She swung around to see compassion in her mother's eyes.

"As you've found out, Mitch is nothing like David. Just be careful."

"It's too late for that warning. I'm in love with him. But you don't have to worry, Mom. Once the party for you is over I'll be back in school. I'm thinking of going

on to law school. An MBA will be an asset if I specialize in contract law."

A pained expression crossed her mother's face.
"Roger and I shouldn't have gone away to get married."

"Please don't say that!" Annie cried. "I'm glad you
did. Coming up against a man like Mitch was a lesson I've been needing for a long time. So let's not talk
about him ever again. I'd rather take you to lunch and
hear all about the wedding ceremony and your trip."

The party was in full swing, but Mitch didn't know
how long his grandparents would be able to stay awake.
While Marion and Annie circulated with David, he decided now was the time to take Roger aside.

"Could I talk with you alone for a minute?"

"Of course."

Roger followed him into the study. "Marion and I
are crazy about your house, Mitch. It's the kind of place
we'd like—right on the beach, and a moderate size."

Mitch leaned against the closed door. "How would
you like to buy it from me at a reduced price?"

Roger did a double-take. The two men had been in
business too long not to read between the lines.

"What's going on?"

"My grandparents arrived yesterday. As you can see,
even with their canes they're both too feeble to have
made the trip. I bought this place with the idea that
they would live here, where I could take care of them.
But it's not going to work. They're happy to be here for

this occasion, but they want to go home. They want to die there, and I can't blame them. It's too late for such a big change in their lives. Under the circumstances, I'm afraid I'm going to have to resign."

The word hung heavy between them.

Roger grimaced. "I understand. But I have to admit I'm staggered by your news."

"I'm sorry. If there were any other way… But there isn't."

Roger pursed his lips. "Maybe this would be the best time for me to sell the company. Marion and I have been talking about spending more time together."

"Do it while you have your lives and your health!" Mitch said fiercely.

Roger eyed him with concern. "After losing Hannah when you did, it's a damn shame you wasted all these years working with no woman to go home to."

"Many times I've thought the same thing about you and Marion."

"You know why I didn't propose sooner?"

"I do."

The other man's brows lifted. "So what's this move going to do to you and the woman you've had your eye on?"

Roger knew damn well it was Annie.

"I don't know yet."

"You sound like me, while I was wondering whether it was too soon to propose to Marion or not. Under the circumstances you'd better hurry up and figure it out.

On this trip I discovered all over again that when you've got love, nothing else matters. Pull out that picture of the two of you and take one more good long look."

Mitch had already done that—more times than he was willing to admit.

"Where's the man known to be so decisive he pulls the rug out from under everybody before they know what's happening?"

Mitch made a sound in his throat.

"When it comes to Annie—"

"I know. Believe me, I know. But now I'm kicking myself for the years I denied Marion because I was worried I'd be proposing too soon. Don't repeat history, Mitch."

Annie wasn't Marion. She hadn't been married before. This was all too new to her. Mitch was terrified he'd frightened her off.

"What about my house, Roger?"

"Let me discuss it with Marion. When are your grandparents going back?"

"They want me to take them tomorrow."

"Then go ahead and do whatever you have to. But I'd like one more favor from you."

"Name it."

"Stay on in an advisory capacity until I decide what I'm going to do?"

Mitch nodded. "I already planned on it. I'm keeping the condo. That way I can fly out once a month."

"Thank you, Mitch. Now, I think we'd better join the party. We'll keep this quiet for the time being."

"I'd appreciate that, Roger."

Relieved to have dropped that bomb, Mitch headed for the kitchen, where he'd seen Annie dart seconds ago on those long, gorgeous legs of hers. She looked stunning tonight, in a creamy two-piece suit with a strand of pearls the same color.

She'd been waiting on his grandparents all evening. They weren't the type to warm to other people in a hurry, but he could tell they were charmed by her.

While she was looking in the fridge, Mitch said, "Can I help?"

She pulled out a quart of milk. "Your grandmother wants to go to bed, but first she needs warm milk to take her pills."

He reached in the cupboard for a mug and handed it to her.

She thanked him and heated it in the microwave. So far she'd avoided looking at him directly. All he needed was a sign.

Dammit, Annie. Give me one.

"I think everyone's having a good time. Don't you?"

"How could they not, in a house this beautiful and with food so fabulous?" She retrieved the mug and hurried past one of the caterers to the living room.

She was treating him in that offish way she had once before. But in this case he was gratified by her behavior—because he knew what was driving it.

The physical side of their relationship was not the problem. What if she wasn't ready for a big commitment with him? Several times she'd talked about his being older.

An older man with old grandparents. She probably found the whole thing a turnoff.

He watched from a distance as she helped his grandparents down the hall to the master bedroom. He enjoyed the fact that they'd allowed her to help them. She had a way...

Was it because she was an innately kind person? Or was it wishful thinking that she truly cared for them because she was beginning to care for *him*?

CHAPTER ELEVEN

ANNIE took the empty mug and put it on the bedside table. "Is there anything else I can do for you?"

Mitch's grandmother was tucked in the king-sized bed. His grandfather Donald had just come out of the bathroom, dressed in pajamas and a robe.

"You're spoiling us." Martha laughed quietly.

"That's what Mitch is going to do to you when you move here to live," Annie said, unaware that Mitch had come into the room until he walked over to kiss his grandmother.

"I'm afraid I can't talk them into it, Annie. I'll be taking them back home tomorrow."

Pain spiked through her body, almost incapacitating her.

"If we were younger..." Martha whispered, looking up at her grandson through watery eyes.

Donald nodded. "We've lived in one place all our lives."

Annie moved to the end of the bed, struggling to maintain her composure.

"Then I'll say goodnight, so you can get a good night's sleep before your long flight tomorrow. It's been wonderful to meet you."

Donald stared at her. "Have you ever been to Minnesota?"

"No."

"It's different than here."

Annie forced a smile. "I bet you had a white Christmas."

He nodded. "That, and blizzards, and below-zero temperatures. But we love it."

"There's only one thing missing..." Martha murmured.

"Not anymore," Mitch declared.

His grandparents looked at him in surprise.

"Tonight I told Roger I'm leaving Hastings and coming back home to live with you."

So he'd really done it... Annie grasped the footboard for support.

Donald shook his head. "You can't do that, son."

"I already have. Everything's settled."

"You're not thinking clearly," his grandfather argued.

Even in his late eighties, he could be intimidating. It helped Annie understand Mitch as never before.

She paused at the door. "Even before you came Mitch told me that if you couldn't move here, he was going home. If there's one thing I know about your grandson, it's that he never backs down."

That cruel smile was in evidence once more. "Annie knows me well."

Yes. She did. Too well.

"Are you coming with him?" his grandfather asked unexpectedly.

Her face prickled with heat. She made the mistake of looking at Mitch. His gaze was enigmatic as he said, "I told them we wouldn't be seeing each other again unless you wanted to."

While she reeled from a surfeit of pain, his grandfather said, "What's the problem, young woman?"

"Donald!" his wife cried. "For heaven's sake! What goes on between these two is none of our business."

Annie was sobbing inside. *Nothing* was going on between them. Mitch only wanted a physical relationship.

"Have a safe flight, all of you."

Without looking at Mitch, she stole from the bedroom and ran into the next one to get her purse.

She saw David at the front door, playing host to the last guest. He took one look at Annie and said, "What's wrong? You look ill."

"Where's Mom?"

"She left with Dad. He said he had something important to talk over with her and wanted to leave. They asked me to drive you home."

"Could we go now?"

"Sure."

She dashed past him and hurried out to the street, where David's car was parked.

He was right behind her, and used the remote before helping her inside. In a few minutes they'd reached the freeway. He looked over at her. "How about telling me what's going on? That's what a brother is for, you know."

"You're very sweet, but there's nothing to tell. I'm in love with Mitch, and he's not in love with me. He's going home with his grandparents for good."

"I heard. Dad told me before he and your mom left the house. Have you told Mitch how you feel?"

"He knows without my having to say anything." Her voice wobbled. "After seeing that picture taken at the party, *everyone* has to know."

"You were certainly caught out, all right. Just remember there were two people in that picture. An objective observer would say you weren't the only one swept away."

She groaned. "So swept away he's leaving and never coming back."

"We're talking about Mitch, remember? As long as I've known him, he's liked all his 'i's dotted and his 't's crossed. He never goes for the clinch until he knows the competition's bottom line."

"A woman shouldn't have to say it first."

"Where did you get a strange idea like that? I have a hunch he's afraid you're using him to get over me. Since our folks left on the cruise, he's been sabotaging me right and left. He needs to know you mean it."

Mitch's words came back to haunt her. *Don't come*

near me again unless you mean it. But he'd been talking about something else.

"Mitch knows I had a crush on you. Nothing more."

"Knowing Mitch as I do, he's not going to be convinced until he hears the words he's waiting for."

"You honestly think he's waiting for a declaration of love?" she scathed.

"What do you think's the reason he called Elaine instead of you to help him out when he got hurt? He was terrified to call you, only to find you came to him out of pity."

Her head jerked around. "Pity? But he couldn't possibly think that! Not after— Well, not after we got stuck in the elevator."

"Well, well, well… Now it all comes out. Don't you know you've tied the great Mitch Reynolds into knots? Give the poor guy a break and let him know how you feel!"

A feeling like an electrical current charged through her body. She could hear Mitch's words. *You're an intelligent woman. One day you'll figure it out.*

Was that what Mitch had meant?

"Still want to go home?" David prodded. "Or shall I turn the car around?"

Maybe she'd be making the biggest mistake of her life, but she had to find out.

"Do you mind? Turning the car around, I mean?"

"What do *you* think?"

He pulled off at the next exit and they got back on the freeway once again, headed for San Clemente.

"Got your excuse all figured out?"

"Yes. I was in such a hurry to get out of there, I ran off without my coat."

"You mean the way Mitch left you when you were still wearing his? That excuse works every time. Mel told me you returned it to Elaine's office—and then who should show up in your mom's office but the big man himself, carrying it with him?"

Annie made a face. "Is there nothing sacred at the office?"

"No." He took the exit and headed for Mitch's street. "Isn't that Mitch's car, screeching around the corner toward us?"

Annie's heart leaped. It *was* Mitch.

Oh, please let it mean he was coming for her because he couldn't help himself!

David started to slow down. Mitch pulled up right next to him. Both men lowered their windows.

Annie didn't dare look at Mitch.

"Where were you going like a bat out of you-know-where?" David spoke first.

"Annie left her coat," came Mitch's deep voice.

"Hear that, Annie? We were just coming back for it. Want to hand it through the window?"

"Not unless you two have other plans for the rest of the night." Mitch's voice sounded so fierce it was almost frightening.

"No, Mitch. Dad asked me to drive her home."

Before getting out of the car, Annie squeezed David's arm to thank him. Then she hurried around to the passenger side of Mitch's car. He'd already opened the door for her.

The warm interior felt good. He reached in front of her to close it, brushing her midriff in the process. Any time he touched her, she trembled with desire.

When she dared a glance at him, his profile looked chiseled. "If you don't mind, I don't want to go home yet. Could we park down on the beach for a while?"

The tension was palpable. "I don't think that would be a good idea." His voice rasped.

"I do. Otherwise I won't have your full attention."

She felt the shudder than ran through his body. "Annie—"

"I know—" She broke in on him. "You told me not to seek you out again unless I meant it."

"Is that why you asked David to bring you back?"

She sucked in her breath. The time for honesty had come. "Yes. I used my coat for an excuse."

His hands had tightened on the steering wheel until she could see the whites of his knuckles.

"You still need an excuse to let him down gently?"

"No. It was the excuse I was going to use on you, so you'd let me in the house. Luckily for me I didn't have to ring the bell and wake up your grandparents. Please could we just drive down to the beach to talk?"

She heard a sharp intake of breath before he turned the car around, causing his tires to screech once more.

It didn't take more than two minutes to find a spot near the surf. He stopped the car, but kept the motor running for warmth.

"Your grandfather said something that made me realize how hard it's going to be when you leave."

"Hard on whom?"

She moistened her lips nervously. "Me, of course."

"Really? I wouldn't have guessed."

"You didn't know my father, but I'm like him in temperament. He took a long time before making a decision, even a small one. But once he did, he never ...ed back. I've been thinking about you and me."

"And?" he fired.

"I've decided I want to be with you if *you* really mean it."

His chest heaved. "You think I don't?"

"I'm not talking about just going to bed together. Here's my proposition. We get married in Minnesota. The family will come out for it. We'll live with your grandparents. I'll finish up school there. By late spring I hope to be pregnant. Your grandparents are waiting for at least one great-grandchild. There's no time to waste.

"Think of all the time Mom and Roger wasted when they could have been happily married for the last two or three years. Instead they tiptoed around each other, afraid to speak their minds because of David and me.

It's made us both feel terrible. And another terrible thing—you're going to be thirty-three pretty soon. It's long past time you settled down, with a wife who loves you more than life itself. What I can't figure out is why you didn't kiss me under the mistletoe at the company party *last* year, after David left? Instead you sat there fuming at me. Surely you realized I'd have been putty in your hands? We'd be married by now.

"And when I think how honorable you were in the elevator. After you put your coat around me I kept waiting for you to kiss me again. I never wanted you to stop. And the afternoon I made dinner just for you. I wanted to show you I could cook. Of course I thought you'd start kissing me in the kitchen while we did the dishes. Then you took off and it killed me. If your leg hadn't been hurt, I probably would have crawled into bed with you that day, too.

"What I'm trying to say is that I want to be near you forever. But, since you haven't said a single word this whole time, I guess our ideas of 'meaning it' are two different things. You can drive me home now."

She was in so much pain she couldn't bear it.

"Would you like to put your coat on before we go?"

"No." Her voice shook, because David had been wrong and she wanted to die. "It's plenty warm in here."

"Suit yourself, but there's something in the right pocket you might want to see."

"If it's a gift for helping you with the party, I'd rather

not accept it. Under the circumstances, I'm sure you understand."

"Then I'll get it out for you." He reached in back and pulled out a scroll tied with red ribbon.

The pain was excruciating. "I already have one for a souvenir."

"This one's a little different," he explained. "I'll do the honors."

He slid the ribbon off and opened the parchment.

Clearing his throat, he said, "'Twas the night after New Year's and all through Santa's house, not a creature was stirring, not even a mouse. Mr and Mrs Claus were all snug in their bed. With their arms wrapped around each other, they had nothing to dread.' Darling?" he whispered, "you know how much I've loved you all these years."

"I do, dearest," she answered, her voice full of tears.

"Will you agree to marry me and become my true wife?"

"You're asking me to marry you *now*, when I've been waiting all my life?"

"'I know I'm not perfect, even if children think it's true. Will you forgive this one flaw and just say I do?'"

"Oh, Mitch—" Moved deeper than tears, Annie pulled the paper away from his hands. Wrapping her arms around his neck, she pressed her lips to his and told him the words he needed to hear. "I love you, my darling, darling Mitch. Let me tell you the ways."

Her words went on for a very long time.

"Annie," he cried exultantly, crushing her so tight she couldn't breathe. "Where have you been all my life?"

"Right where I was supposed to be, until you found me waiting for you. I want to marry you, Mitch Reynolds. I adore you. You don't even begin to know how much."

"That'll do for starters," he said, before sliding a diamond ring on her finger. "Before you ran out I had big plans to give this to you tonight. But I was afraid you'd think it was too soon."

She cupped his handsome face in her hands. His eyes blazed with blue fire. "Now you know otherwise. Let's get this sleigh back to the house, Mr Claus. There's a lot of work to be done before morning."

He gave her a hard, hungry kiss. "I think we'd better have a definition of terms first."

"Well—" She smiled provocatively. "With the negotiations over, I'm in your hands now. It's all up to you. Didn't you say something at the office party about going home for a long winter's nap?"

* * * * *

A Kiss for Mr Scrooge

LUCY
GORDON

Lucy Gordon cut her writing teeth on magazine journalism, interviewing many of the world's most interesting men, including Warren Beatty, Charlton Heston and Sir Roger Moore. She also camped out with lions in Africa and had many other unusual experiences, which have often provided the background for her books. Several years ago, while staying Venice, she met a Venetian who proposed in two days. They have been married ever since. Naturally this has affected her writing, where romantic Italian men tend to feature strongly.

Two of her books have won a Romance Writers of America RITA® Award. You can visit her website at www.lucy-gordon.com.

CHAPTER ONE

DAWN STUDIED THE sky and found it heavy with un-fallen snow. Surely, she thought, it would fall in time for a white Christmas? She couldn't decide whether to be glad or sorry. The kid in her, who still flourished at twenty-seven, insisted that it wouldn't be Christmas without snow. The veterinarian in her pointed out that her work consisted mostly of driving the countryside to visit sick farm animals, and snow would create problems. The kid won.

She got back into her ancient car and drove the few miles to Hollowdale, the village where she was the most junior member of a three-person practice. She'd arrived just before last Christmas, and had been instantly charmed by the old-world atmosphere of a place where all the time-honored traditions were kept up.

It had taken a while for her to be accepted in a country practice. Jack and Harry, the two partners, had talked about the rigors of dealing with hefty farm animals, but had finally been persuaded to give her a chance.

The farmers had been even harder to convince. A young woman with a slim, elegant frame, a mass of glossy dark hair and large brown eyes wasn't their idea of a vet for a recalcitrant bull. But Dawn was stronger than she looked and she soon proved herself capable of dealing with everything. Her dedication to the animals in her care and her willingness to turn out on freezing nights had finally won the community over to her side, and she now felt as much at home in Hollowdale as if she'd been born there.

Her route back took her past Hollowdale Grange, the huge house that for centuries had been the heart of village festivities. The carol singers always called there halfway through the evening, and sang their hearts out for Squire Davis, who gave them hot drinks to refresh them for the work still to come, and placed a generous donation in their box. And every year he'd let his home be used for a Christmas party for deprived children, just as his ancestors had done. But Squire Davis had died earlier that year apparently leaving no heir. The house had been closed and had stayed shuttered all summer and autumn.

Now, as she passed, Dawn noticed something that made her brake sharply and reverse to get a better look. Lights were on in the house. Men were carrying things in from a removal van. Dawn drove on, feeling cheered.

Harry, the younger partner, came in as she was writing up her notes. He was a pleasant-faced young man whose eyes were always warm when they rested on Dawn. She often flirted with him in a cheerful way that she never allowed to get too intense, although she knew Harry wanted more.

"Jack tells me you're going to work over Christmas," he said, sounding scandalized. "You really want to do that?"

"Somebody has to," Dawn pointed out. "Animals get sick even then, and with so many farms around here, there's every chance that someone will need a vet."

"Of course. But why should it be you again? You volunteered to be on call last year. And it was your first Christmas in Hollowdale, I remember."

"Harry, I really don't mind," Dawn assured him. "Jack's got a wife and children, and you've got your brother's family to visit. You know your little nephews and nieces count on 'Uncle Harry.'"

"Oh, I may drop in and keep you company," he said with studied casualness.

"I'm sure there's no need."

"Well, you don't think I'm going to pass up the chance to be with you, do you?" he teased.

She looked up at him, laughing, and he leaned down to kiss her lightly, vanishing before she could either encourage or reject him. Dawn sighed. It would be lovely if she could respond to Harry, a nice man if ever there was one, but one who couldn't excite her.

Only one man had ever made her heart beat strongly, and he had also broken it. That had been eight Christmases ago—long enough for any reasonable woman to recover. And she *had* recovered. It was just that she'd never fallen in love again since, and the festive season had lost some of its savor for her.

Jack, the senior partner, had just finished taking the morning surgery. He was a middle-aged, thickset man with an amiable face, and he grinned when he saw her.

"There's someone moving into the Grange today," Dawn said. "I saw the van as I passed."

Jack's grin vanished abruptly. "You don't have to tell me," he growled. "I've already had a brush with him, and come off worst."

"Why, what happened?"

"I approached him early this morning, about the children's party. I know there are only three days left, but that would still have been enough time to organize something if we worked fast."

"You mean he said no?" she asked in dismay.

"I mean I got shown the door. 'No party. Not this year, not next year, not ever. Get out! Don't come back!' That was the message."

"But the Grange parties are legendary. If he's a Davis, surely he knows that."

"He isn't a Davis. The lawyers finally traced the old man's heir living on the other side of the world. All he wanted was to turn his heritage into money as fast as possible. He put it into the hands of big-city auctioneers, who know nothing about Hollowdale and its traditions, and care less. They sold it to the highest bidder."

"Does this man have a wife? Perhaps she could talk him around?"

"He's unmarried, which has doubtless saved some poor woman from a terrible fate. His guard's impenetrable, like granite. I tried every argument—it's Christmas, the children will be heartbroken. I was still talking as he steered me to the door. This man doesn't care about children's hearts. He doesn't care about Christmas. All he cares about is being left alone. It was like talking to Scrooge. I almost expected him to wave his walking stick and say, 'Bah! Humbug!'"

Dawn gave a faint smile. "Scrooge turned out to be just an old softy at heart," she reminded.

"Anyone who thinks this man is a softy at heart is in for a nasty surprise," Jack growled. "By the way, I've had Harry on to me about letting you work over the holiday again. Did I jump at your offer too quickly? Would you rather be going home somewhere?"

"I've nowhere to go," Dawn said. "My parents are dead, and I've no close family. Don't give it another thought."

"But you're too young to be spending Christmas alone. That's for curmudgeons like 'Scrooge' at the Grange. You should be hurrying off to a lovers' tryst."

Dawn laughed. "I'm quite happy to keep trysts with sick cows and pigs."

But although she smiled, she left Jack quickly

after that. She was afraid her feelings might show in her face.

Once, there really had been a Christmas of lovers' trysts and eternal vows, of blazing happiness and eager hope for the future. But it had also been the Christmas of shattered dreams, cruelty and bitter disillusion.

The man whom for a few brief, glorious weeks she'd thought of as her lover, had been the son and heir of a family of wealthy industrialists. His first name had been—Well, no matter. She'd never used it after she discovered the secret of his middle name, a secret he tried so hard to keep hidden. "Ebenezer?" she'd cried in delight. "You mean, Ebenezer as in Scrooge?"

"Yes, and *stop laughing.* And don't tell anyone, either."

She'd kept his secret, but she'd shortened Ebenezer to Ben, and thereafter that had been her name for him. *A Christmas Carol* had become their special book. They'd read it aloud to each other. Dawn had been struck by the scene where Scrooge's fiancée broke their engagement, saying she no longer believed he could love a poor girl.

But Ben had reassured her, "There's no rich or poor between us. Scrooge was a fool to let her break it off. If he'd known what I know, he'd never have let her go."

Ben had been as different from Scrooge as he could possibly be—a handsome, generous, lighthearted young man whose boyish looks had made him seem younger than his twenty seven years. But beneath his

laughter he had a mature side. He took his family obligations seriously, and that was the only shadow on
Dawn's happiness. For all his protestations of fidelity,
in a careless moment he'd let slip that his parents were
urging him to marry Elizabeth, the daughter of the
firm's biggest customer.

"Hey, don't look like that," he'd urged when he saw
her pale face. "I don't normally like to disappoint them,
but this time I'm just going to have to—except that they
won't be disappointed when they've met you."

"If they've set their hearts on Elizabeth and a profitable tie-up between your two firms, they'll be disappointed with an impoverished first-year veterinary
student," she'd observed wryly.

"Not when they get to know you," he'd said, cutting off further argument by taking her into his arms.

His kisses had sent her reeling, blotting out further
thought. When they could talk again Ben had slipped
an engagement ring on her finger, saying, "I feel
as though Christmas Past was all the Christmases I
wasted not knowing you, Christmas Present is now,
and Christmas Yet to Come is next year when we'll be
married, and all the years after that, years we'll have
together."

That moment was one Dawn still found hard to think
of. It hurt too much when she recalled what had come
after.

Ben had returned to his parents in the third week of
December, intending to tell them everything. The plan

had been that Dawn would then join them for a visit. All during Christmas she'd waited for his call, but it hadn't come. When he'd finally called, a whole week later, it had been to suggest a postponement— "Only a few days, to give them a little time. I'll be in touch."

In her heart she'd known the truth then. Ben was a good, loyal son who couldn't bear to hurt the parents who loved him. Probably he'd arrived to find Elizabeth visiting, and after that he'd fallen further and further into the trap. But she'd clung to the last shreds of hope right up to the moment he'd called her again a week later, and had said it would be better if they never saw each other again.

She didn't blame him for that, but she blamed him for what had happened next. Ben, whose love letters had once burned the pages, had written to her wishing her luck for the future, and enclosing a large check to help cover the cost of her studies. As she'd read that letter, Dawn had almost hated him. She'd given him her first love—fresh and young and wholehearted. And he'd turned out to be no more than a rich man's son, trying to buy her off.

She'd written a stinging reply, returning the check and her engagement ring, saying she could forgive him for ditching her, but not for poisoning her memories of him with an offer of money.

Then she'd gotten on with her life.

The years that followed had their own triumphs and pleasures. She was always in the top quarter of her class, and her warm nature brought her many friends and admirers. She worked hard, and went to parties, flirted, laughed and sometimes kissed. But it seemed that she couldn't fall in love again, and the reason for that was that she no longer believed in the beauty of love. It had been destroyed for her.

She ranked high in her class and had several job offers. She'd chosen to join the Hollowdale practice as an assistant, with the chance of a partnership later. Her first December here, a year ago, had delighted her. The white fields and little cottages had a picture-book beauty. She saw the harder side of country life, too, working in cold barns and helping to dig animals out of snowdrifts. But nothing could spoil the enchantment of listening to pure, treble voices raised in carol singing on Christmas Eve, or helping to organize the children's party at the Grange.

And this year there would be no party because of the intransigence of one man, she thought grimly. Well, perhaps he could be made to think again.

That afternoon she stepped out to walk the few hundred yards to the Grange. Large white flakes were coming down thickly, making it hard to see more than a few yards ahead. As she walked, she tried to picture the man she'd come to challenge. He sounded embittered and he walked with a stick, so he was probably older; but however old he was, he'd been a child at some time. Perhaps, in that way, she could reach him.

The Grange stood at the top of a slight hill, dominating the village. By the time she reached it the ground was already covered with a white carpet. Glad to see lights on in the house, she hurried the last few yards up the long drive, then climbed the steps and rang the bell. She had to ring three times before the door was opened by a grim-faced woman who looked at her without welcome. "Yes?"

"I've come to see—I'm sorry, I don't know his name."

"He ain't expecting you, then?"

"No, but—"

"If he ain't expecting you he won't want to see you. Appointment only. That's his rule."

"But if you could just ask him—"

"Well, I couldn't. I did that once before and got the sharp side of his tongue. He ain't a man to fool with, I'm telling you." The granite features softened, just a fraction. "It ain't my fault. I'm just the housekeeper. I do what I'm told. Is it about that party?"

"Yes."

"I swear he'll throw something at the next person who asks him. Do yourself a favor and be off." She began to retreat back into the house, closing the door until only her face was showing. "I say," she called through the crack.

"Yes?" Dawn looked back hopefully.

"If any of your friends are going caroling, warn them not to come here." The housekeeper shut the door firmly.

So that was that, Dawn thought. She began to walk away from the house, pulling her thick jacket about her. Then she stopped in her tracks as her spirit rebelled against tamely going home. Impulsively she turned and made her way around the house. It was worth a try.

The far side of the house looked out over extensive grounds that fell away down the slope. A man stood there with his back to her, looking out over the country-side in the fast-fading light. In his right hand he grasped a walking stick that he half leaned on. This must be the man she'd come to see, the man who seemed to hate the rest of the world. If she couldn't persuade him, she could at least give the old curmudgeon a piece of her mind. Ducking her head against the wind that blew snow into her face, she began to make her way deter-minedly toward him.

She got to within a few yards before a twig cracked beneath her feet and gave her away. The man turned, scowling. "Get off this property or you'll be sorry," he growled. "I won't have trespassers, d'ye hear?"

Something about his voice sent a frisson through her. It had a faint half-remembered quality that brought an onrush of pain. Through the driving snow she could make out very little—only that he was tall, and younger than she had expected, and that his face was faintly scarred.

She dismissed the thought that had flashed on her. It was impossible. "I didn't mean to trespass," she said, "but it seems to be the only way to get to see you."

He limped a step forward. "I gave orders that no one should see me. Don't you understand plain language?"

The snow swirled about her, creating strange, half-perceived shapes, making the impossible possible. In the dim light she could sense that he'd grown as still as herself, as though incredulous understanding had burst on him, too. Dawn stood rooted to the spot, torn apart by joy and pain at the shattering discovery she'd just made.

"Ben," she whispered. "Oh, God, I can't believe it! *Ben.*"

She came closer but he took a step back. "Get away," he snapped.

"But it's me—Dawn. Don't you know me?"

The wind dropped slightly, and although the flakes continued to fall between them they could discern each other's faces. Now Dawn wondered how she'd ever recognized him. He'd aged more than eight years and his eyes were sunken. She pushed back her hood to give him a better view of her own face, and saw him flinch. Then his expression hardened. "No, I don't know you," he growled. "And I'm telling you for the last time, get off my property and don't ever come back."

"Ben, wait, please—"

She went forward, hands outstretched, but he took a step back, one arm held up as if to ward her off, and the next moment he'd lost his balance and was sprawling on the ground. Dawn hurried to help him but found her way barred by his stick, which he was holding out, pointed at her. "Get away," he grated.

"Let me help you—"

"I said, get away!" he shouted. "Don't touch me, do you hear? *Get out of here!*"

Dawn could bear no more. Choking back the sob of pity that would have burst from her, she turned and fled.

She went to bed early that evening, and lay trying to blot out the sound of carol singers tramping merrily through the village. Her heart was in turmoil. Her love for Ben was over. Nothing was more certain than that. Yet it had hurt her badly to see him reduced to a shadow of his former self. Old emotions and sensations, incredibly painful, came flooding back to invade her, destroying her peace.

For eight years she'd thought of him married to Elizabeth, fulfilled, running the family business, a contented husband and probably a father. When she'd put a face to that image, it had been like the face she'd last seen—young, handsome, full of hope.

But the face she'd seen just now was marked and withered with despair. It was the face of a solitary man, a man not merely unmarried, but profoundly alone within himself.

She thought of the stick that he used as both a support and a weapon against the world, and wondered what had happened to turn a vigorous, athletic young man into a limping recluse. And when had it happened?

Could this be the answer to the mystery that had tormented her for eight years?

At last she got quietly out of bed. What she was about to do might not be very wise, but she couldn't rest until she'd seen Ben again. She got dressed and slipped out into the night. The snow had stopped falling and lay in a thick, white, moonlit carpet all the way up the high street.

The gates to the Grange had a lock that hadn't worked for years, and Squire Davis, a convivial man, hadn't troubled to mend it. But tonight someone had secured the gates by twisting wire around the bars. It took all the strength in her fingers to untwist the wire, and she finished with some nasty scratches, but finally managed it. She pushed one of the gates quietly open and slipped through. The house was almost in darkness, except for a light coming from an upstairs window. Now she realized how late it was and her heart almost failed her. It was no use appealing to the grumpy housekeeper. She must find another way. She began to walk around the house.

At last she came to the library at the rear where the old squire had often sat in the evening with a brandy and a cigar. Her heartbeat quickened as she saw a faint light coming from within. Softly she crept up to the French doors. To her relief, the curtains were still drawn back and she was able to look inside.

A fire burned in the iron grate, making shadows dance on the walls and giving the room its only light.

Beside it Ben was slumped on the sofa. Praying hard, Dawn tried the handle of the French doors, and to her relief it yielded. She stepped inside and closed the door silently behind her. Ben gave no sign of knowing she was there. His head rested against the high side of the leather sofa, and his eyes were closed.

Dawn moved closer to him, then stopped, unable to decide what to do next. While she thought about it she pulled up a chair and sat down opposite him. From this angle she had a better view of him. Sleep had smoothed away his anger, leaving a face more like the one she remembered. It was younger, though still too old for a man of thirty-five. But it was grief and suffering that had aged him, not years. She clasped her hands tightly over her breast, as though by that means she could silence the anguish that seized her.

He stirred, and she held her breath. He didn't awake, but a sheet of paper slipped from his hand and fell into the grate. Dawn picked it up quickly before it could burn. Then she grew very still as she realized she was holding her own letter, written to him in dreadful bitterness of spirit, eight years ago. The cruel words seemed to leap out at her— *"despicable...unforgivable..."*

She'd written those words to a healthy, hearty young man who'd callously tried to buy her off; but the man who read and brooded on them tonight was ill and oddly defenseless. Against all reason she felt guilty, as if she'd struck him a brutal blow.

He'd denied her that afternoon, but he'd come

straight back and reread her letter—a letter that he'd obviously kept so close by him that even in the turmoil of moving he'd known where to find it.

He stirred again, and this time he opened his eyes so that he was looking directly at her. For a moment he didn't seem to react, but finally a gleam of life appeared. "Who are you?" he asked in a voice that barely rose above a whisper.

She'd wondered what she would say to him, and it was only now that the right words came to her.

"I'm the Ghost of Christmas Past," she told him.

CHAPTER TWO

"THE GHOST OF CHRISTMAS PAST," he echoed, and memory seemed to return to him. With an effort he asked, "Long past?"

"No," she said sadly. "Our past."

After a moment he nodded. "I didn't imagine you this afternoon, did I? You came out of the snow and you went back into the snow, and you might have been a dream. I prayed that you were nothing but that, that you wouldn't return—"

"Was that why you secured the gates?" she asked.

"I suppose it was. Yet you were always bound to come back to haunt me." He sat up straight, rubbing his eyes, then poured himself a whiskey from a decanter on a low table near him, and drained it quickly. "Do you drink much of that stuff?" Dawn asked gently.

"What I do is my own business," he growled.

"Once, you never touched it," she reminded him.

He shrugged. "Once! Once a lot of things were true that aren't true any longer." But he didn't pour another glass. "You shouldn't have come," he said wearily. "Things were better as they were."

"Of course I had to come. I had to find out what happened. This afternoon I got the biggest shock of my life. I could hardly believe it was you. You look so different."

"Yes, I wasn't a crock the last time you saw me, was I?" he said with a grim smile.

"The last time I saw you was the evening you left to visit your parents. We said goodbye…." She fell silent, remembering that goodbye, the suffocating kisses, the pain of being apart even for a few days, the promises of eternal love. Looking up, she saw the same memory in his eyes. He looked away quickly.

"Yes, we said goodbye," he agreed gruffly. "We didn't know it was a final goodbye, but that's how things worked out."

She stared at him, reluctant to believe what she was hearing. "Can you really dismiss it so easily, Ben?"

He shrugged. "It was eight years ago. We're both different people. We didn't even recognize each other today."

"Only for a moment—because of the snow. But I knew you soon enough, as you did me." When he didn't answer she said angrily, "I won't just be brushed aside, Ben. There are things you *must* tell me, things you should have told me eight years ago."

"I imagine you've guessed quite a bit," he said wearily.

"Perhaps. I'd like to know when this happened." She indicated the stick.

"Eight years ago, minus one week," he replied simply.

"What happened? I want to know everything. I *have* to know."

"I got to within two miles of my parents' home…." His eyes seemed to focus on the distance as if he were reliving the moment. "I was thinking of you—of us— of how you'd kissed me at the last moment. Suddenly I was skidding. The road was icy. I went down a bank, and woke up in hospital with scarcely an unbroken bone left in my body."

"Oh, God," she said softly.

Ben went on in a dispassionate voice. "I heard afterward that it took them three hours to cut me out of the car, but I knew nothing about that."

"But why didn't you send for me?" she asked passionately.

"For a week I was floating in and out of consciousness. I didn't know where I was, or recognize any of my family. When I finally came 'round I was paralyzed from the waist down, and I thought I was going to be that way all my life. When I called you I was flat on my back, with someone holding the phone up for me."

As she thought again of the eager, bright faced young man she'd loved, tears filled her eyes and began to slide down her cheeks. She tried to brush them away unobtrusively, but she wasn't quick enough.

"What are you doing that for?" he demanded irritably. "It's all over now."

"Yes," she agreed huskily. "It's all over."

"If you think about it reasonably you'll see I did you a favor. I wasn't a pretty spectacle, I can tell you. And my temper was vile. Nurses came and went. None of them could stand me."

"But you didn't stay paralyzed."

"No. It took more operations than I can remember, but I got there. I've been out of a wheelchair for two years now."

Dawn clenched her hands as she thought of the lonely, painful struggle he'd chosen to endure without her. She could have loved him for better or worse, but he'd brushed her out of his life at the first crisis.

She wiped away the last of her tears and straightened her shoulders, managing to give a wry little laugh. "To think that all this time I've pictured you married to Elizabeth," she said.

"Elizabeth married a stockbroker. They have five children. Things have worked out for the best, all the way around."

"*All* the way around?" Dawn said with a touch of anger. "Do you really think things have worked out for the best for us?"

"I didn't choose the hand I was dealt. I simply played it in the way that seemed best. What should I have done? Called you and asked you to tie yourself to a cripple?"

"I *loved* you, Ben. I thought we were so close—and

now I wonder if you even knew what love meant. If we'd been as close as I thought, you'd have sent for me."

"And what then?" he demanded harshly. "When the first shock had passed and you were left contemplating a man with no body to speak of—*what then?*"

"I'd have loved you no matter what. You should have trusted my love. You should have trusted *me*."

"You don't understand," he said angrily. "In the state I was in, I didn't want your love. I didn't want anything except to crawl away and hide. I don't know if I did the right thing for me, but I do know I did the right thing for you."

"You know nothing of the kind."

"Whatever your life has been, it's been better than what you'd have had with me. You're young and beautiful. I'd have turned you into a gray-haired old woman by now. I was strong for both of us. Be glad of it."

"Oh, Ben," she said helplessly. "You don't understand. It's not just that you sent me away when you needed me most, but you lied to me about the reason. When you sent me money I thought—"

"Yes, you made it very clear what you thought," he interrupted. "It was a very plainspoken letter. You have a pretty turn of phrase when you're angry."

"I wish I'd cut my arm off before I wrote you such words when you were ill. But your letter was so short and curt—"

"It was short because writing was agony. I wasn't trying to buy you off, Dawn. I just wanted to help. I know studying to be a vet takes a lot of money, and you didn't have any. Did you ever make it?"

"Yes. I'm with a practice in Hollowdale now."

"Good. Then life has worked out well for you."

She thought of the ache of loneliness that had never left her, night or day, since she'd lost him. She thought of her own barren heart that had never flowered for anyone but him. "Yes," she said bleakly. "Life has worked out well for me."

"How long have you been here?"

"Just over a year."

"But you're already a part of the place, I'll bet. I remember your gift for empathy. It was one of the things I—one of the things likely to make you a good vet."

"Yes, I've become a part of Hollowdale. I love the people here. They're kind and sincere, and they believe in values that other people seem to have forgotten. Jack says it's as though Hollowdale was caught in a kind of time warp so that the world could have a living reminder of how things ought to be."

"Who's Jack?"

"Jack Stanning, he's my boss."

"Stanning? I've heard that name."

"You met him this morning. He came to ask if we could have the children's party here, and you showed him the door."

"I remember. So he's your boss."

"One of them. The other one is Harry. He's the younger partner."

"Are you married yet?" Ben demanded abruptly.

"No, I'm not married."

"You should be. You were born to be married."

"I was nearly married once," she reminded him. "I fell in love with a man—fell so completely in love that nothing else in the world existed. I thought he felt the same, but I was wrong. When trouble came he didn't want my help. I guess there was no help I could give him."

She jumped as Ben slammed the point of his stick on the floor, hard. His face was harsh with anger as he got to his feet and began to pace about the room. "That's just sentimentality," he said. "Nothing lasts forever. Relationships die and you just—form other relationships."

"Did you?" she challenged.

"My attention has been taken up with other things," he said ironically. "The world doesn't look the same to me anymore." He gave a short bark of laughter. "We used to joke that I was Scrooge. Maybe it's not such a joke now."

"I don't believe it," she said urgently. "I can't believe that the man I loved has become so different. You were gentle and sensitive—and loving—" Her voice wavered perilously.

"And I used to laugh a lot," he reminded her. "Don't forget that, Dawn. I've forgotten how to laugh, just as I've forgotten how to love."

"Don't say that," she pleaded. "Perhaps you can't love me—that doesn't matter. But you must love someone."

He stared at her bleakly. "Why must I? I live very well without it."

"Hiding away from people? Hating the whole world?"

He shrugged. "I don't hate the world."

"No. It's worse than that. You're indifferent to the world. You want to drive it away."

"I want to be left alone."

"People shouldn't be alone. It isn't natural."

"It suits me."

"I don't believe it really suits you. It's just what you've settled for."

He shrugged. "Well, everyone settles for the best terms they can get."

"But do you really call it living?"

"It's better than what I had two years ago."

"But it can't ever be enough," she argued.

"It'll do!" he shouted suddenly. "What do you expect of me? That I'm going to open my arms and say let's turn back the clock? The clock never goes backward, however much we—" He took a shuddering breath. "What's done is done. For God's sake, let's put an end to this. It achieves nothing. It's a pity we met again. It opens up old wounds that were healed." He caught her looking at him and said roughly, "Let's face the truth. Neither of us gave a thought to the other until our chance meeting this afternoon."

"Did you really forget me?" she whispered.

"Completely," he said with a blank firmness.

She sat, stunned, knowing she should get up and go, yet unable to move. Whatever she'd expected, it hadn't been this brutal rejection. At last she pulled herself together and got to her feet, and as she did so, the letter she'd picked up when she first came in slipped to the floor. She retrieved it hastily.

"Where did you get that?" Ben demanded.

"You were reading it when you feel asleep," she said. "It fell out of your hand."

He snatched it away from her. The movement brought him close and Dawn looked into his eyes, seeing there everything he'd tried to hide. He'd been lying when he said he'd forgotten her, and the letter proved it. The revelation stripped him defenseless.

"All right," he grated. "I was reading your letter tonight. Seeing you this afternoon reminded me of a lot of things, and I reread your letter. Make what you will of that."

"It's not that you read it," she breathed, "but that you kept it by you all these years."

"It's been useful," he snapped. "It was always there to remind me how much I'd made you hate me, and how completely everything was over between us. Yes, I needed reminding. Is that what you wanted to hear? Yes, I went on loving you for a long time, telling myself I was a fool for it, but unable to stop. I was desperate, crazy with longing to have you to hold me and comfort me. Sometimes I was so close to calling you and begging you to come to me...."

"But you didn't," she breathed. "Oh, you should have called me. Don't you think I'd have come if I'd known you needed me?"

"Yes, you'd have come," he agreed wearily. "But for what? To tie yourself to a man with nothing to give you but his need and helplessness?"

"I wouldn't have asked for anything better than to be needed by you," she said.

"I know that. I once saw you taking care of a sick dog, remember? Caring for helpless creatures is your special talent, but it's put to better use as a vet. Thank God I had too much self-respect to let you use it on me."

"Self-respect?" she echoed. "Or stupid, stubborn pride?"

"Well, perhaps a bit of both. When stupid, stubborn pride is all you have to cling to, it can become dreadfully important. I wouldn't let the wreck of my life become the wreck of yours. I loved you too much for that. Don't blame me for the decision I made. Remember what I saved you from. Now, I think you'd better go."

"Can't we talk some more? There's so much I want to understand."

"What is there to understand? We loved each other, but life didn't work out for us. It was nobody's fault. It just happened. Now it's over."

"Over," she repeated softly, as if trying to understand the word's meaning. "No, Ben, that's not true. It'll never be over as long as we're both alive. It'll never be over as long as you keep my letter by you, and as long as I—" She clasped her hands to her breast, feeling an ache there that almost overwhelmed her.

He watched her face, transfixed by its mixture of sadness and joy. There was a pain in his breast that had been threatening ever since they'd met that afternoon, a pain he'd fought not to feel. But now it overwhelmed him, half agony, half joy at being with her again. He reached out and took a step toward her, but he didn't notice a table in his path. He stumbled, lost his balance and flung out an arm. She caught him just in time, holding on to him tightly. To his chagrin he felt himself clinging to her. She helped him back to the sofa, and sat down beside him.

"You see?" he said wearily.

"Anyone can stumble over a table," she argued desperately.

"I stumble all the time," he told her with a bitterness in his voice that tore at her heart. "And then I have to get my strength back for another effort. And even then I can only walk with a stick, and not very far. I finish the day aching all over and often with a blinding headache. But that's not the worst. I can't even begin to tell you about the dark times—great black, gaping holes of depression that come without warning and swallow me up for days on end. By the time I've struggled through to the end, I'm hardly human. I'm not fit for anyone to live with. I can't bear sympathy, I can't bear pity, and I'm not even sure I could bear love. Don't you understand, Dawn? *I don't want you for my nursemaid.*"

The last words were a shout of agony, and after he'd uttered them he dropped his head into his hands. He was shaking violently as she'd sometimes seen animals shake under stress. The strong protective instincts that governed her whole life made her react at once. Without thinking what she was doing she put her arms about him, enfolding him in a comforting embrace, laying her cheek against his head and caressing him tenderly. "There, my love," she whispered. "I'm here. Hold on to me."

His hand came from somewhere and seized hers in a fierce grip. She winced with pain but made no sound, holding him tightly and rocking gently back and forth. Tears streamed from her eyes when she thought of the wasted years when she hadn't been there to do this for him. He'd chosen to fight alone, rejecting her comfort, but the battle had devastated him, and he couldn't reject it now.

At last he stirred, and seemed to realize what was happening. Dawn felt him grow tense and draw away from her slightly, and she remembered his words, "I don't want you for my nursemaid."

"I'm all right now," he said stiffly. "It's very good of you to—I assure you there's no need—Dawn—"

The last word was a whisper, uttered just before she took his face between her hands and laid her lips on his.

It was the gentlest kiss she'd ever given him. There was no pressure, no intensity, no passion. It was as though he were an injured animal lashing out at the world, who must be calmed before she could help him. When she'd finished she realized that some of her own tears must have brushed off on him, for his face was wet.

Ben spoke with a great effort. "It's a myth that suffering ennobles. It hasn't ennobled me. It's made me an ill-tempered swine. It's good of you to be so friendly still, after the way I've behaved to you."

She managed a smile. "I was always your best friend. I still am. I always will be."

"Thank you." He sighed. "But I think you'd better go now."

Dawn realized with despair that she hadn't made the breakthrough she'd hoped. There was nothing to do but accept her dismissal. She turned toward the French doors through which she'd entered, but Ben said, "Not that way. I'll show you out through the front door. I still have a few manners left."

She allowed him to escort her through the house. As they reached the hall Mrs. Stanley appeared, looking worried. "Oh, sir, I wonder if I should call the police. There's a man hanging about the front gate, and he looks ever-so-suspicious."

Ben grunted and pulled open the front door to look at the man who was still standing there. He turned at the sound of the door and came toward the light. "Why, it's Harry," Dawn said, surprised.

"Is that you, Dawn?" he called from the path.

"Come here," Ben growled, "and stop acting as though you were 'loitering with intent.'"

The young man came closer to where they could both see his good-natured face. "My only intent is to make sure Dawn gets home safely," he said. He addressed her directly. "I saw you come in here and—Well, it's dark and the roads are getting slippery."

"How very chivalrous," Ben said with grim irony. "Miss Fletcher is just leaving. Good night."

Dawn bade him good-night, then went out to where Harry was waiting for her. She gave a last glance back at Ben but he'd already closed the front door.

"You didn't mind my hanging about, did you?" Harry asked anxiously. "I just got a bit worried about you after what Jack said about him."

"That was nice of you," she replied, trying to sound cheerful and not succeeding.

"Hey, what's the matter? You're not crying, are you? Yes, you are."

"No, I'm not," she insisted in a muffled voice.

"Is he that much of an ogre? Damn him for making you cry." He slipped an arm around her shoulder as they walked down the drive to the gate, and hugged her. "Come on, darling. Let's get out of the cold, and you'll feel better."

He hugged her again and drew her out into the road. They didn't look back, so they didn't see the curtain drawn aside a crack until they were out of sight.

CHAPTER THREE

"HARRY TELLS ME you went to beard the lion in his den last night," Jack said, keeping his eyes on the snow-covered road ahead. They were making farm calls together.

"I— What was that?" Dawn took her attention from the white fields and tried to concentrate.

"I hear you went to see the new occupant of the Grange. Harry says you were upset when you left, so I suppose you didn't manage to persuade him about the party."

With a sense of shock Dawn realized she hadn't tried to change Ben's mind about the party. She'd been completely shattered by meeting him again and discovering what had happened to him; everything else had simply gone out of her head.

She'd spent a sleepless, desperate night. All the old pain of thinking he'd abandoned her was as nothing to the new pain of discovering what had really happened. Their love had meant everything to her, but he'd prized it so little that when tragedy struck, he'd simply set it aside. From whichever angle she looked at it, that was the brutal truth.

It was useless to reason that it made no difference now that her love for Ben was in the past. It was true that the intense feeling that had made her take him in her arms and kiss him last night had been little different from what she would have felt for any hurt creature. But the echo of love persisted, along with the memory of high hopes and blissful happiness when the world had been young and full of promise. That glorious time had finally died last night, and the knowledge was tearing her in two.

"No," she said now to Jack. "I didn't persuade him." She forced herself to concentrate on the present. There was work to do. "We'll be going near Haynes's farm," she observed. "I'd like to call in and look at Trixie, just to be on the safe side."

"There's no need," Jack said. He added wryly, "If there was even a hint of anything wrong with that spaniel, Fred would have been on the phone in a panic. I've never seen a man set so much store by a dog."

"I'd still like to have a look. She's getting close to her time."

Jack grinned. "Admit it. The truth is, you just feel sorry for the old boy."

"I suppose I do. He always seems so alone—just those pictures of his family, and his memories."

"I know. It's sad. Mind you, it's his own fault he's alone. He could have his children around him now if he hadn't quarreled with them both."

"Why?"

"Chiefly because he's as stubborn as a mule. Everything has to be done his way. His children had to think his way. They couldn't take the pressure, they escaped. Now all he's left with is Trixie, and she's his ideal companion because she never answers back."

"And he's terrified in case he loses her," Dawn observed.

"There's no reason for him to lose her. She may not be in her first youth, but she's as fit as a fiddle. If you like, though, I'll drop you off there while I'm on my way to see Carney's bull, and collect you on my way back."

She saw Trixie as soon as she went in through Fred Haynes's gate. The spaniel was waddling through the snow, swaying from side to side. Dawn greeted Fred with a smile and received only a grunt in return. But he immediately put the kettle on to offer her a cup of tea.

"Not long now," she said as she knelt by the fire, gently feeling Trixie's stomach and fondling her ears. "Soon after Christmas, I'd say."

"And she's gonna be all right?" he demanded in a belligerent manner that Dawn knew masked fear.

"She should be. I know you're taking excellent care of her, and she's perfectly healthy."

The old man grunted. "Reckon I shoulda put a stop to it when I found out," he growled. "Dunno what got inta me."

But Dawn knew. Trixie had apparently mated with a stray she'd encountered on the moor, and Fred had known nothing about the pregnancy until it was well advanced. To have terminated it then would have involved some risk to the spaniel, and he hadn't wanted to chance it. Now that the birth was almost due he was regretting his decision. Dawn reassured him as much as possible, and sipped her tea, looking around at the old-fashioned room, with its photographs of his children.

"That's my son, Tony," Fred told her, following her gaze. "He went to Australia. Got married."

"He looks very young," Dawn said, studying the picture.

"That was taken before he went."

"Don't you have anything more recent, showing him with his wife?" she asked, curious.

Fred shrugged. "He's got his life and I've got mine. He did send me a picture years back, just after his young 'uns were born. Twins, they were. But we've never seen eye-to-eye. I don't hear from him now. Don't want to, either."

Trixie made a grumbling sound and he bent down to pat her. The harshness left his voice as he murmured to the animal with a tenderness Dawn guessed he'd found hard to show to his children. She watched them, feeling sad for the old man in his self-imposed loneliness that he no longer knew how to end.

She heard the sound of a car horn in the yard. "That's Jack," she said. "Goodbye, Fred. There's nothing to worry about, but give me a call, night or day, if you feel she needs it."

He grunted. "Don't forget to send me your bill for this visit."

She smiled and shook her head. "What visit? I just dropped in to have a cup of tea."

He grunted again, but she thought she saw a flicker of pleasure on his face.

"It's so sad," she told Jack on the way home. "Even if Trixie comes through this all right, dogs don't live forever, and she isn't young. What will he do when the time comes?"

"Hey, you're a vet, not a social worker," he reminded her gently.

"But people's animals don't exist in isolation. They're a part of the rest of their lives."

"I know. I'm merely saying that you can't shoulder everyone's burdens for them. In the end, we're all alone."

"Yes," she said after a moment. "I know that."

Harry had just finished the morning surgery when they got back. "There's a visitor for you," he told Dawn. "It's the fellow you went to see last night."

"Good heavens! Not 'Scrooge'?" Jack demanded with a grin.

"I wish you wouldn't call him that," Dawn said, more sharply than she intended to.

"Sorry," Jack said hastily. "Perhaps this is a good sign. Maybe your charm worked on him, and he relented."

"What actually did he say when you asked him about the party?" Harry inquired.

"Well I— That is— Where is he?"

"In the waiting room."

She found that her heart was beating hard as she opened the waiting-room door. Ben glanced up as she entered. He looked terrible, as though he too had spent a sleepless night. There were black circles under his eyes and tension about his mouth. He rose awkwardly as she entered. "Ben, what's the matter?" she asked urgently. "What's wrong?"

"There's nothing wrong. I came to see you because—" He hesitated. "I understand you've been out visiting farms this morning. Am I taking up your lunch hour?"

"That's all right," she said dismissively.

"No, it isn't. You need all your strength for this work. You'd better come and have some lunch with me. Then I'll have nothing to reproach myself with."

She was about to say he had nothing to feel badly about, anyway, but she stopped herself. There was something unnatural about Ben's manner, as though he was forcing himself to appear casual against enormous odds. If she could get him away from here, perhaps he'd be more at ease. "All right," she said. "Thank you." They went to the little café where she often ate. There were still some empty places. "We have to get our food from the counter first," Dawn said.

"Would you mind getting it?" he asked quickly. "I'll find us a spot." He thrust some money in her hand and turned away in search of a table, keeping his face averted. Dawn hastily collected some lunch and brought it across to the table he'd found by the window. She almost wished they hadn't come, because the harsh daylight gave her a clear view of his face. It was more battered than she'd realized in the dim light the night before. The scars showed, although they hadn't pulled his face out of shape. In that he'd been lucky. He was still handsome, still recognizable as the man she'd once loved so passionately. But she realized that he didn't know this, that he was morbidly self-conscious about his face. He was deliberately turning away from the room, but then some passersby looked in through the window, and he turned back again.

"Ben, it's not so bad," she said, trying to reassure him.

"Isn't it? I don't know anymore. I remember what it was like at first, and I can't get that picture out of my head." Some other customers gave him a passing glance and he averted his face again. "I shouldn't have come here. I should have invited you to the house."

"Why didn't you?"

"I was afraid you wouldn't come."

She smiled. "I'd have come."

"Even after the way I behaved last night?"

"You're entitled to be a bit niggly after what you've been through."

"Don't," he said with a soft violence that startled her.

"What?"

"Don't make allowances for me, Dawn. Don't make excuses. It makes me feel pathetic."

She cursed herself for tactlessness. "I'm sorry, Ben."

"And don't apologize when I'm in the wrong," he snapped.

She opened her mouth and closed it again, stumped for an answer. He gave a faint grin. "You see what you escaped?"

It was in her heart to say that he wouldn't be like this if he'd turned to her, for her comfort would have enveloped him and eased his pain. Then she remembered that he'd said he hadn't wanted her love. "All right," she said. "Just tell me what you want."

"It's just that I realized I'd forgotten my manners yesterday. I never asked why you came to see me. I don't mean in the evening, but earlier—when we first met. You didn't know it would be me, did you?"

"I had no idea. I just came to see the new owner of the Grange."

"Why?"

"I wanted to try to persuade you to agree to the children's party."

"Oh, I see."

"Jack told me you wouldn't even consider it."

"I've only just moved in and you want me to let the place be disrupted."

"Is that the real reason, Ben? Or is it just another way of shutting out the world?"

"Does it matter?"

"It matters to the children who'll lose their treat. They aren't ordinary children. They come from institutions. Most of them are too old to be adopted and the ones that aren't—well, they have other problems." He was silent and she went on, "You used to enjoy children, Ben. You'd pick babies up and press your face against them. It was one of the things I loved most about you. I don't believe you've really changed that much."

"I've had to change. When you see people flinching away from you, you can't inflict yourself on them. You don't understand, Dawn. I've seen the way children look at me, and I can't bear it."

Dawn was silent, wondering if she dared play her next card. At last she decided to risk it. "Well," she said, apparently casually, "you were never the most consistent of men. That's one thing in which you haven't changed."

"What the devil do you mean?"

"You want to deny these children one of the few treats they have because of your feelings, because you're morbidly conscious of being damaged. And you expect me to be understanding about that. But it was only five minutes ago you told me not to make allowances for you. You said it made you feel pathetic." She took a deep breath. "You're right. Your attitude is pretty pathetic."

He scowled at her, but after a moment his expression changed to a reluctant grin. "Caught with my own argument. You always knew how to give it straight from the shoulder."

"So, straight from the shoulder—are you going to forget about yourself and think of these deprived children?"

He hesitated. "If I say yes, who will be doing all the organizing?"

"We will. You won't have to do a thing."

"But who is 'we'? If it means you, that's all right. I just don't want to find myself in the hands of total strangers."

"So if I promise to be responsible for everything—you'll agree?"

After a long, painful pause he said, "I guess I will."

Ben held his breath at the look that swept over her face. It was a look of total joy, and it seemed to bring her back to him as she had been eight years ago. He gripped the edge of the table. "After all," he said after a moment, "I don't actually have to be around during the party, do I?"

"Not if you don't want to. But I hope you'll want to."

"We'll see. When is this party to take place?"

"December twenty-third."

"That's going to give you a tight schedule. Wouldn't it be better to put it off until Christmas is over?"

"It's always December twenty-third. That's a Hollowdale tradition, and absolutely sacred."

He gave her a wry smile. "It's just as well I gave in, then, isn't it?"

She finished eating and tucked away the remains of a roll in a paper towel. "If you're not going to finish that sandwich I'll have it," she said.

He gave it to her. "Are you really that stuck for food?"

"It's not for me, silly. I give it to the ducks on the pond. They have a hard time right now. I've just got time before I have to get back to work."

He went to the pond with her. Suddenly he'd found himself relaxing. The casually fond way she'd said, "silly," just as she'd sometimes done in the old days, had seemed to strip away the years. She looked little older than the girl she'd been then, he thought, watching her standing by the water's edge and clucking to the ducks. They came slithering over the ice to her to snatch the bread from her outstretched hand.

That was how she was, he realized—always with hands outstretched. In their eight years apart, that was the picture of her that had lived in his mind; the way she'd reached out to him with love. At every meeting she'd run to him with her arms open. At every parting she'd reached out for one final caress. At their last ever parting she'd backed away from him slowly, holding on to his hands until the last moment, unable to tear her eyes from him. He'd never forgotten her look, so full of intense, passionate love. It had haunted him so persistently that it had been almost like a living presence. And last night the Ghost of Christmas Past had finally come to challenge him, reviving memories he'd tried to bury because that was the only way he could stay sane. In a few moments she'd undone the work of years, and when she'd laid her lips on his it had taken all his self-control not to embrace her and beg her to come back to him.

He'd lain awake all night, trying to banish her and failing. Only at dawn had a measure of peace come to him with the realization that they hadn't discussed the reason for her first visit, and that consequently he had an excuse to seek her out. They would talk, he would see her by daylight and perhaps exorcise the ghost. But it hadn't worked out like that. In the short time they'd spent in the café he'd been reminded of everything he'd loved most about her—her warmth and tender compassion for suffering that never became sentimental because it was tempered by humor and robust common sense. Strange that common sense should seem an enchanted quality, but it was a part of *her*.

He watched her laughing as she fed the ducks. He was mad to agree to this party, but if he'd refused she would have thought badly of him. That alone would have been enough to take him back eight years, when he'd often curbed his young, male thoughtlessness out of a longing for her good opinion. Did anything really change? he wondered. Ever?

He followed her down to the edge of the pond. "I'll have that sandwich back," he said. "Let's see if they'll take it from me."

Laughing, she held it out to him but something

caught his attention. He seized her hands and examined three long, ugly scratches. "How did you get those?" he demanded.

"Last night, undoing the wire on your gate." She tried to lighten the atmosphere by adding, "I'd forgotten to bring my housebreaking tools, so I had to use my hands."

But his face was full of horror. "I never meant to hurt you," he groaned. "I could never willingly do anything to hurt you. Tell me that you know that."

"Ben, of course I know. It was an accident. I guess it's just hard to slam a door on the world without jamming somebody's fingers."

He was swept by fierce emotion. In another moment he would have kissed the scratches. He was saved from it by the furious quacking of the ducks, and hastened to toss the bread to them. The realization that he'd nearly made a fool of himself caused him to go hot and cold. He moved hastily away from her, and rummaged in his pocket. "Here's my spare front-door key," he said, giving it to her. "It'll get you into the house if Mrs. Stanley happens to be out when you arrive to set up things for the party."

"But won't you be there to let me in?"

"No, I shall have to be out all day. I've just remembered that I have a thousand things to do."

"But Ben..."

"You don't need me, Dawn. Just treat the house as

your own. Do whatever you want. Have a good party. Now I really must be going."

While she was still trying to think of a way to protest that she wanted him at the party, he limped away and soon vanished from sight.

CHAPTER FOUR

ON THE DAY before Christmas Eve, Ben had an early breakfast before getting out his car. He drove off, deliberately choosing a direction that wouldn't lead him past the veterinary surgery. He told himself he'd done everything Dawn could possibly expect, and now he wanted nothing more to do with the whole business. It was time he inspected his new property, which included several small farms whose tenants he had yet to meet.

He started with Martin Craddock. He knew nothing about Craddock except what the books had told him—that he was often late with his rent. In fact most of the tenants were. All the rents had struck Ben as being on the high side for small acreage, but there might be some compensating factor, like land of exceptional quality.

But nothing he saw on Craddock's farm encouraged this view. If anything, the land was stony and looked difficult to work. The house was empty when he arrived so he began to look around the other buildings. Everything was in a poor state of repair, possibly because the estate had been in limbo for several months.

While he was inspecting the cow shed he saw a battered car lurch into the yard and stop. An apparently endless supply of children poured out and into the house, creating a merry riot and dragging their parents with them. Ben saw a middle-aged man, laughing with his children, then suddenly stop laughing as he noticed Ben's car. Ben stepped out into the open and the man began to hurry toward him.

His face struck Ben as pleasant and well-meaning, but indecisive. Right now it also looked nervous. "I'm sorry not to have been here when you called," Craddock said quickly when he saw his landlord.

"Don't apologize," Ben told him. "It's my fault for coming without warning you."

If anything, Craddock looked even more worried. "Perhaps you'd like to come into the warm," he suggested.

The inside of the house was spotlessly clean but very shabby. There was a multitude of homemade paper chains attached to the walls and ceiling, and a tree in the corner, hung with baubles that might have glittered once but now had the tarnish of age.

"Of course, the farm doesn't look its best at this time of year," Craddock said defensively. "If I'd known you were coming I'd have tidied up a bit."

Ben spoke without thinking. "Don't worry. I prefer to see things as they really are."

It was meant as reassurance, but the whole family stopped and looked at him, each face wearing the same fearful expression. What on earth had he said to make anyone look like that? he wondered.

"I see you've been Christmas shopping," he observed with an attempt at heartiness. He didn't know that his forced manner made the words come out sounding like a threat. He only wondered why the family seemed to draw together against him. Mrs. Craddock contrived to shift her bulk so that it covered a bag bearing the name of a toy shop.

"Just a few things for the children," Craddock said hastily. "They don't get many treats, and they're ever so good about it—but at Christmas—you see—"

"Of course." Ben cut the man short out of pity for his stammering nervousness. "I expect you want to get on with your preparations. I won't stay. We can discuss everything in January when I've got the books at hand. Your lease is up for renewal soon, isn't it?"

"Yes but—I mean, perhaps you'd let me show you the place properly—when I've had a chance to—"

Ben realized that the youngest child was staring at his face with frank curiosity. He repelled them. That was it. That was why they drew together and made him feel like an alien. Suddenly he couldn't wait to get out. "No, thanks," he said curtly. "I've seen all I need to. Good day."

He left the house quickly, almost slamming the door in his haste. He didn't begin to relax until he'd driven several miles. His hands were tense on the steering wheel and his body was aching with strain.

He thought of the mean little place and the excessive rent that Squire Davis had been happy to collect year after year, while giving back as little as possible. The Squire might have been an apple-cheeked old man who kept the picturesque Christmas traditions in his home, but he'd been a tightfisted landlord, indifferent to his tenants' hardship. He wondered if Dawn knew that.

He'd have to make changes on the farms, starting with a reduction in rent, and probably interest-free loans to the tenants to help them get new farm machinery. Or perhaps he could buy the best machinery himself, and rent it to them cheaply when they needed it. Absorbed in these thoughts he got lost in the unfamiliar territory, and after he'd driven around for an hour and found his way again, he discovered he'd returned to Hollowdale. He hadn't meant to come back, but his own house was just ahead and it seemed pointless to drive away again. Besides, he ought to look in to see what sort of a bear garden they were making of the place; and if it meant talking to Dawn, was that his fault?

He turned into the drive and immediately found his way partly blocked by a large, battered car, from which someone was lifting boxes and carrying them inside. Ben recognized the young man who'd come to collect Dawn the other night. The newcomer gave him a cheery wave and went on with his work. By the time Ben had limped up the stairs and into the front hall he had finished his task. "We haven't met properly," Ben said politely. "You can hardly call the other night a meeting."

"I'm Harry," the young man explained. "I'm a vet, in the same practice with Dawn. She asked me to start bringing stuff over for the party. She said it was all right with you."

"Perfectly all right," Ben replied. He studied Harry and found him slightly displeasing. He wasn't quite sure why. Harry's face was handsome and good-humored, his manner cheerful and courteous. But he worked with Dawn. He saw her every day and was happy to run her errands. He followed her so that he could see her home through the snow. There was a coziness about the relationship that Ben didn't like. Not that it was any concern of his. Eight years ago he'd released Dawn just so that she might one day find someone like this. But now that he'd met Harry, he didn't like him. "You'll have to excuse me," he said. "I know nothing about the arrangements. I've left everything in Miss Fletcher's hands."

"Fine. Fine. We'll get on. But first—" Harry checked himself. He seemed embarrassed. "I want to apologize for the other night," he said. "Heaven knows what you must have thought of me, hanging around your house like that, and I wasn't very polite to you."

"More polite than I was to you," Ben observed with accuracy.

"It's just that I was worried about Dawn—"

"Vanishing into the house of the village ogre," Ben said with grim irony.

Harry went red. "I guess I overdid it. I can't help worrying about her, you see—"

"Perfectly natural." It must have been a desire to torment himself that made Ben add, "You're very much in love with her, aren't you?"

Harry gave an awkward laugh. "I suppose it's obvious. I just can't help it. I mean, no one could know Dawn—I mean, really know her—and not love her."

"Indeed?"

"Of course you don't know what she's like, but when you do you'll discover what a wonderful person she is."

"I doubt I'll be getting to know Miss Fletcher any better," Ben told him coolly. "She's achieved her object in getting me to allow this party."

"She's very persuasive, isn't she?" Harry asked eagerly. "When she sets her heart on something she puts everything she's got into it."

"Quite," Ben said coldly.

"Everything means so much to her, and that's how she convinces other people that—"

"You must excuse me," Ben interrupted him. "I have work to do."

He limped away quickly, already passionately regretting that he'd agreed to this. But before he'd quite left the entrance hall he heard a light footstep behind him and turned to see Dawn hurrying through the front door. He stayed back in the shadows, hoping she wouldn't notice him, and saw how her face lit up when she saw Harry. But that was nothing to how Harry's face lit up at the sight of her.

"Harry, bless you for being so prompt," she said, smiling at him. "I'm afraid it's going to be a long job."

"Your knight in shining armor awaits, my lady," he replied. "Give me any task. No challenge is too great in return for one of your smiles."

"Fool," she said fondly. "But here's a challenge for you. Go and collect the cakes from Mrs. Turnbull."

"I said a challenge, not an impossibility. Dawn, please, have mercy. She's a terrible woman."

"She's never done you any harm."

"Never done me any—? She calls me 'young man' in a voice that wouldn't disgrace a sergeant major. And she makes me stand and listen while she tells endless stories about how her cakes always win prizes at the fete, and—"

"She's old and lonely," Dawn said. "Be nice to her."

"For you, anything." He kissed her lightly and vanished. Dawn stood looking after his departing form with a tender smile on her face. Ben remained absolutely still in the shadows, not moving until Dawn had picked up a box and taken it into the next room. Then he limped away into the library and closed the door behind him.

But he couldn't shut out the sound. There was a nonstop stream of cars arriving, doors slamming, cheerful voices raised. He tried to concentrate on studying account books, but Dawn's face kept getting between him and the page. He saw again the tender smile she'd given Harry. There was no passion in that look, he reassured himself. Just friendly affection. But perhaps she was ready to settle for friendly affection. Passion had only broken her heart.

He remembered the light, gentle kiss she'd given him the other night: the kiss of a friend, full of compassion and sorrow. And pity? God forbid! But had all love and desire been destroyed in her? He hadn't meant that, when he'd shut her out. He'd thought of her as forgetting him, marrying, having children, finding fulfillment. Instead, he'd taught her a brutal lesson about the uselessness of love.

Suddenly she seemed to be there with him, her younger self reincarnated, smothering him with wild kisses that tasted of honey. He groaned, trying to shut out the torturing vision, but she wouldn't be shut out. Her lips were on his and her arms were about his neck, reminding him what he'd once possessed and thrown away through pride. He groaned and let his head fall into his hands.

A knock on the door made him sit up sharply. "Yes?" he called in a ragged voice.

"May I come in?" It was Dawn.

At that moment he would rather have faced anyone in the world but her, but he controlled himself enough to say, "Yes, come in."

"I came to ask for the key to the double doors," she

said, approaching him. "If we open those we can throw the two big rooms together."

"Mrs. Stanley has the key," he told her curtly.

"She says you have it." She smiled and spoke gently. "I'm sorry to trouble you."

He found the key and gave it to her, resenting her bitterly. Why didn't she go away and smile at Harry who was in love with her, who could marry her?

"Oh, by the way, I had to leave this number at the surgery. Jack's on duty, but if he's called out, people need to know where they can contact Harry or me. Is that all right?"

"Of course it is."

"I'm glad you managed to come back," she said warmly. "It'll be wonderful to have you at the party."

"I'm not going to be at the party," he growled. "I told you, I want nothing to do with it. Now, if you don't mind, I'm very busy."

She was silent a moment, and he wondered if she would come forward and put her arms around him, as she'd done the other evening. But the silence lengthened, and when he looked behind him she'd left the room.

Just as well, he thought. The less they saw of each other, the better. But against his will he found himself listening for the sound of her voice in the din of noise coming from beyond the door.

At last the noise died away to a low murmur, which lasted for half an hour. Then came a sound that made

him flinch—vans crunching along the drive and dis-
gorging children who streamed into the house chatter-
ing excitedly. He took down the estate accounts and got
to work on them, scowling with concentration as he
tried to shut out all consciousness of the party.

He managed to work for an hour, but finally reached
the point where he couldn't proceed without a book he
knew he'd left upstairs. There was nothing to do but
fetch it. As he opened the door he almost collided with
Harry, who had a bundle tucked under his arm and
seemed almost furtive.

"Sorry," he said quickly to Ben. "I've been roped
into playing Father Christmas and I'm looking for
somewhere to put this on." He indicated the bundle.

"You can use the library," Ben said, standing back
to let him pass. He limped away quickly to avoid Harry's thanks, and headed for the stairs. On the way he
passed the double doors that led to the big front room.
They were standing open, and through them he could
see a long table, loaded with food and packed with
children wearing paper hats. He hurried past in case
someone saw him.

When he returned a few minutes later he could see
"Father Christmas" making his way around the two
long tables, pulling crackers that the children held out
to him. Dawn was there, acting as a waitress, making sure there were second helpings of jelly for any
who wanted it. She looked happy and absorbed. Ben

watched her for a moment, feeling a curious aching sensation, before moving quietly away.

The door of the library was open. He was about to close it behind him when he realized there was someone else in the room. A little girl was perched on the library steps, turning the pages of a book. Annoyed that his privacy had been invaded, he spoke sharply. "You shouldn't be in here. Didn't anyone tell you this room is private?"

She seemed to flinch, and when she looked up Ben was shocked and angry with himself. She looked about ten, and had the round face of Down's syndrome. In the same moment he became aware of the caliper splint leaning against the wall. "It's all right," he said quickly. "I didn't mean to snap at you. You can stay here if you want to."

She looked anxious. "Is it really all right? I'm always in trouble for being where I shouldn't."

"You're not in trouble now," he said firmly. "You just took me by surprise."

He'd heard that Down's-syndrome children were notable for their gentle, affectionate natures, and perhaps it was true, for the smile she gave him was the sweetest he'd ever seen. He found himself smiling back. "Was it hard to get up those steps?" he asked with a glance at the caliper.

She shook her head. "I just held on to the shelves. It's quite easy, really. I'm good at holding on to things."

She spoke quite unself-consciously and it made him

answer her equally naturally. "I wish I was good at holding on to things, but I hate people to know that I *need* to hold on."

"Is that your stick over there?"

"Yes."

"Have you always had it?"

"No, just a few years. What about you?"

"Since I was little," she said, unconcerned. "People are funny, aren't they? I mean, if you've got a stick they don't know what to say to you."

"The ones that think they do know are the worst," Ben reflected gloomily.

"They always seem to get it wrong," she said wisely.

They looked at each other in fellow feeling.

"My name's Carly," she offered.

"Mine's—" He hesitated, then gave her the name that only Dawn had ever used. "Mine's Ben."

They shook hands with solemn courtesy.

"Is this your house?" she asked.

"That's right."

"Then why aren't you at the party? Don't you like parties?"

"Not really," he confessed.

She looked anxious. "Don't you like people?"

"I—I don't feel easy with them."

"But why ever not? I think people are lovely."

"Even the ones who say the wrong things?"

"They mean to be kind," Carly said simply.

"I've rather got out of the habit of being with people," he said. "I'm always afraid they're going to look at my face."

She looked at him, puzzled. "But there's nothing wrong with your face."

He was about to say, "Nonsense," in his usual impatient way, when he realized that to her his fears would seem crazy. Her own troubles were so much greater, and she bore them so lightly that suddenly he felt ashamed. "Isn't there, really?" he asked, speaking more naturally than he had to a stranger for a long time.

She studied him more closely. The steps put her almost at his level. "You only have a few lines," she said reassuringly. "And everyone has lines when they get old, don't they?"

"I'm not that old," he said, startled.

Carly gave a little choke of laughter. She was irresistible, and before he knew it he was laughing with her. Absorbed, he didn't notice Dawn come to the door, stand watching them for a moment, then vanish quickly.

"I guess I am that old after all," he said with a grin.

"A hundred?" Carly asked mischievously.

"Less. Not much less, but a bit less. Now let's forget my age. Why don't you tell me what you're doing here? Weren't you enjoying the party?"

"Oh, yes, it's a super party. I'd never been to a Grange party before, although I'd heard all about them. Everyone said there wouldn't be one this year, but I hoped and hoped and hoped. And if you hope that much, it always comes true."

There was a sudden pricking against his eyelids at the courage with which she fended off despair. Despite the blows fate had dealt her she'd somehow clung to the belief that life was good, and it was he who'd nearly destroyed that belief. "Of course it does," he said. "But if you like the party so much, why are you here?"

"We were told not to go anywhere else in the house—" She looked at him, as if trying to decide whether to say the next bit.

He saved her the trouble. "So you just had to go exploring. I know the feeling. I was just like that at your age. Telling me not to do something was like a red rag to a bull. Do you want to see the rest of the house?"

The impish look was back in her eyes. "Thank you, but there's no point now."

"No—? Oh, I see. I spoiled it by saying yes. Then why not go back to the party? You're missing Father Christmas."

"Are you coming?"

"No, I—" He stopped. Her eyes were on him.

"It would be lovely if you came, too," she said earnestly.

"In that case—yes."

He helped her down and handed her the caliper. "Are you bringing your stick?" she asked.

He shook his head. "Suddenly I don't feel as if I need it."

They left the library hand in hand and made their way to the party. As they entered, the noise suddenly died and heads turned in their direction. For a terrible moment the old self-consciousness assailed him. Then he felt the little girl's hand tighten on his in a wordless message of comfort.

"This is Ben," she told everyone happily. "He's my friend."

CHAPTER FIVE

FOR A MOMENT he couldn't take everything in. The meal was over and the tables had been cleared away, leaving a space where children were sitting and standing. Glittering tinsel decorations hung in giant festoons from the ceiling, and around the walls. At the far end of the long room rose a giant Christmas tree whose base was almost totally obscured by presents, and in front of it sat Father Christmas. But for the moment no one was looking at him. Ben's arrival had riveted everyone's attention.

As his mind cleared he realized that most of the children here were disabled in some way. Some had crutches, three were in wheelchairs, and many had Down's syndrome. Their round, smiling faces beamed at him in welcome, and they stretched out their hands to draw him into the circle, as if he were only another child who, like them, looked different from other children.

Under the tree Harry boomed, "Ho-ho-ho!" And

when he had everyone's attention he cried, "Is everybody ready to play games?"

He was answered by an excited cheer. The youngsters crowded around him. A touch on Ben's arm made him look down. A little girl was standing there with a piece of Christmas cake on a plate. "You didn't have any," she said anxiously, holding it up to him.

He thanked her gravely and took the cake. She continued to watch him until he'd taken a bite and pronounced it delicious. Then she smiled and seemed to relax.

He'd had so many nurses—paid professionals who'd done their duty and departed when he became unbearable. The child's gentle concern for him pierced his heart. He'd forgotten that such care could be had freely—except for one person.

Dawn and the other helpers were putting chairs in a circle, asking everyone to sit down. Following the urgings of his new friends, Ben found himself sitting between Carly and a little boy in a wheelchair. He had no idea what was going to happen until Santa produced a huge parcel, which he handed to the nearest child. Someone began to play the piano, and the child promptly passed the parcel to his neighbor, who gave it to *his* neighbor. Suddenly the music stopped and the little boy who had the parcel began to tear off the shiny red paper, revealing shiny blue paper underneath. Before he could go further, the music restarted and it was time for the parcel to move on again.

Good heavens, Ben thought. He'd played this as a child, but not thought of it for years. The parcel came to him and he passed it on quickly. At last it stopped again and the child who had it began tearing at the wrapping. He got another layer off before the music started.

The next time the music stopped the parcel was in Ben's hands. He was embarrassed, not wanting to win the prize, but the packing was still thick, and he made a show of removing some while the children cheered. It was a relief when he could send it on its way. He could see Dawn, doubled up with laughter. He mouthed, "What's so funny?" and she mouthed back, "You."

And it *was* funny. Suddenly he could see that. Why had he stayed away from the party when there was so much fun to be had?

Reflecting thus, he almost got caught with the parcel again, but managed, at the last moment, to thrust it into the hands of the boy in the wheelchair. The child tried to pick at the wrapping but one arm was weak and he had difficulty until Ben came to the rescue, holding everything steady so that the boy removed quite a lot of wrapping. But there was still some there when the music restarted.

Round and round the parcel went, getting smaller while the cheers got louder. With one layer to go, it reached Ben again. This time he worked frantically, so that just before the music started he could thrust the gift into the hands of the little boy, with only a tiny scrap of wrapping left. As the child removed the final wisp of paper, Ben was leading the cheers.

The boy opened the box, revealing an adventure book. From his expression he'd clearly never won anything before in the whole of his short life. Ben was euphoric with triumph and exhilaration. He groped around in his mind for the last time he'd felt like this, but he had to go back a long way to come up with the answer.

It had been eight years ago, when a young woman with dark eyes and soft lips had told him she would love him forever. It had been a glorious victory, achieved after desperate efforts to fend off other men attracted by her beauty and her sweet nature. She could have had anyone she wanted, but she'd chosen him, and he'd felt akin to the gods. Nothing was going to part them. *For better or worse,* they'd promised each other, echoing the words of the marriage service they were planning. *Through thick and thin. Until death.* But he'd betrayed that promise by not allowing her to keep it.

A malaise gripped him. The afternoon that had been so happy a moment ago was dimmed. He looked at Dawn, standing with a small child in her arms, and to his eyes all warmth and light, all joy and harmony streamed from her. If only he'd had more faith in her, they could have had their own children by now. She could have been standing there as his wife. The Ghost of Christmas Present had visited him, and it was a merry ghost, dancing and singing, with children clutching its hand and the hem of its flowing robes. But it was a melancholy ghost, too, reminding him that this might have been *his* present, and he'd blindly thrown it away.

After several more games the party moved on to the serious business of presents. Father Christmas sat under the tree, booming, "Ho-ho-ho!" taking the gifts Dawn handed to him, and reading the names out. Every child had a gift individually labeled and, as far as possible, chosen to fit. As yet another child whooped, "I really wanted this!" Ben made his way quietly around to where Dawn was selecting parcels to hand to Santa.

"How did you know what everyone wanted?" he murmured.

She smiled at him. "Some nifty liaison work with the people who look after them," she said, talking and working at the same time. "Most of them live in homes and hospitals. Their caregivers are wonderful, but even so, individuals tend to get submerged in the crowd. This is our chance to make up for that."

She was like a perfect bell, he thought. Strike where you would, the sound was always clear, sweet and true. It might all have been his own, but now she was smiling at Harry as she handed him the next gift, and Harry was smiling back with the unmistakable glow of a man in love. Quietly Ben moved away, choosing a moment when she wouldn't notice.

He retreated to the library and closed the door firmly, shutting out the sounds of the party, and settled down to wait for it all to finish.

But it was no good. His spirit was still out there with them, watching her jealously. He, who had no right to be jealous!

He endured it for half an hour, but then the low hum that still reached him through the thick oak door died to almost nothing, and the quiet was the worst thing of all. He went to the door and opened it a fraction. The party was still going on, but it had reached the cocoa stage. In the big room he could just see children sitting around drinking out of mugs. Some of the younger ones were beginning to nod off.

As Ben watched, Father Christmas came creeping out into the hall. He was looking around him as though afraid to be seen. When he was sure he was alone he slipped a hand into his robe, and drew it out clutching a sprig of mistletoe, which he lodged in the top of a picture frame in a dark corner of the hall. Then he went down the passage in the direction of the kitchen and when he returned, he was leading Dawn by the hand.

Ben gritted his teeth. He was enraged but helpless. A man could hardly attack Father Christmas, and nothing else would stop the inevitable. Except Dawn herself, perhaps? She might push him away.

But Santa was cunning. Holding her tenderly he inquired, "Have I done everything you wanted?"

"Everything," she assured him. "You've been absolutely wonderful."

"In that case—" Santa pointed up to the mistletoe "—it's time for my reward."

Dawn allowed herself to be drawn closer into his arms to receive his kiss. Her manner wasn't loverlike. She even giggled and said his beard tickled, but Ben's frantically searching eyes couldn't detect any sign of her pushing him away. He retreated and closed the door again, wishing he'd never opened it.

A short while later there was a knock on the door and he opened it to find Carly. "The bus is here," she said with a shy smile. "I didn't want to go without saying goodbye to you."

"It was a pleasure talking to you," he said sincerely. "I hope we meet again."

"Perhaps we'll meet at next year's Christmas party?"

"Yes, perhaps," he agreed.

He watched as she and a small group of others were shepherded through the front door to their waiting bus. At the last moment Carly turned and waved vigorously, and he waved back. Dawn came and stood beside him, also waving. "I'm so glad you two got on well," she said. "It's such a pity that they have to go so early, but they've got quite a distance to travel."

"The party's still going, then?" he asked.

"Another hour, I should think. Is that all right?"

"Perfectly. I told you, I leave everything in your hands." Somebody called her and she turned away to chat with a child. Ben's jealous eyes searched the surroundings and finally located Harry in the big party room, munching Christmas cake. He saw him glance up at Dawn, catch her eye and blow her a kiss from behind his beard. She didn't blow a kiss back, but she waved to him cheerfully.

The phone in the library rang. Ben answered it and found himself talking to a strange woman who introduced herself as Mrs. Calloway. "I need a vet," she explained. "Mr. Stanning's been called out but I was told I could find the other two at this number."

"That's right. I'll fetch someone for you now."

He could see Dawn only a few feet away. Logic might have dictated that he summon her, but something made him walk right past her to Harry. "I'm afraid you're wanted," he said. "You can use the phone in the library."

He followed Harry back through the hall, noticing almost subconsciously that Dawn was walking away in the direction of the kitchen, and couldn't see them. Harry's conversation was brief. Ben heard him say, "Fine. I'll be there in half an hour." As he hung up he was already pulling off the Father Christmas costume. "I've got to dash," he said. "Hang this beard! It was murder to put on and it's murder to take off." He gave a grin of happy reminiscence. "And there was one part of the evening when it was very inconvenient."

"Really?" Ben said, fighting an impulse to do violence to poor Harry's well-meaning person.

Harry was still tugging at the snowy whiskers. "Can you give me a hand?"

"Delighted." Ben took hold of the beard and removed it with one wrench.

"Ouch!" Harry rubbed his chin. "No need to take my chin off, as well."

"Sorry," Ben said untruthfully. "Is there anything else I can do for you?"

"Yes. Shove the costume back in the box, and tell Dawn I had to dash away, would you?"

"You can leave everything to me."

The hall was empty as he saw Harry to the door. He watched him drive away and stood for a moment, reflecting on what he'd just done. It wasn't exactly dishonest, he reasoned. Harry was the senior vet and many customers would have considered him preferable. But the truth was Ben had seized on the chance to get rid of him.

He heard Dawn's voice coming from the kitchen. She seemed to be talking to one of the children. "Don't worry, Gary. You can talk to Father Christmas now and explain, and I'm sure he'll be able to—"

Ben felt a cold hand clutch his stomach. He'd thought no further ahead than removing Harry, but now the full enormity of his action burst upon him. *He'd sent Father Christmas away.*

Now Gary—whoever he was—would be disappointed, and Dawn would reproach him for not fetching her instead. This was disaster.

Moving faster than he'd done in years he crossed the hall, vanished into the library and shut the door. For extra safety he locked it. He was only just in time. The next moment he heard Dawn's voice directly outside. "Does anybody know where Father Christmas is?"

Desperate situations called for desperate measures. Ben surveyed the red-and-white costume, relieved that he was about the same size as Harry. It took him a moment to toss aside his jacket and pull on the garment. Luckily it was the old-fashioned kind—a massive flowing robe that came down to the ground and concealed almost everything. The real trouble lay with the beard. Having been wrenched unceremoniously off, it declined to take any further part in the proceedings, and lay there, torn and useless. The glue Harry had used had dried, and Ben couldn't find any more in the box. But he did manage to find another beard. This one didn't need glue, but hooked on over the ears. He fixed it as firmly as he could, pulled the big hood over his head, checked in the mirror over the mantel-piece to be sure he was unrecognizable, and unlocked the door.

Dawn was outside, alone. "Thank heavens," she said, smiling and seizing his hand. Ben's heart burned within him. Her smile and her touch were both for Harry, damn him! He inclined his head in a questioning manner, but didn't dare risk speaking.

"We've got a crisis," Dawn explained. "It's Gary Briggs. He's a last-minute addition. His father's dead and he lives alone with his mother, but she had to go into hospital so he's temporarily in care. Nobody knew he was coming until the last moment, so there wasn't time to get him a proper gift. I put in one from the reserve we keep for emergencies, but Gary's eleven and when he opened the gift it was a child's toy and much too babyish for him. We've got to do something, quickly. There he is. Gary, I've just been explaining to Father Christmas, and he's going to put everything right."

For a dreadful moment Ben's mind went completely blank. He pulled himself together and coughed, playing for time. When he spoke his voice was as gruff as he could make it. "Let me see—Gary Briggs." His mind groped frantically around the facts Dawn had given him and seized on one. "Your mother's in hospital, isn't she? Have you seen her?"

"I saw her yesterday."

"Is she feeling any better?"

"The doctor said she'd be out in a month."

"That's good. But it's a sad thing to happen at Christmas. Misfortunes always seem worse at Christmas. I wonder why."

Gary nodded and looked at Ben confidingly, as if he'd touched a nerve. "It's because you make so many plans," he said. "You keep remembering the things you were supposed to be doing instead of what you are doing."

"Yes, that's right. You do. And the distance between them hurts." He said the last words almost to himself, but the sight of Gary's trustful eyes on him brought him back to reality. "I expect you miss her very much," he said. "What do you miss about her most?" He was playing madly for time, seeking the essential clue that would tell him what to do next.

Unexpectedly Gary gave it to him. "Doing jigsaws," he said.

"You do jigsaw puzzles?"

"Mum and me do them together. Really hard ones. She's ever so good."

It had happened, the miracle he'd prayed for. "Tell me, Gary, have you and your mother ever done a jigsaw of eight thousand pieces?"

The boy's eyes opened wide and he shook his head.

"Suppose I give you one, and then you can see how much you can manage by yourself, and when your mother comes home you can finish it together."

Gary nodded. He was smiling and seemed beyond speech. "It isn't exactly new," Ben added hastily. "Because I've always loved jigsaws too, and I used to do this one myself when I was a young—a young Father Christmas."

"But how can you be a young Father Christmas?" Gary wanted to know.

"It's a mystery, but take it from me that you can. I've been saving this jigsaw to give to someone who was exceptionally good at them. I want you to wait here with Dawn."

His mind was racing with plans for getting upstairs without actually climbing the main stairway, which would reveal his identity. If he went through the library and out the French doors he could slip back into the house at the side and dash up the back stairs. Pre-occupied, he failed to notice Dawn staring at him as though she'd seen a ghost.

As he hurried through the library he realized what a task he'd taken on. Most of his possessions were still packed up, and he had only the vaguest idea where the jigsaw puzzle was. But his luck held and he found what he was looking for in five minutes. He'd spoken the truth about his lifelong fascination with difficult jigsaws—a hobby that had become almost an obsession in his years of illness. It was still in excellent condition, with no unsightly tears or scruffy patches on the lid, with its brilliantly colored picture of racing cars speeding toward the checkered flag amid cheering crowds. He picked it up and hastened back the way he'd come.

He returned downstairs to find that more children were putting on hats and coats and being shepherded outside to waiting buses. Ben took a moment to stand on the step and wave them goodbye, then hurried back to Gary. He found him sitting under the Christmas tree, looking slightly forlorn in the rapidly emptying room. Ben stopped at the doorway to switch off the chandelier, leaving only the Christmas-tree lights and a few around the walls. There was enough light to give his gift, but no dangerous brilliance to reveal his identity.

He went and sat beside Gary, holding out the jigsaw. The boy gasped and seized it, regarding the picture with wonder. "It's fabulous," he breathed. "And a smashing picture. Not a soppy one."

"That's why I always liked it," Ben agreed, "because it had a decent picture, not a soppy one. Also, because it's very difficult. It'll take you ages." For a moment he forgot his character and spoke as himself: "But I promise all the pieces are there. I always threw them away if any pieces were missing."

"Threw them away?" Gary echoed, aghast. "Just for one piece?"

"There didn't seem any point once they weren't perfect any more," Ben explained. Something in the boy's eyes made him add more gently, "You don't feel that way about your jigsaws?"

"They're all special—like friends," Gary explained earnestly. "I couldn't throw them away just 'cause they were a bit different. I mean, you don't get fed up with people just cuz of that, do you?"

How little he knew of the world if he believed that, Ben thought. The years would teach him differently. But with luck he would cling to his beliefs and would probably make fewer bad decisions than most men.

A middle-aged couple had come quietly into the room. They were Gary's temporary foster parents, ready to take him away. Ben got hastily back into character. They were the last guests to leave and he said booming goodbyes to them and conducted them to the front door. Gary was clutching the jigsaw as though it was the most precious thing in the world. He waved out the window until the car was out of sight, and Ben waved back.

CHAPTER SIX

As HE CLOSED the front door Ben realized how quiet the house had become now the party was over. It was as if he were completely alone.

Then he realized that someone was still there—a figure standing in the shadows of the corner where the mistletoe was still lodged over the picture. She stepped out into better light and he saw that it was Dawn. She came close to him. "Father Christmas, you were brilliant," she said. "It meant so much to Gary." She smiled up at him, expecting a response, but Ben didn't dare speak.

Dawn glanced at the mistletoe. "Come here."

His heart sank. He'd wondered how she felt about Harry's kiss, and this was his answer. She wanted more. She was enticing him, putting her hands into his and drawing him into the shadows—or rather, drawing Harry into the shadows. Terrible temptation assailed him. What he was contemplating was monstrous, unforgivable.

"Dawn—" he said in agony.

"Hush," she told him. "We don't need words. We never did. Only this matters." She was putting her arms about his neck, drawing his head down to hers. He must tell her the truth immediately. It was dishonest to accept the love she meant for another man. But her lips were on his and she was in his arms, pressing close to him, and it was impossible to do anything but hold her tightly, and surrender to her.

His heart burned within him. This was different from the kiss she'd given him the other night. That had been gentle and friendly, a gesture of reassurance such as she might have given to any wounded creature. Now there was desire and urgency in her mouth. The lips that moved purposefully against his were full of sweet promise and infinite delight, as they had been before, long ago; as he had never thought to find them again.

He'd fought his longing for her through the bitter, lonely years, and had thought he'd won. If he couldn't murder his feelings, at least he could master them. That was what he'd told himself. Now that victory was revealed as a sham, a thing of gossamer that could be destroyed by her touch, by the memory of her eager, self-forgetting passion. He'd survived by denying love in order to forget its beauty. But love was invading him, forcing him to recognize beauty and to want it again with a blazing force that shook his battered body like a storm.

"It's true, isn't it?" she murmured against his mouth. "Only this matters."

"Yes," he said hoarsely. "It's true. It's always been true."

The battle was over. He yielded. He was hers again as completely as if there'd been no break. His arms encircled her, drawing her tighter still until she was pressed against the whole length of him. Strength flowed back into limbs that hadn't been strong for years. The body that had seemed half dead was awakening, rediscovering desire and delight.

"My love," she whispered. "Oh, my dear love…"

He murmured her name between kisses, saying the word as a kind of charm to ward off evil, and she answered, "Yes…yes…"

"Tell me that you love me," he pleaded.

"I love you," she responded instantly. "Night and day, every moment…always…until the end of my life…"

For a mad moment he was on the verge of breaking down completely, telling her how he'd always loved her, begging her to forgive him and come back. In another instant the words would have been spoken.

But there was the click of a door opening, a murmur from the kitchen. Before he could understand what was happening, Dawn had quickly freed herself. "Someone's coming," she murmured.

"Dawn," he pleaded.

"Hush," she said urgently.

Her hand brushed across his lips, then she was gone. The arms that had held her only a moment ago were empty again—as empty as if he had embraced a ghost.

* * *

The crib glowed in the soft light. The rest of the church was in darkness. Softly the choir began to sing and as their voices swelled, the congregation joined in. It was Christmas Eve, and most of the villagers were in the little church that had stood there for nearly a thousand years.

Ben had slipped in quietly a few minutes earlier, while the lights were still on, and stood by the door, trying to pick Dawn out in the congregation, but there was no sign of her.

Thirty hours had passed since the party had ended with Dawn in his arms—thirty hours during which he'd soared to dizzy hope and sunk to despair again. At some moments it was clear that she'd known who he was all the time, that it was himself she'd kissed with such passion and longing. At other moments it was so obvious that she'd thought it was Harry that he castigated himself for a self-deceiving fool. Sometimes he remembered that whatever she might have guessed later, it was Harry she'd meant to entice under the mistletoe. And sometimes he just felt he was going crazy.

Everything depended on their next meeting, when he could look into her eyes and read the truth there. All Christmas Eve he'd waited for her to call at the Grange, perhaps on some pretext about the party. But though an army had descended on the Grange to clear up, there had been no sign of Dawn. Nor had she called him.

He recalled that his doctors had advised plenty of exercise, and prescribed himself a walk, which might,

or might not, take him past her surgery. By an odd coincidence, that was exactly where it took him, and he
was rewarded by the sight of Dawn's car vanishing into
the distance. Presumably she was attending a farm, but
when she returned and was less busy, she would call
him. Comforted, he returned home, abandoning his
exercise after a few hundred yards.

The day had stretched on endlessly, with no call
from Dawn. The house seemed unbearably lonely after
the riotous happiness of yesterday. Carly stood out in
his mind, her sweet round face showing no bitterness
at the bad hand life had dealt her. Gary was there too,
with his strange childish wisdom about clinging to what
you loved, even when it had become imperfect. Ben
didn't want to examine Gary's words too closely. They
opened up an avenue of thought that dismayed him.

Once his life had been perfect, and had looked set to
go on being perfect. He'd been a young, strong, handsome man, with an innocent pride in his virility and
his power to thrill the woman he loved. But the perfection had gone. The superb body and looks had been
smashed, and with them his pride. So he'd thrown it all
away. He'd told himself he was acting for her benefit.
But now a child's chance remark had shown him a less
noble motive. Had he been too proud to go to her imperfect—as a damaged man who had to cast himself
on the generosity of a woman's love?

If he'd destroyed her happiness for such a reason,
perhaps he deserved his punishment now. But that

made it no easier to bear. As the lamps in the church dimmed he decided it was time to go, but something held him there, listening to the sweet voices raised in joy—and something more than joy. They were celebrating a human companionship that was alien to him. He'd lost it long ago, on the day he'd decided to bear his burdens alone. Standing there in the darkness, his heart aching with loneliness, he understood all over again what he'd done.

At last he slipped out the door. As he limped across the snow the sound pursued him, growing fainter as he reached his own house.

Mrs. Stanley was still up. He tensed, hoping she'd say Dawn had called while he was out, and was waiting for him, but she only observed that she'd laid out the whiskey decanter in the library. He nodded and bade her good-night.

In the library he settled by the fire and poured himself a glass. But he stopped with it halfway to his lips. *She* wouldn't like it. And she would come. Of course she would, he realized with sudden inspiration. She would be here at midnight. This was why she hadn't called him earlier. The Ghost of Christmas Yet to Come was waiting for the right moment. What a fool he'd been!

There were still ten minutes to go. He got up and checked the French doors to make sure they were unlocked, then he drew back the curtains so that she could see him, and returned to his chair by the fire.

As the last few seconds ticked away to midnight he closed his eyes, straining to hear her. There was nothing. No matter. When he opened his eyes she would be there.

But she wasn't there—not the first time he tried it, nor the second, nor the third. As one o'clock approached he reminded himself that the spirits had come to Scrooge not at midnight, but at one o'clock, and hope revived in him. But one o'clock came and went, and his heart grew cold with despair.

He'd been deluding himself. She'd sweetened him up for the children's party, and once her object was gained she no longer cared. She was probably somewhere with Harry right this minute. He should be sensible and go to bed.

But to leave this room would have been an admission that it was all over, and he couldn't make his limbs move. So he stayed as he was until he fell asleep.

When he awoke the fire was out, and the clock said it was six o'clock on Christmas morning. He cursed himself for a fool, sitting there for hours, waiting for a woman who'd forgotten him. He didn't fancy going to bed now, so he went out to the garage and started up the car. A drive around would clear his head. It was quiet in the sleeping village as he passed through and continued out into the countryside.

As he drove he was making bitter plans. He'd sell and leave here. There was no way he could stay in Hollowdale now. Better to go before he'd properly settled in. But even as he planned, he knew he wasn't going to do any of it. The meeting with the Craddocks had revealed that he had obligations he'd never suspected, and it wasn't his way to shirk his obligations.

He was so absorbed in these thoughts that he was taken by surprise when his headlamps showed a woman straight ahead, trying to wave him to stop. He took a second too long to react. At the last moment he saw Dawn's face in front of him, the eyes wide, the arms stretched out to ward him off. Then she'd vanished.

He braked sharply. Everything in him was screaming in protest as he jumped out into the snow and limped back down the road. "Dawn," he yelled in terror. *"Dawn!"*

"Here," came a faint voice from the ditch.

In his urgency he'd come without his stick. Now he flung himself into the ditch without thinking. Later he was to recall that the movement had jarred him less than he'd expected. At the time he didn't even notice it in his awful dread for her. "Where are you?" he cried frantically.

"I'm just here." Her voice was close and the next moment he had hold of her.

"Are you badly hurt? Oh, dear God! Dawn—"

"I'm fine, honest. I jumped clear in time and landed in the snow. Honestly, Ben, I'm not hurt."

He held her tightly against him. "Thank God!" he breathed. "What on earth were you doing?"

He felt her arms go around him, and her head was

against his chest. "I had to make you stop. Something terrible has happened. My car's stuck in the ditch, and I've simply got to get to the Haynes farm."

"We'll go in my car. It's sturdier than yours."

They helped each other up, and Ben brought his car closer to hers so that she could use his headlamps to see what she was doing. Her vehicle was trapped, nose down in the ditch, and she had to fight to get a door open for her bag, but at last she managed it, and scrambled in beside Ben.

"You're an answer to prayer," she said gratefully.

"What are you doing out here at Christmas?"

"Someone has to be on call. Animals get sick, or give birth."

"I thought lambing was in springtime."

"This is a dog. Fred Haynes has a spaniel who's just about to whelp. He was terrified when he called me to say she'd started early. He adores Trixie. She's all he's got in the world."

After a moment he said, "How long have you been on duty?"

"Since yesterday afternoon. Really, it just means staying at the practice, in case of an emergency. There's a bed there, and I got plenty of sleep before he called."

Her voice was neutrally cordial, but now that the first agitation was over, Ben knew that something was wrong. After her first spontaneous reaction to him a shadow had fallen on her. Even as she spoke she was looking out the window rather than turning in her seat to watch him. He tried to believe he was imagining things, but when she suddenly said, "The road forks in about half a mile—we go to the left," her voice was undeniably distant.

They were climbing higher. Once, when the road turned, he could look down and see Hollowdale, where a few lights had come on. The moon came out from behind the clouds, flooding the snowy countryside with silver light. It was like traveling in a lunar landscape, and he shivered when he thought of her driving up here alone.

At last she said, "That's Fred's farm, just up ahead."

As they came to a bumpy halt the front door opened and light streamed across the snow. The next moment Fred was running toward them. "Quick," he cried hoarsely. "She's having a bad time."

Dawn hurried into the house, leaving Ben to follow her. When he arrived she was already kneeling on the floor beside a spaniel. The bitch was gasping heavily as if in pain, but she was looking up at Dawn with trusting eyes. As Ben watched, Dawn listened to the animal's heart with an intent expression.

"Don't panic, Fred," she said at last. "It's happened a bit sooner than it should have done, but that sometimes happens. It doesn't necessarily mean anything."

"But what are you going to do?" the old man cried. There was a suspicion of a break in his voice.

"I'm going to turn out most of the lights, and then we're all going to keep back."

"But that's not doing anything," he said in outrage. "She needs help—proper help."

"She needs peace and quiet," Dawn said firmly. "She hates these bright lights and people staring at her. Did she try to get away?"

The old man nodded. "She dashed outside and dug herself into the snow. I'd got it all nice for her in here and she ran off."

Dawn squeezed his hand and said gently, "She was looking for a quiet place to give birth. That's all. It wasn't a rejection, Fred."

She switched on a small reading lamp, then turned out the main lights, so that the corner where the basket stood was cast into deep shadow. At once the bitch seemed to relax. Dawn got down onto the floor beside her and stroked her gently, offering the comfort of her presence, but otherwise not intruding. After a few minutes she looked up at Fred who was regarding her with an expression of pure misery.

"If she hasn't produced the first pup in two hours I'll give her an injection," Dawn said. "But she will." She smiled reassuringly at the old man. "Why don't you put the kettle on, Fred?"

He seemed to pull himself together and went out into the kitchen. Ben occupied himself looking around the room. It was a solidly prosperous place, with furniture that was plain but well made. The television set in the corner looked new and expensive. But what struck Ben most was the complete absence of Christmas decorations. There was no tree, no paper chains, no cards lovingly propped on the mantelpiece, no sign of a family that remembered or cared. Nothing. He remembered the home of the Craddock family, full of cheerfulness despite their poverty. "Is the old boy really alone?" he asked Dawn. "There's no one else in this house?"

"No one. Of course he's got employees, but they're not friends. I don't think he has any friends at all. He barks at everyone until they run away. I actually like him, but he works hard at making it difficult."

She said all this still sitting on the floor, never taking her eyes off the spaniel. Her manner appeared normal but Ben had a strange sense that she was using the dog as an excuse not to look at him. It seemed impossible that only the day before yesterday he'd held her in his arms, feeling her passionate kiss on his mouth, her body warm and soft against his. But it hadn't been himself she was kissing. It had been Harry.

The truth was that she'd suspected nothing. Harry was her love now. After the party they'd compared notes and she'd discovered the deception. Now she was angry with Ben, and embarrassed to be with him.

Fred returned with the tea and some sandwiches. Dawn never left Trixie's side, sitting on the floor, watching her, but unobtrusively. Gradually the quiet atmosphere seemed to affect the dog, and she dozed for a few minutes. Then she was awake again, panting harder and straining. And suddenly there was a pup in the basket.

"Look at that!" Fred exclaimed in delight. His face beamed with love.

"They'll come more easily now she's borne the first one," Dawn observed, and in twenty minutes there was another pup. Dawn felt Trixie's abdomen very gently. "That's it," she said. "Just those two."

Trixie was contentedly licking her babies. Dawn steered Fred firmly away. He was over the moon. "Did you see them?" he kept asking. "Aren't they beautiful?"

"They look a bit like sausages," Ben observed.

"Beautiful sausages," Dawn corrected him firmly. "The most beautiful sausages I ever delivered. What are you going to do with them, Fred?"

"Keep them," he said at once. "They're Trixie's. I couldn't give them away. And I'll have them when…" His voice grew husky and he cleared his throat suddenly.

"That's a good idea," Dawn said. "You ought to give them Christmas names, Fred."

"Nay, that'll sound daft," he declared, belligerent in his relief.

"Call them Holly and Cracker," Ben said unexpectedly. "That won't sound daft."

"That's it!" Fred agreed, beaming more than ever. "Holly and Cracker! I'll get some more tea."

CHAPTER SEVEN

WHEN HE'D GONE Dawn threw herself into a chair with her eyes closed. She looked worn-out. After a moment she opened her eyes again and looked at Ben. She smiled at him, but only briefly. The excitement of the moment was over, and once again there was constraint in her manner. Ben had a sensation of floundering, trying to get to her, but being unable to pass a barrier she'd set up. A terrible depression dragged at him. How naively he'd let himself be lured on by the bright dreams that had seemed to dance around him in the last few days. Why, he'd even imagined—

Unable to stop himself, he sat down and buried his face in his hands. The descent back into despair after the rebirth of hope was cruel.

"Ben, whatever's the matter?" She was there beside him, kneeling on the floor, reaching up to him. He pulled himself together.

"It's all right, Dawn. I should have known better."

"About what?"

"About us. When you appeared in my library the

other night—it felt as if you'd come out of my dreams. Stupid, eh? All the things I said to you that night were sensible. They're still sensible. It's just that I—" He forced himself to stop. He'd been about to say, "I don't believe them anymore," forgetting that it wasn't the same with her.

"Just that you what?" Dawn asked in a tense voice.

"They're still sensible. That's how things stand. I just hoped that we could put the bitterness behind us and find a way to be friendly."

"Friendly," she echoed in a blank voice.

He was too absorbed in his own inner struggle to heed her tone. "But ever since the party, you've changed. And I know why."

"Do you?"

"Well, it's obvious, isn't it? You got what you wanted, and I'm glad. You were right all along about that party. Those children deserved a treat, and I'm glad you talked me into it. But I hadn't expected you to change toward me quite so soon. You *have* changed, haven't you?"

She hesitated before saying cautiously, "I don't feel exactly as I did two days ago."

"Of course not. You don't need me anymore."

"That's a wicked thing to say," she told him hotly.

"Why is it? You've just admitted that you have changed."

"Only because *you* have. When I found out what you'd done to the Craddocks, I couldn't believe it. The man I used to love would never have been so mean and hard—"

"Whoa, wait a minute! What am I supposed to have done to the Craddocks?"

"Oh, Ben, please don't pretend," she begged. "I saw them yesterday and they told me all about it. They're devastated. How could you throw them out of the place their family has farmed for so long, and at Christmas?"

"What are you talking about? I haven't thrown them out."

"But you're going to. Mrs. Craddock told me everything—how you went looking around when they weren't there to defend themselves, and implied that they'd been wasting money on the children when it should have gone to the farm, and when Mr. Craddock tried to explain, you cut him short by saying his lease would be up soon. How could you do anything so cruel? How could *you* be so cruel? It's as though I've never really known you."

"It seems you didn't know me if you thought I could behave like that," he said indignantly. "Of course, I'm not going to throw them out. Mrs. Craddock seems to have got hold of the wrong end of every possible stick. I didn't go snooping behind their backs—at least, I didn't mean to. I happened to drop in when they weren't there, and I just looked around to pass the time until they came back. And I never implied that they were wasting money on the children. I remember seeing her trying to hide a bag from a toy shop, but she didn't have to."

"But you said—"

"I was only making small talk about Christmas shopping. I didn't know what she was reading into it."

"And that remark about their lease. Was that small talk?"

"No. I have plans for that farm, but the plans include the Craddocks. Dawn, listen to me. In the few days I've been here I've heard nothing but praise for what a grand old gentleman Squire Davis was, and how he loved to keep Christmas with his neighbors. Tell me, do you know what this 'grand old gentleman' was charging the Craddocks in rent?"

"No."

He told her.

"That much?" she gasped. "But the farm can't be worth a quarter of that."

"I agree. That's why they're so poor and the place is going to wrack and ruin. Davis doesn't seem to have cared about that as long as he extracted the last penny from them. I plan to rewrite the lease, cutting the rent. Then I'll make them an interest-free loan, plus I have a few other ideas that will help get the place back into good condition. I'd no idea how they'd take an innocent remark."

Her face was full of joy. "You never meant to force them out?"

"Of course not. You should have known that."

Dawn's eyes softened. "Yes, I should. It's not a bit

like you as I remember you, but you're so different now, that anything seemed possible."

"A man doesn't change that much," he said gently. "Not inside. Maybe on the surface."

His voice was full of meaning and he saw a light come into her eyes as though she'd understood him. He wanted to say so much more. It was hard to find the courage he needed, but if she would help him—

A clatter announced that Fred was ready to serve breakfast. Ben rose reluctantly, but his heart was lighter.

They ate in the room where Trixie lay in her basket. Every few minutes Fred would rise from the table and go to caress her ears, murmuring words of love. "She really does need to be left alone, Fred," Dawn chided him gently. "Let her get to know her babies in her own way." After that he stayed at the table, but his glance went constantly to the basket. Ben glanced at Dawn, but she was looking at the old man, her eyes filled with infinite pity.

"It's getting light," he said tentatively. "Perhaps—"

"Have some more coffee," Fred suggested quickly. "I was going to make some fresh."

"Just one cup, then," Dawn said gently. "Oh dear," she whispered when Fred had returned to the kitchen. "I hate leaving him when he's so lonely, and on Christmas Day, but we must go soon."

"How come he's all alone? Doesn't he have any family?"

"Oh, yes. He has a son and daughter but he's managed to drive them both away. That's their photos on the sideboard. There's a new one since I was last here. That picture of the two toddlers. He told me his son had sent him that years ago, but he didn't have it on display before. Perhaps Christmas has softened him a bit."

Ben rose and picked up a picture of a young woman just as Fred returned with the coffeepot. "That's my daughter, Linda," he said. "She was a good lass in her way."

"Was? You means she's dead?" Ben asked.

"As good as dead for all I see of her," Fred declared heavily. "I blame that chap she married. He set her against me. We got on all right, me and Linda, before he came along." He stomped back into the kitchen and Ben asked in a low voice, "Did they really?"

"Not according to Jack. I think she married the first man who asked, just to get away." She spoke softly as Fred was coming back.

"I told her she'd regret it if she married him," he said. "And she did. He ran off and left her with two kids. I said she could come back here. I'm still her father even if she did treat me bad. But was she grateful? Not her."

"Perhaps you used the wrong approach," Dawn suggested gently. "Maybe if you'd told her you missed her and really wanted her, she might be more willing to come back."

Fred sighed. "Maybe. Maybe not. I've never been a man for fine words. She knows she can come back if she wants to."

"A man can lose a lot from not being willing to give an inch," Ben said reflectively. "He may even lose the thing he wants most in the world."

Fred grunted. "Oh, aye!" It was clear that he considered this remark in the category of "fine words" and not to be paid serious attention.

Watching him, Ben was appalled. The old man's empty, loveless life seemed like some ghastly parody of his own. *But it was different,* he argued. *He was no Fred Haynes living in bleak isolation in a windswept farm on the moor.*

But the argument wouldn't do. In his heart he knew that his comfortable, rich man's house meant nothing. His true isolation was as bleak as Fred's could ever be, and for the same reason. Instead of seeking human warmth he'd driven it away. He'd been certain, eight years ago, that he'd made the right decision, for Dawn as well as himself; so certain that he'd imposed that decision on her, without reference to her wishes. And now the Ghost of Christmas Yet to Come had raised a curtain, revealing the full horror of his own future.

But was that future set in stone, immovable, unrelenting? Was there no hope?

"Men's courses will foreshadow certain ends...but if the courses be departed from, the ends will change."

"What's that?"

Startled, Ben found Fred's eyes on him. He hadn't realized he'd spoken aloud. "Nothing," he said hastily. "It's just a quote from a book I once read."

"Oh." Fred shrugged. "Books."

Ben realized Dawn was watching him. She'd recognized the words they'd once read together beside a roaring fire, but he couldn't interpret the message in her eyes. He gazed at her frantically, trying to understand, until Fred's blunt voice broke the spell.

"The other picture's Tony," Fred grunted. "He got himself tangled up with a young woman from Australia."

"Fred," Dawn protested, "when you say, 'got himself tangled up,' do you mean he fell in love with her?"

"Call it what you like. I told him she weren't the right lass for him, but would he listen? Not him. Stubborn. Always was."

"I wonder where he got that from," Dawn murmured.

"His mother," Fred declared at once. "She'd never listen either."

"How did it work out for Tony and this woman?" Ben asked.

"He went off to live with her in Australia."

"You told me they had twins," Dawn remembered. "That's their picture, isn't it?"

Fred grunted. "I just came across it," he said. "I can't think why I bothered to put it there."

But they knew. The old man's pride was all that kept him going, but his lonely heart was breaking from the results of his stubbornness. Despite the warmth of the room, Ben shivered.

"It's time we were going," Dawn said.

"Not yet," Fred protested. "Have another coffee."

"We really must go. I'll call back in a few days and see how Trixie is."

He followed them out to the car and stood watching as they drove away. Dawn glanced in the mirror and saw him still standing there, a lonely figure against the sky, growing smaller and smaller.

"Oh, heavens!" she said. "How terribly sad."

"But it's true, surely, that men can change their fate by 'departing from their courses'?" he asked cautiously.

"It would be true if they could do it. But how many people can?"

"Very few, probably," Ben agreed. "But that's because not many people see what they've done clearly enough to understand what they *must* do. But if a man gets that insight—somehow—and if fate gives him a second chance—"

"But that's it. I think in his heart Fred suspects the truth, but I don't think he's going to get that second chance."

"Oh, yes," he said, deflated. "Fred."

"Well, we were talking about Fred, weren't we?"

"Yes, of course we were."

He drove in silence for a few more miles, until Dawn said, "Ben, you've been absolutely wonderful tonight and I— Well, I don't know how to say this—"

"Yes?" he said eagerly.

"I've put you to so much trouble already, but if you

could bear to turn off at that fork up ahead, and go on to the Craddock farm—then you could tell them they didn't need to worry."

Disappointment made him irritable. "It's miles out of the way, Dawn. I'll write them a note."

"But they won't get it until after Christmas and— Oh well, never mind. You're right. I'm really grateful for what you've done tonight."

The sun was up, casting a brilliant light over the white fields so that the glow almost blinded him. He blinked, wondering if he was imagining things or if there really were two figures by the roadside, trying to hail him.

As he drew nearer, the figures took more definite shape as a young man and woman. Ben pulled off and leaned out the window. "Is your car stuck?" he called.

"No, the car's fine, thanks," the woman answered cheerfully. "We just need some directions. Is this the way to the Haynes farm?"

"Right up ahead," Dawn answered. "You've got about five miles to go. But—" An unfamiliar accent in their voices had struck her, and their faces were curiously alike. "Who are you?" she asked with rising excitement.

"I'm Fred Haynes, and this is my sister Jenny," the man said. "We're visiting from Australia and we thought we'd look up our grandfather. We should have arrived yesterday, but we got lost."

Dawn got out of the car and went closer to them.

They were attractive youngsters, tall and strong, with open, cheerful faces, who looked as if they lived active lives. "You're Fred's grandchildren from Australia?" she cried. "Oh, that's wonderful!"

"You know him?" Jenny asked eagerly.

"We've just left him," Dawn told her. "I'm a vet. I've been caring for his dog while she had her pups."

"Do you think he'll be glad to see us?" Jenny asked practically. "Dad's always told us he's a bit of a grump. Will he want strangers bursting in on him at Christmas?"

"He wants you," Dawn assured her. "But he might pretend otherwise because he finds it hard to show his feelings."

The two young Australians grinned at each other and spoke with one voice. *"Just like Dad."*

"Did you say your name was Fred?" Dawn asked the young man.

"That's right. Dad named me after his own father."

"I reckon old Fred will be thrilled about that," Ben said. He'd left the car and come to talk to them.

Jenny looked around at the whiteness. "I think this is all just wonderful. We've never even seen snow before. Dad's always talking about this place, how beautiful it is, and we just had to see it for ourselves."

"You'd best hurry on," Dawn said, smiling. "Straight ahead. You can't miss it."

"Thanks." They headed for their car and got in. Just

before they drove away they waved out the windows, calling, "Merry Christmas!"

"Merry Christmas!" Ben and Dawn called back together.

Dawn gave a crow of delight and jumped up and down in the snow. "That's *wonderful*. Now old Fred really will have a merry Christmas."

Ben grinned. "Not merry," he said. "Happy, I hope, but all the clowns in the universe couldn't make that man merry."

"You're right. He'll grumble like mad, but he'll be happy underneath and that's what matters. And those two won't be upset by his manner because they're used to it in their father and they know how to cope with it. He's been given another chance, and that's the best part of all."

He looked at her, finding himself suddenly misty-eyed. "Other people's happiness really means that much to you, doesn't it?" he asked tenderly.

"Well, you can't be happy all on your own, can you?" she asked poignantly.

"I guess not. Are you happy now, Dawn? Do you have the things you want?"

"Not all of them," she reflected. "But some." Her eyes met his. "And I have hopes of the others."

"Come on." He seized her hand and began to pull her in the direction of the car. "Get in."

"Where are we going?" she asked as she settled into the passenger seat.

"The Craddock farm, of course. Where else?" He was turning the car as he spoke, and soon they were traveling back up the road to the fork.

They arrived just as the Craddock family was pouring out of the house, buttoned up in warm clothes. From the alarmed looks they cast him Ben realized that Dawn had been right. "We were just off to church," Mr. Craddock said. "If—I mean, if you've come to—"

"I've only come for a moment to wish you a happy Christmas, Mr. Craddock," Ben said quickly, anxious to dispel their wretchedness. "Miss Fletcher told me that I'd worried you with my remarks the other day, and I just want you to know that there's no question of you having to leave. When we talk in the New Year you can tell me what you need, and when we've arranged a lower rent for you, I'm sure you won't find it so hard to make ends meet."

It took a moment for them to understand. The Craddocks looked at him, then at each other, then back at him. At last the reality sank in and joyous smiles broke over their faces. Suddenly everything was pandemonium. The children cheered and threw snowballs at each other and everyone else, while their parents threw themselves into each other's arms. That sight brought home to Ben the reality of the fear he'd accidentally created. The memory of how he nearly hadn't come here today made him feel badly.

Dawn squeezed his hand. "Thank you," she whispered.

Mr. Craddock pumped his hand vigorously before yelling, "Come on, you kids! Into the car and get to that church. We've got something to sing carols about, now."

Ben smiled with pleasure as he watched them. "A Merry Christmas!" he called as they all squeezed into the car, and they shouted the words back to him joyfully.

"Merry Christmas, Ben," Dawn said when they were alone.

Now was the time to voice the feelings in his heart. But his courage failed him. He couldn't risk breaking the spell. "Merry Christmas," he told her, and wondered if he imagined a fleeting look of disappointment on her face.

CHAPTER EIGHT

A LITTLE FARTHER along they came across her car stranded in the ditch. "Leave it," Ben said. "I'll send someone to haul it out as soon as Christmas is over. If you get called out again, I'll take you."

"But that'll spoil your Christmas."

"I don't feel as if Christmas is being ruined, Dawn. I feel as if it's the first Christmas I've truly celebrated since—well, since—" He left the sentence hanging in the air.

After a moment she said, "That's how I feel, too."

They could see the village now, slightly below them. Already church bells were ringing out across the snow, and villagers were streaming toward the ancient stone building. Dismay seized Ben as he realized that they were almost there and he hadn't said any of the things he wanted to. But then, he wasn't sure exactly what it was he wanted to say, or whether she wanted to hear any of it.

Now they were entering the village. "Dawn—" he said desperately.

"Could you drop me at the surgery, please?"

It was over. She didn't want him. What was the point of him "departing from his course" if she wouldn't depart from hers? Her "end" was foreshadowed. She would become Harry's wife.

Yet although he said the words inwardly, somehow he couldn't believe them. The ghost that had come to him out of the past was a benign ghost, sent for his redemption. There was only one way it could end. He clung to the thought.

Near the surgery they met Jack walking to church with his family. Dawn explained about the car and gave a brief account of Trixie, then Jack said, "You've done your share. Harry's taking over. Be off and enjoy yourself. Merry Christmas."

When they were alone Dawn said, "I think I'd like to go to church now."

There was an appeal in her voice and Ben immediately responded, "I'll come with you."

Together they made their way along the snow-covered street. He'd left his stick in the car, yet strangely he was no longer troubled by the thought of stumbling. An arm about her shoulder was all he needed—all he would ever need. Gradually they fell into step with their neighbors, all heading for the little church where the bells were ringing out their joyous message. People were looking at him-not staring, but giving him smiles of welcome. Someone called, "That was a grand party!"

He called back, "Wait until next year. Then you'll

really see a party!" There were smiles and cheers, and he wondered why he'd never realized there was such good fellowship in the world.

The road to the church lay beneath a clump of oak trees, stripped bare now. Before they reached the door he slowed and began to draw her aside. He didn't stop until they were both hidden behind the huge trunk of one of the oaks. "Dawn, before we go into church together, I have to know."

"Yes?"

"The other night, at the party, when you kissed Father Christmas the second time—did you know who—?"

He never finished the question. Dawn's arms were around him, her hands drawing his head down until she could lay her lips on his. "Do you think I could kiss you and not know it?" she asked. "Even after eight years?"

Joy flooded through him, almost too great to bear. "When did you realize I wasn't Harry?" he asked hoarsely.

"When you were talking to Gary. I suddenly remembered about your passion for jigsaw puzzles. I was in your apartment once, and you kept the door of the living room locked. You said you had a puzzle with eight thousand pieces spread out on the floor. When you told Gary about an eight-thousand-piece jigsaw I was pretty sure. While you were getting it I looked outside and saw that Harry's car was gone."

He was breathless with hope. "So when you lured me under the mistletoe—?"

"I knew exactly who I was luring. I wanted to kiss you, and I guessed the only way was to let you think you were fooling me."

"I've been so jealous. I thought you loved Harry."

"I do. But only as a dear friend. We had a long talk after the party. He's accepted the truth now. He'll be all right. Half the young women for miles around are in love with him, and he's too warmhearted to stay alone for long."

Looking into her eyes he saw happiness waiting for him. But not yet. First there was one more thing he must say.

"I was wrong," he told her. "All those years ago I was wrong to send you away. In my heart I think I've always known it, but I wouldn't admit it. It was too terrible to face. Can you forgive me?"

"There's nothing to forgive," she said simply. "But we must make the years ahead splendid, because of the ones we lost."

"You kissed me the night you came back to me. And you kissed me again the other night. Will you promise to kiss me every Christmas for the rest of our lives? Otherwise there'll be no hope for me."

"I promise, Ben. It's all I want."

She drew his head down and kissed him again, and they held each other very close in a wordless vow for the future.

High above them the Christmas bells were pealing out across the snow, calling everyone to celebrate the miracle of rebirth. Ben's heart overflowed with joy and thanks too deep for words. Silently he took her hand and they went into the old church together, as now they would always be.

* * * * *

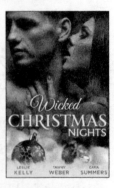

Wrap up warm this winter with Sarah Morgan...

Sleigh Bells in the Snow

Kayla Green loves business and hates Christmas.

So when Jackson O'Neil invites her to Snow Crystal Resort to discuss their business proposal... the last thing she's expecting is to stay for Christmas dinner. As the snowflakes continue to fall, will the woman who doesn't believe in the magic of Christmas finally fall under its spell...?

4th October

www.millsandboon.co.uk/sarahmorgan

Come home this Christmas to Fiona Harper

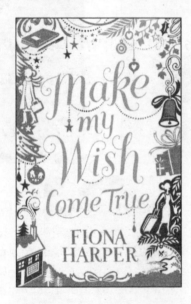

From the author of *Kiss Me Under the Mistletoe* comes a
Christmas tale of family and fun. Two sisters are ready
to swap their Christmases—the busy super-mum, Juliet,
getting the chance to escape it all on an exotic Christmas
getaway, whilst her glamorous work-obsessed sister,
Gemma, is plunged headfirst into the family Christmas
she always thought she'd hate.

www.millsandboon.co.uk

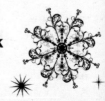

1113/MB442

Meet The Sullivans...